For
Sarah
with warmest regards
Derek Hayden Tait

La Cigale
St. Ouen
Jersey.
30/10/90

EMERGENCY!

Sam pulled open the centre drawer and took out a file which he put on the desk, unopened.

'I want to make you an offer,' he said.

David was intrigued and raised his left eyebrow.

'It touches, but only very slightly, on your professional ethics,' Sam explained. David frowned, and Sam held up his hand. 'Only slightly,' he added.

'That sounds like being just a little pregnant!'

Sam opened the file and spread out a row of photographs. There were six in all, front and side views of each of three men. David studied them.

'They look a pretty bunch,' he observed.

'They raped my Susan. You know the rest. She'll never win another beauty competition, will she?'

David looked up sharply. 'Unhappily that's true. Why don't you get the police on to them?'

Sam shook his head. 'I'm going to deal with them.'

'But why come to me?' asked David.

'I'm just casting the search net wide. There's a drug unit at Manbury Hospital, yes?'

'Correct.'

'Then it's likely that one of these will turn up there some time. They're high risk and could well end up in your casualty department.'

'So?'

Sam's face was like granite. 'So, if they're admitted to your hospital for any reason, I want you to let me know.'

Derek Haydn Taylor was educated at
Marlborough College, Magdalen College, Oxford
and the Middlesex Hospital Medical School. His
training continued as a House Physician at Mount
Vernon Hospital, Northwood, as a Senior House
Officer in a surgical post in Aylesbury and as a
Medical Registrar at the Royal Chest Hospital,
London. He served with the Royal Air Force for
three years and spent two years with the 21st SAS
regiment. Derek Haydn Taylor is now a general
practitioner living with his second wife in Jersey.
He has three children. *Emergency!* is his first
novel for Worldwide.

EMERGENCY!

by

D H TAYLOR

WORLDWIDE BOOKS
LONDON · SYDNEY · TORONTO

First published in Great Britain in 1990 by Worldwide Books, Eton House, 18–24 Paradise Road, Richmond, Surrey TW9 1SR

© *Haydn Holdings Ltd. 1990*

ISBN 0 373 58454 7
10/9010/130749

Printed and bound in Great Britain by
William Clowes Limited, Beccles and London

To Carolyn
who saw the fruit before the flower

ACKNOWLEDGEMENTS

John Donne said that no man is an island and this is as pertinent to writers as to others. Perhaps more so, because writers tend to be isolated and their contact with their fellow men, and women, becomes all the more important.

I should like to thank my publishers for allowing me to present those who have helped me to write this book for your entertainment.

Drs Patric Nisbet and Andrew Borthwick-Clarke, the heavenly twins of the X-ray department in Jersey, must be two of the busiest men I know. Their time is precious, as is their advice, and they have dispensed it with Samaritan generosity.

Silvia Tilman, librarian of the Jersey General Hospital, has the gift of finding what I want when I do not know what it is I do want. Such inference needs not a computer, but a crystal ball. Let no one steal it from her.

Dr John Taylor (no relation, for he can play music) and Dr David Spencer, are pathologists. They have saved me from (some of) the censure of my colleagues when otherwise I would have fallen into a pit of pathological ignorance excavated by enthusiasm instead of expertise.

Dr Martin Barrett, my friend and partner, is a man of infinite patience and encyclopaedic knowledge.

Thank you, Jo, for correcting my errors. As this particular diligence has involved reading over a million words my gratitude is commensurate.

There are others, many of them; it is impossible to thank everyone, but I know they know who they are.

CHAPTER ONE

'WHAT a bloody evening!'

Susan Bennett eased herself back into the padded leather seat of the Bentley Mulsanne as it whispered through the night. From the stereo speakers Benny Goodman's clarinet lilted its way through 'Deep Purple'. Only the needle on the speedometer gave any indication that they were travelling at a hundred and ten miles an hour down the country road.

Sam Bennett flashed her a gold-toothed grin.

'You were great, darling. Just great.'

'Those frosty fart-arses dry me up,' she said coldly. 'That old goat Sir Gerald should be shoved in aspic and kept for posterity.' She mimicked, with an adenoidal upper-class accent, '"Let me help you to a little cold collation, m'dear." All the time the old ram was giving me a feel!'

Sam guided the car round a gentle curve at a steady ninety. The halogen headlights turned the summer night into day for a mile ahead.

'If it gets us twenty millions' worth of the Donnington contract, he's welcome,' he said.

'Sam, you're a bastard!' She slid a hand along his thigh and nibbled his ear.

'Sure. At twenty million a feel I'm a generous bastard. You don't come cheap.'

'If you don't slow up neither of us will ever come again!'

He felt her warm breath on his neck and the speedometer needle eased reluctantly back. His big, builder's hands gripped the wheel more firmly as he felt her hand exploring under his belt.

'Steady, lady!' he warned.

Susan's blonde hair pooled over his lap as she slid down his zip and he sprang out of his trousers like a rutting stag. The Bentley slowed to a majestic roll and Sam's craggy face took on a fixed stare as he looked straight down the tree-lined road. The great oaks and beeches of Savernake Forest, towering high above, made a vast leafy tunnel.

Despite the air-conditioning Sam was beginning to sweat. Susan's head began to move and his face flushed to the tips of his ears. His big shoulders hunched.

'Hang on, Susan, you'll have us in the ditch!'

Reluctantly she straightened up, tucked him back into his trousers and zipped up his fly. She gave him a sideways look, a mischievous glint in her wide almond-shaped eyes. She had big, even teeth, a slender nose and a heart-shaped face that was undeniably beautiful. That and her superb figure had won her the title of Miss Bondi Beach five years ago. Despite the fact that she was such a big girl and blooming into five months of pregnancy, she still looked the part.

Sam had met her at a surfing party when he was investigating a property development on the outskirts of Sydney. The attraction had been mutual between the tough little builder turned developer and the tall Australian beauty queen who, at twenty-five, was twenty years his junior.

In typical style he had married her while completing his property deal and they had flown back to England without even considering a honeymoon. Life had been one long honeymoon ever since. Sam's property empire was now international and she always went with him in their Learjet. Now that she was pregnant, Sam was like a man who has just climbed Everest on his own.

The car slid forward, gathering speed quickly. Sam shook his head.

'Now look what you've done! I'm going to have to drive another twenty-five miles with a stand.'

Susan laughed, her head thrown back, showing the long curve of her neck, her teeth gleaming whitely in the light from the instrument panel. Around her neck was an emerald choker. She was wearing a white evening dress, the folds caught at her left shoulder with an emerald clasp. Sam had never seen her look lovelier.

'Darling, I was so riveted by that old goat I wanted to do that to you after dinner,' she told him. 'Just to break the monotony.'

'Broken up the party, more like!'

'Great. Parties like that should be broken up after the first drink.'

'You're a wicked lady,' he grinned. 'Pregnancy does funny things to you.'

'Right again, sport. It's doing them to me now. Turn in here.'

Susan pointed to a narrow drive leading off into the forest, and obediently Sam swung the wheel.

'What's it doing to you now?' he asked.

She ruffled the back of his neck. 'Turning me into a sexy, preggy lady.'

They rustled into a small clearing. Sam turned the car off the track and cut the engine, then the lights. The summer night came down upon them like a dark mantle. Far away, through the trees, Sam caught the yellow flicker of a campfire.

Susan put her arms round his neck and opened her mouth on his. As her tongue slid and probed at him he felt himself rising to bursting point. He fumbled at the car switches. The two front seats whirred and the backs went slowly down.

Susan took off his jacket and he lifted her dress.

Despite the darkness he could see the gleam of her long legs, the silk of her underwear and the flash of her emerald choker. As his swollen member throbbed in her grip he whispered hoarsely at her,

'What made you do this?'

Her teeth gleamed whitely as she smiled and moved him gently, making him moan with pleasure.

'You did. I wasn't going to let you drive all the way home like that. Anyway, I like it in the car.'

He slipped off her brassiere, cupping the heavy breast with its swelling nipple in his hand.

'Sounds as if you've been around.'

His voice was muffled by her breasts. She tweaked his erection and his head came up abruptly.

'Ow!' he exclaimed.

'Teach you not to be unkind.'

He reached for the elastic of her knickers and, as she raised her buttocks to let him slide them down, the inside of the car was lit up by a bright torchlight beam. A waft of cool air came over them as the car door was opened.

'Get this, chicko. Man, what a pair!'

The voice was hard, aggressive, West Indian. With it came the sweet odour of marijuana. The torchbeam never wavered, the light cascading over them with dazzling brilliance.

Sam raised his hand against it, his tumescence fading, rage fronting his other emotions.

'Get out of it and shut that door!' he snapped furiously.

'Quite the randy little cock sparrow!'

A different voice, the tone high with excitement. Behind it some whisperings he did not catch. There must be several of them. Sam brought his hand down and zipped up his fly. Susan covered her breasts, glaring angrily at the torchlight and the invisible intruders. Sam leaned across her, reaching for the door handle to close it. There was a grunt in the dark as a stick came whistling down, hitting the back of his wrist. Sam heard the bone crack before he felt the pain that jolted up his arm. The arm dropped limply across Susan's thighs and Sam looked at it as though it belonged to someone else, unable to believe what was happening.

'Hey, China, let's see the chick.'

A black hand, long and skinny, reached forward and gripped her arm. Susan felt the back of the sharp knuckles against the side of her breast and shuddered. The hand tightened and pulled at her.

Sam opened the driver's door with his left hand and scrambled out, his right arm dangling by his side. The pain stabbed up at him, sickeningly. He ran around the front of the car. There were several of them, two of them carrying hurricane lamps.

China was the one with the torch, and by now he was pulling hard at Susan, who suddenly kicked out at him. Sam grabbed China by the shoulder, gripping the blue denim jacket and twisting him round. He had a brief glimpse of a lean, ravaged face, prominent teeth with long canines and greasy black dreadlocks hanging in a dirty fringe.

An arm came around his neck from behind, jerking his head back and pressing on his windpipe. His breath came in a high-pitched wheeze. He jabbed backwards with his good elbow and felt it hit something hard. There was a grunt of pain.

'Shit you, Cock Sparrow! Grab his arms.'

It was a short bullet-headed Scot with red hair shaven closer than the black stubble on his chin and a bottle scar running down his left cheek. He grabbed Sam's right arm and twisted it. The pain lanced up his arm and he shouted in agony.

Susan did not hesitate. She came out of the Bentley

like a spitting hell-cat, oblivious of her near-nudity. China was caught unawares as she cannoned past him and went for the Scot, her long nails raking down his white face, leaving red trails like Indian tribal marks. Her thumbs went up to his eyes and he let go of Sam's arm to defend himself against her furious attack. For a moment it looked as though he would never see again as her strong thumbs dug into his cheeks and slid up to his eyeballs. The pain was intense and he could see nothing. It was China who saved him. He raised a bony hand in a fast downward karate chop, caught Susan on the side of the neck, and she went down in a heap.

Sam heaved forward against the stranglehold on his neck, but the grip was vicelike. China's hand went behind his back and came forward with a knife that shone in the flickering light of the hurricane lamps. He stuck the point against Sam's belly and smiled, the long canines foxlike in the narrow face.

'Sure would like to give this little sticker a push. Feels just like butter. Better than a fuck any day. So shove it, friend.'

His eyes glittered. Despite his half-choked state and the pain in his arm Sam could see that he was high on something. The pricking knife point stopped him moving.

Out of the shadows a big black man appeared, wearing a red shirt and dark trousers. He put his arms round Susan from behind and lifted her up, his big hands gripping her breasts. As she regained her feet she came to life, turning and hitting him across the side of the face with her hand. She was a big girl and it was a hefty swipe that must have hurt, but it made no impression on the black. The big lips just split into a wide grin as he caught her wrist and expertly twisted her arm behind her back. He grabbed her other wrist, forcing her to bend forward. With one massive hand gripping both wrists, he pushed them higher behind her back. She bent further down, crying with pain.

Sam stepped forward. The knife point went half an inch into his belly muscle.

'Jesus, you bastard! Let her go or I'll kill you!'

Sam's craggy face was a vision of tormented rage. The black lifted a single finger at him in an obscene gesture, then tucked it into the elastic of Susan's silk knickers. With a single vicious pull he tore them down. The tattered remnant caught at her knee on its way down and hung there. Her rounded bottom gleamed whitely in the lamplight. The bass rumble of the black's voice had a throaty edge to it that Sam recognised—the harsh, demanding tone of a male in full rut.

'How's about it, China?'

China nodded, his dreadlocks shaking with excitement.

'Why not, Tinker? It's a piece of ass for everybody.'

The black had his member out, a monumental pink erection still swelling visibly. Susan struggled as she felt it probing up behind her, but the pain in her arms was too much. Tinker looked over his shoulder.

'Hey, Mac, give us a hand.'

Mac ran his tongue over his lips and stepped forward, his pale face tense with anticipation. He stood in front of Susan, straddling her with his legs, gripping her head between his knees. He took her wrists from Tinker and grinned with small blackened teeth.

'Get at it, Tinker lad. She'll not be after running off the noo.'

Susan could not move. Her head, caught in the vice of Mac's knees, was a bucket of blinding pain while her arms felt as if they were on fire. She tensed inside as she felt Tinker's enormous member pushing at her.

God save me, she thought, maybe if I'm too tight he won't get it in.

She was wrong. She was still wet from loving Sam, and with a great shove Tinker was there in a long slide that she thought would end up in her throat. She felt his hands gripping her waist, pulling her towards him as he thrust at her.

Please, God, make him come. Then he'll stop.

He did not stop, just bent his knees and went on harder until she was on fire inside. Her knees buckled and she went down on all fours. Tinker went with her, and it was worse because her face was in the wet earth and she thought she was going to choke.

Once she tried to wriggle away as he was on a back stroke, but his big hands gripped her belly so hard she screamed and was still, and the next stroke hurt her more than ever.

China was so fascinated that Sam caught him off guard. He felt the grip on his neck relaxing. China's interest was diverted to Tinker's performance. Sam butted backwards with his head and kicked him hard on the shin. China let him go. Sam took three steps towards Tinker and kicked the base of his spine. The toe of his shoe hit bone with a solid crunch that he knew must have reverberated up to the black's skull.

There was a stop in the heaving thrusts. It was as though the machinery had been switched off. The massive form turned and the black towered over Sam like a tyrannosaurus. The great black hands came down in a symmetrical chop, edge on to both sides of Sam's neck, and he went down, unconscious before he hit the ground.

The redheaded Scot stepped forward, unbuckling his belt, a tight grin of anticipation on his pale, stubbly face.

'Mah turrn next. Ah'll gie 'er summat to remember me by!'

He tried hard enough, but she never did remember.

His performance was lost in the company that followed as one after the other they took her. She was a big, gutsy lady and she would struggle and sometimes she shouted in rage and pain and fury, but eventually her strength gave out and she stayed where she was. In the end, when one of them turned her over and took her on her back, she did not struggle.

They were all on a drug high, full of the mind-blowing effects of amphetamine, marijuana, cocaine, heroin, diazepam, tryptiline, haloperidol, stelazine; anything that came out of the communal pot by the campfire. Normally they would have stayed in the forest, a trouble to no one. Sam and Susan had been unlucky; they had stumbled on a tiger's feast.

They left her lying on the beech leaves, a semi-conscious white blob on the ground. Her face was muddy and grazed, her body filthy and between her legs streamed a steady trickle of bright red blood. Mac, the rawboned Scot, tripped over her in the dark as they moved away. She did not even stir. As they passed the Bentley, Mac leaned over the boot and drew a knife from his belt. Digging the point into the paintwork, he scratched in spiky letters:

MAC THE KNIFE

He stood back, holding up the lantern, and gave a ferrety grin.

'Ah lak to be remembered.'

He was remembered. Sam remembered him as he opened his eyes and saw him stepping back to admire his handiwork. His arms were still semi-paralysed, but his legs moved. Unsteadily he got to his knees. Fortunately for him they did not see him move. He shuffled on his knees to Susan, who moaned at his touch. Her skin was cold and he staggered to the car, managing to pull out a rug from the back seat.

The power returned gradually to his arms. Pins and needles crawled over them like marauding fire ants. He put his arms round Susan, dragged her to the car and got her on the back seat. His right wrist was useless, the pain from it hitting him like slivers of fiery ice.

The car started with a gentle rumble at the first touch. He kept the lights off until he had turned. Driving one-handed was not difficult with the power steering, and when he switched on the heads he blasted out to the main road, the engine racing and the wheels spinning in the forest loam.

A mile down the road he stopped and looked over Susan. Her face was ashen, her lips blue, and across the leather of the seat was a spreading scarlet pool. Fear surged up in him and he sent the big car hurtling down the road, his mind probing for the location of the nearest hospital.

A fine drizzle of rain had started and he flicked the wiper switch awkwardly with his one good hand. The car veered towards the ditch as he took his hand off the steering wheel, but his fear for Susan kept his foot down, and at the top of the steep curving hill into Marlborough the speedometer needle was passing eighty.

Even one-handed Sam could have got down the hill had it not been for the rain, and the heavy goods lorry parked on the side with a broken wheel. There was a juddering as the anti-lock brakes came into action on the first corner. On the wet surface the car went into a sideways slide towards the lorry. Sam swung the wheel to the opposite lock, grossly over-correcting, and they were into a spin.

The green sides of the cutting went twirling by. It was like a mad dodgem-car ride. There was a bang and a shower of sparks into the night as the front wheels hit the side, and they went over in a cloud of dust and broken glass to the sound of metal shrieking on gravel.

The car lay on its side, postured without grace or dignity. Sam was drooped unconscious on the driving wheel. In the back Susan moaned as she struggled back to reality. Something was frightening her. She did not know what it was. It was just that something was wrong.

Then she heard it.

Dripping.

She lifted her head and sniffed. Shook her head for a second and then opened her eyes wide, reaching up for the door handle in a wild panic because she realised what it was.

Petrol.

Dripping on to the hot exhaust pipe.

CHAPTER TWO

THE MANBURY Accident Hospital sits squarely south of the M4, high on the Wiltshire downs. Solid and functional, it is surrounded by the over-large car parks and lawns beloved by modern planners. Blue notices with clear white lettering label every department. Batteries of signposts point the way to Accident and Emergency, Pathology, X-Ray, Administration, Theatres, Wards 1–10, Nurses' Home, Endoscopy, Nuclear Medicine.

A wide tarmac drive leads the way from the main road to Accident and Emergency with its brilliant neon sign over the wide covered entrance. From a big window overlooking the front area Donald Shaw viewed the approach of an ambulance as it rounded off from the main road, its blue lights flashing. He smiled with satisfaction as he noted the absence of the intrusive gong. That was the result of his recent memo. Quite unnecessary when there was no traffic, and it disturbed the patients.

He was a small man, with a tight foxy face and a toothbrush moustache the colour of sand. A precise man, a meritocrat who had worked his way up through the echelons of bureaucracy to his present senior post as hospital administrator. Patiently he had erased the marks of his humble upbringing. An occasional lapse was to carry his pens in his breast pocket. He had found that as difficult to cure as a Cockney's aspirate.

His intercom clicked. Donna, his secretary, spoke in a low voice with an air of hushed excitement that he knew presaged someone important, or attractive.

'Mr Compton to see you, Mr Shaw.'

'Thank you, Donna. Please show him in.'

David Compton was the new consultant surgeon in charge of Accident and Emergency. He had been in the post for only six months and already his visits to the administrator were becoming a too-frequent nuisance. Donald Shaw regretted that he had not been on the appointments board when the choice for the post had been made.

David was a demanding innovator. His degrees and experience as well as his personal charm had so impressed the board that their choice had been unanimous. Now he was ensconced in his post and his requirements for staffing and equipment had been continuous and exorbitant. Donald Shaw shook his head and tightened his lips. Surgeons had no concept of the importance of budgeting; they were like children in a toyshop, wanting every new expensive machine that appeared on an increasingly sophisticated market. His eye flickered over a glossy brochure from an electronics firm. The prices in their catalogue made Cartier's look like rag and bone merchants.

Donna opened the door, her pretty features were flushed and her eyes bright. Donald Shaw felt a stab of envy and impatience. The new surgeon seemed to have this effect on most women, young or old.

'Thank you, Donna. You'll have the tickets tomorrow.'

The voice was lazy, slow, cultured; the accent English upper class. Donald Shaw stuck his nose out like an impatient shrew.

'Yes, Mr Compton. What can I do for you this morning?'

'Just come to pick your pocket again, my old Shaw.'

David smiled engagingly at him as he sat in a chair before the administrator's large desk and crossed an

elegantly shod foot over his knee. Malborough and
Magdalen had stamped him with a confidence and ease
of manner that Donald Shaw both envied and despised.

'What absolute necessities do we lack now, Mr
Compton?'

'I want a defibrillator in A and E.'

'We already have a defibrillator.'

David nodded.

'Certainly—up on the medical floor. Have you any
idea how long it takes to get it down to A and E?'

Mr Shaw pursed his lips and shook his head.

'Four minutes at the last try. We just lost a young
man with an arrest because they couldn't get the damn
machine down the corridor quick enough. I want one
just for A and E. It's got to sit there, paddles at the
ready and ready to go, twenty-four hours a day.'

'Have you any idea what they cost?' asked Donald
Shaw.

'Not a clue.'

'The sort you will need won't be less than twenty
thousand pounds.'

'So?'

'How many arrests do you have a year in A and E?'

David thought briefly.

'Six, maybe eight.'

'We have to write these things off over three years.
That gives a total of say twenty arrests over the period.
A thousand pounds a time for the use of it. Just for the
machine.'

David spread his hands.

'So what? If we save half of them it's only two
thousand a life. Not bad.'

The little mouth under the sandy moustache went
tight.

'That's not how we look at it, Mr Compton.'

David snaked up out of the chair, his aquiline

features hard. His tall frame leaned over the desk, his hands on the edge, towering over the foxy administrator. Flinty grey eyes stared down and in a voice with a ring of cold steel he said,

'I hope you feel the same way when you have your coronary, Shaw. For your own sake, try not to have it in my department. Four minutes is a long time.'

Donald Shaw looked as though he had been hit. Introducing personalities was definitely not part of the game. He preferred to keep things impersonal, tidy, unemotional. His hand wandered to the pencil on his desk and he tapped his teeth with it.

'I do not feel it necessary to descend to the arena of personal denigration, Mr Compton,' he said coldly.

David brushed back a wave of black hair that had fallen over his forehead in the intensity of the discussion and waved an apologetic hand.

'Just so you know we're talking about people. You want to come down there some day and tell the wife she's not going to see him again. That instead of taking her to the cinema tonight he's gone to the mortuary. That's what the four minutes is about, that's all it takes to buy you a ticket to the cold house.'

The sharp point of the pencil combed accurately through each bristle of the sandy toothbrush.

'Are there any other points you would care to raise, Mr Compton?'

Donald Shaw glanced significantly at his wristwatch. David sat down again.

'Yes. I need a senior registrar. Two housemen and one junior registrar are not enough for my department. We're getting a lot of major trauma. I can't cope with it all and it's not fair to throw it at a junior registrar. If we get a bad multiple there'll be several avoidable deaths, and then you really will have some talking to do.'

Donald went a shade of oyster grey. The addition of

a senior surgical registrar to the permanent staff of a department made a defibrillator look like a give-away. At the same time the thought of being held responsible, however indirectly, for the deaths of several people after a multiple motorway crash made him cringe.

The idea David had so briefly conjured up multiplied in his mind. Adverse press comment, an inquiry perhaps, and if he was criticised his job could be on the line. He began to perspire and mopped his forehead.

'I'll bring it for consideration at the next meeting of the Staffing Committee, Mr Compton.'

David's bleep peeped loudly inside his jacket pocket. He reached forward, shook a limp hand and was gone before Donald had sat down. Donna pinked again as he leaned over her desk and picked up her telephone. The tall new consultant with the charismatic presence and darkly aquiline looks invaded her peace of mind.

'Mr Compton.' The telephone operator's voice came over, crisp and unemotional. 'A and E, Mr Compton. I'll put you through.'

Mark Slater, his houseman in A and E, sounded worried.

'I've got a problem, sir. A couple brought in after a road traffic accident, and she's not good. Could you pop down?'

'I'm on my way.'

Mark Slater was reliable, did not shout easily, and David went quickly. Despite his experience and confidence there was always that hair-prickling tension at such moments. The long hospital corridor was crowded, a flow of visitors added to the usual traffic of stretcher trolleys, patients in wheelchairs, porters, white-coated doctors and uniformed nurses. He turned the corner by the big lifts and as he was about to increase his pace he felt a hand on his arm.

'Mr Compton, may I have a word?'

Frowning with impatience, he swivelled round, and his frown eased into something closer to a smile. Sister Irving could make anyone smile, she had that sort of influence. Bright copper hair haloed her face, which was not beautiful, but attractive with high cheekbones. Her slanted green eyes gave her a Slavic look. The mouth was wide and the voice low. She was tall and under her nurse's uniform her figure was a constant lure to predatory housemen.

She was the senior theatre sister, the one with whom David worked most frequently. In the privacy of the surgeons' room and her office they were Ginette and David, but on parade it was Sister Irving and Mr Compton.

Ginette had come to Manbury from St Thomas's, London, having trained at the Royal Devon and Exeter and spent some time at the Royal Livery Hospital near Glastonbury. After a long theatre training this was her first senior post and she was determined to make a success of it. She remembered when David Compton had been appointed and she had regarded him with deep suspicion when she had been told how young he was.

There had been a small party for the surgical staff and sisters to welcome him, and it had already been a long day for Ginette. She had not had time to change properly and the dress she wanted to wear had a stain on the front. As a result she had to wear an old brown dress that she should have thrown out long ago, or not bought in the first place. Matron had introduced them, and as she did so somebody behind her in the crush had stepped back, bumping into her so that she had slopped her glass of red wine forward and it had spilt on the front of his light suit.

'I'm sorry!'

Her tension and self-annoyance had made her abrupt

and it came out as though she could not have cared less. David had mopped the front of his jacket with a handkerchief from his breast pocket and when he looked up his grey eyes had a hard glitter in them.

'I didn't catch your name, only your wine.'

The group around them tittered and she could have quite happily thrown the remainder of her wine over him.

After that there had been war, but gradually the flames had died between them, and now they worked brilliantly together with only the occasional flash of hostility. Ginette sometimes now found herself wishing that he was not always so remote.

'Certainly, Sister. Make it sharp, I've got a come-quick.'

'I know. Just to tell you that the theatre is ready to go. We've just finished an operation. Shall I keep them on standby?'

'Yes, please. I'll let you know what and when later. . .'

He was away before he had finished. Ginette was not one to stand on ceremony, nevertheless his abruptness irritated her. As he turned into Emergency he immediately sensed an urgency in the atmosphere. In a department where emergencies are commonplace there are occasions which command an indefinable raising of tension. The pointers are tiny, but they are there. The porters stand about instead of seeking the nearest chair, the ambulance drivers linger longer before driving off, the nurses' footsteps are quicker, there are fewer reassuring words for waiting relatives. Sister's voice has an edge to it and the banter goes out of the Casualty Officer's voice.

This was one of those times.

Mark Slater, normally composed, had a hunted look on his chubby face. Beside him a female medical student, buried in the folds of a large white coat, looked wide-eyed. David raised a single eyebrow at them.

'What is it?' he queried.

'You'd better come and look, sir.'

He led the way to the treatment-room and pulled the curtain aside. David approached the figure lying on the emergency trolley. Already there were transfusion bottles swinging above the patient, plastic tubes descending from them like forest lianas, electrodes strapped to wrists and ankles and wires leading across to a trolley that would have looked more in place in the cockpit of Concorde. David took in the sinister gyrating dance on the oscilloscope screen before he even saw the patient.

The nurse in attendance stood aside to let him bend over the patient, saying nothing. David's experience was wide. Senior registrar at the Middlesex Hospital, registrar at the Royal Victoria, Belfast, surgical tutor at the Protestant Hospital, Chicago. These posts had accommodated him to bloody disaster, but what he saw now made him compress his lips, his eyes narrowing.

Susan's long blonde hair was nearly gone. What was left was short and singed, the stumps black at the tips. Her face was red and swollen like a pumpkin, with yellow blisters on her forehead and cheeks. Her lips were blue and her breathing laboured. She was squirming and turning in pain, her tongue rasping drily over her front teeth.

David laid a sensitive hand on her swollen abdomen. It was hard and rigid and she moaned at his touch. He turned at once to Mark Slater.

'Tell theatre to stay on—we're coming up. Now, Sister, what about the other one? Dr Slater said there were two.'

Sister led the way into the adjacent cubicle. Sam was

unconscious, with a black rubber airway between his teeth. David picked up an arm and let it drop. It flopped like a rag doll's. He raised the eyelids with his thumbs and looked carefully at the pupils. One looked larger than the other.

'Ophthalmoscope, please, Sister.'

The black multi-lensed instrument was in his hand immediately. He switched on the light and peered into the right pupil, swivelling the lenses with his forefinger to get the retina into focus. The optic nerve came into view, its surface looking blurred.

David pursed his lips and went over Sam's reflexes with a rubber hammer. His knees jerked briskly—too briskly. He scratched the soles of the feet. The big toe on the left bent down, but the right one hesitated and just twitched.

'Get him into intensive care, Sister. Put out a call for Dr Sandifer. We need a neurologist here, he may have an extradural.'

As he went up in the lift to the theatre he hoped he was mistaken. An extradural haemorrhage was a bleed within the skull, outside the brain, but giving rise to an increasing collection of blood that pressed on the brain surface. If it was it would mean opening the skull, removing the blood clot, finding the bleeding point and tying it off. Difficult, and something he had only done twice. If it was an extradural it would need doing quickly. There would not be time to get Sam to a specialist neuro-surgical unit.

In the surgeons' room he undressed quickly, getting into green theatre garb and questioning Mark Slater.

'What happened?'

'They crashed coming down a hill into Marlborough. One of the cottagers heard it, apparently, but couldn't get them out. The ambulance boys managed it in the end. They got him first, but they had to put an axe into the door to get at her, and that's when she got burnt. They were pulling her legs when the petrol caught. Lucky they didn't all go up at once.'

David looked at him enquiringly.

'You realise she's in labour?'

Slater nodded.

'Peritonism as well, probably from an intra-abdominal bleed. She'll certainly die if we don't go in, and she'll probably die if we do. It's muck or nettles.'

They pulled on white rubber boots and went down the stone corridor of the theatre suite into the scrub area. Sister Irving was already in the main theatre, standing beside a horseshoe-shaped trolley laden with an array of stainless steel instruments. Everything was ready, checked and double-checked, and Sister stood with her hands, in their tight-fitting rubber gloves, clasped before her like a priest at Mass. Above her white face mask her eyes flickered over the operating table at the trolleys, swab racks, nurses and porters, seeking for something missing, something out of place. There was nothing.

David strode through from the scrub area, like her, his hands clasped before him. Over the mask her eyes widened and stayed on him longer than usual. Despite their frequent hostilities there was an affinity between them when they were working, she knew that. They both knew it, but neither had acknowledged it.

She had worked with many surgeons during her training, but with none of them had she had this complete accord. She could anticipate David's every move and requirement. Now he would not have anyone else to take his cases, and when there was an emergency when she was off duty he expected the same from the other theatre sisters. When he did not get it he was difficult and abrasive, and as a result he had gained something of a two-toned reputation.

David Compton and Mark Slater stood opposite each other across the operating table, Ginette next to David. He looked enquiringly at the anaesthetist, half hidden behind the screen in front of Susan's head, who nodded in reply. The sterile operating towels were already in place, and without further delay David drew the Swann-Morton scalpel in a long sweep down the length of the abdomen in a classic para-median incision to allow him easy access to any part of the abdomen; vital when he was not sure what he would encounter.

The skin parted like a pair of wide red lips. The yellow fat under the skin bubbled bright scarlet and a tiny arterial jet fountained upwards until Mark Slater caught the vessel with the tip of his Spencer-Wells. From the head of the table came the repetitive wheeze and knock of the automatic respirator and next to it the cardiac monitor peeped an accompaniment to the dancing peaks and troughs on the oscilloscope screen.

David worked rapidly, locating the tiny bleeding points in the incision and stopping them with a swift click and ratchet of small Spencer-Wells forceps. Soon there was a gleaming row. He swabbed the wound and it remained dry.

He held out his hand without looking and Ginette slapped into it a red stick with a cable attached. One by one Mark picked up the forceps, and David touched each one with the electrode on the end of the red stick and pressed his foot on to a pedal on the floor. There was a brief hiss as the flesh at the point of the forceps writhed and went black. The bleeding point had been cauterised. Mark unclicked it and picked up the next. Within ninety seconds they had all been cleared.

David pressed aside the abdominal muscles and pointed to the blue, bulging membrane underneath.

'There it is. Nearly half a gallon of blood under that peritoneum. Sucker ready, Sister?'

A drumming sound under the table announced that the sucker unit had been switched on. A steel tube with a perforated snout and attached to rubber piping lay beside David's right hand. He slit the thin membrane of the peritoneum with his scalpel and a well of blood appeared, like a dark tarn. There was a gurgling sound as the snout of the sucker went in and the level of the tarn went down as if a plug had been pulled on it.

'Self-retaining retractor.'

It was lying on the small instrument table beside him, and he inserted the rounded lips into the wound and pulled on the ratchets in two directions. The gape of the wound became a square hole. Mark was busy prodding in the hole with the sucker which made louder noises as the remainder of the bloody tarn was finally removed.

'Light. Tilt, please.'

The big shadowless lamp moved without a sound to a different angle, illuminating the interior of the abdomen. Ginette put a large swab, the size of a small towel, into David's outstretched hand and he used it to push aside the slithering, intrusive intestines.

'There it is.'

He took a small gauze swab and Mark craned his head forward to see. In the depths of the square was something that looked like a white watermelon and about the same size. Around it was already a pool of blood, and as David took his swab away Mark could see a large bleeding point. A long pair of Spencer-Wells nosed their way deep down and were clicked on. Another followed and the bleeding stopped. Mark took the handles of one pair of forceps and lifted the nose towards David, who slipped a ligature round and tied it rapidly with one hand. He did the same to the other one and mopped. Mark looked at him, worried creases over the top of his mask.

'What next, sir?'

A good question. Susan was five months pregnant and already in premature labour. In her condition she would not survive a normal labour after the operation, and the baby, if alive, would have very little chance.

'Caesar.'

The razor edge of the Swann-Morton parted the wall of the womb. There was a gush of blood and liquor into the abdominal cavity and David's rubber-gloved hand plunged into the opening. He felt for the baby, found a leg, then slipped his fingers further up until they closed round the tiny body. When he pulled it out, trailing the blue umbilical cord, it lay white and limp in his grasp. Mark clamped the cord with two pairs of forceps and cut between them.

David handed the baby carefully to Ginette, who took it in a sterile towel and handed it over to a gowned staff nurse. Mark played the sucker busily, draining off the liquor and blood. David scooped out the large mass of the placenta, took a long curved needle from Ginette and drove it deeply through the wall of the womb, suturing the incision he had made. His fingers worked nimbly, clicking and unclicking the long needleholders as he put in a running suture.

'The sooner we're out of here the better.'

His words were echoed by the anaesthetist. His voice was crisp and had an edge which was lost on nobody. He was an Australian and not easily flustered.

'You're right there, sport—she's dead crook. You'd better hurry.'

David flicked a glance in his direction. Next to the Australian the oscilloscope pattern wavered. The jagged peaks alternated large and small and became irregular. The anaesthetist injected into the drip line. The peaks settled down briefly, then danced wildly once more. The peeping of the monitor changed and beside it came the strident note of the electronic alarm.

The peaks disappeared and turned into a straight jagged run.

'Bastard!'

The anaesthetist stood up. Next to him was the resuscitation trolley with the defibrillator. The two paddles would give an electric shock to the heart that was now just a quivering muscle, not pumping at all. With luck the shock would set the muscular pump back into action. He took the paddles, set the buttons on the face of the machine and looked around.

'Stand back, everybody.'

Anybody in contact with the patient would get the shock as well.

He placed the paddles on Susan's bare chest. There was a buzz and her body reared convulsively on the table. Everybody stared anxiously at the oscilloscope. The straight line continued; there were no peaks, no troughs. There was a dead silence in the theatre. A death on the table was a rare occurrence, but now it was a possibility. The anaesthetist put one of the paddles down, turned the current setting to two hundred joules and put the paddles back on Susan's chest, pressing the button immediately. She convulsed again, higher this time, and there was a clatter as some instruments fell to the floor. The flickering green line on the screen gyrated wildly, produced two Everest-like peaks, and David was about to smile when it went back to the deadly sustained tremble of ventricular fibrillation.

'One more and it's over to you, sport.'

The adenoidal Australian tones were flat and unemotional. If the next shock did not work, there was no point in doing more. It would be up to David to try direct cardiac massage by opening the chest, gripping the heart in his hand and squeezing it rhythmically to restart the natural beat.

'Stand back.'

Instinctively Ginette moved her steel-laden instrument trolley away from the table. She saw David's hands, clasped in front of him, tighten as the shock wave convulsed the body on the table once again. Already she had the large scalpel and other instruments ready for the chest incision should it be necessary. When David stepped forward she knew it would be necessary without looking at the oscilloscope screen. It was the urgency in his step and his stance that told her.

The Swann-Morton slapped into his outstretched right hand as his left hand felt along the rib line under Susan's left breast. Mark Slater held the breast back and David made a swift incision between the ribs. The fingers of his left hand ran along the incision line and the scalpel went after them, parting the rib muscles. He slid the fingers of his right hand between the ribs. It was difficult—they would not part easily. He pushed, fingers extended like a karate pose, and then his hand was into the chest, the rib bones gripping his wrist like a vice.

The heart felt like a warm peeled avocado without a stone. He squeezed it, feeling the blood inside squelching into the lungs and the aorta. He had to squeeze hard and then, when it felt empty, he let go and squeezed again. He went on doing this, but as he did so he knew there was something wrong.

Seconds went by before he knew what it was. The chambers were not refilling properly; the return circulation was not there. The organ felt small and limp in his grasp. He stopped his rhythmic squeeze, hoping to feel a squirm from the heart in his hand. There was nothing. It stayed inert. He looked at the anaesthetist, who shook his head.

'It's a no go, sport.'

David pumped harder and faster, his hand paining with the continued effort. He was sweating under his theatre garb. He looked at the monitor, but got no solace.

'Keep the oxygen high,' he ordered.

The anaesthetist shrugged and nodded. David felt his wrist breaking with the strain. He was about to give up when he felt a movement. The heart in his hand, slithery and slippery, gave a squirm that was not of his making. He felt it swell slightly within his grasp and gave it a squeeze when the swelling stopped.

It squirmed again.

He squeezed and waited. This time it swelled faster. He looked at the anaesthetist, his eyes bright above his mask.

'Intracardiac adrenalin.'

A syringe was slapped into his hand and he plunged the needle into the heart muscle, keeping the pumping going with his left hand. There was a rounding heave and he felt as though he was holding a struggling fish.

The heart was beating on its own.

He let it go and watched, marvelling as he saw the contraction waves convulse the glistening brown organ. On the oscilloscope the straight green line was a dancing wave again. The anaesthetist nodded approvingly.

'Nicely, David.'

Rare praise from an Aussie. Working rapidly, David sewed up the chest cavity, then returned to the abdomen. There was only the abdominal musculature to close, and he did this in layers, his fingers flying, the knots tied so quickly that Mark was hard put to it to keep up with him. Finally he stepped back from the operating table and turned to Ginette.

'The baby?'

She shook her head and he could see that, despite her training, her eyes were moist.

'He never even cried.'

CHAPTER THREE

AFTER the operation, Ginette went to her office. The dead baby had upset her. She swivelled her chair round and looked out at the blue sky over the Wiltshire downs and her mind went back to her training days—the days that should have inured her to this sort of thing. That they had not done so was due in part to the softness of her nature and in part to her past.

Her father was a general practitioner in Exeter and her mother had been a dancer with the Ballet Rambert until she married. From her Ginette had inherited her long legs and copper hair. From her father had come the interest in medicine and her love of art. When she was seven her godfather, William Bodger, had died. An ageing bachelor with no family, he had left her his entire estate. Apart from bequests to friends everything went to his goddaughter, whom he adored.

William Bodger had been a typical North Country business man. Both Yorkshiremen, he and Ginette's father had been friends as boys in Sheffield. John Irving had gone south to study medicine and William Bodger had stayed up north to make bicycles, but they had remained close friends for over thirty years. John Irving was comfortably off as a country doctor, but when William Bodger died he was a millionaire.

Ginette had not known about her inheritance until she was twenty-one, and by then it had grown. Generally speaking she found it more of a nuisance than an advantage. Most of the time she was careful to keep a low profile, because she had found by bitter experience that when people discovered that she was

very rich their attitude altered, even if they were nice.
If they were not nice they tried to borrow, and she
never knew if the men she met were interested in her or
her money.

Not until Simon Falconer.

Her first post, after completing her training, was as a
theatre staff nurse at the Royal Livery Hospital near
Glastonbury. She enjoyed theatre work and discovered
that she had a flair for it. The required precision suited
her tidy mind and she enjoyed laying out instrument
trolleys with meticulous care. She liked the air of
excitement and the moments of tension when there was
a dangerous turn of events during an operation.

Simon Falconer had been the surgical registrar at the
Royal Livery Hospital. He was tall, lean and saturnine
and his black hair was brushed straight back from his
forehead. He was quick and dedicated and suffered
fools not at all. Most of the nurses were frightened of
him, and with his air of dark demand it was not
surprising.

One of them had said that he reminded her of a black
Doberman not quite off the leash. As a surgeon he was
nearly brilliant and was undoubtedly headed for top
rank one day. Because of his manner he was not
popular with the nurses. They had warned Ginette
about him when she arrived. On her first day she had
been prepared to meet a black Machiavelli with real
hooves, horns and a tail, and had relished the thought
of giving him a taste of his own medicine.

Instead she had met a handsome man of thirty, with a
gleam in his eye that spoke of humour restrained and a
smile that, though rare, was devastating.

She fell in love with him.

She did it, not gradually, but at once. She did it as
she did so many things, precipitately and without
thought. She did it with the whole of her generous and

spontaneous nature, in a fashion that at first excited the laughter and then the sympathy of the nursing fraternity. The laughter came because she was obvious and innocent, wearing her heart on her sleeve for all to see.

For all, it seemed, except Simon Falconer. That was what elicited the sympathy. He was such an egocentric, career-minded, cold-hearted dog that everyone felt sorry for the gentle and beautiful new girl who had the misfortune to think he was wonderful.

He took no notice of her. Ginette did her best for him in every way. Never did he have to ask for an instrument. When she knew there was to be an operation with which she was unfamiliar, she checked with her books in order to make sure there was no special instrument to be included. He always had the correct gloves, and woe betide the junior nurse who was not standing ready to tie his strings when he had donned his sterile gown and was ready to glove up.

She discovered his favourite brand of coffee in order to serve it during the breaks. She made sure his theatre whites were ironed to perfection when the other surgical staff picked up theirs with the laundry creases still in them. She cleaned his white theatre boots after every session and made sure they were prominently labelled with his name on the inside.

Eventually he realised that the attractive copper-haired staff nurse in theatre was soft on him, and with typical surgical directness he asked her out for a drink at the local pub. He asked her one evening after a long drama involving a boy with multiple lacerations down the length of his arm. Simon had put in no fewer than a hundred and sixty-seven stitches, the last with the same care and precision as the first. When he took off his tight-fitting latex gloves there was blood on the inside, and as he threw them into the stainless steel waste drum Ginette saw it.

She glanced at his hands and saw him mopping them on the edge of his sterile gown. He had worn blisters on the needle-holders, with the repeated opening and closing, and the blisters had burst.

He saw her looking at him, and that was when he had asked her out for a drink. Perhaps it had been the sympathy in her expression, perhaps fatigue had eroded his customary saturnine guard.

'Feel like a drink at the King's Head?' he asked.

It was a command as much as an invitation, but Ginette had been too flustered and delighted to notice. They met in the entrance hall, and she remembered how tall he was. They had gone into the only bar in the pub and sat by the fire, and she had listened to him avidly. He talked incessantly and he talked well. He talked about surgery, music, theatre, books, travel, religion. He spoke with the authority of knowledge, and Ginette was entranced. He spoke rapidly, like a man who had not talked for a long time and wanted to get it out of his system. Only occasionally did Ginette say something, and then it was only to point the way for him to continue. After that evening she was his for ever, although there had been nothing more between them that night than a fireside chat. After that evening they had a tacit understanding, and the next weekend they had driven off to an inn in the Cotswolds where they spent their time walking during the day and making love through the night. Ginette had returned to the Royal Livery Hospital like a woman whose wildest dreams have been fulfilled. Which indeed they had. Work had become more absorbing than ever, although Simon never let his mask drop for a moment. The whole hospital knew of their affair, and the general consensus was one of approval. Ginette was blatantly in love, and Simon had become so much more approach-able that everyone benefited.

Even now she remembered the delight of those days with nostalgia. She had been so dazed with love that she had not noticed that she had missed a period until she was four months pregnant. It was only when she had felt the hook on her skirt bend that she had looked at herself in the mirror and seen an obvious roundness to her belly. Panic-stricken, she had fluffed the pages of her diary, trying to remember when she had last come on.

Her first panic was replaced by delight. They had never discussed pregnancy or marriage, but she knew that the first thing that Simon would do would be to buy her a ring. She held up her hand and stuck out her third finger in a gesture of appreciation.

To be certain, she took a specimen to a friend in the pathology lab who did the test for her while she stood by. The friend had looked at her mischievously.

'No prizes for guessing who's Daddy?'

Ginette had grinned back at her.

'No, none at all.'

'Does he know?'

'I'm going to tell him,' she said.

The friend had put a hand on her arm. Ginette could feel the pressure of it now.

'Ginette, don't be hurt,' she had urged.

'Hurt? Why should I be? He'll be delighted!'

Nevertheless the words had put the worm of doubt in her mind as she walked down the long corridor of the Royal Livery to the theatre block. She almost ran in the excitement of the moment, but even then her training took over. Nurses never ran. Never. Not in an emergency or for a fire. Running denoted panic, and that was something that did not exist. Nevertheless she went like a Louisiana trotting horse. Simon was writing his notes in the surgeons' room when she appeared, flushed and bright-eyed with excitement.

'Simon. . .' She hesitated. Something stopped her
from blurting out her news. Here was too clinical, too
public for such a wonderful piece of private news. Any
moment one of the surgical staff might wander in.
Simon quirked an eyebrow at her.

'Yes?'

'Simon, could we have supper together tonight?' It
was not one of the usual evenings they spent together.

'I'm giving a lecture to the local medical society at
eight.' His voice was uncompromising, but she was not
to be put off.

'How about after? We could always go to
Giovanni's.'

Giovanni's served pasta suppers until midnight and
they had lingered there many times. Simon eyed her
briefly, smiled and nodded.

'OK. I'll try and keep question time brief. What's
up?'

She gave him a smile and tapped him on the nose.

'Tell you later. Ten o'clock?'

He nodded and went back to his notes. Ginette went
to her room in the nurses' home to bath and change and
get ready for their ten o'clock tryst. She remembered
she had chosen the red dress with the upstanding collar
and the bear brooch that her parents had given her for
her twenty-first.

Simon was not there when she arrived at Giovanni's.
She sat at a table with a blue and white check cloth and
ordered a lime and soda. Usually she had a Kir, but
now she took a delight in making the first conscious
decision affecting her newly discovered pregnancy – no
more alcohol.

When Simon arrived she could see that he was in a
difficult mood. He sat down and picked up the menu
without saying hello. When Giovanni's daughter,
Giannina, bustled up he curtly demanded a Scotch and

soda. When it arrived he took a long drink, sat back in his chair and looked at her appraisingly.

'Now tell me what this is all about.'

Without waiting for her to reply he went on.

'God, those bloody GPs get up my nose! The damned stupid questions they ask! Anybody would think they'd never been to medical school.'

Ginette put her hand over his as he gripped his glass.

'Calm down, darling. Not everybody is a specialist in surgery. Maybe they know more about how to treat heart failure.'

It had been the wrong thing to say.

'I know bloody well how to treat heart failure!'

Ginette felt the moment getting away from her, but she pressed on.

'Simon, I've got some wonderful news.'

'Thank God for that! It's about time something good turned up.'

'Darling, I'm going to have a baby. I'm pregnant, Simon! Isn't that wonderful?'

She was so keyed up, so happy to tell him her news, that she did not at first divine his reaction. She was used to the saturnine expression on his features that so rarely gave away what he was thinking, and was not disturbed when he did not smile. He was looking at the menu and continued to do so for a long time before he put it down and faced her across the table. As he did so, a cold emptiness grew inside her. She knew what he was going to say. She felt a sense of having been through the scene before, and when it came it was as if the reel had already been played. He placed the menu carefully on the table between them.

'How far on are you?' he asked.

No loving surprise, no expression of delight. Just a straight technical question. Ginette shook her head.

'I don't know quite. I've missed a couple of periods.'

'A couple? Dear God, you must be nearly three months!'

She nodded.

'Could be. I haven't worked it out yet. I've only just found out.'

'How bloody careless can you get!'

It was as though he had slapped her in the face. She felt her eyes watering and blinked furiously.

'Simon, aren't you pleased?' she faltered.

'Pleased? You must be joking! What are we going to do with a baby?'

'Do? What do you think we're going to do?' She felt herself getting angry and gripped the edge of the small table that was between them. 'We're going to have it and love it and bring it up between us. That's what we're going to do.'

Simon eyed her levelly over the rim of his glass.

'That's what *you're* going to do. Don't include me in that little scenario.'

Ginette stared at him incredulously.

'You mean you don't want. . .'

He interrupted her.

'I mean just that. I do not want to know. I'm a surgeon. I have a career to follow, and that doesn't include bringing up babies, or getting married, or any other tenuous liaison you may have in mind. I have one goal, and one only, and that's not it.'

Ginette felt her breath leaving her and thought for a moment she was going to faint. She sat, gripping her lime and soda, and the moment passed, only to be replaced by a cold anger the like of which she had never known.

'Do you really mean what you say, or is this one of your fancy academic jokes?' she demanded.

'No joke.'

She knew then it was true. He meant what he said,

and in those few moments Ginette changed from a girl to a woman. She stood up.

'Goodbye, Simon,' she said, and walked away.

As she did so she wondered within herself whether he would come after her. When she reached the door and felt the night air on her face she knew he would not. As she lay in bed that night she wept. Not because of her condition, but because of Simon. She had loved him unutterably, still did, and her heart was breaking over the smashed idol that she had worshipped so devotedly.

He had been, for her, the epitome of all that was good and graceful in every sense, and she could not believe, even now, that there was this cruelty in his character. She was not worried for herself. She knew she could cope with her baby alone if necessary. It was the loss of the man she loved that demented her.

Ginette was not a girl to do things by halves. The following day she was occupied with the eye and ENT lists and did not see him. The lists were so busy she did not have time to think about herself and she went through her duties with a mindless efficiency.

It was when she came off duty that she began to wonder whether Simon really meant what he had said. Maybe she had caught him at an off moment when he had been aggravated by the meeting. Perhaps his lecture had not gone well. She knew how egotistical he was and how he hated not to be the prima donna. Maybe he would have a change of heart when he thought about it more carefully. After all, she could be a help to him in his career if only he would realise it. She was too proud to go to him and plead, but perhaps he would come to her?

To her surprise and heart-stopping delight he did come to her. It was after a late list when he stopped by the office where she was writing up the stores requirements for the following day. She felt his presence in the doorway, but pretended she had not noticed until he spoke. When he did she felt butterflies in her stomach and firmed her lips to stop them quivering.

'Will you talk to me?' he asked briefly.

She did not turn to look at him, but nodded. They were alone, the rest of the staff had gone. She could not see him, but the vibrations of his presence enveloped her like the basso profundo of a church organ.

'As a form of low life I could crawl under a snake's belly,' he went on.

Ginette gripped her pencil and gave another little nod. Was this an apology? If so, she was not going to give it to him on a plate.

Simon took a pace towards her and put his hands on her shoulders. They burned through the thin cotton of her uniform and she felt the movement of his thumbs on the rigid muscles of her neck and shoulders.

'Why?' The one word was all she could say.

'Darling, I'm sorry—I truly am. It was just the end of a bad, bad day. I have some problems apart from the hospital, the list was a bugger and those twits at the lecture got under my skin. I just wasn't myself.'

Somewhere, at the back of her mind, a bird began to sing, but she kept her head firmly fixed, not looking at him.

Simon was right when he said he had problems. Despite his surgical dedication he had a weakness. He was a gambler. At first his debts had been within reason, but gradually they had crept up and up, and he had gone to the loan sharks in the end. For a man of his intelligence it was madness, but the gambling urge was something he could not control. It was an addiction as real as that engendered by heroin.

The previous night, in a moment of weakness, he had

confessed his problems to his friend Tom Jenkins, the
senior orthopaedic registrar. Tom had laughed and
slapped him on the back.

'Simon, you dog, you must be joking! What's
happened to that unprincipled rakehell pal of mine?
With that little doll wrapped in your cot sheets what
does it matter? Five grand is tuppence to her.'

'What do you mean?'

Simon was uncomprehending. The thought of
Ginette having money had never occurred to him. She
certainly never showed it, and nurses were notoriously
poverty-stricken.

'That lovely little staff nurse you keep so closely in
your pocket, Ginette Irving. She's so loaded it's a
wonder she can walk.'

'Tom, what the hell are you talking about? She's a
doctor's daughter and there's not the sniff of dough
around her.'

Tom Jenkins put an avuncular arm across his friend's
shoulders.

'There are times when you amaze me, Simon. For a
hard-nosed hound you're occasionally naïve. That
young lady is more than a millionairess in her own
right.'

'What makes you think so?' Simon's voice was low
with suspicion.

'I know so. I play golf with her father every weekend
and he let it out to me after a few drinks at the
nineteenth a long time ago. Asked me not to say
anything, but in view of your plight I think you should
know.'

Simon smiled at him and wrung his hand.

'Tom, you're a pal! I owe you one.'

He stood behind her, gently smoothing her muscles,
and as he did so Ginette felt the tension and the grief go

from her. She tried to sustain a distance from him, but it was useless. She felt happiness returning, banishing from her the black dog of misery that had stood over her for what seemed an age but had only been forty-eight hours.

Slowly she turned in her seat and looked up at him. The satanic curl of his eyebrows and the lock of black hair falling over his forehead captivated her again, as did the rueful smile on his face. She stood up, and as he put his arms around her the tears rolled down her cheeks and she could not stay away from him any longer. She held her face up to him with a smile that belied her tears.

'Oh, Simon, it's been such a long two days!'

Gently he stroked her hair.

'I'm a sod. I must have been mad.'

'We're all a little mad sometimes.'

'I'm glad,' said Simon, 'because I want you to do something mad.'

She looked up at him, eyes wide and wondering.

'What's that?'

'I want you to be mad enough to marry me. Not cross mad, but lunatic mad. Are you that mad?'

For a moment her mouth opened in sheer astonishment and then she flung her arms around his neck.

'Oh, Simon! Of course I'm mad, madder than a March hare. I was cross mad with you, but now I'm lunatic mad, and it's lovely. Just lovely lunacy!'

It was around the hospital in a flash, long before Ginette appeared, self-consciously wearing the sapphire and diamond engagement ring that Simon produced the next day. She was giddy with excitement.

It lasted a week.

Perhaps it would have lasted longer had it not been for the building alterations in the theatre block. The surgeons' dressing-room had been moved temporarily to the linen-room. From the linen-room the duct air system had been moved and now a wide pipe connected the linen-room to the sister's office. The end of the pipe was temporarily open.

Ginette was sitting in the office with Sister Cray. The orthopaedic list had finished and the general list was about to start. Their conversation was interrupted by voices coming through the air-duct as through a megaphone.

'. . .didn't take you long to act on it, you old reprobate, but you don't have to go overboard and marry the girl. Surely she'll let you have it anyway?'

She recognised Tom Jenkins' voice and wondered whether men ever discussed anything other than sex when they were alone. Simon's voice replied, and she flushed as the thought hit her that Tom must be discussing her sex life with Simon.

'She wouldn't come across with it any other way, Tom. I know her well enough to be certain of that.'

Her eyes glinted. She would teach him a lesson for that! Tonight she would not come across with it at all. She would make him go hungry and afterwards tell him why, and then they would laugh and make up.

The next moment her feelings went from loving indignation to cold disbelief. She was not an eaves-dropper, but the conversation was forced upon her, and later she was often to feel that she would rather not have heard it.

'Don't tell me you're going to go through with it?'

'If I have to, but with luck I'll get all I want before we reach the altar. If she's as rich as you say it shouldn't be difficult, but I could always ask for a lump sum to shut up and not be difficult about the brat if we did get married and then divorced.'

Ginette felt sick. This was worse than before. She felt like a boxer who has been knocked down, got up and

then been given the coup de grâce. Simon had found
out about her money. That was what had produced his
change of heart. She thought of their loving moments,
their soft pillow talk and what she had regarded as the
exquisite delicacy of their relationship. Now it revolted
her, and she wanted nothing more than to be rid of
him, never to see him again. She tasted to the full the
bitterness of treachery and went to the lavatory to be
sick.

That had been her last day at the Royal Livery
Hospital.

She saw the Matron the next morning, told her the
facts, and explained that there was no possible way she
could continue there, working in close association with
Simon, with everyone knowing about her pregnancy
and the break-up of their relationship.

The next morning she was on the bus to Exeter. She
did not see Simon and hoped bitterly that it would hurt
him.

Her parents had been wonderful, as she knew they
would be. She took a job at the local health clinic, and
when her baby arrived she christened him Peter and
was glad that he had inherited her copper hair. He was
a happy baby, always smiling and with round, bouncy
cheeks and blue eyes that followed her everywhere.
Ginette lavished on him all the love she had lost for
Simon and he became the centre of her world.

On the birth certificate she wrote 'father unknown'
with a grim sense of discomfort, determined to give
Simon nothing to claim should he ever change his
mind.

Her mother made the finest nanny she could wish
for, and Ginette pursued her career as a theatre nurse
with an even greater sense of dedication. Simon's
callous treatment of her, his indifference to his son
during the ensuing years and his lack of support, put

her into an emotional straitjacket from which she was not to emerge for a long time.

CHAPTER FOUR

DAVID COMPTON took his old Triumph Vitesse down the hill towards the village of Aldbourne at a speed that would have earned him a hefty fine had there been a police car behind him. The gearbox whined protestingly as he double-declutched and went through the corner in a style reminiscent of Nigel Mansell. David liked cars and he liked driving, finding in it a release from the tension of the operating theatre. Like most other activities, he did it well. Unhappily for him he could not afford to indulge his passion.

James's school fees and Laurel's tastes precluded anything more exotic than his Triumph, which he serviced himself at weekends. That way he knew he would be safe from mechanical failure when he pushed the old car to its limits, which he did often.

Apple Tree Cottage stood at the edge of the village, alongside the river. It was the old gatehouse to the Manor which belonged to the Abelsons. David had taken a ten-year lease on his appointment to his consultant post. It was a cottage, in Cotswold stone, with a steeply pitched roof and leaded casement windows. A backdrop of green pastureland led uphill to a beech wood, and with the apple tree in the front garden, it looked like a setting for *The Wind in the Willows*.

The Regency clock in the hall showed nearly six as he opened the front door, and whistled. Laurel called back from the bedroom. She was sitting at her dressing mirror, winding her long black hair into a chignon and pinning it expertly into place. From her tight little smile and the tone of her voice he sensed an icy welcome.

When David married her, twelve years before, he had thought she was the perfect beauty, and he had not been far wrong. Now time and selfish dissatisfaction with her lot had turned the Sugar Plum Fairy into the Wicked Queen. She buffed her nails vigorously and arched her eyebrows at him.

'I thought you were coming home early?' she drawled.

'I know, darling, I'm sorry, but you know I can't always do things to order.'

She stood up, smoothed down the front of her red taffeta cocktail dress, and pouted her lips at him. He pecked dutifully, careful not to smudge her lipstick.

'Now, be a good boy and put out the cocktail snacks. They're all ready in the kitchen.'

'Dear God, surely I've got time for a wash and brush-up?' he protested.

Laurel adjusted the gold wrist-watch he had given her for their tenth anniversary and tapped it with her forefinger.

'The Colonel will be here in three minutes exactly. You know him.'

David sighed and went into the kitchen. The snacks were laid out, with clinical precision, on the serving top. Slivers of celery, carrot, green peppers, and cauliflower fleurettes surrounded a central blob of mayonnaise. Tiny rolls of smoked salmon were flanked by rows of stuffed olives and white onions. A forest of wooden cocktail sticks skewered minute rafts of pineapple surmounted by minuscule morsels of mouse-trap cheese. Laurel did not believe in breaking her rigid dietary discipline for the benefit of her guests.

David picked up the plates and carried them into the living-room. It was furnished elegantly with a Knoll suite upholstered in gold brocade, a white carpet and light green velvet curtains swagged back under deep pelmets. A watercolour of Arles by Marcel Dyf surmounted a white Adam fireplace and over a satinwood Sheraton sideboard hung a modern piece of artwork by Jonathan Quinn, a rising young artist David favoured.

The effect was one of studied elegance. There was no television in sight. Laurel had wanted to secrete it in a Georgian reproduction chest of drawers, but David had put his foot down. He would have the real thing or nothing, and he was not going to desecrate a piece of genuine Georgian furniture for a telly. So it ended up hidden in a cupboard by the fireplace.

In the corner of the rectangular room was a Blüthner grand piano. It had belonged to David's mother, and he played it less frequently than she would have liked, mainly on Sunday mornings and when he was cross. The lid was down and on it was a photograph, in a silver frame, of a boy with a smiling face and fair hair cut in a fringe. It was his son, James. Next to it was a photograph of a black-haired Jewish violinist playing to a petite blonde woman seated at a piano. They were looking at each other and the photographer had captured an intimate moment. David's parents.

He looked at it often, because he had not seen them since he was ten. They had drowned when the Greek cruise ship the *Lakonia* had caught fire and sunk in the Mediterranean. His adolescent years had been spent with his remote but caring Aunt Harriet.

David put down the plates of canapés and looked at the photograph of James. He had taken it on James's eighth birthday and never looked at it without a pang of remorse. The wide blue eyes looked at him with a trust and devotion that tore him apart, and the smile gave the impression of an intelligence that he knew was not there.

James had been born with a spina bifida, a bad one. He had been saved by a rushed flight to Great Ormond Street Hospital and a brain operation. This had saved his life, but not his intelligence. James was not demented, but he was retarded. He was also partially paralysed. He walked only with the aid of crutches, and he was doubly incontinent.

It had all been too much for Laurel. James had needed repeated operations, each one a drama with both of them wondering whether he would survive. He did survive, but the difficulties of nursing, the smell and dirt and constant washing, the fouled clothes and bedlinen, had so offended Laurel that she had retreated into an hysterical fugue.

It had taken a month in a nursing home to get her over that while James was looked after in an institution for handicapped children. It had been a nightmare for David. Most of the children in the public institution were severely mentally disabled, crying and shrieking without cause, unable to speak or communicate, and frequently hurling themselves into bizarre postures. James was slow, but beside them he stood out as an intelligent child.

Laurel's diction was perfect. She spoke daintily and precisely and James, as a result, spoke like an angel. No one, listening to him read, would believe that he was not perfectly normal.

David put the plates down and went back to the bedroom. He had arrived home tired, the thoughts of James had not helped, and now he was angry.

'Is that it? That's all you could find time to produce? There's not enough there to satisfy an anorectic shrew, and what there is wouldn't tempt a lick from a famished fox!'

A pencilled eyebrow went up in protest.

'They're here for drinks, not a buffet supper. There's

a dinner party at the Abelsons' later this evening, anyway. And these little eats are expensive.'

'Anybody would think we're on the breadline!' snapped David.

'With James's school fees we nearly are. Do you know when I last had a new dress? Or the last time we went out to dinner?' Laurel demanded.

The door bell rang, signalling the end of the round. Laurel rustled past him, a picture of red elegance, and as he straightened his tie in the mirror David heard her beautifully modulated tones greeting Colonel Southey and his wife. Dick Southey was the archetypal colonel of Gurkhas—tall, ramrod-straight, hair short, a pencil moustache, and clipped speech that made a chance remark sound like an order. He wore his houndstooth suit like a uniform and his check shirt was of a pattern only to be found in the windows of Gieves. The burnished elegance of his black brogues bespoke hours of batman's labour. David wasn't sure whether he heard his heels click as he greeted Laurel.

He held out his hands to Molly Southey, who moved towards him with a smile. She had been a model with Laurel and it still showed in her stance. She was prematurely grey and used it to great effect. With her violet eyes and classic features she looked striking in a navy blue suit. The Gurkha emblem, a pair of crossed kukris, decorated her left lapel.

The clock in the drawing-room struck six.

'Dick the stickler—always on time!' smiled Laurel.

'Correct, m'dear. Can't stand laggards.'

Molly stood close to David and sniffed.

'Still the busy surgeon? I swear you smell of anaesthetic. Aldbourne's own Dr Kildare. I rather like it.'

Molly liked David and never lost an opportunity to show it. Direct, attractive and forceful, Molly was apt to call a spade a shovel. Sometimes David wondered just how much was on offer. He grinned at her.

'Come with me and I'll give you something you really will like.'

'Ooh—lovely!'

'It's a gin and tonic.'

'Spoilsport!' she laughed.

David was eyeing the pattern on the black stockings covering her long legs when the doorbell went again. On the step was a vision resembling an old English sheepdog. It reared up at him and he was engulfed in a mass of woolly coat and shaggy brown hair. A wet kiss smacked on to his cheek.

Daphne Webber was Laurel's old school chum. Unlike Laurel, she was short and round and demonstrative. She taught English at the local school. Her husband Martin stood beside her. He looked like a whippet; a furtive, cunning and secretive whippet. A whippet with sleek black hair, a toy moustache, and a tight blazer. The badge on the breast pocket made Dick Southey wince. As some people smell of tobacco and others of fish and chips, Martin Webber smelt of pot. Cloying, sweet and sickly, it was unmistakable.

Equally unmistakable was his fishy, damp handshake that made David's flesh creep. Martin was a teacher. He taught at the school of further education at night and ran an art shop during the day in a little alleyway off Marlborough High Street.

He sipped a glass of white wine and his narrow eyes darted round the room.

'Nice bit of Dyf you got there, David. Pity about the Quinn.'

Martin tried to needle David every time they met, and David always rose to the bait. Frequently it ended in an acrimonious exchange, and Laurel would have a go at him later.

'Don't you see the little scut is just jealous of you? He puts the needle in because you're everything he isn't. And you, you great booby, you rise to it every time!'

This time David restrained himself, smiled at Martin and said, 'Laurel likes it.'

Martin stripped a piece of salmon off its square of brown bread and poked it beneath the toy moustache.

'I expect she likes *Comic Cuts* too.'

With a controlled effort David put the plate down and went to answer the door. Disdaining the bell, the caller was banging the heavy brass knocker, making the cottage reverberate like a bass drum. As he passed Laurel she whispered to him,

'Must be the Abelsons.'

He detected the anxiety in her voice. Laurel was ambitious—ambitious for him, for them both. Not in the professional sense, but socially. She was glad of his professional success, but only in so far as it brought them social advancement. To her the Abelsons represented advancement. They were the local gentry, owners of the Manor and their landlords. Sir Ralph Abelson was on the board of Schwarz and Sassoon, a major merchant bank, and his wife Penelope, apart from breeding cocker spaniels, was the acknowledged leader of the local county set.

David opened the front door before it splintered and was engulfed in a miasma of whisky fumes. Sir Ralph Abelson, tenth baronet of his line, stood flushed and foursquare on the doorstep, his hand still raised to hold the knocker. At six feet four and built to size, he towered over David although he was on the lower step. A gap-toothed smile from a heavy-featured face preceded a greeting by a voice like a foghorn.

'Good to see you, David. Right on time today, you see. Didn't want to be late on you twice.'

Behind him, Lady Abelson, gaunt and horsy, whinnied concurrence. A massive hand came across in a sideswipe, clapping him on the shoulder. David hoped fervently it was not dislocated and attempted to smile through the pain.

'Delighted you could come over, Ralph. Good evening, Penelope.'

There was no doubt that the Abelsons had style. It came from ten generations of aristocracy. Their easy manner arose not from self-confidence but from the fact that they did not have the slightest care what anybody thought of them. His double-breasted chalk-stripe suit bore the stamp of Savile Row, but was creased. His Huntsman's shirt was slightly frayed at the collar and his old Etonian tie had obviously never been cleaned.

Penelope Abelson was all twin-set and pearls. The twin-set was cashmere and too big for her and the pearls were real. Her court shoes were unfashionable, but they were handmade by John Lobb. When she smiled and gave a loud laugh, which she did often, David was reminded of a seaside donkey. He saw some dog hairs clinging to her skirt and was tempted to offer her the clothes brush off the hat-stand, but thought better of it and escorted them into the drawing-room instead. Their crumpled style made Colonel Southey resemble a senior prefect and Martin Webber look like a racetrack seller of dirty postcards.

Martin lifted a pointed nose towards Sir Ralph.

'What price that bang on the hill, eh, Sir Ralph?'

A benevolent smile came down upon him.

'I'm afraid I don't recall. . .'

'A right wallop. Bentley Mulsanne comes screaming down the hill and bangs into a truck. Nobody about. Then when the ambulance arrives it goes up in a flamer. They were dead lucky to get out.'

David arrived with the Abelsons' drinks.

'Not so, Martin,' he corrected.

The black toy moustache twitched, aggrieved.

'Why not?'

'She wasn't lucky, she was burned. They're both in intensive care.'

This brought a bray from Penelope Abelson.

'God! Who was it?'

'Chap called Sam Bennett and his wife.'

Sir Ralph lowered his glass slowly in astonishment.

'Not Sam Bennett of Properties International?'

David shrugged. 'Don't know. He's a short, stocky chap—craggy face, black hair.'

'That's him. He's on my board of directors. Pretty tough sort. He only recently married her—quite a beauty, she was.'

'Not any longer.'

Penelope Abelson raised a pair of eyebrows and compressed her lips.

'I remember him. Didn't like him a bit, he kicked one of my dogs.'

Sir Ralph boomed out a laugh like a barrel-organ.

'Don't blame him, m'dear. Pomeroy bit his ankle, and Sam's not one to sit down under sufferance.'

Colonel Southey clipped in, 'You operated, David?'

David nodded. 'Afraid so. She nearly died on the table.'

Molly Southey put a hand on his arm.

'My poor David! That must have been very distressing for you. Now there'll be all sorts of questions, I suppose?'

'That's right, especially as she'd been assaulted. That was the cause of most of her problems, not the accident.'

There was a sudden hush, then Daphne Webber spoke up, her small voice emanating from a round face framed by sheepdog curls.

'Are you talking about attempted murder, then, David?'

David shrugged his shoulders.

'Not for me to say, but that's what it looks like.'

There was a total silence at this until Sir Ralph spoke up.

'Is he going to survive?'

'Yes. He should be OK soon. As you say, he's a pretty tough character.'

'I didn't mean tough physically, David. I meant tough character-wise. He's a hard man, and if his wife's been half killed I wouldn't want to be around when the reckoning comes. And knowing him, it will come. He's not a great forgiver.'

Molly Southey waved an elegant hand at her husband.

'I think that's right. You wouldn't forgive someone if they tried to murder me, would you, Dick? What would you do?'

'Kill him.'

Nobody doubted the brief answer. Daphne spoke to Martin.

'There, dear, that's lovely and gallant and mediaeval. What would you do?'

The toy moustache twitched sideways to and fro.

'Give him a pension.'

Nobody doubted that either, despite the general laughter. Laurel fussed around Sir Ralph. Penelope and Daphne got deep into dogs. Dick Southey suffered an art lecture from Martin Webber on the deficiencies of popular artists like Quinn and Molly Southey led David into a corner, giving him the benefit of her widest eyes and a whiff of Arpège. She sat on a window seat, crossed her long legs and leaned towards him.

'Tell me, David, how is James getting on?'

He knew Molly was genuinely fond of the boy and did not recognise it for the ploy that it undoubtedly was.

'He's doing well, Molly. Very happy, walking better, and he can read. Since his last operation he's had to have some intensive physio, and now he can manage without his crutches for part of the time. We're going over to see him this weekend.'

'Wonderful! So you think St Athelstan's is worth it?'

'Every penny. It's damned expensive and every extra costs, but so what?'

Molly eyed him over her glass.

'How much does it cost you, David?' she asked.

'Twenty thousand a year basic plus extras. Not a lot of change out of twenty-five.'

'My God, that must keep you poor!'

'It does. I have an overdraft that can only be described as handsome—depending on how you look at it.'

Molly quirked at him, her violet eyes mischievous. 'From where I'm looking that's just how I would describe it.'

David grinned at her.

'Don't say that too loud, I've no desire for a caress from a kukri.'

'Not even a baby one?' she said, fingering the tiny brooch on her lapel.

He laughed. 'Maybe just a little.'

Their tête-à-tête was interrupted by Daphne.

'David, can't you come and operate on my labrador? He's got a lump on his poor old belly and the vet says it has to come out.'

'Why not let the vet do it, then?'

Daphne grinned impudently at him.

'Because the last time the vet touched him I got a bill for a hundred quid, and you could do it for nothing.'

'Thank you, young lady. I like your honesty. For half

an hour's free labour you'd get me struck off?'

'But think of poor Rover's belly!'

'I will, in my prayers.'

Molly stood up and breathed warmly into his ear.

'I can think of half an hour's free labour on another belly that would also get you struck off.'

She moved across the room to speak to Laurel and Sir Ralph with a graceful swaying elegance that had Daphne looking after her enviously.

'Why are some women given it all?' she sighed.

David patted her gently on the cheek.

'Never mind, my pet, you have a lovely nature, and that's a lot, lot more than looks.'

The sheepdog curls shook violently.

'Bugger the nice nature. I'd swap it all to look like her for twenty-four hours.'

David laughed and took her arm.

'The way you sound you'd never live it out!'

Daphne's round, lugubrious face looked so miserable for a moment that he regretted saying it.

'Look at your Laurel,' she went on. 'She's another one that looks like something out of *Vogue*.'

'If you were dressed in your nature you'd outshine the pair of them,' he assured her.

She looked up at him with big brown shining eyes that shimmered.

'David, you do say nice things to a girl!'

Sir Ralph's foghorn blasted at them from three feet away.

'David. This lass of yours is coming to join our little circus.'

From the colour of her cheeks and the brightness of her eyes David could sense that Laurel was excited.

'Ralph has offered me a job, David. Isn't that marvellous?'

'It is if you want to do it.'

Despite himself, David knew that he sounded churlish.

'Well, of course I want to do it. It's going to be much more interesting than the job at the library.' She smiled at Sir Ralph. 'And a lot more money too.'

Sir Ralph handed his glass to David for replenishment.

'We can always arrange to pay you less,' he told her.

'Do you get a company car as well?'

David said it with a trace of sarcasm. To his astonishment Sir Ralph nodded his head.

'Right. There's a little three series BMW that goes with it. You'll have to be mobile, Laurel.'

Daphne, who had overheard this last part of the conversation, turned to Martin.

'Must be nice to live like that. Lots of money, no worries, winter in the Bahamas, everybody taking off their hat to you.'

Martin took a sniff of white powder from a snuffbox in his waistcoat pocket and looked disparagingly at Sir Ralph.

'That braying twit! I wouldn't piss on him if he was on fire.'

David suddenly felt exasperated. He had heard Martin's remark, did not like him, liked his comment even less, and when he and Laurel were briefly alone in the kitchen he said to her,

'He's the bottom. I don't know why we have to ask him.'

'Because his wife has some very good connections.'

'Do we have to do everything with an eye to the main chance?'

'Somebody has to try to get on here,' Laurel argued. 'We wouldn't do much if it was left to you.'

'You seem to have been getting on well. What's that job you've got with Ralph?'

'I'm a personal assistant. Fifteen thousand a year, a car and free insurance. Not bad.'

'That's good. At least we'll be able to pay for James without going deeper into the red.'

Laurel turned to him, her face whitening, her lips tight.

'I'm not using my earnings to pay his fees!'

'Well, what will you use them for? You know we can't keep up with them on my salary. Our overdraft's going up like a rocket.'

'That's your problem. My earnings are my own, and I'm not going to chuck them away on keeping our son in a posh establishment we can't afford.'

'You'd rather he went back to that appalling institution he was in when you were in the nursing home, I suppose?'

He saw her eyes narrowing. Something that only happened when she was losing control.

'As long as I don't have to cope with him I don't bloody well care where he is.'

'Well, I do, and he'll stay at St Athelstan's.'

'Not with my money!'

'I don't care whose money, but he's staying where he is if it means mayhem and murder to do it!' snapped David.

He walked out with a fresh tray of canapés, seething beneath an affable smile as he offered the tray to Penelope Abelson, who greeted it with a toothy woof of delight.

'My dear David, you have the most delicate touch with. . .'

The telephone shrilled at his elbow. He put the tray on top of the piano and picked up the receiver.

'David Compton.'

'Just a moment, Mr Compton. I have Dr Slater for you.'

He recognised the voice of Walter, the hospital telephonist. There was a purr and a click and Mark Slater's agitated voice came on.

'Sorry to disturb you, sir, but that chap with the head injury is causing concern.'

'What is it?'

David sighed inwardly. It seemed that every time they had any social function laid on at home he could guarantee a call from the hospital.

'That chap in the motor smash. We've got problems.'

'What sort of problems? Has he had an intracranial bleed?'

'No, sir, but there's something very wrong with his neck and his breathing is obstructed. I'm afraid it's a come quick.'

David recognised the signs and asked no more questions. He put the telephone down and raised his voice slightly.

'Sorry, everyone—have to love you and leave you. Thanks for coming.'

The next moment he was into the Triumph and speeding up the road towards Manbury Hospital.

CHAPTER FIVE

DAVID stood in the anaesthetic-room, looking at the patient's notes. This was a ritual before every operation, and in this instance it was particularly important. He closed the folder and turned to find Ginette standing behind him. The stark simplicity of the green theatre garb with its straight skirt, round-necked shirt and green turban set off her slim figure. He could not help noticing the deep tan of her long legs and wondered briefly if it went all over.

He smiled at her, his eyes crinkling at the edges and his left eyebrow lifting in a way that made her forget momentarily what she was going to say.

'David—ah—Dr Sandifer wants to speak to you. He's in the surgeons' room.'

He stood up. Tall as she was, he towered over her. The room was small and in the confined space they had to stand close to each other. Despite the steely discipline of her training Ginette was disturbed and her green eyes had big, dark pupils. He could feel the warmth of her skin and smell the sweetness of her breath.

They turned at the same time and bumped into each other. David felt the softness of her buttock against his hip and put his hand on her waist to steady her. Instinctively her back arched and he felt a surge within him.

'Steady there!'

Ginette did not know whether it was an apology or an admonishment and marched quickly up the corridor, her cheeks flaming. She prided herself on her cool and detached attitude in her work so that she was never flustered, and this involuntary reaction disturbed her. She had developed a respect and admiration for David as a surgeon that she had not felt for anyone since the days of Simon Falconer, but the burn in her cheeks was a reaction not engendered by admiration. It bothered her because she sensed a lack of control to which she had not succumbed for a long time.

Since Simon her attitude to men had been too forbidding to encourage advances except from the most predatory males, and these she had dealt with in a manner that was as curt as it was uninterested. There were no scars on her body, but on her emotions they were deep and wide.

She had sought and found solace in the perfection of her work, and that was why she held a senior post at such an early age. It gave her a deep sense of achievement to be at the sharp end of repairing bodies broken by accident. With her money she could easily have spent her days shopping and attending coffee and cocktail parties. Instead she had chosen a way of life involving long hours of standing in the operating theatre and going home dog-tired, her back breaking, her feet on fire, but mentally satisfied.

Patrick Sandifer was a tall, thin man who reminded David of a secretary bird. He was standing by the window overlooking the car park, dipping his beak into a cup of coffee, when David entered the surgeons' room. His voice was as dry and precise as his manner.

'This chap's had a haemorrhage into a thyroid cyst, in my opinion. Nothing serious neurologically. Needs evacuating at once, he's going down steadily. Look here.'

He put his coffee down, picked up some photographs and put them on a viewing screen. They were multiple shots taken of the ultrasonic scan of the thyroid. Patrick

Sandifer pointed a long finger at one of the images. At the side of the print was a dense white area.

'The scanner shows it in the right lower pole of the thyroid. Probably a ruptured twig within the cyst. Shouldn't be too difficult.'

'Thanks very much!'

Patrick Sandifer looked at his colleague closely, not missing the sarcasm.

'What's the matter, David?' he enquired.

David grinned back at him amiably.

'You don't have to do the digging. With you physicians it's all just an elegant exercise in logical inference. Like doing *The Times* crossword.'

Patrick Sandifer looked genuinely hurt.

'I don't see what's wrong with *The Times* crossword. I do it every day.'

David sighed, gave up the struggle and turned to Ginette.

'Sister, are we laid up for a thyroidectomy?' he asked her.

'Yes, Mr Compton. And there's a call for you on the corridor phone. Your wife.'

David put his head into the telephone booth and picked up the instrument. Laurel's voice came across the wire like iced crystal, the refined accent clear and penetrating.

'David, do you hear me?'

'Loud and clear.'

'I want to know if you're going to be back before everybody has to go.'

'No, I won't.'

'Are you sure?' she demanded.

'Sure I'm sure. Look, the chap's almost dying, I haven't started and you're arguing about when I'm getting back.'

She lowered her voice.

'The Abelsons could be important to you. You know he's on the Public Health Committee.'

'Bully for him,' drawled David.

'I can see you're in one of your difficult moods. Please do your best to be home soon.'

'Do you mind if I start now,' David said in frustration, 'or do we give the job to the undertaker?'

There was a noise of exasperation from the instrument as David put it gently back into its cradle. In the theatre Ginette was preparing the instrument trolley with Staff Nurse Gotch. They were both masked and gowned in green, Staff Nurse Gotch tall and angular, her beaky nose pushing her mask well out from her face.

Ginette had never warmed to her, but she was efficient and a glutton for work. She was also a great pursuer of young housemen, who knew her as 'Gotcher Gotch.' Sandra Gotch put a handful of forceps on the trolley, laying them out in a precise fan shape.

'Quite a feller, our Mr Compton, eh?'

A typical Sandra comment—insidious and linking them both to him. Ginette said nothing.

'I wouldn't mind five minutes with him on my half day.'

Ginette put a retractor down with a bang on the trolley.

'Mr Compton is married, Staff Nurse. And your half day is Wednesday, when we have a major list. Even with the inclination I doubt he could spare the time.'

Sandra was not one to be put down.

'With a wife like his I reckon he ought to be grateful for a bit of anything. Skin, bone and ice right through.'

Having seen Sandra in the shower, Ginette nearly laughed.

'I've heard that she's very glamorous,' she said.

'Glamour isn't everything, and what about that kid of

theirs?' Sandra was obviously intent on a thorough dissection.

'What about their child?' asked Ginette.

'She keeps it in a home—spina bifida. That doesn't say much for her. She should stay at home and look after it herself.'

Ginette had not heard about David's boy and she felt a wave of compassion. At the same time she felt angry at Sandra.

'Please tally all the swabs, Staff Nurse.'

There was an unmistakable edge to her voice, and Sandra reluctantly detached herself to the other side of the theatre to count the swabs they were about to use. Ginette tightened her lips. In her less charitable moments, which came rarely but her patience was being tested now, nothing would have given her greater pleasure than to get rid of Sandra Gotch on grounds of incompetence, but unfortunately she was very efficient. She made a mental note to review the duty times so that Sandra could take the ENT lists, which were timely and fiddly.

By the time David had scrubbed and gowned, Mark Slater had the preliminaries completed. Sam Bennett was lying on the operating table covered in sterile sheets. Only the whiteness of his shaven throat gleamed through a square within the green.

David flicked an enquiring glance sideways at Ginette and got a nod in return. He picked up the scalpel and drew an arc across Sam's throat. By now there was an obvious swelling in front of his Adam's apple. David knew that Patrick Sandifer had been right. Sam had probably had a small cyst in his thyroid for a long time and as a result of his accident an artery had ruptured within it, blowing it up like a balloon and causing pressure on the trachea behind and obstructing his breathing. Much longer and he would have choked to death. As it was, as long as David could isolate the bleeding point and remove the cyst, Sam would be as good as new very quickly. He picked up the bleeders beneath the skin and turned to Ginette.

'Retractors, please, Sister.'

She handed him the fine-pointed retractors which he used to hold back the tissues covering the thyroid gland and the trachea. Gently he dissected around the gland and mobilised a plum-coloured tumour the size of an orange.

'Ready with the sucker.'

He knew that when the cyst ruptured, as it inevitably would, there could be increased bleeding from the ruptured artery within. The pressure within the cyst had slowed the haemorrhage down, but when it was released it could restart like a gushing oil well.

The cyst ruptured at that moment and there was an immediate outpouring of blood over the operation site. Mark Slater was waiting for it, had the sucker there at once, and the field gradually cleared. David put his finger into the cyst, feeling the extent of it and hoping to locate the bleeding artery. He could feel little within the soft, gelatinous interior, but when he withdrew his finger a fine scarlet fountain pulsed between his fingers and above his head. He took the sucker from Mark Slater, played it within the cyst and peered into the cavity, eyes narrowed, searching for the bleeding point which he had to find.

It seemed to come from nowhere. He probed with the beak of the Spencer-Wells and clicked them together when he thought he had the artery, but the bleeding continued. The cyst was not neatly defined and went into the body of the thyroid in a formless mass.

David began to feel alone.

Gently he moved the gland aside in a different

direction. Nothing happened. He thought rapidly, his mind going over the anatomy of the thyroid gland and its blood supply and the possible aberrations to it. He did not want to remove the whole gland and subject Sam to a lifetime of replacement thyroid tablets, but it would have been easier than trying to get the cyst alone: added to which it was lying uncomfortably close to the carotid artery. One nick into that with the razor point of his scalpel and the bleeding would be catastrophic. The anaesthetist's voice, muffled behind his mask, came through.

'Hundred and ten, seventy. He's coming up.'

Suddenly it was there—a scarlet thread of silk that fountained and flowered on to the surface with a deadly elegance. David smiled under his mask and brought down the steely nose of the fine Spencer-Wells that cut off the fountain with the first click of the ratchet.

'Got him!'

There was a wealth of satisfaction in those two words and the atmosphere in the theatre relaxed noticeably. The fine catgut ligature went on with care, and as he pulled the knot tight, pressing down firmly with his left forefinger, David nodded at Mark Slater.

'Off, very slow.'

He completed the knot, swabbed and watched the area carefully. There was no leak. Now it was going to be easier. He removed the wall of the cyst, oversewed the hole within the gland, his fingers flying like a demon fiddler as he tied one-handed knots with fine catgut.

'Let's get out of here.'

The skin flap was re-positioned and carefully aligned so that there would be no residual puckering, and suddenly they were finished. As they walked out of the theatre, ripping off their rubber gloves, David turned to Mark.

'I want him in intensive care. The full routine for the next forty-eight hours.'

'How do you rate him, sir?' asked Mark.

'As long as that ligature holds he'll be fine.'

'What about the woman? Do you think she might make it?'

David nodded.

'She should do—she's a tough lady. Do you know what happened?'

'Not really. The ambulance crew took them to the Cottage Hospital, who patched them up and transferred them this morning. Difficult to see how the woman got that pelvic bleeding in an RTA.'

'You can get anything in an RTA. I knew a woman who said one got her pregnant.'

Mark's eyes opened wide.

'You've having me on!'

'No. Absolute truth. They were having it off in a layby. A van blew a tyre in the wet and cannoned into them just as he was coming out at the moment critique. Instead of out it was in, and that was it.'

'I can't believe it. How did you hear about it?'

'She got a head whip injury at the same time and came into my casualty. It was in Chicago. She had a ratty little lawyer with her, I remember. He wanted her to sue for both, but the boyfriend wouldn't have it.' He patted Mark on the shoulder. 'You don't know how lucky you are, old son. You could have been fathered by a van!'

Mark went off to supervise Sam's removal to the intensive care unit, and David looked at his watch. Through the open door of her office Ginette caught sight of David's spare figure. He looked as though he needed a good square meal. Impulsively, she called out to him.

'Mr Compton!'

He turned, and as he did so she regretted her action, but by now she was committed. She smiled at him with a confidence she did not feel.

'Would you care for some sandwiches? Dinner will be off, even in the consultants' dining-room.'

She indicated a plate of freshly cut chicken sandwiches on the desk. She never invited any of the other consultants to do this. Why him? It was a precedent, and she did not like setting precedents, especially with men with whom she worked.

'Sister's perks,' she added. 'There aren't many, but this one still holds.'

David hesitated, looked at his watch, then went in and sat down. Down the corridor Staff Nurse Gotch tapped a porter on the arm and dabbed a finger in his direction.

'How about that, Jim?'

Jim Baker, a family man who had more years as theatre porter than Sandra had been alive, leaned on the trolley.

'How about what? If he can't sit down for five minutes after what he's been doing without dirty-minded women pointing the finger he's a fool to be here.'

Sandra lifted a bony chin.

'Be like that!' she snapped.

David looked at Ginette as he munched his sandwich, grateful for her concern and thinking she really was a remarkably attractive woman. She poured him a cup of coffee from a thermos flask.

'Quite a day.'

As she said it her teeth gleamed and he noticed, inconsequently, what a pink tongue she had. Most of the time they worked together she was wearing a mask and shapeless theatre clothing. He recognised that the figure under her shirt was now far from shapeless.

'Like the curate's egg, good in parts,' he said.

'Who said that?'

'I don't know, but it's so often true.'

They both laughed together.

'You don't look much like a curate,' Ginette remarked.

'I don't feel much like one.'

'What do they feel like?' Ginette was surprised to find that her breathing had become ragged.

'Never like this.'

He found himself looking at her intently and the laughing stopped. They just sat, faces close and opposite. He could feel the gentle draught of her breath on his face and excitement surged within him. There was a long silence and he began to move towards her. Her mouth was parted, her lips moist and glistening. She did not move as his face came nearer. She could see, in fine detail, his grey eyes and the tiny crinkles at their corners. A lock of black wavy hair had fallen over his eye and she wanted to move it. Involuntarily she was putting her hand up to do so when the telephone rang.

She moved her hand to the instrument and David sat back, the spell broken. He took a sandwich as she spoke crisply into the telephone, glad he was not on the other end. In action, Ginette's gentle features took on the firmness he had seen in theatre. She had more colour than usual, however, and he noticed that she was drumming her fingers on the desk.

He stood up, looking at his watch. Time to go. She was still talking. Gently he placed his hand over her drumming fingers.

'Thanks for the sandwich.'

He walked thoughtfully to the lecture theatre in a warm and erotic haze. Back in the tiny office Ginette put the telephone down and looked out of the window.

'Damn,' she said, 'damn, damn, damn!'

She was, beneath her professional exterior, a warm but shy person, and the thought that David might have guessed at the effect he was having on her made her curl her toes with embarrassment. Why, for instance, had she insisted that the kitchen send up chicken sandwiches? They had complained about having to do so. She would not have asked any of the other surgeons to join her, so why him?

Despite their protests she had come the heavy on the kitchen staff, knowing that she was stretching their resources. She excused it to herself on the grounds that David would undoubtedly be hungry after a long day and a late emergency.

Sometimes, in the privacy of her flat, she had indulged in daydreams about David, although they had never had any form of social contact. She wondered what he liked to eat and what were his tastes in music. Did he wear pyjamas or sleep in the nude? She had heard that his wife was glamorous, but was he happy? Presumably not, if the last ten minutes were anything to go by. Somewhere she thought she remembered somebody saying that his wife was a bitch. She hoped she was; it would ease her conscience.

Ginette stood up suddenly. What was she doing? She hardly knew the man, and she certainly was not trying to put the hex on his marriage. She pulled the duty rota viciously off the wall and started to amend the names in the boxes with a red pen. There was a lot of movement around the boxes with the name Gotch.

She wondered about David's boy. The fact that he was disabled gave her a fellow feeling. Despite the years the memory of Peter was keen within her, and the fact that they both had children who were disabled seemed, in her mind, to put them closer. She looked in the mirror and tucked in some stray curls under her turban, trying to restore the groomed and disciplined look that was so much her style. It was time she stopped letting her mind wander around in a direction she was not sure she wanted to go. She had not felt attracted to anyone for a number of years, but that was no reason to get hot under the collar about a man she hardly knew.

David fancied her, she could tell that by the indefinable chemistry that exists between some people. She was attracted as much as he, but men were different, especially married ones. She was not going to be trapped into an affair again just because a man gave her the eye and set her blood racing whenever he looked at her. Simon had instilled many things into her, the final one being a deep cynicism concerning the motives of men.

The church bell reached her from the village in the valley of the nearby Og and she looked at her watch. She was due at the Manor for dinner in forty-five minutes with her cousin, Ralph Abelson. Mercifully she had had the foresight to bring her change of clothes with her. She looked swiftly down the recovery-room to make sure that all was in order and disappeared into the changing-room.

When she emerged no one would have recognised the clinically efficient theatre sister in the elegant young woman in the red velvet dinner dress concealed by a nurse's cloak. The mixture of uniform and civilian clothes was not allowed, but Ginette was not going to walk down the long hospital corridor in her dinner finery.

In the hall of the Manor a small group were assembled by the fireplace—the Abelsons, Colonel and Molly Southey, Daphne Webber and a square-built Dutchman who was introduced as Dirk den Pol, an art dealer. Ginette liked Ralph and Penelope and was amused by their matchmaking tactics, which were conducted with the delicate grace of a wallowing hippopotamus.

She went out rarely, and this was something of an occasion for her.

The butler served them fluted glasses of champagne, and Penelope whispered aside to Ginette,

'Attractive fellow, Ginette. Family connection to the Dutch royals, I'm told. Doesn't breed, though—pity.'

Ginette smiled inwardly and wondered what the guest would have thought about her last comment if he was unaware that Penelope was dog-daft.

Through dinner, at an oak refectory table black with years of polish, Ginette found herself being entertained by the quiet Dutchman, whose reserve vanished whenever he spoke of pictures. She was interested in art and antiques, and one of the advantages her money had brought her was the ability to indulge this interest. As a result her flat was beginning to lose wall space for pictures and top space for bronzes and objets d'art.

Daphne was as flouncy and happily noisy as ever.

'He's a sod, that husband of mine. Wouldn't come tonight—says he has to go to town on business.'

She shook her Muppet-like curls in disgust. Ralph brayed from the other end of the table,

'Coming to watch the polo with us next week, Ginette?'

'No, thank you, Ralph. Duties galore.'

If there had not been she would have invented them. Socialising at Hurlingham was not her scene. The soft-accented tones of Dirk den Pol reached only as far as her ears.

'How about a trip to the Royal Academy to see the Toulouse-Lautrec exhibition?' he was asking.

She turned and smiled at him.

'Yes, that would be lovely, but I'd have to fit it in with my schedule.'

He had large brown eyes and the look of a soulful saint, but it was not that which attracted her. It was his articulate knowledge about pictures, and visiting the Toulouse-Lautrec exhibition with him as her guide would be an experience.

'Make it a morning and I'll lunch you afterwards at the Ritz,' he promised.

As she was leaving after dinner Daphne whispered to her in the hall,

'If you can't make it, let me know and I'll go as your stand-in. Do you think he'd notice?'

Ginette gave her a hug and laughed.

'Daphne, dear, I'm sure he'd notice, but I'm equally sure he wouldn't mind a bit.'

Molly Southey appeared beside them looking gorgeous, but petulant.

'What happened to David and Laurel?' she wanted to know.

Ginette shrugged her shoulders. She had not known they had been invited to the dinner that night, but was glad they had not turned up. Somehow she did not relish meeting David's wife. Although they moved in the same social circle she had never seen Laurel, much less spoken to her. They were newly arrived, Ginette went out very little and doubtless Laurel did not consider her important enough to pursue socially.

Daphne pursed her lips.

'Another row, I expect. Nothing new.'

CHAPTER SIX

STAFF NURSE Crisp, efficient as her name implied, stood looking at the oscilloscope screen beside Sam Bennett in the intensive care unit. A naso-gastric tube emanated from his left nostril and was strapped to his forehead. From his left upper chest a thin polythene tube led to a drip line into which two bottles poured a steady stream of glucose-saline and citrate.

Sam was breathing slowly and easily, there was a gentle dew of sweat on his brow and upper lip, and he was unconscious. Staff Nurse Crisp checked his pulse and wave reading on the screen and the flow rate on the drip line; then she wrote briskly on the clipboard that hung at the end of Sam's bed.

The intensive care unit was designed to provide just what its name implied—intensive care. It was staffed by two carefully chosen nurses trained in all resuscitative procedures. The unit itself had every form of equipment for nursing patients who were extremely ill. No visitors were allowed in the unit. The care was magnificent, but the price of admission was high. You had to be desperately ill.

The staff nurse took a large syringe, attached it to the naso-gastric tube, and drew the plunger back firmly. A greeny-yellow liquid foamed into it. She drew out three full syringes and after that it stopped coming. Sam stirred fitfully. His eyelids fluttered and opened. He looked at her without focusing, closed them, then opened them again. He licked his lips and as the nurse leaned over him he said,

'Who the hell are you?'

She smiled.

'Good morning, Mr Bennett. I'm your nurse. How do you feel?'

'Terrible,' said Sam, and closed his eyes again.

David Compton entered the unit. Staff Nurse Crisp noted the strain lines at the corners of his eyes and the firmness of his mouth. He did not appear as relaxed as usual.

'How is he, Staff?' he asked.

'Recovered consciousness just a minute ago, Doctor. Not much back from the tube, drip running freely. Fluid balance matches. He's doing nicely.'

David looked over Sam briefly and nodded, satisfied. Now that the pressure was off the trachea and the bleeding stopped, Sam was likely to make a rapid recovery.

'We should have the tube out and the drip down by tonight, Staff Nurse. I'll be in after the list.'

The nurse watched his tall, athletic figure go out through the swing doors and wondered what it was that had put the unaccustomed steel into his voice that morning.

Staff Nurse Best came out of the observation cubicle and stood beside her.

'Something up with Boy Wonder this morning, then? What's got up his nose?'

'Too much on his plate, I expect. He doesn't get much rest.'

Staff Nurse Best, fat and homely, sniffed.

'That I doubt. He's dedicated, he is. Work won't worry him. More like it's the cold breeze from that iceberg wife of his. She wouldn't melt in a furnace, that one.'

'She's a fool,' said Staff Nurse Crisp. 'Somebody'll take him off her one day if she doesn't look out.'

Best looked knowing.

'And there's someone ready to do just that, if you ask me.'

Crisp laughed at her.

'Don't tell me you're in the running with everyone else, Besty?'

Best put her nose up.

'Not me. I've got better things to do than run after doctors. No, it's that theatre sister—the one with the red hair and long legs.'

'You mean Sister Irving?'

'That's her. And him not above smiling at her as well, you'll notice.'

'Go on with you, Besty! She's got ice in her veins. You're just jealous.'

'Better her than that other one in theatre—Sandra Gotch—she's a real man-eater.'

Staff Nurse Best shook her head firmly.

'Not a chance. She's not in his league. She feeds on young housemen.'

They both turned at a noise from Sam. His eyes were open and more alert. Best swabbed his mouth and moistened his tongue and lips. His craggy face looked grey and drawn under the heavy bandaging round his neck, but he was now very much awake.

'Thanks. Where's my wife?' he wanted to know.

A quick look passed between the two nurses. Staff Nurse Crisp laid a hand on his wrist.

'Just try and relax. Do you have any pain?'

'I'm dying and she tells me to relax! How is my wife?' Sam repeated hoarsely.

'Do you have a headache?'

'Of course I've got a headache, it hurts like hell. Now where is my wife?'

He struggled in the bed, trying to sit up, and failed. There was a silence as he looked anxiously from one nurse to the other. Finally Best said to him,

'I'm afraid she didn't do very well.'

'Not very well? Is she bad?'

'Yes, Mr Bennett, I'm afraid she is.'

'God Almighty, how bad?' There was alarm and anxiety in his voice and in his face.

'She's alive, Mr Bennett.'

The lines in Sam's face went even deeper. He seemed to sink into the bed and grow smaller. When he spoke again it was in a whisper.

'The bastards. Those bloody bastards!'

The oscilloscope screen flickered uncertainly for a second and his eyes closed. Once again he became unconscious.

In a side ward Susan Bennett awoke to an agony of mind worse than the pain in her belly and the torture of her burned head. Through the mists of morphine she knew that she had lost her baby, and the pain of that loss superseded all others. Her head was bandaged and her face was like red meat covered with the gloss of anti-inflammatory cream. Mercifully she had only suffered first-degree burns to her face and she would not be scarred, but she had lost her hair and there were patches where it would not grow again.

The ward sister, Monica le Feuvre, came into the room.

'Good morning, Mrs Bennett. How are you feeling today?'

'How would you feel?'

Susan was in no mood for pleasantries. Monica le Feuvre nodded sympathetically.

'You're right—it must be bloody. The good news is that your husband is doing well.'

Involuntarily Susan tried to smile, but her face hurt too much to crease it, so she nodded back. She was relieved that Sam was doing well, but immediately her mind went to herself. Not out of self-pity, but because she knew Sam's weakness as far as injury and deformity were concerned. He could not bear it. It was an obsession with him. Even a lame animal revolted him.

What would he think about her, with a red face and no hair and bald patches? And no baby?

In her low state, confused by the morphine and faced with a future uncertain, the tears rolled down her face. Carefully Monica mopped them away, knowing they would sting on her burned cheeks.

In the theatre block Ginette was pinning the operating list for that day on to the notice board in her office. There was a long list and she would be assisting David at all the operations.

She ran her finger down the list – cholecystectomy, femoral graft, breast lumpectomy, repair of subclavian aneurysm. A wide range, and it was going to take time. There were some old notices high up on the board and she was standing on a stool to take them down when David walked into her office. She did not hear him until he was directly behind her, taking the opportunity to admire a length of brown leg.

'Good morning, Sister Irving.'

She recognised the voice at once, turned and lost her balance. There was nothing to hang on to and she would have fallen if David had not caught her. He held her firmly. Her breasts were pressing against his chest, she had one foot on the floor and the other leg bent behind her on the stool. Their faces were close and she could feel his warm breath on her cheek. They stayed like that for a moment, both of them feeling their hearts beating hard under their thin cotton shirts. He smiled at her, not letting her go.

'You'd never make a living in the circus!' he told her.

'Not on the tight wire,' she agreed.

'Clown, perhaps?'

'Perhaps. My leg is aching,' Ginette told him.

'So am I.'

His head was slowly lowering towards her, their eyes locked. An adenoidal voice behind him stopped the movement.

'First case is up from the ward, Sister. Do you want me to. . .? Oh, I'm sorry.' Staff Nurse Gotch's voice held a tone of malicious delight. She stood in the door of the office, hand on hip. 'I'm sure I didn't mean to intrude, Sister. It's just that. . .'

'You didn't intrude, Staff Nurse. Mr Compton has just saved me from a nasty fall. No, I do not want you to scrub for the first case. I shall take it myself. You can check the instruments for the antral washout in theatre two.'

Ginette's green eyes were bright, her chin high and her cheeks flushed. David looked on with quizzical amusement. When Gotch had disappeared Ginette turned to David.

'I wouldn't grin like that if I were you. She'll have it all over the nurses' home at lunch that we're having an affair.'

'So we're branded, Ginette?'

'We soon will be.'

'Paying the price without the party?'

She nodded, her lips full and tempting, her colour still high.

'In that case. . .' he took her gently by the shoulders and turned her to him, '. . .it would be a pity not to. . .'

His mouth descended on hers, warm and firm. Involuntarily she opened her lips, their tongues met and she clung to him, feeling the heat rising from her legs into her belly. It lasted only seconds, but felt like an age. Then he was gone, leaving her looking out of the window at the blue sky with a lifting heart and a prayer on her lips.

David went through the morning list with a speed

and precision that brought a comment from the anaesthetist.

'Christ, David, if you ratchet on like this we'll have nothing to do after the coffee break!'

Far from distracting them, the incident in the office seemed to have sharpened their senses. They did the whole list together, working in concert with almost telepathic communication. Sandra Gotch was kept on the instruments all morning, much to her disgust. Ginette realised she was treating her unfairly, and at that moment she didn't care.

At the end of the list David changed and stopped outside her office on the way to the wards. Her heart thumped as she looked up from her writing and saw his tall figure, the wavy lock of hair falling over his right eye. He gave her a rakish smile and a little salute.

'Thank you, Sister. That was really quite splendid.'

She blushed and nodded, not knowing what to say. He turned and she watched as he walked down the long corridor away from her.

She thought of the way he had coped with the emergency the previous day and shook her head. You did not often see that class and breadth of surgery done now. It showed what a depth of training he had to be able to deal with such divergent emergencies. On the spur of the moment Ginette decided to look in on Susan Bennett when she went for her lunch break. It was not her responsibility any longer, but she felt an interest in and a compassion for the woman who had gone through such an ordeal. It was common knowledge in the hospital that Susan had been raped, and Ginette wondered how she herself would be able to face everybody if she was aware that they all knew it had happened to her.

Susan was dozing when Ginette quietly opened the door, but she opened her eyes immediately she heard the click of the latch. They opened wider in query when she saw the sister's uniform. Ginette smiled at her.

'I'm Ginette Irving—I'm the theatre sister. I've come to see how you are.'

Susan nodded impassively at her, her skin too tight to move.

'Thank you. I owe you a lot, I'm told.'

'No, you don't. It was Mr Compton who saved you.'

'What's he like?' Susan asked.

'Wonderful. He's the finest surgeon we've got. He saved your husband too. He's. . .'

'OK.'

Ginette blushed, realising her gaffe. She also felt an empathy with Susan. Somehow she knew she was not one to swap empty words, and she was right.

'How do you feel about the baby?' she asked quietly.

'Bloody, but I can cope with that.'

'What about your husband? Will it upset him?'

'Not the baby—me. He hates deformity, and I'm not going to look pretty for a long time. If ever again.'

'He'll get used to it,' Ginette assured her.

'Not Sam. I'll be lucky if he doesn't give me the push.'

Ginette was horrified at what she heard.

'Surely not?' she protested.

'You don't know Sam,' said Susan bitterly.

'Your face won't show anything eventually, and you can wear a wig for your hair if it doesn't all grow back.'

'In bed?'

The voice held a bitterness Ginette could not believe. She patted Susan's hand and made for the door, unable to produce the reassuring words her nursing teacher would have expected of her.

'I'll pop in and see you tomorrow,' she said, and was rewarded by a gleam in the eyes within the fixed red face.

As she walked down the hospital corridor to the canteen she wondered how she would feel if she were in Susan's place. It was unimaginable, and she put it out of her mind as her bleep went off.

Alone once more in the single room, Susan thought about Sam. They had had such a fine time together since they were married and had built up a close relationship. As close as one could with a man like Sam. He was tough and relentless, and because of his feeling about deformity she could not see them getting back to their old relationship unless they were given a better than even chance. Sure, he'd try, but they'd both know what he was thinking, and that would be the beginning of the end.

She was under no illusions about Sam. He was a fit and sexually demanding man who was accustomed to getting what he wanted when he wanted it. He was not going to get anything from her for a long time, and it would not be long before someone put in an appearance on his horizon if she did not get better and look better very soon.

Slowly she started to move her feet under the bedclothes and wiggle her toes. She lifted her arms in the air several times and made circles with her wrists. It was not much, but it was a start.

Professor le Masurier was dark and intense. He never wasted a word or a moment. His visits to Manbury Hospital were short, but they always bore fruit. His speciality was vascular surgery, and David had been his registrar at the Middlesex Hospital for two years. The Professor's training had enabled him to save several limbs and fingers in his present post in traumatic surgery. He had sewn them back and maintained their blood supply by micro-surgery.

The afternoon outpatient session was over. A series

of selected patients had been brought before the Professor for detailed appraisal. Some of them, requiring advanced investigation, would be transferred to the Middlesex. For the rest, it was the Professor's opinion about procedure and technique that was required, and it was David who would carry it out.

'David, these results of yours on manual restoration are really excellent.'

David flushed at the rare praise and shrugged.

'I've been lucky.'

The Professor shook his head and regarded David with piercing black eyes.

'No such thing. Luck doesn't exist—especially in this field. Would you like to go to Lyons?'

David blinked at the unexpected turn.

'Lyons?' he queried. 'What for?'

'The French are interested. I've been invited by their Societé Medicale to demonstrate there in a few weeks' time. Unfortunately it conflicts with a meeting in Rio de Janeiro. Will you take my place? I've spoken to them and they would welcome it.'

For a moment David was lost for a reply. Apart from his natural interest the prestige value of such a trip was enormous. He raised his hands upwards.

'What would I be expected to do?' he asked.

'Demonstrate our new micro-dissection techniques. Perhaps some immediate trauma. They're close to the Autoroute du Sud, so there's always something coming in.'

David thought briefly.

'Tricky in a strange set-up,' he commented.

The Professor nodded.

'You'd be better with your own anaesthetist and theatre sister. Not a problem.'

David thought quickly. The Professor was right about having one's own theatre sister instead of working in entirely foreign surroundings, but how would Ginette react in such a situation?

She was good, the best theatre sister he had ever worked with, but how would they get on outside their professional milieu? On this sort of trip there were many other considerations. There would be much more in the way of social contact. He had sworn at her in the past for handing him the wrong instrument, and she had responded with a frigid silence and manufactured such an atmosphere that it had been discussed with relish in the nurses' dining-room before the operation was over.

The last thing he wanted on foreign soil, when he was on show to the surgical fraternity in Lyons, was Ginette making things difficult for him. In theatre they were a fine team most of the time, but what about outside those porthole doors?

Inevitably they would be thrown together a great deal more when they were in France. If their social relationship deteriorated what would happen to their work? Their early coldness towards each other now seemed to be a thing of the past, if their unexpected kiss was any indication, but David knew he should continue to make an effort to improve their relationship.

He thought about it and began to enjoy the prospect.

'How about the administration here?' he asked. 'They wouldn't like it if I'm away with half the staff.'

A confident smile greeted that one.

'I'm sure you'll find them very helpful when they get my letter.'

David did not doubt it. The Professor's influence extended into many spheres other than clinical medicine. The corridors of power in the medical world were no different from those in politics. He did not hesitate.

'Thank you, I'd like it very much.'

The Professor stood up and held out his hand.

'Good. My secretary will send you the details. Goodbye, David.'

He was gone, almost before David could reply. A few moments later a chauffeur-driven black Rolls-Royce went past the outpatient block. In the back the Professor was sitting with a file on his knee and dictating into a microphone.

He did not look up as they went by.

CHAPTER SEVEN

THE MORNING sun slatted through the gap in the chintz curtains of Apple Tree Cottage, waking David. Beside him Laurel lay on her back, her long black hair spread on the pillow. He leaned over and kissed her gently, sliding his hand over the pink satin nightdress to cup her breast.

It was the weekend and he was off duty. They had no pressing timetable. He kissed her again, more firmly this time. She awoke and felt his urgency, but lay there and said nothing. He held her, his lips on hers, pressing her close, but she put her hands to his chest and pushed him away.

'Please, David! I'm not up to that sort of thing at this time of the day.'

He stopped, deflated, his tumescence fading. His feeling of care and closeness evaporated.

'I'm sorry.' He threw back the duvet and swung his legs over the side of the bed. 'I'll make the tea.'

It was a scene he had played all too often. In the kitchen, he turned on the cold tap to fill the kettle and looked out over the garden. How many times had he done this? How many times had he stood here, stifling his emotions with the mundane act of tea-making? To argue about making love was something he could not do. It was not something he would ask for, like a dog pleading for a bone. It was either there or not there.

Laurel had never been a sex kitten, but in the early days of their marriage she had enjoyed it in a clinical fashion. David sighed, lifted the lid of the Aga and put the kettle on to boil.

The clock in the drawing-room chimed seven, inconsequentially reminding him that today they were driving to Henley to see James. He cheered at the thought and lifted up the model yacht he had bought in Swindon the previous day. It was a racing yacht with adjustable sheets and halyards, and white linen sails. The tiller had several different settings and the flying keel gave it a sporty look. It was a nice toy, not too complicated for James to manage, but with enough extras to make it interesting.

St Athelstan's had a lake and a river where model yacht sailing was a popular pastime. David looked forward to giving the toy to his son. He never failed to enjoy the delight in the child's face when he took him a present. It was, in a sense, an atonement for not having him at home.

He took the tea tray into the bedroom. Laurel was sitting up doing her nails. They were long and filbert-shaped and she waved them in the air to dry.

'You haven't forgotten it's the shoot tomorrow?' she queried.

'No. You haven't forgotten we're going to see our son today?'

There was little doubt in David's mind which event took priority with Laurel. Not that she was interested in shooting—she wasn't. She could not tell a pheasant from a cuckoo, but it was held at the Abelsons' and that was enough. Also she looked good in tweeds.

As if on cue the telephone rang. Laurel picked it up and before she could utter a word David heard Sir Ralph's foghorn making the instrument vibrate. Laurel held it a foot away from her ear to avoid being deafened.

'We're meeting at ten tomorrow, David.'

'It's not David, it's Laurel. Good morning, Ralph.'

'Sorry, m'dear. Where's that husband of yours?'

'Right here—I'll put him on. See you tomorrow.'

David took the telephone.

'Morning, Ralph.'

'Just wanted to make sure you'd be there at ten. Got a gun for that young feller you're bringing along?'

David remembered, guiltily, that he had promised Mark Slater a day's shooting and that he had forgotten to organise a gun for him. Ralph was, for all his other failings, utterly precise with anything pertaining to his favourite sport.

''Fraid not,' he apologised. 'Can you let him have something out of your armoury?'

'Right. Have to get it cleaned and ready for him, though. Thomson will do it first thing. Don't be late. G'bye.'

David was left holding an instrument giving forth a dialling note. Sir Ralph was not one for the little niceties.

'Who is it we're taking along?' Laurel wanted to know. 'One of your wretched down-at-heel housemen, I suppose?'

'Quite right. Except that he's not down-at-heel or wretched. He's bright, hard-working and dog-loyal. He works a hundred hours a week, and a day out shooting is like a trip to Mars for him.'

Laurel, standing before the mirror to judge the look of her military-style costume, did not reply.

David took the old coaching road that led from Bath to London to get to St Athelstan's, disdaining the M4 motorway. The school was three miles outside Henley-on-Thames, and as they drove through the wrought iron gates David saw a row of cars parked on the raked gravel of the front courtyard. He put the Triumph at the end of a row that consisted of two Jaguars, a Mercedes, three BMWs and a Rolls-Royce.

As they walked towards the main doors Laurel

inclined her head at the cars.

'Makes me feel like the poor relation,' she remarked.

'Poor relations don't pay the fees at these places.'

David knotted his hands in his pockets and Laurel rang the bell.

'Mr and Mrs Compton! It is nice to see you. James has been so excited all morning.'

The Matron was short and homely, with a quick eye and a lilting Welsh accent. She wore a blouse and skirt and there was not a hint of uniform. The policy of St Athelstan's was to be relaxed and informal. She led the way through the building to the lawn at the rear. They went through some french windows, and David could see James sitting on top of a square climbing frame. There was a mock battle in progress and James had his crutch to his shoulder, juddering it to imitate a machine-gun. As he brought it round in a sweep of fire he saw them, and the next moment was off the frame and hop-skipping across the lawn, his face shining with delight.

'Daddy, Mummy! I've been waiting for you!'

David knew that if it had been dawn they would still have been too late for James. Laurel proffered her cheek to be kissed and then David swung the boy off his feet into the air.

'You've grown, my son,' he smiled.

'Matron says I've gone up an inch. She says I'm going to be as tall as you.'

Laurel tightened her lips. Not surprisingly Matron was quoted frequently, but Laurel found it galling.

'Matrons aren't always right, James,' she said coldly.

'Ours is, Mummy.'

There was no answer to such desperate confidence. David was just grateful that they had left the Matron behind in the main house.

'What would you like to do today, James?' he asked the boy.

'Can we go on the river?'

'Of course.'

'Can I bring my friend Nicholas?'

'Certainly, if Matron says so.'

Matron did say so, and Nicholas turned out to be a reserved boy of James's age with black curly hair, who would only look at his feet. His total vocabulary consisted of yes and no, but he was a fast runner and this was what had raised him to dizzy heights in James's estimation.

When they got to the car David produced the yacht, and the delighted reaction from his son made his chest ache. It reminded him of the last present he had received from his father before the fateful cruise. It had been just such a yacht and was still one of his treasured possessions.

Aunt Harriet had been good to him, but she was a spinster, his mother's older sister, and not well versed in bringing up young boys. There had been no lack of money for his education and he had never been deprived, except of his parents. Now his own son was coming dangerously close to the same fate.

James had the mast up and down, the sails off and on and the tiller adjusted, in moments. Nicholas also evinced an interest, and there was a tense moment when he put it between his knees and refused to let it go.

They drove to the river and David hired a skiff. It was a big one. Laurel sat in the stern with the boys and steered by ropes attached to the rudder. David rowed them up-river, pointing out the stretches and marks where the Regatta was held. They passed Phyllis Court, then turned and idled back to moor outside the Angel. David lifted James ashore, because he could not manage to climb over the side of the skiff without letting go of his yacht, which he refused to do.

They lunched at the pub in a room with windows overlooking the river so that the boys could watch the procession of boats up and down the Thames. At lunch Laurel was stiff and anxious, her whole demeanour rigid and unbending. She viewed James with obvious distaste. Nicholas said nothing, but James chatted happily to his father.

David recognised the signs in Laurel. She could only keep up the mother pretence for so long. Now she was worried that James was going to have one of his 'accidents', and she would be humiliated in public. She did not consider how James would feel about it, David thought, and he became angry, but tried not to let it show to his son.

After lunch they drove back to St Athelstan's. James was desperate to sail his new boat on the lake. After parking the car he led them down a path through a small group of tall trees and over a wooden bridge that spanned a stream leading to the lake. There was a small jetty with a rowing boat moored to it. A pair of swans by the rushes at the far end completed a quiet and delightful setting. Close to the jetty was an area that had been concreted to the water's edge to allow the children easy access. Within moments the little boat was scudding across the lake in a wide circle that David hoped would bring it back to where they stood.

Inevitably it did not. Instead it lodged against the edge of the jetty, and James was up and making across the planking with his crutches at a great rate.

'James!' There was steel and command in David's voice. The boy stopped as if he were on the end of a wire. 'Come back. I'll get the boat.'

David walked to the end of the jetty, leaned over the water and pulled up the yacht by the tip of its mast. He walked back to the concrete apron.

'I do not want you to go on that jetty again—ever!' he told the boy sternly.

James looked downcast and just nodded. Later, as they walked back to the main house, Laurel said to David,

'Why did you have to be so tough on him just now?'

'Can he swim?' asked David.

'You know he can't.'

'If he can't use his legs, and with those heavy calipers on them, what sort of chance do you think he'd have if he fell in?'

Laurel said nothing. James took them into the gymnasium, a large room lined with wooden wall bars. There were ropes looping down from the ceiling, parallel bars and vaulting horses standing alongside coir mats and about it all a faint smell of sweat and athletics. James went to the ropes.

'Watch me, Dad!' he called.

He undid a rope which was nearly two inches thick and gripped it with both hands. A moment's hesitation and then he was going up it, using only his hands, his legs swinging loosely beneath him. When he got to the top David clapped.

'Well done, young man!'

For a ten-year-old it was an impressive feat. When James got back to them, red in the face, David patted him on the back.

'I just wanted to show you I could do something well, Dad,' James explained.

As Laurel led the way out David was too choked to reply.

The Matron stopped them in the hall as they were about to leave.

'I presume you've had the secretary's letter, Mr Compton? I'm so sorry.'

'No, Matron, I've received nothing from the secretary. What's it about?'

The Matron looked embarrassed.

'It's the fees, Mr Compton. They're going up.'

David made a rueful face.

'Nothing new about that these days. I expect we shall cope.'

'It's rather a substantial increase. I wondered whether you would have liked to have spoken about it.'

The Matron was a discerning lady. She had a shrewd idea of how difficult it had been for the Comptons to keep up with the fees.

'What is this increase, then, Matron?' David asked.

'Depending on the arrangements it's going to be between forty and fifty per cent. One of the problems is that we've lost our grants from two major sources.'

David just nodded.

'Thank you, Matron. I'll wait until I get the letter, and if there's a problem I'll telephone you.'

'I'm sure the governors would try to come to some sort of arrangement if necessary.'

'Thank you, Matron.'

There was a silence as they drove back to Aldbourne. Laurel was the first to speak.

'Well, that's it, then,' she said briefly.

'What is?'

'The fee increase. We can't afford it. That will mean another seven thousand a year at least. That's twenty-seven thousand a year. It's going to be nearly all your total earnings.'

'So?'

'So it's not bloody well on!' Laurel skewed round in her seat, gripping the dashboard. 'I'm not going to stay in poverty just to keep him at that school when there's another place he could be at for practically nothing!'

'You'd have him in that appalling institution?' demanded David.

'Yes, I would, rather than have us go broke.'

David took the car through a sharp bend with protesting tyres and a revving engine.

'I'd rather go broke.'

There was a silence as he drove the Triumph viciously through a series of bends that had the small car heeling over. Laurel took no notice, but sat looking at the countryside as if she were on a coach outing. David clenched his teeth.

'By the way,' he told her, 'I'm taking Professor le Masurier's place at the Lyons conference. I'll be away for the best part of a week.'

Laurel shrugged.

'When you're like this I wouldn't care if you never came back.'

The morning had still the delight of summer about it, but with that hint of freshness that foretells the impatience of autumn in the wings. David looked out of the window of the garden shed, noting the golden-blue sky with satisfaction. It was going to be a good day. He opened the gun box and took out his twelve-bore shotgun. It was a finely made Holland and Holland with a single-trigger action, two pulls on one trigger serving to fire both barrels. The stock was beautifully chased, depicting a hunting scene. It had been his father's and was his most cherished possession.

Carefully he lifted out the barrels, fitted a mop to the wooden cleaning rod and smoothly slid it up and down them, mopping out the gun oil. He put in two dummy cartridges, went outside and tried a few dry shots at the sky. His father had been the same build as he, and the weapon fitted snugly into his shoulder as he brought it up and swept it round in mock action.

'David!' Laurel's voice from the bedroom window. He looked up. 'There's somebody stopped outside the front gate looking lost. You'd better go.'

David sighed. Last night had ended in a flaming row, a development from their conversation as they left St Athelstan's. They had not made it up, and he could feel that today was going to be prickly at least. Doubtless Laurel would put on a front for Ralph, and that might help. He only hoped there would not be a scene in front of Mark Slater. Laurel was quite capable of doing that if she thought it would serve her purpose. As he went outside he thought to himself that life with Laurel was becoming more than he was prepared to stand. Only the fear of losing James and the effect it would have on him made him stay with their marriage.

It was Mark Slater, sitting astride an old Matchless motorbike, clad in a loud tweed jacket, green corduroys and a cap to match with a sewn-down peak. A pair of green gumboots were tied to the pillion. He looked relieved when he saw David.

'Thank goodness! I thought I was lost and going to miss the start.'

'Bring your bike through the gate, Mark,' David told him. 'You can park it round the back.'

'Thank you, sir.'

'David will do.'

Mark's pink and chubby face went pinker.

'Thank you. . .er. . .David.'

Mark wheeled his bike round the side of the cottage and looked round appreciatively.

'Lovely place you've got here, David. Sorry I haven't got a gun to bring.'

'Don't worry, our host is going to lend you one. Tell me, any problems in the wards? How's that chap Bennett?'

'Up and running. Got half the ward organised round him and played hell with Sister when she told him there was no private room to be had. Fit for discharge, I'd say, otherwise we'll lose a ward sister!'

David laughed.

'Amazing how some people bounce back,' he said.

Mark nodded. 'He's a rare one, though. Especially after the damage to his wife and losing the baby. The police still haven't been able to track down their attackers.'

David clapped him on the back.

'Enough shop for now. Come and meet my wife.'

Laurel was coming down the stairs as they entered the front door, dressed for the part as ever and superbly elegant in a tweed suit and boots. She greeted Mark with just enough coolness in her manner to discourage any familiarity.

They climbed into the Triumph, and Mark sat in the back clutching David's gun in a canvas carrying case. It was a few moments' drive to the Manor, and as they went up the drive lined with giant rhododendrons and swept into the courtyard there was a gasp from Mark.

'What a place!'

Aldbury Manor was an impressive sight. A large Tudor building, it retained most of its original features, with tall leaded windows surrounded by exposed woodwork within the walls. Huge double oak doors carried the original ironwork decoration, lockwork and latches.

The Abelsons' Mercedes estate car was parked with the tailgate up. There were numerous dogs jumping around it, barking loudly. Several other cars were there already, among them the Southeys' Sunbeam-Talbot and the Webbers' battered Rover.

'I didn't know Martin Webber went shooting,' remarked David.

Laurel sniffed. 'He doesn't. They're only asked because of Daphne, and he tags on for the drinks.'

'Thoomsoon, Thoomsoon!' the foghorn bray came

reverberating through the oak doors. Sir Ralph at full throat was formidable even at a distance. He appeared through the front doors, enormously magnificent in a green Norfolk shooting jacket, knickerbocker trousers, long brown stockings and full brogues.

Thomson, the gamekeeper, appeared as if out of the ground, a gun in the crook of each arm—a small, lean man with a quiet face who wore a cap too big for him and leather gaiters over shiny brown boots.

'Right here, Sir Ralph.'

'Where is everybody? Those guns cleaned and ready?'

'Most of 'em is gathered by the old oak, and I see Mr Compton's party has just arrived.'

David was taking his gun out of its case as Laurel made her entrance across the gravel courtyard.

'Ralph, I do hope we haven't kept you waiting,' she smiled. 'This is Dr Slater. He found our house at last and we brought him up.'

Somehow she managed to imply that it was Mark's fault that they were late. Sir Ralph's florid, once good-looking features broke into a smile.

'Not at all, m'dear. Glad to see you here, Doctor. Thomson has a gun ready for you. Only two rules— don't drop it and don't swing inside the line. Come on.'

He strode off with seven-league boots and they chased after him, Mark nervously breaking the gun as he did so to make sure that it was not loaded. Thomson saw him do it and looked suitably offended, but was too polite to say anything. The guns were standing in a group under a huge oak tree at the side of the Manor, accompanied by several followers.

David did not know them all, but managed to introduce Mark to Colonel Southey and Molly and Daphne. When Martin Webber appeared Mark Slater looked surprised.

'You two know each other, then?' David queried.

Mark nodded. 'We do.'

Martin was equally short, but the brief tension of the moment was broken by Sir Ralph raising his voice, above which speech was impossible.

'We'll move off now, everybody.'

The guns moved off first. Mark stuck close to David.

'I'm not sure what to do here, David,' he muttered. 'What does swing inside the line mean?'

'If a bird comes over you mustn't bring your gun round behind you if there's anybody to your right or left. It's dangerous. Especially if it's a rabbit or a hare on the ground.'

Mark looked relieved.

'Thanks. Anything else I should know?'

'Yes. Don't pinch someone else's bird. If it's at the end of your range don't try and be clever. Leave it to the next man.'

'Don't worry—I'll just be glad to make it go off,' grinned Mark.

'It'll do that all right. Keep your safety catch on and break your gun when you climb a fence. What's he lent you?'

Mark peered at the side of his gun. 'Difficult to read, I think it says Purd. . .'

'Purdey? Good grief!'

Mark looked puzzled. 'Something wrong?' he asked.

David looked at the gun Mark was carrying. 'No, not a bit. Only that gun you're hanging on to is worth all of fifteen thousand pounds or more.'

Mark went almost white.

'No wonder he told me not to drop it!'

Thomson was a little ahead of the party. He stopped briefly and faced them as they walked towards him.

'Cock birds only today, if you please, gentlemen,' he instructed.

Mark looked worried again. 'How can I tell a cock bird?' he asked David.

'He's only referring to cock pheasants. If it isn't big, with a long tail, a red head and a white collar, don't shoot it. Easy.'

They spread out and covered several fields. Mark, despite his fears, did creditably, and by lunch had bagged two pheasant, a woodcock and a hare, and nobody had shouted at him. For lunch they all picnicked. Folding tables were set up, white tablecloths laid out and in no time there were plates of cold fresh salmon, foie gras, game pie, fresh bread rolls and a whole Stilton. Krug 1966 came out of a cooler and there was Clos Vougeot 1971 to go with the pie.

Mark tucked in happily, talking to David between mouthfuls of Stilton. He waved a glass of the red wine.

'I hope none of the guns get tucked into too much of this before we start off again,' he remarked.

David nodded and was about to say something when he was engulfed by Daphne, who flung her arms around his neck.

'That Martin of mine is getting so tiddly on Ralph's fizz I've left him to meet your nice young friend,' she announced.

Mark grinned uneasily, took another slurp of champagne and held out his hand.

'We just met at the house—under the old oak tree,' he reminded her.

Daphne laughed.

'Yes, I know we did. I meant I came over to know you better. You looked nice.'

David laughed, and Mark went the colour of a turkey's neck.

'Don't worry, Mark. Daphne's everybody's friend, but she's quite harmless,' David assured him.

'Well, I'm not, but I'm never given the chance.' The

words were spoken by Molly, casual and elegant as ever, who had walked over from the Abelsons' car where Laurel was gazing up at Sir Ralph. David smiled at her.

'Hi, Molly. Not shooting today?'

'Only from the hip, darling. Are you staying at the Manor?'

'No, our house is only a mouse's throw away, you may recall.'

'Pity. I just love making those old floorboards creak after dark.'

David kissed the tip of his finger and put it lightly on the tip of her nose.

'Molly, one snap from me and you'd make the welkin ring.'

'Just you wait, 'Enry 'Iggins!'

Molly walked off in pretended disgust. Mark's gaze followed her admiringly.

'Wow! I never get that sort of woman saying those sort of things to me,' he sighed.

Daphne gave a sheepdog flounce.

'Well, of all the cheek! And I thought I gave it a real go.'

The next moment she was off to help Penelope corral her dogs back into the car. Mark looked crestfallen.

'Now you see it, now you don't. I don't seem to have the touch,' he remarked ruefully.

David patted him on the shoulder.

'I'm sure you have. Let's go—Thomson is marshalling the guns.'

The afternoon went even better for Mark, who brought down three cock pheasant before he found himself stationed at the end of a copse with David.

'We'll just stay here to catch the odd pigeon if we're lucky,' David told him.

They were not lucky. The pigeons stayed away and

they stood there together for some time. Mark fidgeted a little, then said,

'David, I've got a problem I'd like to talk to you about.'

'Go ahead.'

'I think I may have caught a dose,' Mark confessed.

'So?'

'It only started this morning, but I'm pretty sure of it. I had a swab and VDRL done this morning before I came out.'

'It's easily cured,' said David. 'You should know that.'

'Yes. It's not that that worries me. It's where I got it.'

'You mean you know?' David could not help the gentle jibe.

'Yes. I haven't had a girlfriend for a long time, but the other night I went to a party in Marlborough. It was a pretty wild set-up and they were handing out all sorts of things like hash and coke as well as the booze.'

'And you got tucked into the coke?' David was genuinely horrified, but tried not to show it.

'No, it was hash. They were handing it out in the soup. I'd had a fair bit to drink and it seemed a good idea at the time.'

'And this led you into the arms of a little doll who was kind enough to give you gonorrhoea?'

'More or less, only it was the doll who led me there in the first place, and she's into it all the time, apparently. Together with that husband of your pal Daphne.'

'Martin Webber?'

Mark nodded miserably.

'Right. We had a row on the night of the party because he wanted the girl I was with to go into a threesome with him and I wouldn't let her.'

'So my greedy young friend wanted her all for himself and collected?'

'That's about the length of it.'

'And do I know your secret siren?' asked David.

Mark looked more miserable than ever.

'That's the trouble. It's Sandra Gotch.'

'And both of you on parade tomorrow for a major surgical list?'

'Yes.'

'Not from now you aren't,' said David firmly.

'Of course. That's easy enough for me, but how do we get her out of it?'

'Tell her to go sick. Telephone her tonight.'

Mark brightened visibly. Just having David to make decisions had cleared the air. There was a halloo from Thomson and they trudged together back to the Manor. The shoot was over.

Laurel was standing by the front doors when they returned to the Manor.

'David, Ralph wants us to stay to drinks and then go back for dinner,' she announced.

'Fine, but first I must run Mark to the cottage. He has to be back this evening.'

They got into the Triumph and were off past the rhododendrons before Mark realised he had not thanked his host for the day.

'What shall I do, David?' he wanted to know.

'Phone Sandra Gotch first, then come back and do it.'

At the cottage Mark got through to the hospital. David purposely left him in private and went to clean his gun. Mark came back in a very short time, his face grim. David raised his left eyebrow at him.

'Tell me the worst. What did she say?'

'She told me I was a dirty little scaremonger. She said she was OK and I could get lost.'

'Did you tell her you'd told me?'

Mark shook his head.

'Mark, there's no way I'm going to have that woman in theatre tomorrow morning,' David said firmly. 'If you can't fix it tonight I'll see the Matron in the morning before I start the list, and you know what that will mean—all hell let loose, with screams about confidentiality and victimisation. You'd better try hard.'

CHAPTER EIGHT

GINETTE was tucking her hair inside her turban when David's voice gave her an unexpected thrill. She turned and saw him framed in her office door. When he was smiling and relaxed he could give her a look that made her flutter. This morning he looked serious. There was none of his enviable, easy manner.

'Is Staff Nurse Gotch on duty this morning?' he asked.

'Yes. She's changing now. She's taking the first case.'

'I want her out of the theatre. She's to report sick.'

'What on earth for?' queried Ginette.

David told her. Ginette's wide green eyes opened wider.

'This isn't going to be easy, David. She may object strongly.'

'She can burst into blue flame for all I care, as long as she doesn't appear in my theatre as a source of infection.'

'That's very unlikely anyway.'

'Unlikely isn't good enough. I want it to be impossible.'

She looked at the firm line of his mouth, the set of his chin, and knew there was no room for compromise and respected him for it.

'I'll do my best,' she told him.

'If you don't, Sister, I will.'

Ginette watched him as he strode down the theatre corridor. Despite her irritation she knew he was right. She sighed and raised her voice as she saw the rangy figure of Staff Nurse Gotch emerge from the nurses' changing-room.

'Staff Nurse—a moment, please.'

Sandra Gotch was tall and bony, but superficially attractive. Her eyes narrowed as Ginette spoke.

'Where did you get this information?' she demanded. 'Who told you this?'

'I'm not at liberty to say, and it's irrelevant. The fact is you may have a communicable disease, and we can't run the risk of wound infection.'

'What if I won't?' said Sandra Gotch truculently.

'I shall have to bring the matter before the Senior Nursing Officer.'

Sandra pointed forward at her like an angry hound.

'This is a bit of your doing! You're frightened I might show you up because I'm faster and better than you. You want me out—that's it!'

'It is not,' Ginette assured her. 'Your work is good and I welcome it.'

Sandra gave her a sly smile.

'Frightened I might get to your precious Mr Compton, perhaps? Scared I'll tread on your patch?'

Ginette started to get angry. Her cheeks reddened and her eyes went as hard as emeralds.

'Nurse Gotch, are you going to report sick or not?' she asked coldly.

'Very well. I'll go sick, but if they give me a clearance I'll be back with an official complaint and you'll be on your way!'

Sandra disappeared back into the changing-room and Ginette found David in the recovery area. She was flushed after the encounter.

'I've done as you said,' she told him. 'But I can't say I liked it.'

He looked at her so fiercely that her heart gave a thump. In his work he was so demanding, so unrelenting on any point that departed from surgical perfection that in these moments he was a different man. There was a relentlessness about his personality that frightened her. Since their kiss he had intruded upon her thoughts in a disconcerting way. Now she could hardly believe it had happened.

She became conscious that they were standing close enough for her to feel the warmth of his body. When he was not before her she cursed herself for her girlish stupidity and vowed not to let it happen again, but it always did.

'We can't always do what we want, can we?' he said. 'Right now I can't do what I want.'

Her mouth parted breathlessly.

'What's that?'

'I want to kiss you, but I can't. Not here. So let's start the list, shall we?'

He turned and was into the scrub area before she could answer, and she was gowned and scrubbed before she had got her senses back. Pat Coppard, the Australian anaesthetist, had the patient anaesthetised and ready on the table. His slangy, penetrating accent came from under the mask.

'No Slater, no Sandra this morning? What's happened, the whole place going crook?'

'Just the luck of the draw, I suppose,' said David evenly as he made the first sweeping incision to remove a diseased gall-bladder. 'How's your French?' he added.

'Pretty fractured, sport. Why?'

'We're off to Lyons. Demonstrating our vascular micro-surgery.'

'Sounds OK. Who's going?'

'Just you and I and Sister here.'

Ginette's hand hesitated momentarily as she reached for the instrument David was passing to her.

Pat Coppard was a short, hollow-cheeked individual who looked as though he ate razor blades for breakfast.

Nothing rattled him and his comments could be pithy and biting. The sort of man who would only need five minutes' notice for a trip across Antarctica.

'Tell us more?' he invited.

'Just a little entente cordiale. Professor le Masurier was asked, but he's going to Rio de Janeiro. Asked me if I would take his place. We've got to go as a team—I can't do it alone.'

'Nice of you, sport. Sounds good—I'm for it. When is it?'

'In about a month.' David turned to Ginette. 'How about you, Sister?'

'This is the first I've heard of it,' she said.

She was being deliberately prickly. Just like him to drop this bombshell in the middle of an operation without the slightest discussion or enquiry about what her views were! How did he know she would be available? He didn't. He just took it for granted that she would be there.

She threaded a needle-holder and slapped it into his outstretched palm with more than usual vigour. They discussed it further over coffee.

'How long shall we be away?' she wanted to know.

'A few days, perhaps.'

'What about the office boys and girls?' Ginette was referring to the administrative hierarchy.

'The Professor says he can look after them. Nice to have a boss high in the pecking order.'

'Right, sport,' said Pat. 'We'll bring him back a good few bottles of wine. Wives included?'

David shrugged.

'I suppose so, although I don't think Laurel will be along.'

Ginette did not know what to think when she heard that.

'What's it going to involve?' she asked him.

'I'll be giving a lecture, and we can demonstrate our instruments. Then they'll have some cold cases for us, plus whatever trauma that turns up off the motorway. That's why I want you two along. I don't want to be at the end of a bleeding femoral with an anaesthetist I don't know and a scrub sister I can't understand.'

Ginette nodded to Pat Coppard.

'Isn't he a thoughtful doctor? He only wants us there to keep him out of trouble.'

Pat looked at her keenly.

'I reckon we might have a job at that, with you along.'

Ginette blushed, stood up and fiddled with the coffee cups.

'The next case will be up from the ward now, Dr Coppard,' she said stiffly. 'I'm sure he'd rather be asleep when he's wheeled into theatre.'

Pat Coppard grinned at her. 'Good on you, sheila. Never take it lying down.'

He drifted out of the room, and David laughed.

'See what I mean about paying the price?'

'It's time you went to scrub,' Ginette reminded him.

'Have you ever been to Burgundy?' he asked.

'I've never got as far as Calais.'

'Splendid, you'll love it. We might even get a chance to whisk into Provence.'

'Won't your wife be going?' she queried.

'Very doubtful. She doesn't like that sort of caper, and she's got a new job.'

Ginette deputed one of the theatre nurses to take over as instrument nurse and she assisted David in Mark Slater's absence. The rest of the morning's list went like a sewing machine. They had never been more attuned. The instruments clicked like typewriters, the sutures went in at speed, and every move was without hesitation. There was never an anxious moment.

David took off his rubber gloves and dropped them in the bin together with his cap, mask and gown as they left the theatre.

'Thank you, Ginette,' he said as he walked away.

She was disturbed. Nothing gave her greater pleasure than to be working with him, but what about playing with him? In France there would be that much more opportunity for play. Did she even want to play? Silly question—the feeling in her quivering stomach gave her the answer to that. She sat in her office and looked at herself in the mirror. She looked good and she knew it. Her eyes were bright, her copper hair, tumbling over her shoulders before she put it under her cap, framed a face that was alive with excitement and interest and something more. She pointed at herself in the mirror.

'You,' she said, 'are being a fool.'

She knew it, and she didn't give a damn. She wondered what the trip to France was going to involve. If it was going to be a week there would certainly be some socialising, so she would need more than her uniform to wear. Ginette loved clothes, and here was a great opportunity to indulge her weakness. She looked at the calendar. Tomorrow was her day off and now she knew precisely what she was going to do with it. She gave a little wink at the mirror.

'Bond Street, here I come!'

Not only was it Bond Street, but the Ritz as well, because Dirk den Pol telephoned her that evening with his promised invitation to the Toulouse-Lautrec exhibition and lunch. The following day she was in London early and had her shopping finished by eleven o'clock, when she met him on the steps of the Royal Academy.

Dirk was polished, suave and articulate and, in his own Dutch way, good-looking. He stepped forward to greet her, wearing a brown double-breasted jacket, and a white tie. His teeth gleamed as he smiled and Ginette

noted that he was wearing a heavy gold ring on his left
little finger. They walked up to the ante-room on the
first floor, Ginette absorbing the atmosphere of the old
building, redolent with years of dusty culture.

Dirk was well informed. It was his subject, and he
made the walk round the exhibition an hour of intense
interest for Ginette. They gazed at posters of the
Moulin Rouge with the high-kicking La Goulue and
Jane Avril with hair that matched Ginette's.

The pictures and Dirk's comments brought to life for
her the atmosphere of Parisian café society before the
turn of the century. She admired the disdainful hauteur
of Aristide Bruant and sympathised with the abandoned fatigue in the figure of Cha-u-Kao, the woman
clown. As they walked down Piccadilly in the sunshine,
Dirk took her arm.

'And now I keep the rest of my promise,' he
announced.

She looked at him with a raised eyebrow.

'What's that?'

'To lunch you at the Ritz, of course.'

They sat in the Regency elegance of the high-
ceilinged dining-room overlooking Green Park, and
Dirk entertained her with the gossip of the art world.
He regaled her with inside stories of the Van Meegeren
fakes, and the sad fate of Tom Keating. He was so witty
with his penetrating comments she was kept laughing
throughout the lunch. When they were having coffee he
put his hand over hers.

'Ginette, would you care to finish your coffee in my
suite? I always keep one here when I am in London.'

She looked at him directly over her coffee cup.

'Does that mean what I think it means?'

He quirked at her.

'You are a very direct young lady, but since you
ask—yes.'

Ginette smiled at him. It was a kindly smile, although not an inviting one. Dirk was a nice man, but he held no attraction for her. Beside David he paled into insignificance.

'You're very kind, Dirk, and perhaps I should be flattered, but I think the coffee would go cold upstairs.'

He shrugged and nodded, resigned, but good-humoured. Ginette inwardly heaved a sigh of relief.

'Someone else, perhaps?' he asked her.

She nodded.

'Once isn't making a habit of it, you know.'

'It is for me.'

Inside her a voice taunted her that there was no one else, that she was making it up. She smothered the voice with the thought that it was as good an excuse as any to avoid going to bed with Dirk den Pol. Dirk was a good loser, however, and when she drove back they had parted friends. He was a nice man, but he was not for her, although, for once, the prospect of getting away from the routine of the hospital was alluring.

What worried her was her ambivalent feelings towards David Compton. He confused her when they were close outside the theatre, and if things were not exactly as he wished when operating he could upset her to such an extent that she was near to tears. At the hospital she was able to get away if that happened, but what about this trip? Of necessity they would be in close proximity most of the time, both in and out of the theatre. In a foreign country she would feel less sure of herself.

It was quite possible that under the strain of being so much in the public gaze David would be more demanding than ever and she would find it difficult to cope in such unfamiliar surroundings. Or would he be less arrogant away from his home ground? Maybe he would be more relaxed in France.

David, in the meantime, was talking to Sam Bennett, who looked a different man. His face, previously craggy, now had the look of a savage dog. He was no longer ill, was wearing a scarf to hide the scar across his throat, and there was a hard, cold look about him. David looked at his charts and examined the scar.

'How do you feel, Mr Bennett?' he asked. 'I think you're fit to go home now.'

'Fine. I could run a mile.'

'I wouldn't try that just yet!'

Sam stood up beside the bed and held out his hand.

'Thank you, Mr Compton. In a little while, perhaps you'd come and have lunch with me?'

'Thank you.'

David smiled, nodded and carried on with his round. Sam got out of bed and slipped on his silk dressing-gown and his slippers. He had some difficulty in getting the plaster cast on his broken wrist through the sleeve, but managed it with perseverance.

Susan was in a single room further down the corridor, and she tried to smile at him when he entered her room.

'How are you, Sam?'

He felt his stomach knot with rage as he looked at her and forced himself not to show his feelings.

'I'm pretty good, Beauty. How's yourself?'

'Laughing all the way, sport. Takes more than this to keep a good girl down, when she's from down under!'

Her voice was the same, but her speech sounded clipped through the tightness of her lips. He took her hand in his and squeezed it gently, trying to control the rage rising within him against the men who had done this to his lovely Susan. The men who had robbed them both of their first and only son, because they had been told that there would now be no more.

'It's going to be all right, Su-Su,' he said gently.

The tears dripped down her cheeks at that. He only called her Su-Su in moments of special tenderness or emotion. Maybe, she thought to herself, maybe it *is* going to be all right. She nodded at him, unable to speak. She tried another smile, but gave that up because it hurt too much.

'I'm going out tomorrow, Susan,' he told her. 'David Compton's happy now that he's cut my throat and says I'm wasting his time and bed space. I'll be in every day, Beauty.'

He bent to kiss her, realised it would be too painful for her when she flinched and gave her hand another squeeze instead.

Outside her room his expression changed, and a passer-by would have stopped in horror at the look on his face. That night he did not turn on the television or listen to the radio through the headphones. He sat in a chair by the window with the curtains open and gazed into the night sky. The stars were brilliant, and he stared long at Orion's sword and the Plough and saw neither of them. Only the flicker of his eyes and the bitter expression on his face gave any indication of his thoughts.

CHAPTER NINE

DAVID thought no more of Sam's invitation until a month later, when there was a telephone call for him one afternoon.

'Sam Bennett.'

'Good afternoon, Mr Bennett.'

'Lunch next Saturday?' asked Sam.

'I'm sorry, that's difficult.'

'Dinner suit you better?'

David nodded into the telephone.

'Yes, it would.'

'Seven-thirty, then. Will you bring your wife?'

'Thank you.'

'You know my place? Offa's Hall, on the main Cirencester road just before you reach the Highwayman. If you get stuck ask at the pub.'

The instrument went dead before David had time to reply. Like Ralph Abelson, Sam Bennett did not waste time on frills.

Laurel received the invitation with all the enthusiasm of a bride in a brothel.

'Who is this man anyway?' she wanted to know.

'He's a chap I operated on recently. He was in that smash outside Marlborough.'

'Was that the man with the Bentley?'

Her tone was more interested. David nodded.

'International property developer, and nobody's fool. Ralph said he was on the board of Schwarz and Sassoon.'

Laurel tossed her head.

'Oh well, I suppose it will give me an opportunity to

air my red dress again. Who else is going?'

'Don't know, could be only us. Maybe it's just a thank-you dinner, but I had the feeling there was a little more behind it,' said David.

They found Offa's Hall without difficulty. It stood, screened from the road by a small wood, on the side of a hill. As they drove through the wood and it came into view, even David whistled.

It was ultra-modern and large by any standard. Built entirely in Cotswold stone, it was roofed with dark Welsh slate, sloping up from ground level in a clean sweep on either side of the front of the house, which was entirely of glass. It looked, from a distance, like a monstrous bat that had landed and was trying to claw its way up the hillside.

Sam Bennett met them at the front door and a maid in uniform took their coats.

'Come through and meet some friends of mine,' he invited.

He led the way into a long room with a giant fifteenth-century stone fireplace halfway down one wall. On the opposite wall were several paintings, one of which David recognised with a shock as Renoir's 'Femme au Corsage Rouge'.

Then came a foghorn bellow from a figure on the leather chesterfield.

'Laurel, my dear girl!'

The leviathan frame of Sir Ralph Abelson arose and Laurel was engulfed. David noted that her frosty expression was replaced at once by animated pleasure. Sam Bennett looked on with benevolent amusement as David greeted Penelope, who whinnied her delight at seeing them. David turned to Sam.

'How did you know we were friends with the Abelsons?' he asked in surprise.

Sam winked knowingly and tapped the side of his nose.

'It's not only surgeons who know it all, y'know.'

Susan was standing beside the fireplace. Her face still bore the dull red flush of healed burns which she had concealed as far as possible with make-up and she wore a long blonde wig. In a blue satin dress with long sleeves and a heavy pearl choker she looked brilliant. Only David and Sam knew how much damage she had concealed.

She wore a wide, winning smile as she came forward to greet Laurel, whom she had not met before. David looked at her carefully. There was a new hardness in her eyes, doubtless born of the suffering she had undergone, but perhaps of something else as well? The maid served champagne before dinner and they dined off an immense marble table. Laurel admired it as she put her wine glass down, and Sam nodded appreciatively.

'Sixteenth-century Florentine—came out of the Farnese Palace. Susan likes it because it saves her a lot of polishing. She isn't much of a one for housework.'

It was the first time he had made any reference to his wife, and David felt that it did not augur well.

They ate avocado pears stuffed with cottage cheese and fresh caviar. David was fascinated by a fifteenth-century mille-fleurs tapestry on the wall opposite him, depicting scenes of village life, and was on the verge of asking Sam about it when the maid took their dishes and brought in a wooden platter bearing a saddle of lamb. Sam carved and the maid served. When he sat down he raised his glass.

'Here's to our new employee.'

They all raised their glasses, including Laurel. Ralph patted her on the arm, and David hoped privately that he had not broken it doing so.

'Can't do that, m'dear. Drinking your own health.'

For once Laurel was nonplussed.

'Oh. . . .I'm sorry. I didn't know you meant me.'

Sam leaned forward.

'Of course. Schwarz and Sassoon is one of my banks.'

David wondered whether he owned the bank or just used it. From what he had recently seen of Sam he thought the former was the more likely. They toasted Laurel, who recovered herself and queened it demurely.

Susan looked across the table and smiled.

'I didn't know you were joining our staff.'

She made it sound as though Laurel had just been engaged to clean the lavatories. David saw Laurel smile icily and incline her head.

'I think all firms work on a need-to-know basis now. Perhaps that's why.'

Susan felt herself flushing at the icy put-down. Instinctively she knew Laurel was a woman to watch, even to be feared. She had the flawless features and elegance that she knew Sam admired. Already she had caught him looking at her and paying her those little extra attentions that gave him away.

Since her discharge from the hospital her thoughts and fears had not gone away. If anything they had increased. Sam had not been close to her. She had missed the little pats and touches he would give her when they were together. Now he was like a stranger, and she knew why. He was offended by her injuries. No longer was she a flawless beauty. Susan had worked hard at her convalescence and had recovered well, but she was far from being back to full strength. Now she was angry. Her face flushed redder than ever, which made her worse.

She looked across at Laurel, and felt a savage ire rising within her at this woman who was so blatantly sitting at her dining table, in her home, and putting out the vibrations strength five at her husband. A husband, moreover, who had just agreed to employ her. In her agitation she picked up a fork and tapped the end of the handle on the marble of the table-top. She eyed Laurel, her wide full mouth a hard line for once.

'When you own the business, as we do, there's always a need to know everything. I hope you won't lose sight of that in the course of your duties.'

'When I'm apprised of my duties I shall be in a better position to know how to interpret that requirement.' Laurel was not one to be put down easily.

Susan glared at her.

'Interpretation isn't what we're talking about. We're talking about duties and orders and doing as you're bloody well told!'

There was a sudden silence at the table. Susan's outburst had penetrated even the foghorning of Sir Ralph Abelson. Sam looked across at Susan with a savage expression.

'Susan—do you feel ill?' he demanded.

She stood up, tears welling into her eyes.

'Yes, I bloody do! I feel ill and sick.'

She pushed her chair back with a screech on the marble floor and left the room with a patter of feet. Sam looked around the table at the others with a raised eyebrow.

'Susan isn't over it yet, I'm afraid,' was all he said, and carried on as if nothing had happened.

The maid served coffee and liqueurs after dinner and Sam went to find Susan while the others spent the time looking at his collection of gold pocket watches. He found her in their bedroom, lying sobbing on the bed. With unusual gentleness he sat down beside her and patted her back.

'Come on, girl. What's the problem?'

'You know what's the problem. I'm the problem.'

'You're getting better,' he assured her.

'I am, and what good is it? You look at me as if I was a whore! Without my make-up I look like something out of the Chamber of Horrors. And you spend your time sniffing at that porcelain doll who looks as though she's come out of a china shop!'

'I couldn't care less about her,' said Sam. 'I've only just met her.'

'That's enough. You can't face making love to me because I've been fucked by those fellows. That's it, isn't it?'

Sam's hands gripped the bedclothes. She was right, and he hated himself for it, and he *was* attracted to Laurel. Had been from the moment she walked into the hall and swung her wrap off her shoulders with the practised ease of a professional mannequin. He did not hate himself for that; Sam was too much of a man of the world to let a minor question of morality disturb him. What did bother him was that he could not fancy Susan after her gang rape and with her burns. It was illogical, selfish and immature, but it was there.

'No, it isn't,' he said. 'You're just not well enough yet to do anything.'

'No? How do you know? You're a doctor? Have you tried?'

She sat up, facing him, her eyes wide and wild. The tortured memory was still within her, and with a perverse fury at his attitude she wanted to bring it up to hurt him, although it destroyed her to do so.

'Why don't you try now? See if it still works? Shall I tell you something? It does. I'm the same woman— there's nothing different. It's all there, you know.'

She put her hands to her face and wept. Sam stood up.

'For God's sake, Susan!'

He looked down at her briefly and strode out of the room. Susan stayed where she was for a few moments, then stood up and went into the adjoining bathroom. She washed her face in cold water and put on more make-up. Gradually her movements became slower and more controlled. She compressed her lips after applying her lipstick and looked at herself in the mirror.

'Can't afford too much of that, my girl. Now get down and get among it.'

Susan was nothing if not a fighter. When she appeared downstairs there was a momentary silence. She smiled at them all.

'Sorry, everybody—I just went over the top. Must be the change in the weather!'

There was a general laugh and the atmosphere relaxed. Sam patted David on the shoulder.

'Excuse us a moment—I have something I want to show David here.'

Susan sat and watched them leave, and surprised herself at the way in which she conjured sweetness and light out of a mind teeming with fury and a natural antipathy towards the cold beauty of David's wife.

Sam took David into his study, a room lined entirely by books except for one area which was occupied by a rack of shotguns and sporting rifles. In the centre of the study was a leather-topped partner's desk. Sam pulled open the centre drawer and pulled out a file which he put on the desk, unopened.

'I want to make you an offer,' he said.

David was intrigued and raised his left eyebrow.

'After that dinner and wine, how can I refuse?'

'It touches, but only very slightly, on your professional ethics,' Sam explained. David frowned, and Sam held up his hand. 'Only slightly,' he added.

'That sounds like being just a little pregnant!'

Sam opened the file and spread out a row of photographs. There were six in all, front and side views of each of three men. David studied them.

'They look a pretty bunch,' he observed.

'They raped my Susan. You know the rest. She'll never win another beauty competition, will she?'

David looked up sharply. There was no point in beating about the bush.

'Unhappily that's true. Why don't you get the police on to them?'

Sam shook his head.

'And get them six months' suspended sentence? Those guys are for me. I'm going to deal with them. Those pictures are only the first step, they cost me an arm and a leg from a detective agency, and worth every penny.'

'How did they get these?' David wanted to know.

'I gave them a description of them—not only visual, but voices and accents. They say they're certain it's them. Money talks its way into a lot of places, even the police computer.'

'Why come to me?' asked David.

'I'm just casting the net wide. There's a drug unit at Manbury, yes?'

'Correct.'

'Then it's likely that one of these will turn up there some time. Also, being druggies, they're high risk and could well end up in your casualty department.'

'So?'

Sam's face was like granite.

'So money buys me a contract, and that's a lot quicker if I know when and where they are.'

'How can I help you?'

'By helping yourself. David, I'm not going to beat about the bush. I know you've got financial difficulties. I think I have a way you could ease them off a little.'

David looked at him suspiciously.

'What makes you think that?'

Sam took him by the arm.

'Look, David, don't get on your high horse. It never helps. I have ways of finding out things; especially in the financial world. I talk about overdrafts as easily as you do about the pox, so don't let's mess about. I want you to study those pictures until you can recognise them anywhere. Then, if they're admitted to your hospital for any reason, I want you to let me know. I'll pay you three thousand each one.'

David thought quickly. It was hardly a breach of the rules that Sam was suggesting. Not really wrong, but not quite allowed either. Perhaps, in a court of inquiry, it would be criticised, but nowhere else. With his savagely rising overdraft it would help to stave off the problem of James's increased school fees.

He looked up at Sam. He was the only person who would be able to give him away, and that was not likely. There was no other source of money to help him.

'OK,' he said casually, 'that shouldn't be a problem.'

'Fine!' Sam closed the file, put it into a leather zip case and handed it to David. 'Here's your homework.'

They went back to the others. Penelope was fussing about its being late, the long drive and the dogs that needed to be bedded down when they got back, so the party broke up. As they shook hands on leaving Sam looked at David.

'I look forward to hearing from you.'

David nodded, and they set off back to Apple Tree Cottage. On the way back he went over his conversation with Sam and wondered what he intended to do with the information about the men if he gave it to him. A picture came into his mind of a mini-invasion of the hospital by thugs with machine-guns, intent on carrying out a contract, and he shook his head. Not in today's society. Nevertheless the uneasy feeling remained that he had lent himself to something unpleasant and over which he would have no control. Sam was a no-messing individual.

He spoke to Laurel as they drew up outside the cottage.

'When do you start your new job?' he asked her.

'Next week.'

'What sort of money did you say they're paying you?'

'Fifteen thousand and the car.'

'Good lord!' exclaimed David. 'What do you have to do to earn that?'

'Don't worry—nothing you wouldn't approve of. Sam Bennett's a hard one, isn't he?'

'Not surprising after what happened,' shrugged David.

'I wouldn't like to get on the wrong side of him. Do you think he's really as wealthy as he seems?'

'I do. Mega-rich, I would say.'

'Well, I shall be able to buy some nice clothes at last!' Laurel remarked.

'You couldn't see your way to helping with James's fees out of your new-found wealth?'

'No, I will not. I've told you, David, I've scrimped for too long already, and there is an alternative.'

'There's no alternative. I will not have him in that dump!'

'I'm going to need a new wardrobe and we can have some new curtains for the cottage. I think a holiday on the French Riviera might be nice.'

They finished the journey in silence. Only when they had got into bed did Laurel speak.

'By the way, I shall be out for the day on Thursday. I'm going up to Town.'

'Shopping?' asked David sarcastically.

'No. Sam has asked me to have lunch with him. He wants to discuss my new duties.'

David looked at her sharply.

'Is that meant to be a sick joke, or do you mean it?'

'I mean it all right. You don't imagine a man like Sam Bennett is going to pay me fifteen thousand a year without getting his pound of flesh?'

'That's probably just what he *is* after. And I thought it was Ralph you were working for?'

'He gave me the job, but they're both in the same bank and Sam thought I'd fill the post as his PA.'

She appeared unconscious of his barbed comment in her preoccupation with her new horizons, so he let it pass and enquired gently,

'When are you coming back?'

'Friday. I thought I might look up Joanna Blackburn and do a show. Why? Does it matter particularly?'

David sighed to himself.

'Not especially. Only I'm off to France on Saturday morning at the crack of dawn.'

Laurel looked sideways at him.

'Well, in that case I might as well stay up for the weekend.'

'You do that.'

As they lay silent side by side, David began to wonder where it had all gone wrong. What on earth was Laurel going to do to justify such a salary? A worm of suspicion entered his mind as he thought of Sam's expression as he had spoken to Laurel at the dinner table.

He knew something she could do to earn her keep; something that, to judge from his expression, Sam would find vastly entertaining. There was no doubt in his mind now that she was after Sam for his money, and he smiled grimly in the dark.

Two could play at that game.

CHAPTER TEN

DAVID gave Ginette only three days' notice that the trip to Lyons was definitely fixed. Aggravated at the short notice, she snapped,

'How am I expected to organise a theatre suite and duties if you only tell me at the last moment that we're traipsing off to the Continent?'

'With your customary despatch and expertise, I should hope. There's no need to manufacture difficulties.'

She scowled at him under her turban, at the same time intrigued at the prospect of being with him away from the hospital.

'What are we supposed to be demonstrating in our guise of the international surgeon?' she asked. 'There are the instruments to think of. They may not have what you use. What am I to do when you ask for an Ellis and it's locked in the cellar with the Nuits St Georges?'

'Take our stuff with us. For God's sake, what's the problem? We're not going to the moon!'

She sighed deeply and said, 'Try and be sensible. How do we get there?'

'Pat's Volvo. He's got an old estate car half the size of a London bus and it will take us and all our gear.'

'Isn't that the long way round? Couldn't we fly?'

'Not so easy with our stuff, and we can be there the same day, and more fun too,' said David. 'Especially if we manage a night stop on the way back.'

Ginette looked at him quickly, but his face gave nothing away.

'You still haven't told me what operations we're to do,' she said.

'Not easy when I don't know what they have to do. I can't organise motorway accidents to order for our convenience.'

She felt herself getting cross. When she had arrived at Manbury she had become recognised as a highly efficient theatre sister, dedicated to her work and seemingly with no particular interest outside it. No one at Manbury knew anything of her private life and she was careful never to refer to it. She hated sympathy, and her relationship with Simon and its consequences was not something to be exposed to public view.

She felt as though she was getting out of her depth into an area where she did not know the ropes, and David was being deliberately unhelpful. Furthermore, he would still require the same standard of theatre technique when they were abroad as there was at Manbury, more, probably, if they were on show to the French surgical fraternity.

They were due to leave on the Saturday morning, and Ginette compiled lists of instruments they would need. She sent requisition forms to the stores and there was the usual complaint from the stores manager.

'If these are going out of the hospital, Sister, then you'll have to sign. I can't accept any losses incurred outside the hospital.'

'Very well, Mr Smithers. Where do I sign?'

Ginette had long ago learned not to argue with the stores manager, who was under the impression he was the guardian of King Solomon's mines.

When Saturday dawned they met early in the hospital courtyard. The Volvo had been packed the night before. Pat and David were there before her, despite her six a.m. arrival. She handed her bag to Pat, who hefted it over the tailgate of the car. He groaned.

'What have you got there, lead books?'

'Just filmy silk, Dr Coppard. You should take more exercise,' she replied sweetly.

David patted her on the shoulder.

'Passport?'

She nodded.

'Then let's go.' He was in one of his no-messing moods.

Pat Coppard drove, with David beside him and Ginette in the back. They took the M4 towards London, skirted the metropolis and drove past Canterbury to Dover where they drove on to a British Rail Seaspeed Ferry. The giant hovercraft, taking over four hundred passengers and more than fifty cars, was far from full and they drove down the concrete pad straight on board.

Thirty-five minutes later they were on French soil. At the *péage* they took a ticket and were soon skimming along the Autoroute du Nord towards Paris. Ginette looked at her watch. It was not yet ten o'clock.

They stopped for coffee and croissants at a service station near Bethune and filled the petrol tank. David took over the driving and Ginette went to sit in front. He winked at her.

'Think you can manage the navigating?' he asked.

'Just keep your mind on your job, David. I'll take you on, mile for mile, on a two-hour driving stint, if you dare?'

David turned in his seat to Pat.

'How's that, Pat? OK with you? It's your car.'

'Give the girl a chance, David!'

They checked the clock and the mileometer and were away. The Volvo was smooth and, for its size and age, surprisingly fast. David kept his foot down and most of the time they were doing between five and ten miles an hour over the ton. The traffic was mounting and they had to slow frequently.

The morning sun was hot, but the car remained cool and Ginette saw that the air-conditioning was switched on. After two hours they logged the mileage. A hundred and sixty miles. Ginette nodded coolly.

'Not bad, Mr Compton.'

'Your turn now,' he told her.

She shook her head. 'Not now. I'll take my turn later.'

She had heard all about the *péripherique*, the motorway around Paris, and David was not going to railroad her into that one. Typical of him, she thought, to try and win by giving her the slow part of the route! She firmed her lips and determined that this was one occasion when he was going to take a back seat. It was only when they had turned on to the Autoroute du Sud and were well away from the city traffic that she turned and said,

'I'll start now, *monsieur*.'

They slid into the next service station, filled up, had a wash and a walkabout, and Ginette climbed into the driver's seat. She had never driven a big Volvo before, and it felt enormous. As they cruised down the slope out of the service station she switched off the air-conditioning. She had read that it took ten per cent off performance. David was talking to Pat and did not notice.

She took it easy at first until she had got the feel of the car, and then she put her foot down. Slowly the speedometer swung round to a hundred. The car felt rock-steady and her foot was not on the floor. A hundred and five, ten, fifteen, twenty. Her foot was hard down, the road reeling up like a fast-moving ribbon. She had never driven so fast in her life. She kept to the outside lane and learned to flash her headlights when a car ahead signalled to overtake. Her hands were wet with tension and excitement.

David sat beside her and said nothing. It was his very silence that gave his concern away. She remembered Harry Truman's words,

'If you can't stand the heat, get out of the kitchen.'

She smiled to herself. A voice behind her rose querulously.

'Christ, you could roast a pig in here! What's happened to the bloody air-conditioning?'

'I turned it off. Didn't want to spoil the performance of this racing machine.'

'My God—never trust a woman! If she doesn't kill us on the track, we'll die roasted!' groaned Pat.

The hills of Burgundy rolled by, with pictures of owls, rabbits, wild boar, and stags on the sides of the motorway. Ginette drove the fleeing Volvo hard. She became used to the speed and started to enjoy herself. She flicked brief glimpses at the clock and the mile-ometer.

Past Beaune they hit the two-hour mark and David read the mileometer like a dirge.

'A hundred and eighty miles.'

When they stopped alongside the pumps of a service station the fuel gauge was in the red, and Pat reared up from the back seat.

'I'm asserting owner's rights. My nerves can't stand you two hellhounds competing!'

Ginette vacated the driver's seat gratefully, but revelling in her triumph. She felt tired and wrung out after the fast run in a car that was foreign to her and was delighted to relax in the back seat. She avoided rubbing in her victory. David, she could see, was clearly surprised by her turn of speed.

The motion of the car was soothing, and she watched the French countryside through the side windows and dwelt on the thought of being with David on this trip that had sprung out of the blue so delightfully. She wondered if he would have much time to spend with her, or would he be gobbled up and lionised by the French medical community? Would there be any women doctors at the symposium? She hoped not. At least, not pretty ones.

She felt alert and excited as she turned over in her mind which of her new outfits she would wear and when. She hoped they would get an opportunity to be alone at least part of the time. She wondered if David would kiss her again. She could remember the way their lips had met and the memory of it sent a delicious *frisson* through her.

Would he try and make love to her?

Was she going to let him?

She lingered on the thought, but could not arrive at an answer. In front of her she could see the back of his head through the bars of the head-rest and wondered what he would say if he knew what she was thinking, only inches away from him. She was glad she had spent that ludicrous sum on silk underwear. Apart from feeling nice it gave her confidence. After all, she thought again, you never know. She tried not to think about his wife and his son.

They drove into the Place Bellecour in the centre of Lyons at seven o'clock and found their hotel, the Royal. As Ginette relaxed in the foam of a hot bath and felt the travel aches disappearing, there was a knock on the door.

'*Entrez!*' she called, remembering to use her school-girl French.

There was the click of the door latch, the rattle of glass on metal and a man's voice said,

'*Merci, madame.*'

Then she heard the door close.

Intrigued, she got out of the bath, wrapped a towel around herself and went into the room. On the table was a tray carrying a champagne bucket and glasses. The foil-covered neck of a bottle rose out of the bucket and a ticket on the tray read,

'TO THE VICTOR—THE SPOILS. LEAVE A LITTLE FOR ME.'

Ginette smiled to herself, gave the neck of the bottle a twirl and went back into the bathroom. She put on a blue silk dress with a flared skirt and full sleeves and shoes to match that had brought a gasp from the vendeuse when she had tried it because it had suited her so perfectly. She had not asked the price, and only when she had proffered her gold Mastercard and seen the figure did she wonder whether the card would catch fire.

There was a knock on her door. She twitched the latch, called, 'Come in, David,' and went back to the mirror.

She thought there was a delay in his reply and looked in the mirror to see what he was doing. A man was standing by the champagne bucket and looked at her back with an amused smile. Ginette gasped at first and then gave a laugh.

It was not David.

He was about the same age, but shorter, slim and brown-haired, smooth-faced with large brown eyes and an air of assured elegance. He smiled at her in the mirror, his amusement obvious.

'Your welcome is most generous, Sister Irving. I wish I could deserve it. I am Philippe Duval, pathologist of the Institut Pasteur. I am here to welcome you on behalf of the conference committee and to introduce you to our members. I hope you will permit me.'

He gave a charming bow, and Ginette, who had been staring at him in the mirror, turned and held out her hand. She could feel herself blushing in front of this good-looking Frenchman and cursed inwardly.

'It's kind of you, Doctor Duval, to come and introduce yourself.'

'I would not have presumed, but it is late and there is a function to attend. And my name is Philippe.'

'Thank you, Philippe. I'm Ginette. May I offer you a drink? I'll telephone the others to tell them you're here.'

Philippe had the cork out of the champagne with typical Gallic grace and the ease of long practice. He raised his glass to her.

'To a pleasant meeting and to future pleasure.'

Ginette inclined her head and raised her glass, conscious of the suggestive gleam in his eye.

'I've enjoyed the one and look forward to the other, Philippe.'

She knew she was being provocative, but it was harmless fun and she enjoyed it. The telephone rang. It was David.

'What are we doing?' he asked. 'Are you ready?'

'Yes, I am. Come and join us, both of you.'

'Us? What do you mean "us"?' he queried.

'Come and see. And thank you for the champagne.'

There was a click as he put the phone down without further comment and seconds later there was a knock on her door. David stood there, lean and rakish in a grey pin-stripe suit, and behind him stood Pat Coppard wearing an Australian blazer. Ginette saw David's eyes wander over her shoulder and felt a twinge of irritation that he was not admiring her new dress. He was only interested in who else was in the room.

'Come and meet Dr Philippe Duval,' she said. 'He's going to introduce us to the conference.'

The two men came into the room and shook hands with Philippe. Ginette could sense a bridling atmosphere between David and Philippe as they sized each

other up. She poured the champagne and David
offered her a toast.

'To the winner.'

Philippe raised an eyebrow and David explained.
The Frenchman turned and raised his glass to her.

'How splendid to find so able a driver·in a lady so
beautiful!' Somehow he managed to convey that she
would not have won the champagne had he been in the
competition. 'And now I must take you to the welcome
party to meet everybody, and especially Professor
Langevin.'

They left in Philippe's Citroën. The reception was at
the Sofitel in the Quai Gailleton which was only round
the corner, but as Philippe remarked, Ginette could not
be expected to walk there in her high heels.

The party was in a large room on the first floor, and
Ginette had a shock when Philippe opened the door for
her. The room was crowded. Waiters, with white-
gloved hands, were moving to and fro bearing trays of
glasses brimming with champagne. Philippe made for a
small group surrounding a distinguished-looking man
with silver hair and a goatee beard. He wore half-moon
spectacles and had the air of a pensive and forgiving
mole whose mind is on other things.

'Professor, may I present our friends from England?
Sister Ginette Irving, Mr David Compton and Dr
Patrick Coppard.'

The Professor beamed at the men distantly, but
greeted Ginette warmly, holding her hand in both of
his.

'I am *enchanté*,' he told her.

He looked around. Standing behind him was a
devastatingly attractive young woman. With her short,
dark hair and gamine features she could have stepped
straight out of a fashion magazine. She was wearing a
tight-fitting mauve and silver dress with a short frill

above the knee, possible only on a young goddess with a matchless figure.

The Professor took her by the hand and introduced her.

'My niece, Anne-Marie. She is studying medicine here. Soon to qualify if she spends as much time on her studies as she does on the motorbikes of the young men.'

They all laughed and Anne-Marie pretended to be angry with her uncle. It was obvious from the Professor's looks and manner that she was the apple of his eye. As she shook David's hand she dimpled at him and said,

'I have heard a great deal about you, Mr Compton. You are to lecture here, *oui*?'

David was flattered.

'Yes. Just a short address.'

'On micro-vascular surgery, I think?'

'Yes, but how did you know that?'

'Ah, I read the journals, and here is the conference agenda.' She waved a sheet of paper at him with an amused smile. He was acutely conscious of her pale mauve lipstick which matched her finely manicured fingernails. Her scent too he could not miss because she was standing so close.

Ginette, talking to the Professor, missed nothing. David groped for words before the sophisticated young lady.

'When do you qualify, Miss. . .er. . .' he began.

'Langevin, but I would prefer you to call me Anne-Marie.'

'Anne-Marie, yes—when do you finish your studies?'

'This year, I hope.'

'And then?'

'I study to become an eye surgeon. It is my ambition since I was a little girl.'

'I hope you're successful,' he told her.

'Thank you, David. I think I shall be. It is not very often I do not get what I want.'

She laid a delicate hand on his arm and he felt the warmth of it under the fabric of his suit. Ginette happened to look across at him at that moment, saw the mauve nails contrasting with the grey pin-stripe and gave him the benefit of a fractionally raised eyebrow.

'I think Philippe is anxious to introduce you to somebody else,' Anne-Marie told him.

Philippe was indeed standing beside him, and as he was whisked away to meet other members of the French medical society David wondered whether or not he had been smoothly dispatched by the assured young Anne-Marie.

Ginette was firmly engulfed by Professor Langevin. He enquired about her work and their technique and told her that there was an operating session the following day when he had arranged for them to do two cases.

'We shall all be interested to see your technique, *ma chère mademoiselle*.'

Ginette, surprised by her sudden feelings of jealousy, hoped that her technique was up to his niece's, otherwise there was the possibility of blood on the walls, and not in the operating theatre. The Professor pushed up his spectacles and peered at a gold watch which he drew out of his waistcoat pocket.

'*Tiens*, it is late! I have given myself the pleasure of entertaining you to dinner. We are going to Daniel et Denise. You approve, I hope?'

'We are in your hands, Professor. Who are they?'

'They are a restaurant, *ma chère*. *La cuisine magnifique*, you will see. I have arranged it all.'

The Professor looked more mole-like and benevolent than ever, but not a bit as though his mind was on other things. Ginette decided that his interest in her was not entirely academic. Despite his silver hair the Professor, in his smart black jacket, pin-striped trousers and a blue flower in his buttonhole, was something of a *boulevardier*.

At Daniel and Denise, in the Rue Tupin, they dined magnificently off a menu the Professor had arranged beforehand. Ginette was not surprised to be sitting next to him, nor was she surprised to see that Anne-Marie was next to David.

The Professor was talking. He never seemed to stop.

'. . .not good to give a choice to a party like this. Too many decisions and we never eat until the appetite is gone.'

Ginette decided he was right when the dinner was served. They ate *terrine de homard* that tasted of fresh lobster, and *filet d'agneau en croute*. When she bit into the delicate slices of lamb surrounded by their pastry case Ginette knew she was in the real France. There was a pause when they digested a sorbet Jacques Cartier, the cooling water ice covered with *marc* helping to digest the lamb. Finally, after an interval, there arrived, with great pomp, six *soufflés au Grand Marnier*.

Ginette guiltily enjoyed every mouthful of the soufflé that dissolved so lightly upon the tongue. David looked across at her just as she was putting her spoon into the mountain of frothy delight and gave her a look that made her feel like a schoolgirl caught in a naughty prank.

She deliberately turned to talk to the Professor. Trust David to make her feel guilty when he was the one who was stepping out of line with the ultra-smart Anne-Marie, leaning towards her and putting his hand on her arm as they talked.

Ginette was not normally a jealous person, but she

felt it now, and when Anne-Marie stood up soon after the coffee and announced that she must go Ginette was relieved. The Professor peered benevolently at his niece over his glasses.

'Where are you off to, *chérie*? More late study?'

Anne-Marie pointed an elegant and tiny finger at him.

'No, Uncle, you know perfectly well. I have a rendezvous with Jacques for *le disco*.'

'And where is it tonight?'

'A new place he has found at Grenoble.'

'Grenoble? But that's miles away!'

It was David who had spoken, and Ginette glared at him.

'It is only *cent kilometres*, David. Not long on a BMW. In fact, the journey is half the fun. I like the danger, it is stimulating!'

She blew kisses to them all and was gone, and somehow the party was diminished.

'On a BMW?' queried David. 'Do I understand she's going there on a motorbike?'

'Yes, many young people today enjoy the thrill of motorbike riding,' replied the Professor.

'I hope she gets back in one piece. We have more major physical damage from motorcyle accidents than any other single cause in England. I think they're lethal.'

David's concern was obvious, and Ginette felt a sudden hurt that shocked her with its intensity. What was he doing? He had been bowled over by that gorgeously attractive young Frenchwoman and now he was being protective towards her.

How could he?

CHAPTER ELEVEN

GINETTE awoke and wondered for a moment where she was. The sun was streaming through a gap in the curtains and she looked at her watch. It was seven a.m., and she remembered, with a sigh, the remainder of the previous evening.

She and David had taken a taxi back to the hotel and had said nothing to each other. She had been cross with him for acting like a schoolboy with Anne-Marie and he had made one curt comment about smarmy, good-looking Frenchmen. They had not had a row. She had collected her key and gone up to her room before it could develop, but there had been a coolness, a *froideur*.

She felt miserable. She had been so looking forward to this trip with David, and as soon as they were on to French soil they were being difficult with each other. When other people appeared on the scene he was different. Ginette lay thinking, in her half-waking world. He was so charismatic, so good-looking, everybody's friend, and everybody wanted a piece of him. Was she being stupidly jealous and over-demanding?

She decided she was.

That made her get up and run a bath, determined to look her best before these *soignée* Frenchwomen. Furthermore, they were due to look over the operating theatres first thing and see the layout. Philippe Duval had promised to come round at eight-thirty and guide them to the hospital in the Volvo so that they could unload all their gear. She smiled to herself and wondered how David felt about 'smarmy Frenchmen' this morning!

After her bath she riffled along the rail in her wardrobe and picked out a smart little white suit with navy revers. She was certainly not going to wear uniform. The suit followed the lines of her figure well and the skirt was fashionably above the knee and showed off her long legs.

When she arrived in the breakfast-room the two men were already into their croissants, and Pat whistled when he saw her.

'That'll give the French somethin' to think about, Ginette!'

David got up and pulled a chair out for her. Obviously on his best behaviour, she decided, and gave him a wide smile.

'*Merci.*'

'What time are we on parade?'

'Eight-thirty Philippe arrives.'

'And then?'

'We get ourselves acquainted with the theatre layout. You're due to examine the patients at nine-thirty and we cut at eleven. Gives you time to have a discussion with the Professor and his circus.'

David turned to Pat Coppard. 'OK with you, Pat?'

That was one of the nice things about David. He was always one to include everybody in decisions, even though they were not strictly theirs to make.

'Sure, David. You know me—I can sleep any-where.'

Pat's humour was dry and self-denigrating. Philippe arrived, full of vigour and anxious to be off. He sat in the back of the Volvo and guided them to the hospital through the traffic. Pat drove and Ginette sat between David and Philippe.

The operating theatre was large and modern. The senior sister was Souer Camille; a smart, brisk woman with the leathern look of the inveterate skier. She spoke some English and they soon established a rapport. Ginette had been worried that she might be difficult over a stranger coming in to show off, but Soeur Camille was above that.

They went over the instruments together and apart from some of David's special toys there was nothing they did not have. Ginette felt a sense of relief. It was apparent that they did almost everything here that was done at Manbury, but as Soeur Camille explained, 'They like to see other people's tricks, and for the micro-vascular surgery your Monsieur Compton has the big name.'

Ginette glowed. Praise for David gave her more pleasure than praise for herself. She warmed to the kindly French sister with the creased face. Here was a woman with whom one felt at ease, perhaps a woman in whom one could confide.

Down in the outpatient department Professor Langevin, his registrar Michel Drouin, houseman Jean Potier, together with a gaggle of students, were discussing David's method for replacing a diseased popliteal artery in a diabetic lady. It was striking nine o'clock when the telephone rang. Jean Potier picked it up and listened.

'It is for you, Professor.'

The goatee beard twitched in a half circle and the benevolent mole became a fiery shrew.

'Tell them I'm busy.'

'It is the police, Professor. They are urgent about it.'

The Professor grabbed the instrument.

'Langevin.'

There was a silence and David saw the Professor's reddened face go pale. He nodded several times and then said,

'Oui, tout de suite.'

Slowly he put the telephone down, and when he

looked up at them there were tears in his eyes and he looked bewildered. David glanced at Pat and they waited for him to speak.

'It is Anne-Marie. She has been in an accident.'

He stopped, unable to speak, and David leaned forward.

'She's not dead?'

The Professor shook his head.

'No. She was on the back of the motorcycle. They were coming home from the disco and they hit a lorry. She was trapped by her hand under the wreckage. They were afraid it was going to catch fire and it would fall on her.' He shook his head and put his hands over his eyes. Michel Drouin put his hand on his chief's shoulders.

'But they managed to get her out?'

'*Oui.* And to do it they cut off her hand.'

There was a sudden shocked silence in the room. For all their familiarity with disaster, this was close to home. David spoke first.

'Where is she now?'

'She is on her way in an ambulance.'

The telephone rang again. After the last message the tone had the shrill sharpness of disaster. The Professor picked it up. As he listened his face relaxed and his eyes brightened.

'*Oui—certainement. A toute vitesse.*' He put the telephone down and turned to them. 'They have rescued her hand from the wreck. It is coming in a police car.'

There was an immediate atmosphere in the room. Stark tragedy was replaced by sudden hope. They all looked at David, and with an acute sense of discomfort he knew what they were thinking and what they were going to say. Professor Langevin looked at him over his spectacles. It was a long, long moment. Unquestionably it was David's field. He was the expert in

amputation trauma and limb replacement. Nevertheless it was a chancy and difficult business. Unless it was
done with speed and expertise the patient would be
worse off than with a simple amputation and an
artificial limb.

He looked at the Professor's pleading expression.
Gone was the surgeon, gone was the academic. What
was left was an agonised uncle.

'You will help?'

It was not a command, it was a request, but the three
words were more than a command to David. He looked
at the Professor.

'How long ago was the accident?' he asked.

It was a loaded question. The length of time the limb
had been severed was of vital importance. If it had been
without blood supply for too long there would be no
question of attempting a limb coaptation.

'Half an hour ago.'

'Let's move!'

He had barely said the words when Michel Drouin
picked up the telephone and spoke rapidly. He was a
tall, thickset man, but his reflexes were faster than a
striking heron. He handed the instrument to David
with a single word.

'Theatre.'

There was a pause and Ginette came on the line.

'Hello. David? What's going on?'

Briefly he told her.

'Lay up for a limb graft. It's possible the limb may
arrive before the patient and if so we can start on it
right away as long as the condition is satisfactory.'

'Right.'

The line clicked. Ginette was not one to waste words
in an emergency. David turned to Michel Drouin.

'Perhaps we should get to theatre? I hope you will be
able to assist?'

David did not like being assisted by someone whom he did not know. Ginette provided all the assistance he normally required. His invitation to Michel Drouin was not only a courtesy but a necessity, as he was not formally registered under French law and theoretically he would be assisting Michel Drouin. Michel Drouin nodded and led the way to the theatre suites. As they followed, Pat Coppard put it in his pithy Australian fashion.

'Christ, David, it's coming off the fan faster than you can duck!'

They were walking along a corridor on the top floor, which overlooked the approach to the hospital. There was a commotion far below as a police car, siren hawking and lights flashing, heeled round the entrance into the courtyard. A uniformed policeman leaped out carrying a box. Pat pointed.

'I bet that's her hand arriving. They certainly don't mess about!'

Laurel Compton smoothed the front of her immaculate skirt and viewed herself in the mirror of the women's room at Langan's Brasserie. The elegant red dress and her black hair vied with each other in their severity to produce a combination of elegance that made her smile with satisfaction.

The devil's colours, she thought. Well, why not?

After all, she was on a devil's mission. Laurel was no mealy-mouth and self-deception was not one of her weaknesses. She saw in Sam Bennett an attractive man who was available, and she was going to avail herself of him. With luck that availability would be permanent and take her out of her present situation, which she regarded as inadequate, and put her on a different sphere. One of limitless wealth and an international life-style; something she had always coveted.

When she had arrived Sam was not there and rather than sit alone she had gone to the powder-room. She glanced at her watch. Ten minutes after time. He would not be later than this. Laurel walked past the long bar and saw him sitting at a table looking at the motley picture collection on the walls of the bar-room.

He bore no signs of his recent accident. Even the plaster cast on his wrist had come off. He was wearing a double-breasted blue suit with a broad chalk stripe and a cream tie. He looked craggy still and with his broad shoulders and big spatulate hands he looked what he was, a tough and determined man with an underlying ruthlessness given away by his mouth and eyes.

He waved and pulled a chair out for her. She noticed he did not get up.

'Smart lady. What'll you have?'

'Campari soda, please.'

Sam waved and it was before her. She did not really like it, but the colour was right for her outfit. Laurel did nothing without thought, and this was a battlefield where all the moves had been carefully considered.

'I want to tell you about my next business trip. I shall want you along.'

She nodded slightly and eyed him quizzically.

'What do you want me to do?' she asked.

'I'll tell you over lunch. How are you for time, by the way?'

'No problem when I'm working. And I am working, am I not?'

The maître d'hôtel handed her a large menu card and with her usual care for her figure Laurel ordered melon and then halibut. Sam waved the menu away and ordered bangers and mash with onion sauce.

'Can't stand these fancy new dishes. Stick to the simple things well done.' He looked up at the waiter. 'A bottle of Krug in the bucket as well.'

They sat at a window table close to the entrance. It
gave Laurel a chance to see who was coming and going,
and those who did she found intriguing. A succession of
showbiz personalities and a smattering of society with
the occasional politician; they were all treated to Sam's
special and abrasive brand of commentary.

'See that fat little guy with the willowy blonde? Harry
Bronstein—property dealer. He owns more whore-
houses than the Church of England.'

Over lunch he told her about his proposed trip to
Arizona to set up a deal involving the building of a
major shopping precinct.

'I want you there to help with the organisation,
mainly social, partly administrative,' he explained.

'What do I have to do?' Laurel asked.

'Anything that's necessary. This isn't a Brownies'
outing, and you're a grown-up girl.'

As they talked she felt an almost mesmeric fascination for this arrogant, mannerless, demanding man
who had torn what he wanted from the world and was
now, despite his recent catastrophe, back into battle.
On the spur of the moment she interrupted him.

'Sam, how much are you worth?'

He looked at her sharply.

'What does it matter?'

'It must be many millions.'

'Maybe, but you know the saying, "A guy who knows
how much he's worth ain't worth much".'

'Then why do you still go on building more and
more? Why not take it easy and count your shekels?'

He grinned at her out of his craggy features.

'I like to fight. I like to take up a challenge, any
challenge. And I like to win. Most of the time I do.'

He said it simply and without a trace of boasting.
Laurel believed him, and it gave her a thrill to be with a
man who was so dynamically charged. He reminded her

of the black knight in *Ivanhoe*.

He poured her more champagne. Laurel normally drank little, but today she was enjoying herself and felt on a high plane. Sam obviously expected her to enjoy it, and she was not going to let him down. When they emerged from Langan's a taxi drew up and as they sat back Laurel shook her head.

'I'm amazed! Whenever I want a taxi it takes half an hour and a mile of walking.'

'You shouldn't be. It's my taxi. It's the easiest way of getting around London, and when I don't want him I tell him to go off and earn some money.'

She laughed. It was so typical of the pragmatic Sam. They drove through the maze of Mayfair and emerged into Park Lane. Sam handed her out of the taxi, to her surprise, and led the way into the foyer of a tall block. There were two banks of lifts, but Sam ignored these and stopped by a smaller door. He slid in a plastic disc, the door opened and they stepped into a small lift. There were only four buttons, she noticed—Up, Down, Doors, Alarm.

When they emerged it was into a large room overlooking Hyde Park. The furnishings were discreet, but lavish—antique French furniture, a Savonnerie carpet, a picture over an Adam fireplace that she recognised as a Breughel, and a coloured horse on a Buhl table that could only have been made by the Chinese potters of the Tang dynasty. She walked to the window and looked over London.

'Quite a view,' she remarked.

'I agree.'

Sam was standing behind her, and as she turned she saw that he was smiling mockingly at her.

'Are we talking about the same thing?' she asked.

'I was talking about what I was looking at, and I wasn't staring out of the window.'

Laurel felt an electricity in the atmosphere and prickles ran up and down her legs. The game was on, she knew it. This was put up or shut up time. She knew also that she did not have a decision to make. She had made it long ago. Sam put his hand out to her. She took it and he pulled her to him with a harshness that surprised her.

Accustomed as she was to David's gentleness, Sam's direct, almost brutal approach took her by surprise. Her head went back as his mouth came down on hers and she felt the stony hardness of him as he held her so tight it took her breath away. She felt his hand slide down her back and hold her buttock in a grip so fierce that she felt a *frisson* of painful pleasure sear through her. The frightening strength of the man brought her to an electrifying awareness of his animal approach. There was no question of her being in charge. She was in a situation over which, for the first time in her life, she had no control.

She began to tremble.

Sam felt it, recognised it for what it was and pulled off her dress. He did it, not with grace and finesse, but with a single action that had the tiny buttons at the back popping like baby balloons. It left her standing in her bra and silk french knickers before the plate glass window overlooking Hyde Park.

'Sam!' she protested. 'Somebody'll spot us!'

'Not from down there.'

He was unbuckling his belt, his jacket on the floor, and Laurel thought for a moment he was going to use it on her and stepped back towards the window, her eyes wide. He looked at her and grinned.

'Now they can see you.'

Involuntarily she stepped away from the window towards him and he caught her round the waist. The roughness of his hand against her skin excited her as it slid under her bra and gripped her breast. She felt herself growing moist, knowing that there was no way she was going to stop the roller-coaster of this man now.

'Take it easy, Sam!'

It was a plea. By way of an answer he put his foot on the sofa, bent her over his knee and gave her a smack on the bottom that brought tears to her eyes. Twice. She writhed round in his grasp and tried to bite his wrist. Instead she found herself on the sofa with her french knickers to her knees.

'Sam, please!'

He was above her and the sight of his member, blue and pulsing and emerging between thighs like tree-trunks, made her gasp.

'Wait, Sam—please! I'm not ready.'

There was no reply, and she knew from the look on his face that there would be only one reply. She tried at first, with weakening resolve, to fend him off, but she might as well have tried to stop an express train. She relaxed. Slowly he put his member into her hand as he knelt over her, looking her in the eyes.

'You do it.'

As if in a dream she took him in her right hand, thinking how incredibly hot he was. She could feel herself wet, but at the last moment something inside her panicked and she tried to push him aside. Instantly a pain in her groin flared as his thumb dug into her. His voice gritted at her.

'Go on!'

The pain had been so brief and intense she was glad, anxious even, to do as he said, and with a surge he was inside her, thrusting with the momentum of a steam engine. Laurel had never had an orgasm in her life. Pleasure, yes, but she had never allowed David to break through her control in their sexual encounters. As she felt herself carried over on the tide of Sam's passion she had no idea of what was happening to her. Only that there was an electric battery in her that was pulsing to explosion.

Automatically she thrust back at him and they moved faster in a demonic rhythm that finally erupted into a cataclysmic orgasm for them both.

'Saaaam!'

Swiftly as it came, it went. The fire and the passion passed and they lay panting side by side. He was the first to move and whispered in her ear,

'How about that, then?'

For Laurel it had been a first.

For Sam it had been yet another challenge.

The hand arrived in a thermo-pack. Someone had had the forethought to pack it correctly in twin polythene bags so that the skin did not come in contact with the coolant of the thermo-pack. David examined it minutely, and despite his surgical training he felt a twinge as he recognised the distinctive mauve nail polish and realised that these were the fingers that had lain so delicately on his arm the night before.

There lay Anne-Marie's ambition to be an eye surgeon. If he succeeded there was a faint possibility she might still achieve it. The stump was clean and fresh. It had been removed expertly. There was none of the tangled trauma of a limb that had been torn off, ruining the chance of putting together the fine arteries and nerves. Here was a situation offering the best possible chance of success.

Carefully he put the hand back in the cool-box and with a flick of his head indicated to Michel Drouin that they should scrub. Pat had disappeared into the anaesthetic-room. The preparation of the hand would take time, and there was now no more precious commodity.

The ambulance bearing Anne-Marie would arrive a little later. David did not doubt that she would be on a drip, and that would slow them down. In the theatre the hand was put into a flexible lead splint that would hold it in any position. David swabbed it carefully with antiseptic and started on the meticulous exercise of cleaning, identifying and setting up the arteries, nerves, muscles and tendons for coaptation.

This was far from completed when Jean Potier appeared at the entrance to the operating theatre. As they looked up he nodded and disappeared.

Anne-Marie had arrived.

She was lying on the trolley, pale, petite and semi-conscious. A red blanket with a black stripe covered her. A drip line from a plastic bag of saline draped down from above her head to her right arm. Her left arm ended in a white, bulbous bandage. David was relieved to see that there was no tourniquet. The bleeding had been controlled by direct pressure, which gave him a better chance of restoring the circulation. He looked at Pat Coppard.

'How is she?' he asked.

'Better than you or me with a grasper gone.'

'What's she had?'

'Morphine and thiopentone—the local doctor did it on the spot. I reckon he deserves a medal.'

David thought rapidly. A second anaesthetic in so short a time was undesirable, but essential. The less she had the better. He looked at Pat.

'Brachial block and thiopentone?'

It was going to be a tiring operation and would take hours. A brachial block, local anaesthetic into the nerves supplying the arm, would totally anaesthetise the whole arm, but Anne-Marie would need to be kept asleep by small and repeated doses of intravenous thiopentone. She had been through too much to endure hours on the table awake, even if she could not feel what was going on.

Pat Coppard felt along her collarbone with his thumb and found the point that guided him to the brachial plexus, lying beneath the bone like a leash of reins.

'Just a little prick, Anne-Marie.'

He injected a small amount of lignocaine with adrenalin 1/200,000 until there was a bleb under the skin.

'I'm going to give you a small injection in a second. You'll probably feel a little electric shock down your arm, but it will only be a quickie and then you'll feel nothing. OK?'

There was a murmur from Anne-Marie, and Pat slid the needle deep down through the anaesthetised bleb into the tissues beneath the collar bone. She gave a tiny start, and he nodded with satisfaction and pushed the plunger slowly down. Her reaction had told him he was in the right place. Now her whole arm would go numb. He withdrew the needle when the syringe was empty and gently pricked her upper arm.

'Feel that?'

She shook her hand. He went further down to the edge of the bandage.

'How's that?'

'Nothing.'

David saw a nurse leaving with a tube of blood and a form in her hand. Pat had already taken blood for cross-matching in the laboratory. The sooner Anne-Marie had a transfusion of whole blood the better. David gently took her right hand and she opened her eyes and smiled at him. Despite everything she looked brave and attractive.

'David, are you to be my knight hero?' she whispered.

'I'll do my best.'

'That should be easy for you. You are the best.'

The long eyelashes fluttered uncertainly and her eyes closed. Ginette, standing at the theatre entrance to the anaesthetic-room, felt only compassion. Pat Coppard held Anne-Marie's right hand and gave it a gentle and reassuring squeeze.

'Now I'm going to put you to sleep.'

The nurse handed him a twenty-millilitre syringe full of pale yellow thiopentone. He found a vein in her arm, slid the point of the needle into it, withdrew and saw the dark venous blood come welling back, then started to inject, saying to her,

'I want you to count to ten, Anne-Marie.'

'Un, deux, trois, quatre, cinq. . .six. . .sept. . .huit.'

She was asleep. David went to scrub again and re-garb. By the time he returned to the theatre Michel Drouin had completed the hand and Anne-Marie was on the table. A non-sterile nurse took off the bandages before they put on the sterile drapes covering Anne-Marie and her arm, leaving only the stump revealed.

David flicked away the stitches that had been inserted at the accident and sat down to identify the bones and arteries. The bones were easy. The fine spicules of the radius and ulna appeared like white coral within the wound. He had to obtain bone fixation first and freshen the bone ends so that they would oppose correctly.

'Rongeur.'

The rasping as the rongeur bit into the bone ends grated around the theatre.

'Raspatory.'

The finer raspatory smoothed the surface made by the rongeur. He obtained fixation of the opposing ends with vanadium steel plates. There would be some shortening of the forearm, but this would assist the arterial and nerve repairs. He searched for the radial artery and found it easily, but the ulna artery was more coy. This was his most urgent task, to restore the blood supply to the hand lying delicately and patiently within the grasp of the leaden glove that held it firmly in position.

He spent a long time clearing the ends of the arteries of their adventitia, the outer coat, to prevent thrombus formation at the junction site. A thrombosis here would ruin the result and end in a gangrenous hand and even the death of the patient.

'Ethilon six-O on a cutting P-3.'

The needle, with its finely bonded filament, was in his hand before he had finished speaking. He picked up the radial artery with fine, single-toothed jeweller's forceps and started opposing the two ends. It had all begun. There was silence in the theatre except for brief requests.

'Adson's forceps.'

When they came to tendon repair,

'Buck-Gramcko forceps.'

'Ethibond ST-4 on a fine straight.'

'Weck sponge, please.'

With the return of the major arterial circulation the hand lost its deadly whiteness. David isolated the big veins and sewed them together, checking that he had more veins than arteries to ensure that there was sufficient blood outflow for the limb. A bottleneck on the drainage side would cause a swiftly swollen hand and breakdown. The fine vessels and nerves required the use of the dissecting microscope. Here David was using ultra-fine sutures. He did not take his eyes off the lens while in the process of doing the finest arteries, but held out his hand and spoke his requirement.

'Ten-O on an Ethilon BV7-3.'

The filament on this was twenty-two micro-millimetres thick.

Ginette watched him like a hawk, trying to anticipate his next requirement. There was a constant demand for normal saline to keep the tissues moist. Soon the operating site began to bear little resemblance to a wrist and hand as the tissues were laid bare for apposition. Occasionally David would take a hook and use it to retract a tendon and glance over his mask at Michel Drouin.

'Flexor pollicis longus?'

The main flexor tendon of the thumb, and Michel would nod in agreement that they had got the right piece of tissue that looked like just another white strand in the midst of so many.

'How about that for the median nerve?'

That was an in-house joke. The median nerve, in its own special tunnel, was so obvious it could not be missed. The dissection went on and on. It was hot in the theatre and David had to straighten up frequently to ease his cramped muscles. Surgery of this nature, like motor racing, demanded fitness even though no intensive effort was required.

From the head end of the table there was silence. One thing David appreciated about Pat Coppard was his ability to keep silent. Nothing destroyed concentration more than a talkative anaesthetist.

Finally it was done and there were only the skin sutures to put in. Ginette had the fine subcuticulars ready. She knew David would want as hairline a scar as possible, and bringing the skin together by inserting the stitches under the skin was a better way of achieving it. When he came off his stool he was conscious, for the first time, that he had been in a modern teaching theatre where there was a gallery above and the operation had been conducted under the gaze of a television camera. They had been on show to the whole of the French surgical fraternity.

With the greatest care the restored hand was put into a splint and bandaged. The next few hours would be critical and the less disturbance to the tissues now being re-oxygenated the better. Ginette looked at her watch.

'Warm ischaemic time one hour and forty-five minutes, cold ischaemic time thirty minutes, Mr Compton.'

He looked at her over his mask and she saw the fatigue lines around his eyes. They had been at the operating table for eight hours. Ginette felt as though her legs were made of stone when she walked through to the changing-room. Now that the tension of the operation was over, fatigue washed over her.

She showered and changed and had a brief cup of tea with Soeur Camille. The Frenchwoman eyed her sympathetically and nodded.

'You have made history here, you know?'

Ginette raised her eyebrows in surprise.

'Oh, yes, they will talk about you both for a long time. Very good, the way you work together. You are lovers?'

She said it so naturally and unexpectedly that Ginette was caught off guard.

'No, not yet.'

Then she put her hand to her mouth and blushed scarlet. Souer Camille laughed.

'Do not worry, *petite*. It is easy to see that you are close together. When it comes to you it will not be difficult.'

Ginette recovered herself and smiled ruefully.

'It's just that he's married and has a young son.'

Souer Camille looked at her, astonishment written large upon her tanned Gallic features. A man taking a lover outside of wedlock in France didn't have the power to shock as it would in England.

'What has that got to do with it? And how about

you? You have been married—I see it in your face if not on your finger.'

Ginette hesitated. She had never confided in anyone.

She closed her eyes and her mind sped back to when Peter was two. She was working at the Birmingham Accident Hospital when she first noticed that he would squat after he had been playing with other children. One day she saw, with sudden alarm, that he was blue around the lips. The next day she took him to see the paediatric registrar, whom she knew slightly.

He examined Peter carefully, tapping his chest, listening with both sides of his Litmann's stethoscope and placing the flat of his hand on the front of Peter's chest. Finally he folded his stethoscope into the pocket of his white coat and beckoned to Ginette to sit down. She did so, feeling that she wanted to run away.

'You know there's something the matter with him?'

It was not a question, and she nodded a lie at him.

'He's got Fallot's tetralogy. Didn't you know?'

It was almost an accusation. Dumbly Ginette shook her head.

'He's never been ill except for the odd sniffle and I've given him something.'

'What about when he was born? Didn't he have a paediatric check?'

Again Ginette shook her head. Peter had been born at home and delivered by the district midwife. No one had ever checked him thoroughly enough to detect a congenital heart defect. Even as she thought about it she felt herself going faint with fright. Fallot's tetralogy – the blue baby syndrome – was a serious heart defect. It meant major corrective heart surgery if Peter was not to die young.

'How bad is he?'

Her voice was as faint as the mew of a newborn

kitten. There were degrees of Fallot's tetralogy, some worse than others. The registrar shook his head.

'He's pretty obvious. Can't really say until we've done angiography.'

Ginette shuddered. Only minutes ago everything had been fine, and now here she was talking about cardiac surgery on her son. After her interview with the paediatric registrar matters progressed with lightning speed. Peter was taken into the cardiac unit for blood tests, X-rays, echocardiograms, electrocardiograms, and cardiac catheterisation. Finally the day arrived when Sir Francis Holmes spoke to her quietly and gently and told her that Peter would need an operation to correct his defect. Despite her training she had questioned him with the desperation of the ignorant.

'Does it have to be?'

'I'm afraid it does. He could go into reverse shunt any time, and you know what that means.'

'What are you going to do?' she asked.

'A Lillehei—a total correction of his defect. It's more difficult than the Taussig-Blalock, but the long-term results are better.'

Ginette shuddered at the phrase 'long-term results'. Already, in her daydreams, she had seen Peter as a tall young man with a family of his own and herself doting on her grandchildren. Was that now not to be?

'More "difficult", Sir Francis? Does that also mean more dangerous?'

'Perhaps, but quite frankly my results are good. You needn't worry.'

She nodded and said nothing. There was nothing more to say; and, with the faith she had in Sir Francis, she had not worried. Peter had his operation the following day. Ginette went with him to the theatre. He was sitting up in the bed, hugging his teddy bear with one hand. Ginette held his other hand, desperately willing strength into him. They stopped in front of the double swing doors leading to the sterile area and he had seen the tears in her eyes.

'You aw right, Mummy?'

His concern was obvious, and she hugged him quickly.

'Yes, darling, Mummy's fine.'

He had gone through the swing doors, holding Teddy and waving to her, and she had walked quickly away and spent the morning tramping over the Levels until she knew the operation would be over. She returned, and as she stood in the lift to the cardiac unit, she felt as though she was going to her own execution.

When she saw Sir Francis and he beamed at her she thought she would weep with relief. Instead she held out her hand in a formal gesture and said,

'Thank you, Sir Francis.'

It did not seem adequate, but it was all she could think of. That night she knelt on the floorboards beside her bed and prayed her thanks to God for the first time in fifteen years.

It was something she never did again, because Peter died the next day.

Sir Francis had been visibly affected, apologetic almost, and lost himself in a maze of technicalities, endeavouring to explain what had gone wrong.

Ginette opened her eyes and looked at Camille. Since the death of her son she had carried the burden of her grief alone. That was why she sometimes appeared cold and sharp to the other nurses. Here was an opportunity to lighten her burden; one that might not recur for a long time. She nodded at Soeur Camille and in a bursting flood of confidence she told her all about it.

She told her too about the immediate aftermath, when she had roamed the streets of her home town, her clothes and hair wild and unkempt, her mind trembling on the verge of depressive madness, not working, unable to hold a conversation. She told her of the patience of her parents, who had stood by and said nothing until eventually she recovered. She told her then of the years after, when she had immersed herself in her work to become what she was now.

The leathern features softened with compassion and Camille said nothing until Ginette had finished.

'And what have you become now?' she asked.

Ginette shrugged.

'Knocking on to be an old maid, I suppose.'

'You are not a one to be an old maid, Ginette. But you have become a tough and lonely lady. Time to let yourself go a bit or you will end like me,' Soeur Camille added with a trace of bitterness.

'You're right, Camille, I do need to open up more, but I haven't been married,' Ginette explained.

Camille shook her head sympathetically.

'*Ma petite*, that is sad.'

'No, Camille. My son's death was the sadness.'

'*Ah oui, le Fallot. Je connais bien.* But here we do not have many who die after the Taussig-Blalock. *Le bon* Docteur Benoit, he has not lost one out of twenty.'

'Peter didn't have the Taussig-Blalock,' Ginette told her. 'They did a Lillehei.'

Soeur Camille clucked her tongue.

'Ah oui, the Lillehei. Very clever, very difficult, if you win it is the best. As you say in England, "double or quits", *non*?'

'Yes.'

'You played for the high stakes for your baby?'

'Yes—no—oh, Camille, I didn't know. It all happened so quickly!'

Camille put her arm round Ginette's shoulder, sensing her mounting emotion.

'*Doucement*. What happened? Your friend, he did the operation?'

'No. It was long before I met David. Sometimes I think maybe if he had done it Peter would still be alive, but that's silly, I know.'

Camille patted her gently and handed her a tissue.

'Here we do the Taussig-Blalock, but they want to do the Lillehei. Only Docteur Benoit, he is of the old school. He likes to be sure they live at least, you know? No matter that they do not last long and die young. With the Lillehei they go on for ever, have a family and die old men.'

Ginette dabbed her eyes and nodded.

'Tomorrow we have a Fallot on the list, but they have not asked your David to help. Benoit is *trop fier*, he is too proud to ask help from anyone. Your man, he does the Lillehei?'

Ginette nodded.

'I'm sure he does.'

She had never seen David do a Lillehei, but her faith in him was total. Soeur Camille looked thoughtful.

'We have never had a Lillehei here. It would be a big first.'

She fussed around Ginette and ushered her out.

'Tomorrow we'll do the list together?' she asked.

Ginette hesitated.

'I think we may be off tomorrow.'

'No.'

There was a firmness in the response that was lost on Ginette.

Pat Coppard drove them back to the Royal. Even his chipped features looked more gaunt than usual. It had been a long, difficult and emotional time for them all. When the operation was over Pat and David had retired to the surgeons' room, but the discussion had been brief. Professor Langevin had not been there, the

168 EMERGENCY!

time and strain of it all had been too much for him and
he had been persuaded to retire. After a brief cup of
coffee they had climbed into the Volvo.

Despite her fatigue Ginette felt keyed up. It had
been a triumph for them all—she had no doubt of that.
Everything had gone smoothly. There had been no
hitches, no raised voices, no delays while everybody
waited in an agonised silence. There was every prospect
of success in a patient who was bound to capture the
attention and sympathy of the whole of the medical
fraternity.

She looked across at David, sitting beside her in the
back of the big car. She could see his face clearly
illuminated in the cold moonlight. He looked drawn,
and yet his features were so fine and his expression so
remote it made her heart ache. Instinctively she took
his hand and gave it a squeeze. He turned and smiled at
her, and the look on her face captivated him. He leaned
over and kissed her, and they stayed kissing, their lips
warm upon each other as the light from the street lamps
caressed them with invisible wands.

When they drew up outside the Royal they came
apart and Pat turned round.

'Come on, chums, this is where the giggling stops. I'll
park the car and see you in the morning.'

They tumbled out and he was away. They crossed the
hall and the concierge found their keys.

'Bonne nuit, m'sieur, 'dame.'

They waved their keys in reply, took the lift and were
walking along the long corridor of the third floor before
either of them spoke another word. David's room was
nearest to the lift and they stopped outside it. Something in his manner alerted Ginette and sent her heart
pounding. She did not know whether it was the sudden
straightening of his figure, the quickened last pace, the
husk in his breath or the way he put his arm around her

waist, but she knew he was summoning something.

She did not have to wait long to find out what he was summoning. It was her.

'Ginette.'

'Yes, David.'

Her voice sounded small and quavery in the dim light of the hotel corridor. He hesitated and said nothing. They stood before each other in silence; both of them taut as violin strings.

'Do you know what I'm feeling, Ginette?'

He was whispering, but to her his voice thundered. She leaned close to him.

'Yes, David, I know.'

His hand went behind her neck and she thrilled. He kissed her, and she went hot as he held her to him in an embrace that had within it all the tenderness of which she had ever dreamed. They stayed like that and she felt thrilled and content, but apprehensive.

'What do you know?' he whispered.

There was a deep silence as he looked down at her.

'I know you want me.'

'Is it the same for you?'

She thought she would not have had to tell him it was the same for her. She felt it screamed around her. Surely he could tell? With an overwhelming sense of bliss she realised that she had before her the man she loved in an act of supplication, not demand. Despite his arrogance, despite his demanding and intolerant surgical attitude, he was standing before her in a gentle and requiring moment. Slowly she put her hands around his neck and put up her lips.

'Darling, it's the same for me too. Like you'll never know.'

He never would know. But for Ginette, the quivering anticipation of that moment was something she would remember for ever. Gone was the girl who had been betrayed, gone were the hang-ups and the bad times. From a nearby café came the strains of 'September Song'. She looked at him quizzically.

'You know what they'll say, of course. It was a shipboard romance.'

'Who will say it, and why should they? Who will know?'

'Affairs are difficult to conceal.'

As she said the word 'affair', it brought her to earth and reminded her of Simon. Did David know about her money? She could not believe it, there had been so little social contact. Furthermore, he was not that sort of man, she felt quite sure, but then she had felt sure of Simon. She felt as though she was tottering on the edge of a precipice and made an attempt to draw back from the brink.

'What about your wife?' she asked quietly. 'She'll be bound to hear.'

'My wife and I aren't on the best of terms. And I wasn't asking for an affair.' His face was set like granite.

'Then what were you asking for?'

'Goddammit, I don't know!'

He stared at her in tortured fury, put his hands in his pockets and, after several tense seconds, turned and walked away.

Behind him Ginette stood in bewildered amazement, tears welling in her eyes, her world rocking around her. As she lay in bed and heard the church bells through the night she tried to think. It had been a hard, emotional day, bringing them both to a pitch of physical and emotional exhaustion.

What did he want? Just a night in bed?

Did he want more than that with her?

Did he want to leave his wife and perhaps lose his son? Where did she stand in the middle of all this?

It was a mess, and she clutched at her pillow in a wave of misery and frustrated emotion.

CHAPTER TWELVE

GINETTE sat at the back of the big lecture theatre. It had a small stage and a podium and the seats sloped sharply up in a semicircle. She had deliberately chosen to sit at the back so that she could see all who were coming to David's lecture and judge their reaction.

At breakfast she had been able to tell, from his taut gestures and clipped speech, that he was nervous. He had confessed as much over the croissants and honey that arrived with giant cups of hot chocolate.

'This is worse than doing a major operation!' he groaned.

She looked at him, her head tilted to one side.

'But you lecture regularly to the nurses at Manbury.'

'This is a different crowd. There are surgeons here from all over Europe, men who leave me behind in the surgical field. I feel presumptuous.'

'Nonsense! You're as good as any and better than most. They may have done similar things, but no one is ahead of you in vascular micro-surgery.'

Ginette's loyalty bubbled to the surface. She was not going to have David sell himself short. As he followed her out of the breakfast-room he walked behind her and watched the swinging walk she had and the upright back which gave her such an air of grace and vitality.

Neither of them had referred to the events of the previous night. David tried not to squirm when he thought of it. Ginette was a woman in a maze. She knew he was in an emotional quandary. She knew he was trying to come to terms with his feelings for her and relate them to his lack of love for Laurel and his marriage vows. He was that sort of man.

The lecture hall was filling rapidly. It was nine o'clock, and David had told her he thought it was too early for the conference members to make the effort to come and listen to a junior colleague. He was wrong. The great lecture hall filled and overflowed. Eminent men from faraway places were sitting on the steps in the aisles. Word had spread about the operation on Anne-Marie, and they were all here to see and listen to the man who had performed what was being bruited as a modern surgical miracle.

Ginette looked around and felt proud for him. When he stepped on to the podium she could see from the way he adjusted his tie that he was nervous. Even his voice was a pitch higher.

He gave a cough. 'Good morning, ladies and gentlemen.' He shuffled his papers on the lectern before him. 'I hope you do not think I am here to teach you. On the contrary, during question time I hope to learn from you.'

He was getting into his stride, and as he straightened up and his voice became firmer Ginette knew everything was going to be fine. He was not a natural speaker and she knew this was a side of surgery that he hated. She was so anxious for him that she almost felt as if it were herself up there.

He detailed the techniques they used at Manbury, with particular reference to limb grafts after traumatic amputation. As he spoke more and got into his subject his enthusiasm and dedication shone through. It was something this critically appraising and academic audience appreciated. Technical excellence was all very well, but heartwarming dedication was the salt that gave the lecture its savour.

Ginette did not listen to half of what he was saying. She was looking around at the audience to get the response, and what she saw brought moisture to her eyes.

They were enrapt.

When David finished there was a tumult of clapping and several people stood up. Ginette had never seen anything like it at an academic lecture. It was some time before David could make himself heard to invite questions. They came like arrows at Agincourt. After half an hour, with the audience still pressing him, a messenger appeared and gave him a whispered message on the podium. Ginette frowned slightly, wondering what it was. David held up his hand.

'Thank you all for your kindness and your interest. Please excuse me—I have to go immediately. I am sure you all understand.'

There was an outbreak of clapping and David walked off the stage. Ginette left her seat and met him outside the lecture theatre. She knew at once from his expression that there was trouble.

'What is it?' she asked urgently.

'Anne-Marie—there's a problem with the graft.'

Together they hurried across lawns and along corridors to Anne-Marie's room. Soeur Camille and Michel Drouin were standing in the corridor outside and Michel's face was serious with worry. Philippe Duval appeared in the distance, carrying his pathologist's tray of syringes and bottles. David wasted no time.

'What's the problem?' he demanded.

Soeur Camille replied as he was looking at her—typically he sought the nursing opinion first.

'This morning the hand was swollen, a little blue, but not unduly. Now it is very blue and more swollen.'

'How is she?'

'Her condition is good—she is young. But she has much pain.'

'Blood pressure?'

'OK.'

Michel Drouin pulled at his lower lip.

'The drainage, it is not keeping with the supply. Too much in, too little out, I think.'

They trooped into the private room. Anne-Marie lay, propped on pillows, drip lines draped from above the bed. She was pale, but her gamine features were lightened by a smile when she saw David.

'Hello, Anne-Marie.'

'The knight himself!' she whispered.

'How does it feel?'

'Bloody.'

'I just want to take a little look,' David told her. 'Shan't disturb it at all.'

Soeur Camille had taken the dressing down and the limb lay in a cradle swung from a monkey pole. It did not look good.

When David had finished the operation he had left a hand that was pink and looked almost normal apart from the encircling line of stitches around the wrist and up the forearm. Now it was big and blue, the fingers like podgy stumps and the hand deeply cyanosed. David looked anxiously at Anne-Marie. She looked strained and peaked, but not really ill.

'Do you feel ill?' he asked her.

'No. It hurts like hell, but I'm not ill like you mean.'

A good point. If the limb was breaking down Anne-Marie would suffer from the toxic effects of disintegrating tissue which would damage her kidneys and push up her blood pressure.

He inspected the hand more closely. The blue colour was from de-oxygenated blood not draining from the limb quickly enough. It was spending too much time in the tissues and becoming more de-oxygenated as a result, and that was the cause of the blue colour. It was not due to inadequate blood supply to the limb. The venous anastomoses he had made so carefully and which took the blood from the limb were not yet coping with the arterial supply to it. It was likely to be a temporary situation, but in the meantime the congestion had to be relieved, otherwise the situation would deteriorate and there would be arterial block and limb death.

He was debating the possibility of further venous grafts when Philippe Duval spoke up. The quick-witted pathologist had also summed up the situation fast.

'How about leeches?' he suggested.

Ginette blinked. Leeches had been in use for relieving congestion years ago, but she thought they had gone out with the Ark.

David snapped his fingers and nodded at once.

'Splendid! As an interim measure it might just stop the vicious circle. Have you got any?'

By way of reply Philippe picked up the telephone and spoke rapidly for a few moments. When he put the instrument down he was smiling.

'The pharmacist here is a proud man—he has many leeches. He is bringing them up himself.'

He had barely finished speaking when there was a knock on the door and a portly man in a white coat entered carrying a jar with a screw top in which were swilling around a mass of pale, slug-like creatures. He handed the jar to Soeur Camille, and disappeared without a word.

David nodded approvingly.

'They've used these in a few centres for relief of venous congestion after trauma, usually for periorbital haematomas. Over to you, Sister.'

There was a squeak from Anne-Marie. 'You're not going to put those horrid bloodsuckers on to me?'

David nodded and smiled reassuringly at her.

'Don't worry, Anne-Marie—you won't feel anything,

and those little chaps may well be your saving grace.'

Soeur Camille was already setting up a dressing trolley to apply the leeches. She looked at David with raised eyebrows on her leathern face.

'How many?' she queried.

He looked back at her solemnly. He had not the slightest idea.

'Droves of ten, I think, Sister. And replace them when they've had enough.'

He went back an hour later. The hand was markedly less congested and covered with a mass of blue-coloured leeches very different from the creatures he had seen swimming in the pharmacist's bottle. These were many times their size. With their tiny teeth, assisted by a local anti-coagulant they produced, they had sucked blood from the tissues and become grossly engorged. They lay over the precious hand like a carpet of dark blue jelly.

Soeur Camille's face showed her delight. She was standing by the bed, long tweezers in her hand, occasionally replacing a dark, engorged leech with a fresh white hungry one. She was very careful when taking them off. It was easy to snap off the fragile teeth, leaving them in the skin to suppurate. David gave her the thumbs-up sign and left with a feeling of relief.

Outside he and Ginette stood facing each other. It was the first time they had had a private moment since their scene the previous night. Ginette waited for him to speak. She could see from the etched furrows in his face that he was disturbed. He put his hands on her shoulders and looked at her in a way that she thought would make her heart break.

'How about a truce?' he asked. 'Just while we're here anyway?'

She nodded, not trusting herself to speak, then found her voice.

'You could show me the city and take me to lunch.'

'Fine! Let's go.'

They walked through the main hall and out into the late morning sunshine. A taxi had just set down an old man on crutches accompanied by a mini-skirted young girl, and on impulse David flagged it. It was a big Citroën, and as they sank into its cushioned comfort David said to the driver,

'Do you speak English?'

'*Oui, monsieur.*'

'Would you take us somewhere where it's pleasant to walk? Somewhere nice to be.'

'*Certainement, monsieur.*'

The driver turned his head, gave them a toothy grin and set the meter. Ginette gazed with fascination at his bright tartan cap with a red pom-pom in the centre.

'That was a good idea,' she said.

'I spent too much time as a student walking miles around dreary parts of big towns to waste any more of it now,' David explained.

They sped down the Avenue Rockefeller, crossed the broad stretch of the Rhône on the Pont de la Guillotière and recognised the Place Bellecour. Ginette laughed.

'I think he's a romantic! I think he knows us and is just taking us back to our hotel.'

David, staring out of the window at the passing scene, was caught wrong-footed.

'Why should he do that?' he asked.

'I can't imagine,' Ginette replied demurely.

'You like *basilique*?'

The red pom-pom swivelled and Ginette gasped as they went over a red light while the toothy grin gleamed at her.

'Yes, of course.'

Anything to make him look back where he was

going. He did, and the Pont Bonaparte took them over the Saône on to the Quai Fulchiron. Above them towered the Basilica of Notre Dame de Fourvière. They drove up through the old quarter of Lyons and when they got out and walked through the cathedral grounds the view of the city and the rivers Saône and Rhône stopped them.

The sun glinted off the surface of the two rivers, and the dull terracotta of the old roofs was relieved here and there by the green of the occasional tree. It had a warm continental feel, and to Ginette it was something new. Behind them the cathedral tolled sonorously the hour of noon.

'Let's go and look inside,' David suggested.

He was beginning to relax. She tucked her arm under his and they walked into the cool gloom of the cathedral. In a corner a battery of slim candles glittered on an iron candelabrum. Beside it was a box of candles of different sizes, glistening white in the flickering candlelight. On impulse Ginette stepped forward, took a tall one, lit it from one of the others and stuck it on an iron pin. David squeezed her hand when she came back to him.

'Can I guess what that's for?'

She nodded and they walked up the centre aisle together. He thought it was for Anne-Marie. He was wrong, but she was not going to tell him so. Close to the cathedral was a funicular railway which took them to the bottom of the hill and they walked through the old quarter until they found a likely-looking restaurant in the Rue Boeuf. It was seventeenth-century, and they lunched off sea-urchin soup and fresh salmon that had the veriest hint of the smokery about it, while the shades of the contemporaries of d'Artagnan looked on approvingly from the shadows.

'What's on this afternoon?' asked Ginette.

David looked thoughtful.

'Lectures, demonstration of embryonic brain implants by the neuro-surgical team for the treatment of Parkinson's disease and a liver transplant. It's all new for old these days, as Aladdin's uncle was wont to say.'

'Philippe Duval has invited me to go round their path department,' she told him.

His left eyebrow nearly hit the ceiling. 'What on earth could be of interest to a theatre sister in a path department?'

The imp of mischief entered into her.

'The pathologist, perhaps?'

It was a mistake. David flushed and his lips compressed. He looked round and waved to a waiter.

'Time we went if we're going to join in this conference at all,' he said stiffly.

It was like Jekyll and Hyde. In no time they were scurrying across the Pont Bonaparte. Ginette had a job to keep up with his long strides.

'Where's the fire?' she asked breathlessly.

He looked sideways at her.

'You don't seem to have any difficulty travelling fast in other spheres,' he said shortly.

She sighed. She had spoken unwisely and she was going to pay. She hoped it would not last.

At the hospital David made for the lifts and after pressing the button said to her,

'I think I'll take a look at the brain implant. I'm sure it won't interest you.'

She was being dismissed, and for a moment she thought anger would overtake her, but she controlled herself and smiled at him.

'No, David, I think I'll go and have a chat with Soeur Camille and see how Anne-Marie is getting on.'

As she made her way to the ward she thought how

touchy he was. Could she cope with this flaring jealousy? In his present state he was about as manageable as a wild stallion. She found Soeur Camille in her office on the ward. The world-weary eyes in the tanned face creased into a smile as Ginette entered.

'*Eh bien, ma petite*. What has he been doing to you now?'

The keen eyes of the older woman missed little. Ginette sat opposite her, unconsciously graceful even in the plain wooden hospital chair. She tilted her head on one side as she did when she was concentrating or embarrassed.

'Nothing. I came to see how Anne-Marie was getting on. He's gone to watch the brain implant.'

'She is much better. The hand has gone down, but excellently. It was a temporary situation and the leeches, they have worked well. That Philippe, he came up with a good one there.'

'Not for me, he didn't,' sighed Ginette.

She could not help telling Camille about her teasing words concerning Philippe, and David's reaction. Camille shook her head and a raised finger at the same time.

'You have a fine man there, *petite*. A tiger. The Chinese say, "He who would saddle the tiger must first learn to ride him," and that is true. You put a barb under the saddle and now you are frightened when he leaps and roars.'

Ginette laughed and felt cheered.

'You're right, Camille. Thank you.'

'Do not worry. If he fancies you he will come back quick. And he does fancy you—I can see it.'

Ginette stayed talking to Camille, finding it refreshing to discuss the work they did under different circumstances. Finally Camille stood up.

'*Tiens*, I must do a round. Come with me.'

Ginette accompanied Camille round the ward, noting the different methods used and the different role she played. They came into the corridor of the private wing and were about to enter Anne-Marie's room when there was a step behind them.

'Have the leeches won, Sister?'

It was David. Soeur Camille replied without falter.

'*Absolument, monsieur le docteur.* Come and see for yourself.'

She was right. Anne-Marie was asleep when they went in. She had been given an injection of morphine. Camille had removed the last of the leeches and the change in the hand was remarkable to behold—not normal by a long way, but no longer blue and over-congested. It looked set fair for recovery. They were about to move quietly away when Anne-Marie opened her eyes. A faint smile appeared when she saw David.

'Thank you,' she said, and closed her eyes.

They halted together outside the door and David inclined his head towards the room.

'The leeches worked remarkably well,' he said with relief.

'True. Your colleague, Dr Duval, has done you a favour.'

David looked at Soeur Camille sharply, but that lady's face was expressionless. Ginette just managed to keep a straight face and asked him,

'How was the implant?'

'Interesting—very. Looked as though it was going to be a long session. I saw all I wanted.'

The tautness had gone and he was back to normal again. As he sat and wrote a note Camille whispered to Ginette,

'You see? He was not long at the operation. Most of the time changing his clothes, I think. You can be happy, Ginette.'

Ginette nodded, her heart singing. Soeur Camille caught her by the arm and took her aside.

'*Ecoute, ma petite*, stay here for a few minutes. The Professor is talking to your David. They all want to see him do the Lillehei, and the Professor has persuaded Benoit to step aside today if your man will do it.'

The crafty Camille had been busy behind the scenes!

Ginette felt a mixture of emotions. She had never taken a Lillehei, and the association with Peter was strong. She would be treading in the steps that had lead to the death of her son. Would she be able to remain quick and precise in her job with such an emotional drain upon her?

The Professor arrived and the two women left discreetly so that he and David could talk alone. They were closeted for twenty minutes before the Professor emerged, smiling. Ginette thought David looked tense and wondered whether there was not too much pressure being put upon him in too short a time.

They all went to a side ward to see the boy. He was a child of three with large brown eyes, dark hair and the same indefinable air about him that she had seen in Peter. He looked anxiously at the imposing deputation around him and reached for his mother's hand. She put her arm protectively around him, and Ginette felt a pang as she recognised herself in the diminutive French mother.

The Professor spoke rapidly to Soeur Camille and two hours later they were garbed in theatre, with Dr Benoit standing over a small form, the bone saw in his hands, ready to cut through the tiny sternum.

The anaesthetist sat beside his bank of valves and flow-meters; drip lines draped into each arm and the upper chest of the child on the operating table. A black naso-endotracheal tube of miniature proportions snaked into the tiny nose and was moored by strapping on the forehead. The heart-lung machine stood like a Star Wars vehicle and beside it squatted its attendant, a technician versed in the intricacies of pump engineering, a slave tending its every robotic whim. When they were on bypass the child's life would be dependent on this massive mechanical oxygenator, a complex box full of pumps, pipes, valves, and membranes.

Dr Benoit pressed the button on the oscillating saw, which chattered like a praying mantis as it bit into the centre of the child's breastbone. It was so designed that it would only go through bone and not damage soft underlying tissues. Red sawdust appeared on either side of the incision. Dr Benoit quickly completed the manoeuvre and the sternum was spread apart in a way that never failed to elicit a feeling of tension within Ginette.

She could not help comparing the steps of the operation with Peter's. It was almost as though it was he under the green wraps. She took a grip on herself and firmed her lips under her mask. Soeur Camille was taking the case, but Ginette was going to have to play an important role when it came to the actual repair, which David was going to do. Dr Benoit was only completing the preliminaries.

While she was watching, and had relatively little to do, she went over in her mind the course of the operation. The tetralogy described by Dr Fallot consisted of four defects. There was a hole in the heart between the two main chambers, the ventricles. There was a narrowing of the pulmonary artery taking blood from the heart to the lungs. The aorta, taking oxygenated blood from the heart to the body, was transposed so that it took blood from both main ventricles instead of just the left one carrying only oxygenated blood. Finally the right ventricle was enlarged.

The Lillehei consisted of putting a patch over the

hole between the two ventricles so that they did not exchange oxygenated and de-oxygenated blood. The other step was to open the narrowing, the stenosis, of the pulmonary artery carrying blood to the lungs. In order to do this David would have to have a clear, bloodless field, and that was where the heart-lung machine came in.

It was going to take over, temporarily, the function of the lungs and keep the blood oxygenated. The child's blood would be diverted before it reached the heart, oxygenated in the machine and returned to the aorta to go round the body. David would then carry out the repairs on a heart that had no work to do and was therefore not beating.

The snag was the bypass time. It could not go on indefinitely and post-operative deaths were frequently allied to excessive bypass time. David, if he worked quickly, could probably complete the operation in three hours of bypass time. The child would never survive five hours of bypass time, even with body cooling. It only needed something to go off schedule and they would be out of time, and however clever the surgery, the bypass time would claim its pound of flesh. Speed, care and efficiency were all essential. No repeats. Everything had to be right first time.

The chest was open and Dr Benoit was smearing white bone wax over the cut edges of the sternum. It was like putty and reduced bleeding from the cut bone surface. Camille produced a clutch of four plastic tubes that were to be used to divert the blood from the heart. Ginette reached to fit them into a clip and felt a snag on her rubber glove. A projecting sharp spicule of bone had torn a tiny hole in it. She put the clip down, turned away, and at once a nurse was there with a spare packet of gloves. She de-gloved and snapped into a fresh pair. It had not taken long and they were not at a critical stage of the operation, but it was one of those silly hazards. During bypass time it could be vital.

The tubes went into the venae cavae, the main veins leading to the heart. The two arteries next, and then came the moment which transformed the relaxed atmosphere within the operating theatre. David looked across at Dr Benoit and nodded.

'Going on bypass.'

The clamps went on and the squatting figure by the heart-lung machine repeated the instruction and set the clock. From now on every minute counted. David took the tiny heart in his hand. It was flabby because it contained no blood and it was not beating. He located the right ventricle and made a longitudinal incision along the outflow tract. As he did so he said, in the flat controlled tone Ginette recognised he always used when he was under stress,

'You may get an abnormally large branch of the coronary artery here. Needs care, and if there is one then tunnel under it.'

Ginette was conscious of the circle of viewing faces from the observation window above them and knew that everything that was said would be going on tape and camera. David opened the chamber of the heart and carefully dissected away tiny bunches of muscle tissue.

'Watch for the papillary muscles of the tricuspid valve when you do this. We don't want to add tricuspid incompetence to the little guy's problems.'

Ginette wondered what had happened at this stage of Peter's operation. Had he lost a papillary muscle and gone into failure because of an incompetent valve? An incompetent surgeon?

David gently splayed open the chamber of the heart and pointed to a small hole inside the right ventricle.

'There it is—that's the septal defect. When it's

beating and full, blood will be squirting through there at one hell of a rate.'

'*Trente minutes.*' The insistent warning from the pump attendant kept them aware that the clock was ticking.

'Patch.'

Ginette had it ready and it was into David's hand, a small piece of Teflon gauze about a centimetre in diameter. He laid it close to the hole in the septum and brought it out and snipped it into shape with a pair of scissors.

Just like a dressmaker, thought Ginette.

Tiny stitches of nylon bonded on to minuscule needles threaded the patch in place. David wore a loop, a pair of magnifying glasses, covering his head like a welder's guard. The nylon stitches were held like shrouds on a sailing ship until he was satisfied the patch was perfectly applied, then they were tied in rapid succession and cut.

'*Deux heures trente.*'

Ginette looked across at Camille, her eyes wide. In the excitement of the operation she had not noticed the monotonous repetition of the time. There was still a long way to go. David's voice cut across her alarm.

'You need to watch you don't put the stitch too deep in here at the bottom end of the patch. Might catch the Bundle of His and get a nasty heart block.'

The Bundle of His, an invisible band of nerve tissue running inside the heart muscle and carrying the excitatory wave that made the muscle beat. If it was cut the wave would not sweep around the heart and it would not beat properly. This was one of the night-mares of a cardio-vascular surgeon, that the heart would not pick up after the operation. Sometimes if it did pick up it did so with an abnormal rhythm. The beat would be so irregular the heart would fail.

She watched David stitch two fine wires into the heart muscle and lay them carefully across the green sheeting.

'Watch these.'

It was fatally easy, in the maze of tubes and instruments and surgical litter, to forget those fine strands. They would lead to the pacemaker and help to start up the tiny pump when the operation was finished and keep the beat regular during the next few days.

Gagool kept no closer watch over King Solomon's mines than Ginette over those wires. There was a movement beside her. It was a nurse with a plastic feeding cup and a straw. Suddenly she realised she needed something. They had now been operating for five hours. She felt the nurse move her mask aside and she sucked gratefully on the straw. Cold, sweet orange juice sluiced refreshingly into her mouth.

'Patch, please, Sister.'

This time it was for the enlargement of the right ventricle so that the blood could exit from the right ventricle more easily to the lungs. David cut it into a pear shape and started again on the exacting process of putting in the tiny nylon stitches to bring it into exact apposition.

'*Trois heures.*'

David was finishing the patch. They still had the tubes to remove. Ginette wondered which part of the operation on Peter had been the one to go wrong. The ratcheting grew faster as the tubes were removed and stitches inserted. Tension in the theatre was rising. Nobody had said anything, but there was that inexplicable atmosphere.

'*Trois heures quinze.*'

She began to hate the sound of the pump assistant's voice.

'Venting.'

It was important to make sure that there was no air in the heart before it was flooded once more with blood. Air emboli could float like clots to the brain and cause disaster. David was inserting a needle into the aorta, letting the air out of the heart and the great vessels the same way as a plumber vents a central heating system.

There was a pregnant pause.

'Bypass off.'

Blood was flooding into the tiny heart and expanding it. The pressure of the returning volume of blood, expanding the chambers of the heart, was normally stimulus enough to set it going. Ginette held her breath and waited for the tiny organ to writhe in the telltale way that showed it was beating.

Nothing happened.

David picked up a syringe loaded with 1/1000 adrenalin and injected into the heart muscle.

'Paddles.'

The tiny paddles connected to the defibrillator would deliver an electric shock to the heart to get it going like jump leads to a dead motor.

'Stand back!'

There was a sudden twitch in the small brown organ which had occupied them for the last several hours and a slow worm-like movement began over its surface. An incomprehensible mutter from the pump technician and Dr Benoit nodded to David.

'We have circulation.'

The writhing grew more enthusiastic, and Ginette heaved a sigh of relief.

'Pacemaker.'

An attendant fiddled with the black box attached to the two fine wires and the writhing became regular. David watched attentively, then turned and raised his left eyebrow in a gesture Ginette had come to recognise so well.

'Looks as though we're home—not very dry, but we're home. Let's close.'

The rest of the operation took time, but the show was over. The atmosphere in the theatre relaxed. There was whispering and the occasional laugh in the background. Camille winked at Ginette over her mask. Later, in the privacy of the sister's room, she looked at Ginette directly, noting her suddenly moist eyes and experiencing sympathy for the younger woman.

'Tell me, *petite*. I know what you are thinking, but tell me. It will do you good.'

Ginette stared at the kindly, brown, leathery features and started to unburden herself.

'I was thinking why he couldn't have been there to do it on my son. Then he wouldn't have died.'

'Maybe. Maybe. Maybe. You will never know. Time to forget, time to start forward.'

'He's good, isn't he, Camille?' said Ginette softly.

'Better than ever I see. Here they will talk about him for a long time to come.'

CHAPTER THIRTEEN

SUSAN lay back in the golden bath with the fish-headed taps spouting a gentle stream of warm water over her toes and luxuriated in the foam. At last she felt better physically. Her athletic body had been quick to recover from her injuries and she was beginning to feel again within her that surge of energy which had deserted her since her ordeal.

She glanced up at the clock on the bathroom wall. It was five-thirty and she expected Sam back at six. Not that that meant anything. She was used to him turning up two hours later than expected without a word of excuse, or with half a dozen business friends whom he had invited at the last moment. She had geared her life to dealing with this sort of thing, realising that it was part of the way of life she had chosen when she married him. She did not regret it, in fact she enjoyed the variety and excitement it engendered, and she met different and sometimes exciting people. It was just that at times like this, when she was not on top, she would have preferred a quieter life-style.

She heard and recognised the crunch of the Bentley's tyres on the gravel courtyard and sprang out of the bath in a panic. True to form, he was doing the unexpected.

Swiftly she towelled and sprinkled herself liberally with his favourite Chanel talc and donned a brilliant blue Japanese kimono which she knew he liked her in. As she tied the sash behind her back she looked at herself in the mirror and was grateful that the pale powder she had used had almost hidden the fading red flush of her facial burns. It went with the garment.

She grinned ruefully at herself as she realised that there was no possibility of her producing the rosebud mouth to complete the picture of a Japanese courtesan. Her generous mouth would never take on that disguise.

'Can't win 'em all, duckie,' she muttered at the mirror, and swirled her long golden hair piece up in a chignon and clamped it with a tortoiseshell comb.

When Sam came into the great living-room she was waiting for him by the fireplace.

Deliberately she had stagemanaged it so that she would look her best for him when he returned. There were fresh flowers throughout the room, roses in profusion so that their scent was overwhelming. Sam loved roses, and like everything else he liked he preferred them in plenty. He stopped in the doorway, and despite his fatigue he could not but admire Susan and the ambience.

'Great thing, doll. You look a lot better.'

'I feel a lot better. Back on the ball nearly.'

She looked at him keenly, noting the fatigue lines around his eyes without appearing to scan him too closely.

'How did the day go with you, Sam?' she asked. 'Any news on the Phoenix deal?'

'So-so. I'm flying down there soon to sort out that crafty bugger Forrest.'

He was glad to turn the conversation to a specific topic away from local interest. Susan was tuned into his wavelength very closely and could pick up the slightest nuance. He came up to her and kissed her perfunctorily, noting still the flush on her face. She turned and poured him a drink. It was a point of honour with her that she always had it ready for him when he returned at night. He took a long drink of the malt whisky and savoured it before speaking again.

'What's on tonight?' he asked.

He left the social calendar to her, relying on her good judgement who to entertain and how often. She did it with great finesse, and it was only when he upset her routine with his unexpected guests that she would occasionally explode when it was over.

'Nothing, darling. Just you and I.'

She had ordered his favourite simple supper, pease pudding and saveloys, a relic of his early childhood which he had retained and ate only when they were dining alone. It always amused her that he would eat this and accompany it with a Château Cheval Blanc.

He finished his whisky and she poured him another which he enjoyed when he had his bath. He returned in casual trousers and a light sweater, and they ate together at the marble table in the dining-room. The supper restored his wellbeing and good humour and he looked at her over his glass. She was still an attractive woman, despite her facial injuries.

Impulsively he put down his glass.

'What time is it?' he asked.

'Nine o'clock.'

'How about bed?'

Susan looked at him directly. It was the first time he had said anything to her like that since the accident. They had always been outspoken to each other, never stood on ceremony, so it was not out of the way between them that he should put it so directly.

Her heart thumped. Maybe she had been wrong about his feelings being cramped?

'If you feel like it.'

'Right I do!'

Together they left the room as it was and went upstairs. When they got into bed Susan prayed within her that she would be better. She was as frightened as a bride to make love after her internal injuries, but there had to be a time to start, and she could have wept with delight that Sam wanted her after all, disproving her fears.

It started well and ended in a farce.

Despite his intent Sam could not achieve an erection. It was a situation he had never encountered, and he dealt with it in characteristic fashion. He got cross.

The more he tried and the angrier he got the more his member retreated in flaccid obstinacy. Finally he turned his back to her and swore.

'Fuck that for a game!'

Susan stroked his shoulder soothingly.

'Tomorrow, Sam. Tomorrow it'll be great.'

He grunted, got out of bed and threw on his dressing-gown and went down to his study. There he picked up the telephone directory and ran his finger down the column until it came to the entry 'Edrich, Claw and Horne, Enquiry Agents.'

He stabbed viciously at the buttons. A sleepy voice answered on the tenth ring.

'John Claw here.'

'Claw, I want to know why you haven't been in touch about my enquiry. Have you come up with anything?'

'Yes, Mr Bennett. We should have some news for you soon.' There was a note of patient resignation in the voice, which did not need to enquire who was telephoning at this late hour.

'What the hell does that mean? I'm not paying you a small fortune to be fobbed off with pat phrases!'

'Mr Bennett, do you know what time it is?'

'I don't give a tuppenny fuck whether it's morning, noon or night. I want some action. I'm paying you to do a job and you're not doing it!'

'Yes, Mr Bennett. I'll be in touch shortly.'

Sam slammed the instrument down and looked through the study door at 'La Femme au Corsage Rouge.'

'Prats,' he said with feeling, 'a load of prats!'

The Professor stood on the steps of the hospital surrounded by a retinue of resident surgical staff, Soeur Camille and her nurses and Philippe Duval. Pat Coppard drove the Volvo slowly out of the hospital courtyard and David and Ginette waved out of the windows. They had re-established their truce after the Lillehei operation and the old rapport was back again. Ginette sensed that he was holding himself in, like a racehorse on the bit, and thought she knew why and loved him for it even if she regretted it. He did not want to drag her into an affair which might affect her career.

She looked out of the car window and what she saw made her grab his arm.

'Look!' she said, pointing upwards.

From an open window, high on the top floor, waved slowly a purple handkerchief.

Anne-Marie.

They left Lyons and headed north on the autoroute. David was sitting in the front passenger seat and Ginette was left to her thoughts in the back. She felt tired and dozed, despite the speed. David's voice woke her up.

'How about taking a different route back? There's no mad rush. If we cut off at Châlon-sur-Saône to Autun we can take the D-roads, with less traffic, and go through the château country along the Loire. Take in a night stop on the way instead of the mad dash we did coming down?'

He sounded enthusiastic, and Ginette sat up. She had never seen any of the famous châteaux. At the same time her heart gave a thump as she saw it as a possible ploy by David for them to be together. Pat grinned and nodded.

'Right by me, David. I'm going back down under

next year and it'll be another thing to tell 'em about.'

When they left the autoroute and drove along the minor roads deep in the Burgundian countryside Ginette felt more in touch with France. The magnificent white Charolais cattle looked mournfully over the hedgerows and there were vineyards everywhere, their vine rows stretching away with mathematical precision. She saw no workers and wondered how they came to be so carefully tended. The rolling countryside gave her occasional glimpses of a château hiding coyly behind wooded hills, the white limestone buildings and grey-turreted roofs conveying an atmosphere of elegant magnificence.

She caught sight of a buzzard hovering over a field, the broad sweep of its brown wings and splayed tail holding it steady thirty feet above the ground while it sought its prey with eyes that could spot the twitch of a mouse's whisker.

They passed a lake and Ginette was sure she saw a fish leap clear of the water. Behind all the enjoyment of the country lay her mounting excitement at the prospect of a stop at a French hostelry instead of dashing straight back to England.

They crossed the wide stretch of the Loire at Nevers, stopping at the end of the bridge to admire the view of the cathedral of St Cyr and Ste Juliette with its decorated Gothic tower and monstrous gargoyles barking and spouting eternally to ward off evil spirits. Pat drove slowly over the bridge so that they could look up the river. Instead of the broad reach of water which she had expected, Ginette saw a multitude of streams split by islands of mud and sand, sparsely decorated with shrubs.

David leaned back and held her hand.

'Not much like the mighty Thames, is it? You can imagine the trouble the old bargees had to get up here out of the rainy season. They spent most of their time dragging their boats over the flats.'

Ginette was lost with delight as she took in the vista of the bridge with its many arches and the mediaeval atmosphere of a town garbed in a grandeur bestowed upon it by the ancient Dukes of Burgundy. She saw an *épicerie* and pleaded for a halt.

'I don't know about you two, but I'm famished!'

David accompanied her and they bought a Camembert cheese, saucisson, three small quiches Lorraine and a bottle of red wine. A few yards away was a *boulangerie* and there they bought a *baguette*—a metre of crispy French bread. Ginette climbed triumphantly into the back of the Volvo with her shopping.

'Drive on, chauffeur, and find us a picnic spot. It is the magic hour of *déjeuner* when all travel must cease.'

Pat grinned and nodded, and ten minutes later they were parked in the shade of tall chestnut trees overlooking the town. Pat produced a scout knife from the glove compartment and they used it to cut the cheese. Sitting on the grass, they ate the quiche and drank the red wine out of disposable beakers. The Camembert with the French bread had a flavour never found on Ginette's table in England. She looked across at David.

'Why is it that food tastes so much better away from home, when you're on a picnic? Here we are, sitting uncomfortably on the ground, no plates, plastic glasses, just bread and cheese, and it's utterly delicious. Doesn't make sense!'

David put his arm around her, making her feel warm and relaxed.

'That's what makes the world go round. There's no logic in delight. Sit and enjoy it.'

It was warm and there was a haze over the plain below. A large blue dragonfly hovered nearby, and

Ginette watched its fairytale beauty briefly before it helicoptered away towards a stream tinkling by the roadside. David was lying beside her, his hands behind his head and his eyes closed. As she looked at him a wave of tenderness came over her for this man who was now such an important part of her life, was absorbing her, not by demand but by his charismatic presence. A curl of dark hair had fallen over his eyes, and she restrained an impulse to stroke his forehead and push it away.

Pat Coppard gathered up the remains of the lunch and stored it in the car. He clicked his fingers at them.

'Time to climb aboard, you sluggards. At this rate we'll hit the land of UK in a week.'

They sped through Bourges and Vierzon along the north bank of the River Cher. The road ran close to the river which, unlike the Loire, was brimming its banks. It was late afternoon when they rounded a bend and saw a road sign announcing the town of Chenonceaux.

David held up his hand.

'Hang on, Pat. There's a château here. How about this for our night stop?'

The Volvo slowed and Pat grinned at him.

'You're the one who knows. In the country of the blind the one-eyed man is king.'

'Let's see what turns up.'

What turned up was a sign on an old building which spelled out 'Chez Barthélemy.' Pat swung the wheel and they came to a halt in the driveway of a hotel with a courtyard dotted with umbrellas, tables and chairs. Through the panelled windows of a dining-room they could see the sparkle of glasses and white napery. There was an atmosphere of subdued comfort. A coloured sign of the Chaine des Rôtisseurs suggested that the food would be above average.

David turned in his seat to face Ginette.

'How does this appeal to you?' he grinned.

After the long journey, Ginette saw it as a little piece of heaven. She smiled and nodded. David got out and disappeared into the reception. Three minutes later he reappeared, looking smug.

'It'll do. Let's have the bags.'

They had been lucky. The last two rooms in the hotel were theirs. Ginette walked through a hall furnished with a studied elegance that spoke of taste and discrimination. Every piece of furniture was antique—no room here for reproduction. The receptionist was faultlessly groomed, her manner welcoming, but with the aloof sophistication that only the French can convey.

Ginette's room was on the first floor, overlooking the courtyard. It was furnished in the Louis Quinze period with a pale blue motif. The wallpaper was continued over the ceiling and ruched net curtains covered the window. A wool Ladik carpet with a pale blue background complemented the swagged blue satin curtains and the bedcover.

The first thing Ginette did was to run a bath and fling in a generous amount of bath salts. After the long car ride her muscles felt stiff, but as she luxuriated in the warm water she felt herself relaxing and the stiffness fleeing. She soaped her arms and legs, contemplating their evening together with a warm sense of anticipation.

After her bath she lay on the bed in her dressing-gown and picked up the phone. It was Pat who answered. He and David were sharing a double room.

'What are we going to do, Pat? Rest, or walkabout before dinner?'

'No walkabout for me, Ginette. My guts have gone crook. I've been here thirty minutes and twenty-nine of them have been in the bog.'

'Poor Pat! Can I help?'

There was a harsh explosion of derisive laughter.

'You're a great girl, Ginette, but not even you. . .'

There was a gasp over the line and it went dead. She put the instrument down, puzzled. A moment later it rang. It was David.

'Poor old Pat's got it bad. He had no time to explain.'

'I hope you've given him something for it?' said Ginette.

'He's got some Lomotil and Dioralyte. I reckon that's going to be his dinner.'

'I rang to see what we're doing,' she told him. 'Rest or walkabout?'

'How about a look at the château?'

'Fine with me. How long have I got?'

'Ten minutes.'

'See you downstairs. Last one down buys champagne!'

She wore a dress in soft green cotton with no sleeves and a low round neck. It was cool and the swing of the full skirt to just above her knees set off her hips and long legs to their best advantage. When she walked down the stairs David was waiting for her, the typical elegant Englishman in fawn trousers, a cream shirt and a lightweight pullover.

He took her hand and they walked out on to the courtyard.

'Poor Pat's had it this evening, I'm afraid. I only hope he'll be well enough to leave in the morning.'

'Is he fit to be left?' she asked.

'Sure. He's best on his own at the moment.'

He led her along the road and they turned down an avenue of grandiose plane trees forming the approach to the château. It was guarded by two stone sphinxes. In the late afternoon there was an atmosphere of massive quiet which the presence of the occasional visitor did little to dispel.

They crossed a drawbridge over the moat and surveyed a pair of white swans guarding four cygnets with an air of watchful pride. In front of them lay the river Cher and before it reared the beautiful château. They stood together on the square of the keep and admired the rounded towers with their turrets and arched windows. To their left was a formal Italian garden. They walked through it and stood by a long wall bounding the river. From here they could view the length of the château, which straddled the river on great stone piers.

The evening sun cast red reflections on the water, giving the château a rosy glow. David put his hand on her shoulder.

'Not bad, even for a king's mistress, don't you think?'

'Who was that?' asked Ginette.

'A lovely lady called Diane de Poitiers. She was the mistress of Henri the Second and lived here for many years until he died. Then his widow threw her out.'

'That sounds pretty tough. Who was she?'

'Catherine de Medici.'

'Sounds right. The Medicis were always a vengeful lot.'

They walked along the gravelled paths of the Italian garden, admiring the scribed formality of the tiny hedges. Against the far bank of the Cher they watched an old man sitting in a punt, fishing. In front of them lay a further formal garden, bounded by tall trees. David waved his hand around to encompass the area.

'In the days of the pleasure-loving kings, like Charles and Henri, they held great parties here. Some of them made our swinging sixties look tame. The ladies of the court acted as serving girls and went topless among the guests.'

'Sounds very sexy. That must have raised the men's blood pressures!'

'It did. What went on was nobody's business.'

'Would that sort of thing get you going?' she asked innocently, looking at him with large eyes. David put his hands on her waist and pulled her gently to him.

'It already has.'

He was pressed close against her, and she did not need to be told.

A couple appeared out of the main doors of the château and were heading towards them. David released her and they walked hand in hand over the gravelled pathway through the Italian garden.

'This used to be a hospital during the war,' he told her. 'The Cher was the boundary between occupied and unoccupied France. Patients could be admitted by the front and discharged through the back into unoccupied territory. It made a great escape route.'

'That's a nice story,' smiled Ginette.

He turned and looked at her directly.

'This is the sort of place where stories are made.'

'That's what I'm afraid of!' She laughed and pulled at his arm. 'Come on. We'd better get back to the hotel or we'll miss dinner.'

They sat in the courtyard before dinner and David ordered a half bottle of champagne which was served with a plate of freshly made brandy snaps. They could see through the kitchen windows from where they were sitting and it appeared to be empty. Long stainless steel surfaces gleamed, but were devoid of food.

'David, do you see that? There's nothing going on in the kitchen at all!'

'Don't worry, that's how it should be. All quiet on the surface and paddling madly beneath—like a swan on a rip tide.'

He was right.

When they went into the dining-room it was full. They were given a window table and dined off fresh asparagus, salmon of the Loire, rack of lamb with potato slices baked with truffles and, discarding the cheese, finished with tiny *fraises des bois*.

As they ate they talked. David was a good talker. He spoke only of what he knew, and he spoke well. Apart from that, Ginette liked the sound of his voice. Their knees touched under the table, and she found one of hers gripped briefly between his, but it did not stop the flow of their conversation. They drank Vouvray with the salmon and Chinon with the lamb and took their time over both, relishing each other's company as well as the food.

There was a closeness between them. They had no need to mention it; it was just there. By the time they had finished their coffee it was ten o'clock. Ginette put her hand to her mouth with a guilty start.

'What about Pat? We haven't been to see him.'

'Don't worry. He'll be fine, the last thing he wants is us waking him to ask if he's OK,' David assured her.

'Don't you think we should at least look?'

He stood up.

'Stay where you are. I'll be back.'

She watched him walk away between the tables and noticed several women cast a glance in his direction, and felt a sense of pride. Their walk in the garden of the château had aroused her, as had their conversation over dinner. Ginette was a sensuous woman and now she felt an erotic warmth within her that made her move uneasily on her chair. Her long fingers toyed impatiently with the slender stem of her wine glass.

When David reappeared she watched his broad-shouldered, slim-hipped figure wending towards her, and thrilled again at the turn of his head and the crooked grin he gave as he inadvertently brushed against a woman's chair.

'He's flat out,' he told her. 'Not a stir.' He sat down

and took her hand. 'Did I ever tell you what an exciting-looking woman you are?'

'No.'

'I'm telling you now. With those high cheekbones and slanted eyes you could have been the daughter of Genghis Khan. A real Tartar princess.'

'You know many?' she laughed.

'Lots. They people my dreams and they all look like you.'

'When you kissed the Blarney stone, you must have licked it all over!' Ginette teased.

'That's what I'd like to do to you.'

She looked around and hoped nobody had heard. In her ears his voice rang like a town crier's.

'I don't know what you mean.'

She did know. She knew only too wonderfully well. Somehow she didn't dare confess it.

'I'll give you the details. I want to. . .'

'It's all right—I've got the message!'

David put his hand over hers.

'Have you? I hope you have, because I want it to come over loud and clear.'

Ginette felt herself getting warm again, her eyes became larger and her breathing shorter. Unconsciously her tongue appeared at the corner of her wide and generous mouth, and David leaned quickly over the table and kissed her on the lips. Then he stood up and without a word she did the same. Hand in hand they walked out and went upstairs. Her room was lit only by moonlight filtering through the net curtains. She reached for the light switch, and instantly his hand covered hers.

'No.'

That was all he said, and she turned to him, her knees weak and her body shaking with apprehensive delight. He brushed the hair from her face and she felt his hands behind her neck, his thumbs brushing her cheeks. Slowly his face came down and their mouths met with a hungry warmth.

They were moving in step, in the dark, towards the bed. Ginette's heart was thudding with anticipation. No decision here for her to take, it had been done for her, and she was glad. She felt the firmness of his hands on her back, pulling her to him.

'Oh, David!'

His hands cupped her neck as he said, 'I want you to know something.'

'Yes?'

Her voice was small in the darkness.

'Would you believe it if I told you that this is not me, not my style?'

'Perhaps.'

'You're so very special. I need you. I need you all the time, just to be with me.'

Foolishly, deliriously, Ginette felt like crying. This was what she wanted, needed to hear. For too long she had been alone, a lonely, isolated, unapproachable iceberg. She leaned against him, her fears melting in a rising tide of joy and desire.

'DAAAAVID!'

The desperate cry was accompanied by a banging on the door. Pat Coppard. The accent was unmistakable.

David reacted with the speed of a Western gunslinger and was across the room and had the door open before she knew what was happening. Pat tottered in and fell on the floor. David switched on the room light. Pat looked dreadful, like a white ghost lying on the floor. Ginette covered him with a blanket and put a cushion under his head. As she did so he recovered consciousness and his mouth contorted in a rictus of pain.

'Sorry, chums. Thought I was going to die alone among the snail-eaters.'

'Take it easy.' David examined him carefully, then shook his head. 'Don't worry, it's when you're afraid you're not going to die that it's bad. Let's get you to bed.'

They helped him to his bed, and David turned to Ginette.

'We've got some pethidine, haven't we?'

She nodded and took the Volvo key. It was in their emergency pack with the instruments they had brought. She was back within moments, and David injected it into Pat's arm.

'OK, Pat, I'll see you don't die alone. Lots of drinks and you'll be great by dawn.'

Pat tried to smile at him.

'You charmer. What is it?'

'Dehydration. Something no Aussie will ever admit to.'

David looked across at Ginette.

'Don't you stay up—I'll keep an eye on him. See you in the morning.'

As she went back to her own room Ginette felt let down as well as disappointed. How could he dismiss her like that? Did he think of her as no more than a plaything? She roughly pulled back the sheets on her bed and threw the pillow at the wall. Perhaps if she had seen David at that moment she would have felt better.

He was looking at Pat, who was asleep, and was shaking his head.

'Pat, my boy,' he whispered, 'you owe me one. A big one!'

CHAPTER FOURTEEN

MARTIN WEBBER stood behind the counter of his art shop off Marlborough High Street. Despite its size he did considerable business, because his wares were varied and not all connected with art. Brushes, paints, paper and canvas and a few prints for the college boys were not enough to live on, much less pay for his sessions at the betting shop.

Like many inadequates, Martin dreamed of riches. Brought up in a Liverpool slum, he had been quicker-witted than most of his friends. His wits had saved him when his mother died. He was just sixteen. His father wanted him out of the way to marry again and young Martin had left for London. He had a talent for sketching and made money going round the pubs and clubs, which was where he had met Daphne.

It had not taken the sharp little Liverpudlian long to assess the advantages of marrying a young lady socially above him. After that the easy-going, demonstrative and affectionate Daphne had been an easy prey.

Daphne's family, however, had not been so easy, and riches had not fallen upon them with the ease and certainty that Martin had envisaged. Betting had been a successful way of funding them for some time, but the odds had swung against him long ago and now he was almost used to visits from heavy gentlemen who said little and looked hard.

So far he had managed to keep ahead of the payments, but only just. That was why he was peddling drugs. Martin was a pusher. He took pot himself, but nothing else. Speed, cocaine, crack and some heroin were his stock in trade. Twice a week he drove to Rickmansworth, parked the Rover and headed on the underground for Notting Hill Gate. A short walk to a house in Kensington Church Street, a drink at a local pub and he was back on the late train.

His other line was pornography. Not in a big way; just a discreet trade in expensive hard-core porn. Enough to make it worthwhile, but not sufficiently widespread to attract the attention of the police. Daphne knew nothing of his sidelines. She would have been horrified.

The brass bell tinkled on its metal rocker as the shop door opened. A bewhiskered middle-aged man in a tweed coat and cap, wearing knickerbockers and brogues, stood in front of him.

'Good morning, Major. I have your order here, sir.'

Martin reached under the counter and brought out a neatly wrapped brown paper parcel, book size. The Major nodded and took it under his arm.

'That will be fifty pounds, Major.'

'Good day to you, Webber.'

A single note was put on the counter and the Major was gone, striding purposefully up the alley as if he were on parade. Martin shook his head as he went. The Major's line was hard paedophilia, and what he spent on it would have kept a family of starving Ethiopians for a decade.

Martin put the note in his back pocket. No tax on that source. He turned his attention to some lithographs and became so absorbed that he did not notice two figures walking up the alley.

China and Mac were frequent visitors and Martin's best drug customers. What they bought depended entirely on their resources. Martin was usually glad to see them because they meant money. Today was

different. He had no stock, and China and Mac were
not into deprivation.

As they came into the shop Martin could see that
China was twitchy and difficult. Mac was silent and
sullen, the scar on his left cheek livid against his pasty
face. He stood behind China, biting his lips, his eyes
flickering.

China put a skeleton-thin hand on the table and
drummed his fingers. His dark, sharp features and
obsidian eyes reminded Martin of a questing snake. His
voice had a soft, penetrating lilt.

'Just crack and dragon dust today, Scouse.'

Martin raised his hands, his shoulders hunched, and
shook his head.

'You caught me wrong today, China. Not a trace.'

The obsidian eyes fixed on him and Martin swallowed with anxiety.

'Good kif I've got. You can have some—on me. Just
to try.' Martin was fumbing in his inside pocket when
Mac slammed the flat of his hand on the counter.

'That's for kids. It's the hard stuff Ah want, and Ah'll
pay mah whack.'

Martin saw the vicious expression, the tiny beads of
sweat on the upper lip and forehead, and recognised
danger signals.

'It's no good asking—I haven't got anything. The
chemist next door has more than me.'

China's expression altered. He looked cunning and
interested.

'Let's have a look upstairs.'

'What do you want upstairs, there's only a couple of
stockrooms.'

'Take us up.'

They tramped up rickety wooden stairs into a dusty
room with a single window. There was no furniture,
just a tumble of cardboard packing cases. China went

to the window and peered out.

'That flat roof the chemist's?'

The flat roof was directly below Martin's window and overlooking it, from the chemist's, was an upstairs window. China gripped Martin's arm.

'Tonight, Scouse, we'll be back. Meet us here, midnight.'

Martin read his mind at once.

'I don't want any part of that sort of thing, China. I live here. You want to try burglary, you're on your own.'

The next moment he was on the floor, the studs of Mac's boot stabbing into the side of his face as the Scotsman trod hard down. The pain was intense. He pushed against the floor with his hands, but the boot pressed harder and he stopped.

'Stop, for Christ's sake! You're crushing my skull!'

'Midnight?'

'Yes, midnight. Take your boot off, take it off. Please, for God's sake!'

He was babbling with pain and terror. Reluctantly Mac lifted his boot and Martin stood up. His eyes widened with shock as he saw Mac click back the blade of a flick-knife and slip it into his pocket. He rubbed his face.

'You didn't need to do that.'

Mac put his face close to Martin's, his rancid breath like a sickening fog.

'Ah'll do what Ah bloody lak, when Ah lak it. See?'

Then they were gone, leaving Martin looking at the clock and counting the hours until midnight. That brief spasm of brutality had unbalanced him. He was not used to it, and yet to China and Mac it was obviously part of their way of life. He shuddered at the thought of the flick-knife and wondered just how close he had been to being cut up.

The lithographs no longer interested him, he was too on edge. To calm down he rolled a joint and took in a long drag, feeling the sweet fumes going down to his boots. He sat on a Windsor chair and looked down the alley as the soothing waves enveloped him. His mind wandered to the chemist next door.

It was a family business. The father, Bill Brotherton, had started it thirty years ago and now it was run by his son Ian. He was a large, friendly lad, keener on rugger and Rotary than he was on pharmacy. Martin's contact with him had only been to collect the vet's prescriptions for Daphne's dogs. He hoped that young Ian would not be doing any late-night stocktaking when China and Mac paid their call.

They arrived at ten minutes to midnight. Martin was sitting in the shop with the lights off. He had left the door unlocked and muted the bell. When the door opened he sat up with a start. They had made not the slightest noise coming up the alley. China's teeth gleamed in the dark.

'You can go home now,' he told him.

Martin got up without a word and closed the door quietly behind him, glad to be away from the predatory pair. China and Mac were out on to the flat roof in seconds and Mac's knife made short work of the hasp on the chemist's window. They were into a stockroom.

'Give us the torch—Ah can't see a bloody thing.'

China flicked on a torch and they opened the door.

'Christ Almighty!'

The landing outside the door overlooked the ground floor of the main shop. The whole area was brilliantly lit by fluorescent tubes. Mac backed into the stock-room, cannoning into China in a panic. China gripped his arm.

'Cool it! Stand still. They keep it lit all night to scare us off. There's nobody there.'

Mac looked dubious.

'Ah don't lak it, China.'

'Come on.'

China went down the stairs into the shop area, crouching behind the display shelves to avoid being seen from the street. At the back of the shop was a counter marked 'Dispensary' and behind it a door labelled 'Private'. China pointed at it, saying nothing. Mac, confidence restored, nodded and they crept to it. China gripped the door handle, turned it gently and pushed it open.

'Who's there?'

Ian Brotherton was sitting at a computer console, his back to the door, when China opened it. He swivelled in his chair.

'What the hell do you want?' he demanded.

Mac, the experience of a thousand street fights in a hundred alleys behind him, came forward like a charging bull. Ian, sitting in the chair, did not stand a chance. Mac's charge carried him over backwards and a boot into the side of his head left him unconscious on the floor. It was all over in less than five seconds.

China prowled round the room, looking for the drugs cabinet. The room was lined with containers of every kind. He went round reading the labels.

'Stelazine, Adalat, Fentazin, Tenormin, Serenid, Ponstan, Captopril. For Christ's sake, where's he got the real stuff?'

They took no notice of Ian's white-coated figure sprawled on the floor. They did not see his eyes flicker open and then close. Ian was a second-row forward, close on fifteen stone, and had been knocked out before. He lay quiet until his head cleared, then got to one knee, grabbed the chair and swung it in an arc at China.

It caught him on the knee, sending him to the ground

with a squeal of pain. Ian followed after it, but was
tripped by Mac, who kicked his heels together. He
sprawled forward, arms outstretched and hands to the
floor.

'Aaah!'

The shout was animal in its intensity, the pain lancing
from his hand to his shoulder. Sharp as a terrier, Mac
had stabbed down with his knife at Ian's outstretched
hand. Now it was pinned to the wooden floorboard,
transfixed by the knife blade. Trying to support himself
on his left arm, Ian looked horrified at his right hand,
blood welling around the blade. Mac grabbed his left
arm and twisted it behind his back.

'Where's the bloody stuff, then?' he demanded.

'What stuff?'

'The hard stuff. Ah want to know where it is.'

Mac gave a vicious twist to Ian's arm, but there was
no reply. He had fainted. China was sitting in the chair,
nursing his knee. He stood up.

'Get him on here. We'll fix him when he comes
round.'

Mac pulled his knife from where it was pinning Ian's
hand to the board and together they lifted Ian with
difficulty on to the chair and Mac resumed his search,
throwing open drawers and breaking glass cupboard
doors in a fury to find the dangerous drugs cabinet.
Soon the room was a litter of containers, spilled tablets
and broken glass.

Ian came round, and as he did so Mac was standing
with his back to him. China was occupied trying to open
a cupboard. Ian used his left hand to pull a handkerchief from his pocket, bent down and picked up a long
sliver of broken glass from the floor. The handkerchief
covered the edge and he held it like a short sword.

Mac turned, saw Ian standing and came at him. What
he did not see, in that brief moment, was the long glass

sliver. As the two men met in the middle of the room he did not even feel it as it lanced through his sweater and shirt into his belly with the ease of a hot needle into butter. Ian was knocked back into the chair by the force of their impact.

China looked up at the commotion and was across the room like a snake, and when Ian was knocked back into the chair he had his arm round his neck in a hammer lock. Ian, dripping blood from both hands, could do nothing. Mac had his knife out in a flash. The tip of the knife grated against Ian's teeth as he put the blade into his mouth. Ian gagged on the bleeding from his tongue.

Mac looked down at him.

'Now where do Ah find it? Tell it or Ah'll. . .'

He stopped and looked down, feeling for the first time the wound from the glass. Bright red blood was pouring down his front. He looked back at Ian, understanding dawning slowly upon him as his strength and blood flowed from him.

'Jesus—you done me. You bloody done me!'

There was an eternal second when nothing happened and then, with a savage thrust, Mac pushed the knife blade forward as far and as hard as he could. There was a grating as the blade hit bone behind the throat. Mac felt his strength going and as he began to fade he gave another vengeful thrust.

It was like an electric current upon a corpse as the blade hit the spinal cord, tearing through nerve tissue, sending messages of destruction to muscles that made the young man convulse like an electrocuted bull. Ian's body twitched spasmodically, then went rigid and outstretched before he slumped in a lifeless heap from the chair.

Behind him China rose like a grey ghost. Mac, his hand pressed to his side, moved towards the door.

'China, Ah'm bad. Git me aht of 'ere.'

China put an arm under his shoulders and they moved across the bright arena of the main shop. The front door had a Yale lock and opened easily from the inside. Headlights came up the High Street as they crossed the pavement. When he saw the blue flashing light on the roof of the car China let go of Mac and ran across the broad expanse of the street and fled down an alleyway towards the river.

Mac sank on to all fours on the pavement. His voice was barely more than a whisper.

'China, don't go. Don't leave me, China. Ah'm goin'. . .'

The police did not see the shadowy figure of China flitting across the road and away towards the River Kennet. They called an ambulance and made Mac as comfortable as possible. From the road the chemist's shop looked undisturbed.

There was nothing to tell them of the corpse that had been Ian Brotherton, lying in the dispensary.

The Casualty Officer at Manbury Hospital saw the blue ambulance lights flashing far away as he looked out of the theatre window. He sighed and called to the staff nurse in a world-weary voice.

'No peace for the wicked this night, Staff, and that includes you.'

Staff Nurse Gotch, covering the duties in Casualty, looked across at him.

'Now what?' she wanted to know.

'Trouble—you'll see. It takes something hot to make those boys come at that rate.'

They brought Mac in on a stretcher. His breathing was shallow, his face white, and he was unconscious. A huge pressure bandage, like a white lifebelt, encompassed his waist. The ambulance men reported to the Casualty Officer.

'Stabbed with a piece of glass in the belly. Enough blood on the pavement to stop up a sewer!'

Staff Nurse Gotch was fast. In seconds she had giving sets ready on a dressing trolley and bottles of Haemaccel.

'Nurse, O-Negative blood, two units,' she ordered.

The Casualty Officer examined Mac briefly and turned to her.

'Venflon.'

Sandra Gotch handed him a Venflon syringe, a needle within a plastic cannula attached to a small chamber. He raised a vein in Mac's arm and smoothly inserted the tip of the Venflon needle. Blood trickled into the chamber.

'I have flashback.'

She handed him a syringe. He used it to withdraw a sample of blood and handed it over.

'Cross-match four units, right away.'

He withdrew the needle from the vein, leaving the cannula inside. Sandra had already attached the plastic sack of whole blood to the giving set. He opened the roller tap and let a crimson stream flow down the tube before connecting it to the cannula. He taped the needle in place and moved around the trolley to the other arm. The Venflon went in. This time he did not take a sample, but attached a bottle of Haemaccel and ran it in fast.

The Haemaccel, yellow and translucent, flowed quickly and easily. It was a synthetic colloidal solution containing the right quantities of electrolytes and volume expanders to offset the effect of shock. Sandra Gotch checked the blood pressure.

'Thirty over zero.'

'Hypovolaemic shock. He's going to need a bucket-ful. Keep it going fast while I take a look at him.'

Cautiously the Casualty Officer undid the pressure

dressing. Below Mac's ribs, on the right side of his belly, was a wound that looked insignificant. It was only an inch across and not bleeding. He felt the abdomen with gently probing fingers, then looked up at Sandra Gotch.

'Alert theatre. He's got internal bleeding, liver probably.' He checked the flow rate on the drip lines and went to the telephone in the office.

'Mr Compton, please.'

David, although asleep, picked up the instrument before the second ring. He could tell from the edge on the Casualty Officer's voice that it was an emergency.

'Sorry to disturb you, sir. Stab wound of the abdomen. He's shocked and probably has hepatic bleeding.'

'I'll be with you.'

David was out of bed and into shirt and trousers in sixty seconds. Within four minutes the Triumph was out of the drive of Apple Tree Cottage and heading over the downs to Manbury Hospital.

Since their return from Lyons life had been hectic. The story of his operation on Anne-Marie had been picked up by the Press and he had been lionised. That had meant more pressure on his time than before.

He recalled a hoarse piece of whispered advice from the leathern-faced Soeur Camille as they were leaving.

'You look after her, *mon brave*. Do not let her go.'

As he drove over the Wiltshire downs through the night he smiled to himself. She was right, and he was not going to let Ginette go, for more reasons than Camille could imagine.

He examined Mac in Casualty. Already, with the inflow of blood and Haemaccel, he was looking better and no longer unconscious. David thought there was something familiar about him, and it was only when he was sitting in the surgeons' dressing-room, waiting for the theatre to be ready, that he realised why.

Sam Bennett's photographs.

He sat up and looked at his watch. It was two a.m. Sam would be asleep, but he had made a point of saying he wanted to know at once. David shrugged and picked up the telephone. Theatre would not be ready for at least half an hour and he had nothing further to do. It was a quick and easy way to earn three thousand pounds.

'Sam? David Compton.'

'Don't tell me one's arrived?'

Sam was not slow. He knew there was only one reason for David to ring him at that hour.

'That's right. And he's bad—stabbed in the belly with a piece of glass.'

'What's going to happen to him?' Sam wanted to know.

'We've got him on a drip, but he's bleeding internally. I'm going to operate in a few minutes.'

'What are his chances?'

'Not good, I'm afraid. Less than fifty-fifty. It depends.'

'What on?'

'A lot of things. Where the bleeding is. If I can stop it. His constitution.'

'Thank you, David. I'll keep my side of the bargain.'

'Very good of you.'

David was about to conclude the conversation when Sam's voice came back to him.

'David, there's something else.'

'Yes?'

'If he doesn't make it. . .' There was a pause.

'Yes?' David queried.

'If he doesn't make it you can add on a nought.'

David felt himself growing cold and angry. 'Do you mean what I think you mean?' he asked stiffly.

'Yes, I do.'

'What do you think I am?'

'We already know that. We're just arguing about the price.'

'There's no deal,' David assured him.

Sam's voice came back soothingly.

'OK, no deal. I'm just telling you what's going to happen, that's all. If the man dies then you'll be credited with thirty thousand.'

'This is an open line, Sam. I don't want anything to happen.'

'We're not all masters of our fate. If he goes under your care it saves me money elsewhere. Good business. Goodnight, David.'

Ginette came into the room as David was putting down the phone. He tried to smile at her.

'Something wrong, David?' she asked.

'Not really. Are you ready?'

'Soon will be. You can scrub.'

She smiled at him, and went out of the room. He watched her go, and even the sight of her long legs and her smile did not help to raise his spirits. Sam's conversation had rattled him, not least because they had been on an open line and could have been overheard.

There was a streak of ruthlessness in Sam Bennett that David could now see clearly and which had him concerned about the use to which he would put the information he was being given. He realised that Sam had been clever in his approach. Manbury had a drug abuse unit and it was more than possible that one of the gang would eventually land up inside the hospital.

If Sam caused the death of one of the gang as a result of information received from him where would that put him in the eyes of the law? He tried not to think about it. Carole, one of the hospital telephonists, was a noted gossip. Probably that was why she had taken the post and where she got it all from.

The thought did not help his peace of mind. If the hospital authorities got wind of it he would be sacked immediately. And what if one died on the table? That didn't bear thinking about. No one would believe that it was not premeditated murder in public.

He thought around it.

It was not impossible to conjure a situation where the patient would die without the blame being put on the operator. What was the life of a rapist and thug like Mac when measured against his son's future?

Without his knowing it his long fingers were entwined in a tightening grip, the knuckles white. His aquiline features looked gaunt as he strode towards the operating theatre. Mark Slater was already there. This was the first time they had worked together since the younger man's infection. David knocked across the elbow tap, wet his hands and filled them with liquid antiseptic detergent.

'How is it, Mark?' he queried.

Mark grinned ruefully.

'Fine. When I die you'll find penicillin writ large on my behind.'

'How about the lady?'

'Acid as a lemon about it, but she went along. I don't think she's exactly in love with Sister Irving.'

David shrugged.

'I'm sure she can ride that.'

'You're right. Sandra's acting as her instrument nurse tonight. The duty nurse can't get in.'

David finished scrubbing, dried his hands on a sterile towel and opened a gown pack. Gowned, he powdered his hands and slipped on close-fitting surgical gloves and snapped them over the cuffs of his sleeves with a single, practised manoeuvre. He walked through into the theatre and a nurse, following after him, tied the strings of his gown behind his back.

Pat Coppard was sitting at the head of the operating table surrounded by a bank of electronic equipment. Multi-coloured lights blinked and peeped like an amusement arcade. An automatic ventilator wheezed up and down, feeding gas and oxygen into a corrugated tube the size of an elephant's trunk. Tubes and leads hung down and disappeared under the green theatre sheets like forest creepers.

'You'll need to be in and out of this one like a long dog,' advised Pat. 'He's pretty crook.'

David looked at him levelly over his mask.

'OK to start?'

Pat Coppard nodded back at him, saying nothing. They both knew. David was not asking if the patient was ready, but whether it was safe to start at all.

Ginette handed him the scalpel.

As he went through the muscle layers there was surprisingly little bleeding. Mac's blood pressure was too low to provide the impetus to create significant blood flow. David snapped the self-retaining retractor into place.

'Suck.'

He put in a big pack, exposing the surface of the liver. Across the upper surface, oozing dark blue, was a jagged rent. This was where Ian's glass shard had torn in. Nearby an artery fountained scarlet as he moved the pack. It was deep down within the cavity. David held out his right hand and into it came a long-handled pair of Spencer-Wells forceps with a slap. Ginette had seen it as soon as he had and knew what he would want.

Meticulously he clipped the beak of the forceps on to the artery and passed the handles to Mark Slater.

'Hold that.'

Mark held it as if it were the tail of a scorpion.

Ginette had a string of catgut stretched between her hands. David took it without looking. His left hand held one end high, the other he took deep into the wound and around the Spencer-Wells. There he tied a one-handed knot, firming it gently against the beak of the forceps. He looked at Mark.

'Off, gently.'

Slowly, as if he were defusing a bomb, Mark unlatched the ratchet of the forceps and eased the beaks off the artery while David tightened the ligature. He completed the knot and swabbed over it gently. The scarlet fountain had ceased. He held up the ligature.

'Cut—long.'

Mark snipped the ends of the ligature, leaving half-inch tails. David turned his attention to the rent in the liver. With a long, curved needle he put in six mattress sutures that brought the edges together without cutting through the friable tissue. He looked at Pat Coppard.

'We're coming out now. OK?'

'Put your skates on, the ice is getting thin.'

For the next few minutes there was only the sound of clicking forceps, the snip of scissors and a laconic command, 'Cut' or 'Hold'.

Mark followed the patient to Intensive Care and Pat Coppard and David were joined by Ginette in the surgeons' room.

'What do you think of him, Pat?' asked David.

'We wasted our time.'

David whipped his head round in surprise.

'What do you mean? He's not that bad.'

The razor-lean face of the Australian chipped out a tight smile. 'No, he should get there if your knots hold.'

'Thank you, Mr Coppard. Then what is it?'

'There's enough police down in Casualty to form a football team. That little bugger stabbed a chemist to death in Marlborough. That's how he got a gut full of glass. They've only just found the chemist.'

'How awful!' Ginette looked shocked. 'You mean we've done this for a man who's just committed murder?'

'That's about the length of it. We've cobbled him up so the rozzers can have him.'

David looked at Pat, slowly shrugged his shoulders, and said,

'Ours not to reason. . .I'm off. Goodnight both of you.' David looked warmly at Ginette as he stepped into the corridor.

He stopped at the intensive care unit on his way down. The nurse in charge nodded and smiled reassuringly at him and he went down the stairs to the front courtyard. In the light of the tall standards illuminating the car park he saw Ginette getting out of her Morris Minor and walked over to her.

'Trouble?' he queried.

She spread her hands.

'Won't start—the battery, I'm afraid. I left the lights on.'

'Don't worry, I'll run you home.'

He felt a sense of excitement, like a small boy going to school for the first time. There was a set of jump leads in his car, but he was not going to say so.

'I'm in Wootton Bassett. It's miles out of your way.'

'Nonsense! Under that modest little bonnet there beats a high-powered racing engine. Have you home sooner than you can say swab.'

It was a clear night and the stars were out. David had the top down and they swooped over the downs and through the lanes, the slipstream blowing their hair. Ginette put a hand on his arm and pointed.

'Turn right here, into the white gateway.'

The white gateway led to the front of a large Georgian house. It had an air of quiet, patrician affluence. As they drew up David turned to Ginette and raised his eyebrows. She smiled.

'No, not all mine. They're flats.'

'Just for a minute I was expecting the butler to come out.'

'Not so.'

She hesitated. She had always kept her hospital life and her private life quite separate. Somehow she felt, sometimes rightly, that the friends she made at the hospital would not welcome her if they knew her wealthy background. Sometimes she felt almost guilty about it.

After Simon she was acutely aware that her wealth might attract the wrong sort of man. She could not believe that David came into that category and, like the tortoise making progress, she decided to stick her neck out.

'Would you like to come in? I have a nice Remy-Martin I can offer you after that kindly drive.'

David looked at his watch. It was a quarter past four. He had decided to refuse, but as he got out to open the door for her he said,

'Thanks very much. I feel the need for a drink.'

Her flat gave him the cosy welcome of an old friend—pink and green chintz covers, rugs and scatter cushions, ballet pictures and some old theatre posters. David noticed one for a performance of *Traviata* at the Theatre Royal, Exeter, dated 1862. On the mantelpiece was a bronze of a ballerina on point, arms extended. Further on he recognised a Georgian silver cream jug by Hester Bateman.

Ginette came out of an adjoining room carrying two balloon glasses, and David saw that she had changed out of her uniform into a green cotton kaftan. Her long copper hair tumbled on her shoulders as she bent to lift a glass decanter from the sideboard. She swirled the cognac in the glass and handed it to him.

'My thanks for the lift, David.'

They toasted each other, their eyes meeting over the glasses. He raised one eyebrow in an unconscious gesture and she smiled at him. Suddenly he did not know what to say. She reached behind her, opened a cupboard door in the sideboard and pressed a switch. The room gently throbbed with the music from *Porgy and Bess*.

'Do you like it?' she asked.

He nodded. They listened, standing together, for a few moments. When it came to 'Bess, you is my woman now' David put his glass down and, like a man in a dream, took her in his arms. She came to him without hesitation, sinking into his embrace with a gentle warmth, her perfume flaming the bonfire of his senses. The moist warmth of his lips on hers and the heat of him on her breasts through the kaftan brought on an urgency that had them both clinging together. He felt her pressing against him and she slipped a leg through his as their tongues met in an erotic duel.

They stood there for an aeon, their mouths locked, their breath hot upon each other, their hands moving and searching. Under the kaftan Ginette was wearing nothing, and by now David was not surprised. Through the thin cotton he could feel her flesh, firm, smooth, curved like a nymph's and warm to the touch.

He felt her hands slip under his shirt to caress his back. The movement of her soft body against him was both erotic and curiously innocent. The snake of his emotions gripped him and he drew back and looked at her.

'Where?'

His voice was hoarse, raspy with need of her. She looked up at him, her eyes as wild as his desire for her.

'Oh, David!'

She buried her face on his chest, sobbing with delight

and relief that he still wanted her. Beside them a grandfather clock struck the hour. The sonorous chimes quietened him and he looked down at her and stroked her hair.

'Ssh! Now I've made you cry. I'm sorry.'

For once he had missed her emotion and the wildness went from him, supplanted by a tenderness that made him enfold her gently. She turned her face to him.

'You big fool,' she said, 'I'm crying with delight.'

He kissed her softly on the nose, the cheeks, the eyelids, the chin, the ears—fluttering butterfly kisses that made her laugh and suffer with delight. Her hands were at his waist, further untucking his shirt.

'Can't have the great surgeon going home hungry,' she smiled.

'I don't want to go'

'I know, and I don't want you to go. We don't have to keep it on ice.'

David smiled and his arms went around her. There was nothing more to say. They danced together to the music and their steps led them into the bedroom. Ginette felt dizzy with excitement.

As they swung around the room David caught sight of a man's silk dressing-gown hanging over the back of a chair. Jealousy arose from nowhere and set his mind to thinking.

He led her out of the bedroom, his thoughts in turmoil. It all came together neatly in his mind. The expensive flat, the furniture, the bronzes and rugs all spoke of the sort of money that no nursing sister could ever earn. It had to be a wealthy boyfriend.

Ginette had to be somebody's mistress.

As the thought struck him he stopped and tapped his watch.

'It really is time for me to go—goodnight. Thanks for the drink.'

Then he was gone, leaving her standing in hurt astonishment. As he drove away he looked up at the front window on the first floor. A figure with long hair made a black silhouette in the moonlight. He waved and the figure raised an arm in farewell.

He drove across the Wiltshire countryside with the abandon of a man possessed, the adrenalin fizzing through his system like champagne. When he coasted into the drive of Apple Tree Cottage dawn was tipping the woodland trees with gold.

He was tiptoeing across the hall when Laurel appeared in a dressing-gown with a face like a fury.

'Where the bloody hell have you been?' she demanded.

David's eyebrows went up to his hairline.

'Emergency at the hospital. What's got into you?'

'Emergency? You can say that again! They want you now. They've been after you since you left, and that was two hours ago. So what have you been up to?'

Without answering he brushed past her and picked up the telephone.

'Mr Compton here?'

'Dr Slater's been trying to get you, sir. I'll put you through.'

He heard the bleep connection over the wire.

'Dr Slater.'

'What is it, Mark?'

'The Scotsman, sir. I've been trying to get you. I'm afraid he's dead.'

David put the telephone down with a feeling of impending disaster. Despite his pre-operative temptation he had done nothing to conjure the death of the Scotsman. Every meticulous surgical manoeuvre had been out of the book. There was only one reason he could think of for the Scotsman dying and that was a failure of a ligature. The one on the hepatic artery. If that was the case and the police found he was thirty thousand pounds better off as a result they would take more than a polite interest. But how could they find out?

His mind went back to Sam's conversation on the open line and a chill went through him.

'Off again, I suppose?'

Laurel's voice had a querulous acidity he had come to recognise only too well. Normally he would ride her petulant comments, but now, after all that had happened, he turned on her.

'No, I'm not. I'm going to bed. And I can do without one of your class one tongue-lashings just now, thank you.'

'It's time somebody said something, the way you're carrying on!' snapped Laurel.

He clenched his fists.

'Who's carrying on?'

'You. You don't give a damn about time and whether you're here or not. You just come and go as if you're in a lodging-house!'

Conscience had led him to misinterpret her comment about 'carrying on'.

'At least in a lodging-house I wouldn't get badgered every time I walk in the door!' he retorted.

'Badgered? You don't know the meaning of the bloody word! I haven't even started. The way I've had to suffer because we spend all our money on school fees is enough to badger anyone!'

'I don't imagine you were suffering much being taken out to lunch by Sam,' said David drily.

'No, I wasn't. I enjoyed it very much. More than I've enjoyed anything for a long time. Ever, in fact.'

'What do I infer from that?'

'You can infer just what you bloody well like.'

He looked at her flushed and angry face, normally so

pale and composed, and realised that she had been making love with Sam. Strangely, it did not now hit him with the force it would have done. The one-time attraction between them had burnt to ash in the fires of domestic conflict.

He just felt angry.

'For God's sake, Laurel! Just calm down and let me get to bed.'

It was five-thirty and he was due to start at nine at Manbury. He walked past her and went up the stairs two at a time. Behind him Laurel stood at the foot of the stairs, her hands on her hips, and screamed up at him.

'At least Sam can send me!'

David stopped at the top of the stairs and turned. There was a mix of frustration and bitterness in his voice when he replied, 'And I would do the same—preferably a long, long way away.'

CHAPTER FIFTEEN

DONNA tilted her retroussé nose and dabbed on some powder when she heard David Compton's voice in the corridor. His 'Good morning, Donna,' in brown and mellifluous tones, sent a tingle up her back. She pinked gently and opened the door to Donald Shaw's office, wishing she was wearing her dress with the low front.

'Mr Compton to see you, sir.'

She threw a dimpled smile at David and disappeared. Donald Shaw twitched his toothbrush moustache and tightened his lips. Donna's mind would not be on her job for the rest of the day. David gave him an easy grin.

'How's the Shavian world this summer morning? What splendid news have you for me? I know—you've persuaded the establishment committee to let me have a senior registrar?'

Donald Shaw paled at the thought, but he was getting used to David's manner. He twiddled the propelling pencil in his breast pocket.

'No, it's about the Press and this murder and the man who died.'

David's ease evaporated.

'What about them?' he asked.

'They've been swarming round the hospital, questioning anyone willing to talk. Obviously it's a good story and they're trying to piece it together with the murder.'

'So?'

'I'd like to make sure that the hospital puts out a proper front. We don't want any undesirable publicity. You know how these things can be misreported and get out of hand.'

'We have nothing to hide,' shrugged David.

David experienced a queasy pang about his night call to Sam, and hoped fervently that Carole had not been on duty that night.

'Of course not. I'd just like to make sure that no one says anything silly to the Press. After all, it'll come out at the inquest after the post-mortem.'

David stood up.

'Is that why you asked me to come and see you? To tell me that?'

'You're the surgeon in charge of the case. I felt it only prudent.'

'My God!'

David walked out without another word and went past poor Donna without a sideways glance, his grey eyes glacial. The sight of him in high dudgeon gave her a delicious *frisson* that lasted all day.

In his office he dictated reports into the pocket recorder ready for his secretary to collect before he started the morning outpatient session. The door opened abruptly and he looked up with irritation.

'David, would you like to see the PM on the Scotsman this morning?'

It was Joe McLean, the pathologist, a raw-boned, bucolic Scot who played rugby first and practised medicine second. He did the post-mortems. In his white-tiled world, smelling of coldness and death and formalin, everybody's errors were laid bare. His was the last court of appeal after disaster.

'Thanks, Joe. What time?'

'We'll have the cadaver open and ready for inspection about twelve.'

Joe grinned, exposing big yellow teeth that reminded David of a yawning donkey. The big red face with the tangled black hair disappeared, and David tried to concentrate on his reports. It was not easy. He kept thinking of a copper-haired woman who clung to him and whose perfume he could smell now. He thought too of a silhouetted figure that raised an arm in response to his wave.

Had he been right in his supposition that she was some wealthy man's mistress? He had a nasty feeling he had jumped the gun to a wrong conclusion. What must she have thought when he disappeared so abruptly when they were on the point of making love? He had a shrewd idea of what her thoughts would have been, and it did not make him feel any better.

These thoughts went from his mind as he slit open his mail which he had brought from the cottage. With a sinking feeling he recognised the familiar long white envelope from his bank, marked PRIVATE in black letters. Rapidly his eyes skimmed the contents '. . .thought it only courteous to inform you that your account is now £60,000 overdrawn, which I am sure you will recall is considerably in excess of your agreed facility. I would be grateful if. . .'

With firm and precise movements David folded the letter and tore it into fine pieces. The day of reckoning was creeping inexorably closer. After the shattering row they had had on his return from the emergency there was no point in speaking to Laurel again about her salary contributing to their expenses. His conversation with Sam rose up and he felt like a man stepping reluctantly towards the edge of a cliff. A sixty-thousand-pound cliff.

What was the alternative?

Ginette?

He wondered just how well off she was.

He sat back and tried to get his thoughts in order. With that latest massive increase in James's fees and the interest on his present overdraft something would have to be done. More private practice, perhaps?

There was practically none at the moment. He had not had the time and opportunity to build up a private practice in his speciality of vascular micro-surgery, there was little enough of it anyway in the private sector. He felt the tide of events taking him with increasing force. No longer was he the master of his own fate.

Exactly at noon he pushed through the swing doors of the post-mortem room in the Department of Pathology. The coldness and the background hum from the big refrigerators were accompanied by a pervasive whiff of formalin.

The death house.

Joe was standing by a white porcelain slab on which lay the corpse of the Scotsman. Had it not been for the flaming red hair David would not have recognised the body. The skull had been cut round and the top removed like a decapitated hardboiled egg. The front of the rib-cage was missing, David saw it standing on end on a nearby shelf, and the abdomen gaped wildly, having been slit from diaphragm to pubis. David though it all looked like an upstage version of a knacker's yard.

Joe beckoned with a red rubber-gloved hand.

'Look in here, David.'

David peered into the cavity of the abdomen, thinking it bore little relationship to the one on which he had been operating so recently. Joe lifted up the bulk of the liver and cut through the pedicle with a long-bladed knife. Beneath it was a large blood clot, the size of a soup tureen. He spooned it out with cupped hands and sloshed it into a stainless steel bowl.

'I've just been reading your operation notes, David. That ligature was on the hepatic artery. Here it is.' He pointed to the open end of a white tube. Beside it was the long-tailed ligature, no longer encircling the artery.

'Looks as though something was wrong with the ligature.'

He picked it out with a pair of forceps and put it on a stainless steel tray. David looked at it like a man staring at a picture of his own execution.

'That's just something extra. The principle cause of death was acute cardiac failure—look at the oedema in these lungs. Couldn't stand the shock and haemorrhage.'

'What will you say at the inquest?'

David heard his own voice, hoarse and dry as sandpaper. Joe toyed with the ligature.

'Do you always use this grade catgut for major arteries?'

David picked it up and felt it between his fingers.

'Difficult to say now. Feels a bit thin. Can I keep this?'

Joe hesitated and then nodded.

'Aye, I'll not be commenting on that. The cause of death was cardiac failure and I'll be saying that it was accentuated by further bleeding internally. Can't be sure of the site of the bleed.'

'Thanks, Joe.'

'Well, I can't be sure, and that's the truth.'

David walked out of the Department of Pathology feeling as though he had spent the morning in a rugger scrum. He took the piece of catgut to his office and examined it carefully. There was something about the feel of it between his bare fingers that he did not like. It had an unaccustomed roughness.

He picked up his telephone and dialled the theatre number.

'Mr Compton. May I speak to Sister Irving?'

When Ginette came on the line he tried to keep his voice crisp and impersonal.

'Sister, I would like a sample of all ranges of catgut

we use in theatre, and particularly the ones we used last night for that stab wound.'

'Certainly, Mr Compton. I'll bring them myself. You're in your office?'

'Thank you, Sister.'

When she arrived in his office she leaned against the door, her hands behind her back. David had not seen her since he had driven away from her flat.

'Well, Mr Compton?'

The voice was husky; somewhere between Marlene Dietrich and Tallulah Bankhead. Not her theatre voice at all. He stood up and went round the desk. Quickly she held up a hand holding several packets in a fan shape, like a card player with a full suite.

'This all you need, Mr Compton?'

Her expression was serious, defensive almost. He took the packet from her and put it on the table.

'Ginette, I'm sorry.'

He put his arms around her. She stiffened against him and he released her.

'Ginette, I said I'm sorry.'

She shrugged, feigning an indifference she did not feel. Inside she felt bruised by his hurtful action at a moment when she had put out the first delicate tentacle of trust.

'What have you to be sorry about?' she said coolly.

'Leaving as I did. It was wrong.'

'Then why did you do it?' Despite herself she had to ask the question.

'I was jealous,' David explained. 'I saw the dressing-gown.'

'Which dressing-gown?' Ginette shook her head in surprise.

'The blue Paisley one in your bedroom. Somehow I didn't think you kept other company.'

She nearly laughed, and then became cross. The

dressing-gown was her father's. He occasionally dropped in and stayed the night and she was about to send it to the cleaners, but what right had David to dictate, when he was married to Laurel? In any case, they had done nothing other than exchange kisses.

'What if I do keep "other company", as you so delicately put it? I'm a single unattached woman and I can damned well keep whatever company I like!'

It had been a very long time since she had had any male company. None at all since Simon, but she was damned if she would tell David that.

'Ginette, I said I was sorry.'

He tried to kiss her, but she pushed him away.

'Don't you know we're overlooked?' she said coldly.

He turned and looked out of the window beside his desk. Ginette was right. Above was a covered corridor with windows that looked into his office. There was nobody on it. She held out the packets of catgut and became serious.

'What do you want these for?' she asked.

He picked up the ligature on his desk and showed it to her.

'Is this what you gave me to tie off that bleeder last night?'

Ginette nodded. 'I remember. Something wrong with it?'

'Look at it. What do you think?'

She turned it over carefully in her fingers, rolling it between them, and looked at him thoughtfully.

'Sure this is it?' she asked.

'Absolutely.'

'This is 000, but it doesn't feel right.'

'Where did you get it from?' asked David.

'I didn't. I took it from the instrument nurse.'

'Sandra?'

Ginette nodded. 'Sandra opened the packet and gave

me the catgut. I didn't check the packet—Sandra knows what to use, it's not as though she's a trainee. I shouldn't have to check her—she'd be insulted.'

David looked thoughtful, twiddling the catgut between his fingers.

'You're right. Give me a fresh packet of 000.'

He ripped the packet open and rolled it between his fingers, his eyebrows going up and down as he did so. After a moment he bent beneath the desk and dragged up a tall mahogany case and from it produced a binocular microscope. With practised ease he slid the two pieces of catgut between glass slides and inserted them under the low power. Under magnification the strands of catgut looked like ropes of yellow tow. One of the ropes had the tight disciplined twirl of a guardsman's moustache; the other as fluffy as a flying officer's first attempt.

He leaned back and beckoned to Ginette.

'Look at this.'

She leaned over his shoulder and peered down the binocular lenses.

'What's happened?' she asked.

David took the opportunity to put his arm around her hips.

'Same 000 catgut, only the one on the left has been thinned—probably by scraping with the flat edge of a scalpel. That's deliberate.'

Ginette took her eyes from the microscope and looked at him in horror.

'Who?' she breathed.

'It wasn't you, was it?'

'Of course not!'

'That only leaves one other.'

'Sandra?'

David nodded. 'Who else?'

Ginette felt herself unable to think properly.

'Why would she do that?'

'Jealousy. Revenge. Bloody-mindedness—you never know. Did you come the heavy on her about reporting sick?'

'Pretty much,' she admitted.

'Perhaps that was it. You know she wants your job. You fall down on it and she steps in. You'd better watch your step from now on,' David warned.

'Do you think that killed him?' Ginette's green eyes were hard and alight.

'Can't tell, but it's my bet. Fortunately Joe McLean isn't sure, so it won't come out like that at the inquest. He was pretty much a goner anyway.'

'David, this is awful! Every moment I shall wonder if that scheming woman has set a trap for me. And what about the lives of other patients? What are we going to do?'

He stood up and put his arms around her, gentling her with his hands, and she let him.

'Don't worry,' he said gently. 'This was probably a one-off. She can't do much when she isn't working in theatre anyway.'

He took her face in his hands and kissed her gently.

'Now pass me a smile please, Sister, and we'll get on with the circus!'

CHAPTER SIXTEEN

THE AXE glinted in the afternoon sun as David raised it high and brought it down in a glittering arc to slice through the log on the chopping block. He was surrounded by a tumbled heap of split wood, the exposed white surfaces enveloping him in an aftershave aroma of the great outdoors.

He placed another log on the block, hefted the axe, got the line of cleavage and swung again. The two halves fell away, clean and satisfying. It made him feel better. Laurel's implied confession that she had been to bed with Sam Bennett had hurt him as well as making him angry. He was not going to seek out Sam for schoolboy revenge, but nor was he going to let the situation get away from him.

He heard a chattering sound and saw a grey squirrel sitting on top of the garden fence. In its front paws was an acorn attached to an oak twig, which it could not remove. David leaned on his axe and watched the little animal with delight. Its fury with the twig had rendered it unaware, or uncaring, of David's presence. He watched for several minutes while the tiny battle raged.

'David!'

Laurel's voice broke the spell. She was leaning out of the upper casement window. The squirrel looked up with darting alarm, left the fence and went bounding over the grassy field, his bushy tail waving like an animated Davy Crockett hat. Irritated at the intrusion, David turned round.

'What is it now?' he asked abruptly.

'What shirt do you want to wear for the party?'

He sighed. Laurel was so organising. He had several dinner shirts and she knew he would wear any of them. She just had to be busy and show it.

'The one with the frilly front.'

'Isn't it time you came in to change?'

'Shan't be long.'

He started to pile the logs neatly under the eaves of the shed. It offended him to leave them in disarray. He enjoyed the simple outside jobs. They gave him an opportunity to relax and think, away from the pressures of the hospital.

The party that night was at the Manor to celebrate Ralph Abelson's fiftieth birthday. Early reports had it that it was to be a grand affair. They had not visited the Manor recently, but Laurel had seen numerous Harrods' vans passing the cottage on their way there.

He went inside and ran a bath. Laurel was standing before the dressing-mirror in their bedroom wearing a silk camisole and holding a flowing white dress. He sat on the bed to take off his socks.

'New dress?' he asked.

'Mmm. Wait till you see it on. I bought it out of my first week's salary. They're a generous lot—very proper and old-fashioned, but money seems to mean nothing when it comes to expenses.'

'They keep you busy?'

'Not really. Depends on Ralph to some extent, but mainly Sam.'

'Sam? I didn't know he had much to do with it.'

'Neither did I when I began, but he's a really big wheel,' Laurel told him. 'They bow and scrape like mad when he's around. You'd think he owned the place!'

'Maybe he does,' said David. 'I wouldn't put it past him.'

'Anyway, I have to arrange their schedules, appointments, make bookings, soothe ruffled clients. Just a high-flying "gofor" girl, I suppose. Ralph doesn't need much looking after, but Sam's a different matter. He never stops—a Catherine wheel of a man.'

David sensed a different tone in her voice and decided to go fishing.

'He never strikes me as much of a dynamo,' he remarked.

'Don't you believe it!'

David went over to the bath and lowered himself into the steaming water.

'Who's going tonight?' he asked.

'All the gang and half the county. Dancing all night. Kippers and bacon and eggs at dawn.'

'Sounds more like a Magdalen Summer Ball,' David commented.

'Ralph after his lost youth, I expect.'

'Can't see us sitting down to champagne and kippers in the morning light. Don't forget we're going to see James tomorrow.'

David emerged dripping from the bath and towelled himself vigorously. He knotted the towel round his waist and went back into the bedroom, his dark hair damp on his head, his skin pink from the bath, his muscles sleek and rippling.

Laurel eyed him speculatively.

'You're quite a hunk of man, David. No wonder the girls go for you!'

She moved across the room, dabbing at her ears with a perfume bottle, and stood in front of him. She put the bottle down on the dressing-table and placed her hands on his waist. Her lips had a pouting expression he recognised, and when her hand went under his towel he was already half erect. She looked up at him, her lips moueing.

'Like that?'

Her hands were busy upon him. He found himself

explosively tumescent, his bare feet gripping the carpet. The towel went to the floor and his hands to her camisole, which joined the towel. She was naked, but as he put his arms around her to take her to the bed, she stopped him.

'No, I'll never get my hair right again.'

She pressed herself against him. Over her head he could see their reflection in the dressing-mirror. Laurel squeezed him gently with both hands and he groaned. Her hand on his testicles filled him to bursting point.

Laurel rarely wanted sex, but when she did she moved like a striking krait, and with the same precision. Nevertheless she never let it interfere with her appearance. His hand between her legs found her swollen and moist. She turned her back to him and bent forward, her hand guiding him in.

'Like a stallion, David.'

He reared at her in momentous heaves that brought forth gasps and forced her to grip the chair for support. The mirror reflected their 'danse erotique' as he held her by the waist and drew her back and forth until his orgasm splurged in a cascading torrent that ran down both their thighs.

They stood still for a moment, out of breath, then came apart. They looked at each other briefly before Laurel sat in front of her dressing-table and picked up her tail comb.

'Thank you, David. That was quite a performance.'

He retired to the shower. As the hot water needled on his back he felt a sense of remorse. His performance with Laurel made him feel that he had in some way betrayed Ginette. He was honest enough with himself to recognise that he did not love Laurel, but she was still his wife. So why not? He turned the jets to cold and came out of the shower half blue with cold.

Downstairs, immaculate in a white dinner jacket,

maroon tie and cummerbund, he poured out two glasses of champagne and awaited Laurel's appearance. James stared at him from the picture frame on the piano and he made a mental reservation to get home early. He knew the boy looked forward to their visits with a desperation that made him feel guilty, and he tried never to be late.

He heard Laurel's footsteps on the stairs and looked round. She came into the room and twirled before him. Her dress was white and swagged in Grecian style. It was decorated with shiny black stones and the back was cut lower than low. On her left shoulder was a tiny brooch that scintillated even in the subdued lighting of the living-room. With her black hair drawn severely back and her face made up like a ballerina the effect was striking.

David whistled and peered at the brooch. It was a tiny replica of a prancing stallion in diamonds with a ruby tongue and a billowing sapphire tail. 'Looks mighty expensive to me. Where'd you get it? Don't tell me your salary stands for that.'

'It's just a little stick-pin in paste,' she shrugged. 'A welcome-to-the-firm present from Sam.'

He looked at her keenly as he handed her the glass he had poured. 'Very generous!'

She shrugged.

'Not really. He's rich as Croesus, and he does owe you one, you might remember.'

David preferred not to remember and sipped his champagne. The thought reminded him of his pressing financial problems.

'What are we going to do about James?' he asked suddenly.

'I don't know. I've already told you what I think we should do.'

'You mean put him in a soul-destroying institution?'

'You're overstating the case!' Laurel complained.

'Over my dead body we will!'

David pointed to the prancing stallion.

'You could sell that thing for a start. It must be worth a small fortune.'

'I damn well won't, and it isn't worth what you think. It's paste.'

'I don't believe you.'

'So I'm a liar now as well as a bitch?'

'You said it!' snapped David.

They stared at each other intensely, quivering like a pair of mongooses straining for a fight. David was the first to speak. He did so with a sense of resignation. This last shot at converting Laurel showed what she really thought, how intransigent she was, and how little she cared for the boy.

'For God's sake, Laurel, this is no good. Let's go.' She snatched up her fur wrap and marched out of the front door before him, taut as a violin string.

As they rounded the drive leading to the courtyard of the Manor they both gasped. The ancient building had been transformed. Shafts of coloured light criss-crossed in the summer dusk, lighting up mullioned windows and dormers. Flags curled lazily from several poles and the two marquees under the beeches glowed with their inside lighting. Red carpet walkways between the giant tents and the Manor were peopled with guests in evening dress. From one of the marquees lilted the strains of *The Blue Danube*. Footmen in full livery bore trays of glasses bubbling with champagne.

Laurel gasped with delight.

'It's like a scene from the court of Louis Quatorze!'

David could not help thinking that the cost of the party would have paid off his overdraft and left enough change to complete James's stay at St Athelstan's. Penelope Abelson greeted them in the first marquee.

She wore an ornate brown dress decorated with multi-coloured stones, and her long face bore a look of lugubrious resignation.

'The party's quite out of my control. Just too many people.'

As they moved away from her Laurel whispered to David,

'A Balmain gown, and she still manages to look like a dog in drag!'

Susan Bennett arrived with Sam, driven by their chauffeur in a new Bentley Mulsanne, and was wearing a magnificent russet ball gown in satin and taffeta with long white gloves. An emerald bracelet on her left wrist matched her emerald choker and two hours before the make-up mirror had concealed most of the ravages of her accident. Nevertheless she felt apprehensive. It was her first outing since she had left hospital.

The first person she saw was Laurel.

Fortunately Laurel was dancing with Sir Ralph at that moment and Susan had time to adjust herself to her presence. She seethed inside at the sight of her. She had felt nervous and apprehensive before arriving at this prestigious gathering, but these feelings evaporated when Laurel approached them with Sir Ralph in tow.

Apart from a brief and disdainful glance Laurel ignored her and sat next to Sam, exuding a proprietorial air of familiarity. Sam was waving to a footman bearing a tray of wineglasses. When he arrived Laurel lifted her glass.

'Happy birthday, Ralph.' Susan saw her look directly at Sam as she continued, 'And here's to us.'

Either Sam missed it or he chose to ignore it. Not so Susan.

'What are we drinking to?' she queried.

Laurel looked at her innocently.

'Our health, and future fun, perhaps?'

Susan smiled back, her face a mask.

'I'll join you in that, sport, for sure.'

She stood up and started to raise her glass, but as she did so her foot caught in the hem of her dress and she stumbled abruptly. The red wine in her glass cascaded over the front of Laurel's white Grecian gown. Susan regained her balance and looked at the ruin of the dress. A huge magenta stain over the front proclaimed an irrecoverable disaster.

'Laurel, I am sorry! So clumsy of me. Let me help you to clean it up.'

Laurel's face was a study in barely restrained fury. Before she could stop herself she blurted, 'Of all the stu. . .' She halted, then smiled glassily. 'If it's all the same, I'll deal with it myself.'

She stood up and walked off. Susan turned to Sam and shrugged.

'Can't win 'em all, can you?'

Sam looked at her, a gleam of admiration in his eye. A man of action himself, he admired it in others, especially his wife.

A little while later, David was taking champagne from a bewigged footman when he felt a tap on his shoulder—Dick and Molly Southey, with Molly iridescent in a fitted dress shimmering with blue sequins. He raised a glass to them both.

'To the most elegant couple of the evening.'

Dick Southey stood resplendent in the dress uniform of the Gurkhas. Ramrod-straight, he looked as though he had stepped off the face of a cigarette card. Molly gave him a brilliant smile.

'Darling, I know you want to talk to Laurel, your uniform goes with her dress so beautifully. I'm taking David off for a dance.'

The Colonel clicked his heels and Molly grabbed

David's arm and led him to the dance floor. She waved a hand at the billowing pink and white candy-striped lining to the roof of the tent, the ornate chandeliers on the walls and the attendant footmen.

'Isn't this too gorgeous? Don't you think Ralph has the biggest ideas?'

'I think he must be off his trolley to spend all this money,' David said shortly.

'Grumpy spoilsport! You're like a dog looking for a lost bone. What's the matter? Rowing with Laurel again?'

David nodded as they swirled into the motley of dancing couples. Molly danced, as she did everything else, with a languorous elegance. She smiled at him with a mischievous look.

'Well, if all else fails you can always come home to Momma.'

David grinned back at her. He was never quite sure how much she meant.

'Have you seen Ralph yet?' he asked.

She shook her head

'No. I suppose we ought to seek him out and wish him a happy birthday before the party gets too frantic.'

As they danced David caught sight of a woman in an emerald dress with a strikingly beautiful back and copper hair who was walking away from the dance floor. He had only a glimpse of her, but for a moment he could have been persuaded it was Ginette.

The likelihood of it was so utterly remote he dismissed it at once. Soon he would be imagining her in every redhead that went by!

They left the floor and saw Ralph standing in a corner of the marquee among a small group. His foghorn bellow was audible even above the dance music. They pushed their way towards him and as they did so he saw them coming and signalled to them with a massive paw.

'Here, you two, come and have a drink and meet my cousin.'

He looked around and from behind his leviathan frame emerged the woman in the green dress.

David stared at her, his mouth agape. It was Ginette.

'What are you doing here?' he asked in disbelief.

The smile of amusement on her face disappeared.

'Much the same as you, I would think.' The tones were her crispest, reserved usually for student nurses who stepped out of line. 'Don't worry, Ralph,' she added. 'Mr Compton and I know each other—very well.'

Beside him Molly raised an elegant and inquisitive eyebrow, but said nothing. They sat down and dutifully wished Ralph a happy birthday.

He responded with a beaming smile, ran a hand over his shining black hair and leaned towards Molly.

'Brought me a present, have you?' he asked.

Just for once Molly looked embarrassed. She had not. Before she could reply Sir Ralph had taken her hand and lifted her to her feet.

'I'll have this dance with you as my birthday present.'

David also stood up and looked at Ginette, still confused with the surprise at seeing her. He said nothing but gave her the slightest of bows, and they were on the dance floor before anyone had noticed they were gone. She felt warm in his arms and there was no shuffling or tripping and treading on toes. They danced together as one.

She smiled warmly, her eyes glinting at him, and his heart went out to her with a leap. Despite this he still had to have some answers. Why was she here this evening? It was not the sort of venue at which he would have expected to meet his theatre sister.

'What's going on?' he demanded. 'Did I hear Ralph say you're his cousin?'

She glanced speculatively at him.

'Yes, you heard correctly. The relationship's on my mother's side of the family.'

Despite her lighthearted reply Ginette felt uneasy, as if she had been caught out in a deception. She was jumpy about disclosing too much of her background to anyone in the hospital, and now that she had allowed David behind her private curtain she was unsure. At the back of her mind also was his abrupt and steely departure the night he had left her flat.

'Why didn't you tell me you were related to Ralph Abelson?' he wanted to know.

'Why didn't you ask me about my family and connections if you wanted to know?'

Her voice was crisp, she could feel herself bridling at his brusque interrogation.

'I'm sorry, I just didn't expect. . .'

'Obviously not. If you had, would you have been here?'

'Of course, more than ever.'

Ginette began to calm down. There were still burning questions David wanted answered by this tantalising woman and, without thinking, drew attention to his inner insecurities and jealousy by asking,

'Do you wear men's dressing-gowns for choice?'

She turned her face up to him, thinking he was being funny, but the expression on his face stopped her pert reply.

'I've never worn one in my life.'

'Then what about the one I told you I saw in your bedroom?'

There was a moment of silence between them, then she laughed outright.

'Just for your information, that belongs to my father.

Although why I should have to explain that to you I don't know.'

She turned from his grip and walked off the dance floor, leaving him to be taken up by Molly Southey, who regarded it as a heaven sent opportunity. Ginette almost ran through the guests to get away before somebody noticed the tears that were welling up. She had known that David would be at the party with Laurel and very much wanted to see what Laurel looked like and how he behaved with her. Seeing them together, she would quickly know whether or not they were happily married.

'Ginette, my girl!' Her cousin's foghorn boomed in her ear, stopping her progress. 'Meet David Compton's wife. This is Laurel.'

Laurel had made a good job of getting the stain out of her dress, nevertheless it was still evident, and the knowledge had done nothing to improve her temper. At first they were both remarkably polite, but the atmosphere was strained. Ginette tried to be friendly, but there was a hauteur about Laurel that she found difficult to cope with. She had no desire to quarrel openly with David's wife, but Laurel was in a vindictive mood.

'You work at the hospital under David, I understand?' she said coolly.

Ginette was not sure whether the wording was deliberate or just unfortunate.

'Yes, we work together in theatre,' she agreed.

'Indeed, how many performances a day do you manage?'

Ginette tried to think of a suitable reply, but could not, and turned away abruptly instead to escape Laurel's viperish tongue. She had not seen David come up behind them and pushed her way blindly through the crowd until she was standing under the great oak.

A twig snapped behind her and she turned with a gasp. He was standing three feet away. In the dark she could not see the expression on his face, but the tone of his voice told her everything.

'Would it be any good if I were to say again that I'm sorry?'

She could not speak, and when he stepped forward and took her in his arms she put her head to his chest and held him tight.

'My princess.'

'Still peopling your dreams?'

David wanted to kiss her. Instead he looked into her eyes and he raised an ear to the music.

'Do you know what they're playing?'

She nodded.

'Schumann's *Traumerei*.'

'Dreams. Never stop them.'

They kissed and strained hungrily to each other. He caressed her neck and ran his thumb gently against her ear. Her voice was husky as she whispered up at him,

'Oh, David, what are we going to do?'

'Ssh, darling! Leave that for tonight. We'll sort it out later. Tonight is just for us.'

Laurel's next dance with Colonel Southey was more like an erratic game of military hopscotch. They circled the floor in a series of hops and leaps and when the dance was over she tottered off the floor and would have tripped on the coconut matting had it not been for Sam Bennett, who caught her in mid-flight.

'My favourite Girl Friday, trying to do somersaults!' he grinned.

'Thank you, Sam.'

She recovered herself and introduced the two men, who immediately went stiff-legged like a pair of dogs bristling for a fight. Typically Sam ended the moment by taking Laurel's arm.

'Show me where they keep the drinks in this pub, Laurel. Good to meet you, Colonel.'

After a few steps Laurel protested to him,

'I don't think that was very nice of you, Sam.'

'I'm not nice—you should know that. That's why we get on.'

Finesse was not Sam's forte, and Laurel liked it. He tapped the stallion on her shoulder.

'He's shining bright tonight. Shall we make him do his little act again?'

Laurel pursed her lips at him.

'That was just for once, Mr Bennett.'

'Then maybe I'd better find you a tiger next?'

'Maybe you had. I like tigers.'

Sam grinned.

'This is turning into a big game hunt. I think we're going to have a ball!'

He looked round for Susan, guiltily aware that he should be staying close to her this evening. His attraction to Laurel was that of the rough hunter after the gazelle. He found her porcelain beauty fascinating, tempting to break, and the fact that she had confessed to him that he was the only man to bring her to orgasm had stirred his machismo.

Susan was standing on the other side of the dance floor, talking to the Colonel. Her long blonde hair was smooth and immaculate, and from that distance there was no trace of her disfigurement. As he looked she threw back her head and laughed, and he saw again the beauty he had married. Despite the fact that she could not see him he shuffled his feet uneasily.

When Ginette and David returned to the marquee they were greeted by Daphne and Martin Webber. Daphne was flouncing up and down in a yellow creation that appeared to have come from a dressmaker without an iron. Martin had the over-precise manner of the partly drunk and this, combined with a generous drag at a toke, had put him into a world half removed from reality.

Since the night of the murder he had thought of little else. Every tinkle on his doorbell heralded the police and his consumption of alcohol and pot had taken a pole-vault. He peered forward at David, his nose twitching over the brush of his moustache.

'How is our surgical friend this eve?' he queried.

'Fine, Martin. What goes in the art world? You had a narrow escape the other night.'

'What? What? Where was that?' The narrow eyes flickered around as if looking for an escape.

'The murder. Next door to you, wasn't it? Lucky they didn't come and do you.'

David was only having a little go at Martin for fun and was surprised at the force of his reaction.

'I don't keep drugs in my place, I'll tell you! That's what they were after. China was after the dragon.'

The band swung into a selection of fast rock music and David and Ginette stood watching the dancers. Laurel went past, trying to cope with Sam's idea of rock 'n' roll. Ginette squeezed David's hand.

'Isn't that the chap we had in who nearly lost his wife?'

'Correct. Now he's my wife's employer.'

'She looks as though she's putting in overtime!'

Across the other side of the room Susan was thinking exactly the same as she watched Laurel and Sam dancing together. The difference was that while Ginette had no particular love for Laurel, Susan had grown to regard her with a hate engendered only within a woman who sees her life, her man and her home, endangered.

Something must have transmitted her thoughts to Sam, because he took Laurel off the floor, returned her to Sir Ralph's crowd and went to Susan. As he approached she smiled at him, telling herself to stay in control, to be nice and not play the jealous wife. Stay cool, girl, she thought, stay cool and get rid of the bitch.

Sam appraised Susan as he was walking towards her. She looked superb in the russet dress, no doubt about it, and those emeralds he had found for her in Burma were something. Her figure was her greatest asset. It had not changed since her days on the beach at Bondi. My curvy blonde, he had called her then, and she was now. His uncomfortable thoughts about his recent attitude made him try harder.

'Let's dance,' he smiled. 'You're looking good.'

She smiled at him in return and took his arm as they walked to the floor. They had always danced well together. Sam was not a natural, but Susan was, and she made up for his deficiencies so that he thought he was better than he was. She was not really up to dancing yet after her surgery, but was determined not to let it show.

They glided off together, and she thanked her stars it was not a rock 'n' roll number. As they twirled she could feel stabbing pains shooting through her pelvis, but she smiled at him and twirled again, treating the ballroom as a battlefield.

David and Ginette together had not gone unremarked. Martin Webber was talking to Laurel along with the Southeys and the Abelsons. He knew Molly had a weakness for David and he could not help dripping poison slyly into the vein.

'Looks like the medics are clinging together tonight.'

He twitched his head in the direction of Ginette and David. Their preoccupation with each other was obvious, even at a distance. Laurel's eyes narrowed fractionally as she followed Martin's indication.

'That's his theatre sister. I expect they're talking about their work next week.'

'She's a beauty and a half,' persisted Martin, enjoying putting the knife in.

'Beauty? It depends what you regard as beauty. I think she's common.'

Ralph Abelson picked that up and snorted.

'Common? Damme, that's one thing she ain't! She's my cousin.'

If Susan had been with them Laurel's put down would have made her evening. David and Ginette, oblivious of all this, went to the buffet tent and stood before a groaning board bearing whole cold salmon, their pink flesh decorated with cucumber, lemon, split olives and yellow mayonnaise. Ribs of roast beef reared up from white damask tablecloths and York hams sat on porcelain carving stools. Vast bowls of multi-coloured salads jostled with plates of scarlet gambas. Varieties of skewered sausage were lined alongside an array of Scandinavian smoked fish. A waterfall of bright red crabs and lobsters cascaded into an ice lake of oysters. Further down the line were bowls of sweets, trifles, fruit and several whole Stiltons, each wrapped around the waist with a white cloth.

Ginette groaned in amazement.

'I've never seen anything like it! A true-blue cornucopia!'

They ate oysters and drank champagne, then went back for salmon and gambas and sat together at a corner table. David showed her how to shell the gambas without tearing her hands. She bit into the delicate white flesh with relish, looking up at him with a smile.

'Delicious! Go on, tell me I'm eating too much.'

'Never. I like to see you enjoying yourself.'

'It's awful. I have an enormous appetite.'

He looked at her over his glass with a quirky smile.

'So have I—truly enormous.'

Ginette looked back at him quickly and smiled somewhat shyly.

'I hope you get an opportunity to satisfy it.'

'So do I.'

From the dance tent came the seductive strains of a romantic waltz.

David listened to the music while watching Ginette over his glass, and the thought came to him that her connection with the Abelsons might well explain her affluence.

CHAPTER SEVENTEEN

DAVID awoke to see the morning sun streaming through a crack in the bedroom curtains. He felt a sense of anticipation. Laurel stirred and David got out of bed and went into the shower. The cold water needling on his skin refreshed him, and as he towelled himself dry he heard Laurel move again. In the morning she was at her waspish worst, especially after a party.

He walked into the bedroom feeling like a torero entering the bullring. She was sitting up in bed, doing her nails, and eyed him frostily.

'What's got you up and doing so early?' she wanted to know.

He looked at the gold carriage clock on the chest of drawers.

'Ten-thirty. It's hardly dawn, and we're already late if we're going to be on time at St Athelstan's. You know how he counts the minutes.'

'You don't think I'm going to bloody traipse all the way there after last night, do you? We can go next week instead. Ring the Matron and tell her we can't make it.'

'No way.' He pointed a finger at her, his voice hard as steel. 'You get out of bed and get dressed. That boy lives for our visits, and I'm not going to disappoint him just because you've had a night out and won't make the effort. Now shift!'

Laurel looked as though she had been hit, but she moved. David seldom spoke to her like that and in a frigid silence she dressed. They were about to leave when the telephone rang. It was Mark Slater.

'David, I'm sorry, but we've got a real problem here. Can you come in?'

David's eyebrows went up like a lift.

'This isn't my weekend on take, Mark—you should know that. Gerry Rodgers is on call.'

'Yes, I know, I've rung him, but his wife says he's just put a garden fork through his foot and can't even stand.'

'What's the problem?' asked David.

'Farmworker got his hand torn off in a thresher and we've got the hand. It's your country.'

David hesitated, although he knew he had no choice.

'I'll be with you.'

He turned to Laurel, who was looking at him with grim satisfaction.

'So it's off to the sick, lame and lazy, is it?' she drawled.

'Gerry Rodgers is on and he's out of action. It's going to mean arterial reconnection, which is my pigeon anyway. You go on in your car and I'll follow later. It's going to be a lot later.'

'Seems hardly worth it,' Laurel shrugged.

'It's worth it. Even for five minutes it's worth it. Give James my love and tell him I'll be along later for certain.'

David parked the car in his customary place. One of the perks of being a consultant was that you had your own parking spot with your car number on it. Mark Slater met him in Casualty and took him to examine the patient.

David was glad to see that Staff Nurse Gotch was not on duty. Since the episode of the frayed ligature the less he saw of her the better. They changed in the surgeons' dressing-room, and as David emerged, tying his mask at the back of his head, he bumped into Ginette.

'Well, don't you meet the nicest people round here!'

She smiled at him and he felt a warm glow as they looked at each other. Last night's aura was still very much with them.

'I thought this was your weekend off.'

They both said it, and then laughed at each other.

'How come you're here?' he asked.

'Same as you. They needed extra staff for your fancy surgery and asked me to come in. I'm second on call today. Anyway, I'm the only one who knows your fussy ways with arterial surgery.'

As she spoke he was conscious of a slight under-current of feeling between them, but could not put his finger on it. She seemed uneasy about something. Seconds later he realised what it was. She looked guilty. He thought about it and with the intuition of people who are close he knew why. She felt guilty about keeping back from him her upstage background. He squeezed her hand gently.

'Just one thing,' he told her.

'What's that?'

'I couldn't care if you lived in the Ritz itself.'

It was meant to reassure her. In one respect it did, but she wondered uneasily how he would feel about her lunch there with Dirk den Pol.

The operation, as expected, took a long time and it was late afternoon before David took his gloves off and walked wearily from the theatre. He declined tea, changed rapidly and was about to leave the theatre complex when Ginette appeared in the corridor.

'I thought you'd like to know that I've been checking through our stocks of catgut 000,' she told him. 'It's all perfect, and I've opened a couple of samples and gone over every inch of them. It was frayed deliberately.'

'You reckon it was Sandra Gotch for sure?'

Ginette nodded.

'Why would she do it?'

'To get back at me because I made her report sick and because she's gunning for my job. If I make a serious mistake and it shows up then I'm out and she's in. Do you think we should report our suspicions?'

David thought carefully about the possible repercussions and shook his head.

'Listen, I've got to go. It's James's visiting day, and I'll only have half an hour with him as it is.'

She smiled and nodded understandingly at him.

'Don't worry.'

He kissed his finger, laid it briefly on her lips, and was turning to leave when a nurse came running up the corridor. She slowed to a walk when she saw Ginette's disapproving look.

'Mr Compton, there's a call for you on the corridor phone.'

David's forehead creased in annoyance.

'Get Dr Slater to take it, would you? I have to go.'

'It's from the school, sir. They said it was urgent.'

He strode past her to the telephone booth and put his head inside the acoustic cubicle.

'Mr Compton.'

'This is Matron, Mr Compton. I'm afraid there's been an accident with your son and your wife.'

David felt ice in his veins and had to clear his throat to speak.

'Is he all right?' he demanded.

'Yes. They both are, but your wife was very shocked. She's in Henley Hospital.'

'What happened?'

'They both fell into the lake. Apparently your wife jumped in when James fell and was in danger of being dragged down by his calipers. They were lucky to be rescued by the groundsman.'

'I'm on my way,' said David tersely.

Ginette saw his expression and looked at him

questioningly. Briefly he told her.

'Ring me when you know more about it,' she said. 'I'm off duty tomorrow.'

He nodded, and clattered his way down the stone steps towards the car park. As James was apparently unharmed David thought he had better see Laurel first to get the story.

He drove at a speed that took him through bends with the Triumph shifting sideways, the tyres at their limit of adhesion. On the straight past Nettlebed his foot was on the floor, the wind noise loud in his ears, the car vibrating protestingly.

He was concentrating so fiercely on the road ahead he did not see the flashing lights behind him or hear the police gong above the wind noise. Finally it was the loudhailer that drew his attention.

'This is the police. . .!'

He slowed and the police car overtook him. It stopped in front of him at the roadside, lights blinking. A burly policeman in a peaked cap walked back to him and leaned on the car as David wound down the window.

'Do you realise you were breaking the speed limit, sir?' The voice had the patient resignation born of a thousand such encounters.

'Yes, I do, Officer. My son has just had an accident and my wife has been admitted to Henley Hospital and. . .' David outlined his problem, and the policeman looked sympathetic.

'May I see your driving licence, sir?'

With a sigh of frustration David fished it out of his wallet and handed it over.

'Do you still work at the Manbury Hospital, Mr Compton?'

'Yes, I do.' David could not think what this had to do with speeding along the Nettlebed road.

'You may remember my daughter, Linda Shawcross?'

David did remember her—a little girl of seven who had fallen off her horse and broken a leg.

'Yes, I do.'

He felt like a parrot.

'She walks a treat now, sir. Doesn't limp a bit.'

'I'm very glad,' said David.

The driving licence was handed back.

'Follow us, Mr Compton. Henley Hospital, you said?'

'That's right.'

The police car moved away, followed by a wondering David. He did not wonder for long. Still with lights flashing, it took off at a speed that had him wondering if the Triumph could keep it in sight. The police driver was a master, and what traffic there was drew aside as they fled in tandem through the dark. There were times when David's scalp prickled, but the lead car never slackened speed. When they drew up outside Henley Hospital the burly policeman wound down his window and waved a hand.

'There you are, Mr Compton, and thanks.'

The police tail-light was away before David emerged from his car. Laurel was sitting up in bed when he arrived. Even in a hospital nightdress she managed to look groomed and glamorous. She gave him a wan smile.

'Hello, David.'

He sat on the bed and looked at her.

'What happened?' he asked.

'James was reaching for his yacht on the pier, lost his balance and fell in. I went after him, but I'm not very good in water, as you know, and it was deep and I got stuck in the weeds. I thought we were both going to drown. Oh, David, it was dreadful!' Her eyes began to fill with tears.

'What about James?' he demanded.

'James is fine. The groundsman pulled him out first.'

'How do you feel now?'

'Just a bit shaky. I swallowed a lot of water and choked a bit, but I'm all right really. They say I can go the day after tomorrow.'

'I told James he wasn't to go on that landing stage,' said David sternly.

'I know, but he was so keen to sail his boat.'

David stood up.

'I'd better go and see him now before he goes to bed. Will you be well enough to get yourself back home?'

Laurel nodded.

'Don't worry about me—I'll be fine.'

At St Athelstan's James was in his dressing-gown when David arrived. He was sitting on his bed, his calipers off, and flung his arms round David's neck as he bent over him.

'Oh, Daddy, I knew you'd come! Did you manage to put that poor man's hand back?'

David gave him a hug.

'Yes, I think so. How are you?'

'Fine. I did get wet, though. Mr Tallboys pulled me out. It's a good job he was there.'

'Tell me what happened?'

'Mummy took me on to the landing stage so I could sail my yacht, and as I was putting it into the water I fell in. I felt her grab me hard on the back to try and save me, but it wasn't any good. Then my calipers pulled me under the water. I was frightened!'

David put his arm round his shoulder.

'Don't worry, my son. It's all OK now.'

James looked at him appealingly.

'Daddy, I don't think I like it here any more. Couldn't I come and live at home?'

David felt as though his heart would break. He patted the boy on the back.

'Not just yet, James. Maybe one day.'

He thought of Laurel and knew that the day would be a long way off, even though the boy was improving all the time. Then he thought of Ginette and what her answer would have been in the same situation. He despaired of ever being able to spend any worthwhile time with his son. Soon the years would flit by, and he would not have known him with that family closeness that only comes with time spent together.

He helped his son out of his dressing-gown and tucked him into bed. As he bent over him and kissed him goodnight he whispered in his ear,

'Maybe that day won't be too long now.'

He would have been less confident had he been able to overhear a conversation between the groundsman and his wife that evening. The worthy Ned Tallboys was relating to his wife the events of the afternoon when he had rescued James and Laurel from the water.

'I tell you, Maureen, I seen it only from a long way, and I don't want you to repeat this to no one, but it seemed to me that she wasn't so much as trying to save him as give the little lad a push.'

Which was exactly what David was wondering as he drove away from St Athelstan's.

Tinker's muscles bunched and glistened under his black skin as he bent, twisted and swayed before the exercise mirror, his fists scribing circles in the air with the heavy weights. He was naked but for a black nylon G-string, and the bright lights in the gymnasium made the droplets of sweat on his skin sparkle like diamonds on a jeweller's velvet.

His bare feet gripped the mat and he grunted with each exertion. The pain of it was mirrored in the tightness of his mouth and the flare of his nostrils, but he did not falter in the precise sequence of the prescribed exercise schedule.

Tinker was a fitness fanatic, and his dedication to it was reflected in the superb condition of his herculean frame. He owed his physical strength and beauty to his Ashanti forebears, and from them too he had inherited a natural arrogance, for his grandfather had been a chief.

He finished with the weights and sprang into an attitude of karate attack, held it for a split second and began a series of lightning-fast moves finishing with a roundhouse kick, a *mawashi-geri*, that would have felled an elephant.

Finally he put his hands on his lean hips, rose on his toes and did a high kick that brought his knee to his forehead. He swivelled on the ball of his foot and kicked backwards and sideways, danced a brief two-step and delivered a similar set of moves with his left leg. An expert in the martial arts would have recognised the moves of *la savate*, the French art of kick fighting, as elegant as the ballet and as dangerous as playing kiss with a cobra. Tinker was watching himself in the mirror, his face expressionless, the flat look in his eyes denying the handsome arrogance of his Ashanti features.

Tinker was clever, intelligent and immensely capable. He was also a psychopath. His fanaticism for fitness was only a means of ensuring the gratification of his two great appetites, drugs and women, preferably unwilling women. Being a psychopath he knew what he was doing and that it was wrong, but was totally uncaring as long as he thought he would avoid retribution, which he always did.

He worked as a computer maintenance technician and lived on the edge of the town in a converted loft, over a garage. He had done the conversion himself and

built the gymnasium into it. The remainder of the flat
consisted of a long living-room, one bedroom, kitchen
and bathroom. The living-room was furnished with a
white leather three-piece suite. Massive loudspeakers
stood like the statues of Rameses at the end of the
room serving a complex hi-fi arrangement alongside
an IBM computer on a white marble table.

The entrance to Tinker's loft was by a wooden
outside staircase. As China tramped up it the sound of
Bach's *Mass in B Minor* from the big speakers made the
wooden walls vibrate. He did not recognise it, and
battered on the door to make himself heard above the
surging strains of the Credo. China stopped hurting his
bony knuckles on the door and gave it a kick.

It was a Sunday morning, he had felt too sick to have
breakfast and the amphetamine he had taken was not
having its customary effect except to give him the jitters
and a headache. When Tinker opened the door,
dressed in a white towelling gown, he pushed past him
into the main room.

'Christ, man, what a row!'

Tinker was a devotee of classical music, but the
intricacies of Bach's Mass were lost on China. The big
black went over to the hi-fi, flicked a switch, and the
ensuing silence was as loud as the previous music.

'You're looking bad, China,' he remarked. 'What's
your problem?'

'Give us a drink, man. I really need it.'

Patiently Tinker sloshed Scotch into a tumbler and
handed it to him. China gulped at it with both hands.

'You heard about Mac?'

Tinker nodded.

'You get some stuff out of the place?'

Tinker's priorities did not include mourning over
deceased friends.

'Nothing. We had to clear out quick.'

'Not quick enough, by the sound of it.'

'They didn't get me,' shrugged China.

Tinker looked at him speculatively, as a snake might look at a rabbit.

'Do you think they will?'

'Christ, no. Not as long as Martin keeps his trap shut.'

'How does he know?'

China told him how they had got into the chemist's shop. When he heard the story Tinker toyed at his lip with a long forefinger.

'You could be in for trouble, China. Drugs is one thing, but accessory to murder is big league. Martin decides to blow it and they'll have you inside long enough to wear out the key.'

China's face turned thinner and a murky grey. Tinker went into the bedroom and changed into jeans and a T-shirt.

'We'll pay Martin a call,' he decided. 'We haven't had a party in a long time, and I could do with some crack.'

China ran bony fingers through his greasy dreadlocks and looked apprehensive.

'Man, you're not looking to do anything special? That Martin, he'll be OK, and there's no other line we got on the hard stuff just now.'

China had seen Tinker in action before— unpredictable and dangerous as a rattlesnake one moment, mellow and full of honeyed words the next. Partnering Tinker in anything had all the attraction of bare-handed mamba grappling. They walked up the hill past the Bear and into Marlborough's High Street.

Sunday morning was rendezvous time at Martin's shop for the drug fraternity, and despite being at the ball for most of the previous night Martin was there. He was fitting glass into a frame when China and Tinker walked in, and his foxy features froze when he saw them.

'How's it, fellers?' he asked nervously.

'Fine, man, just fine. Tinker here just thought it'd be nice if you could fix up a party, and mebbe find us some crack.'

Martin's tiny moustache twitched to and fro with agitation. China made him uneasy, but the big black terrified him. He had seen him, at a party, hold a cat over a fire by the scruff of its neck. The animal had not been harmed because Tinker had put it back gently on a chair with a caress, but Martin knew with unholy certainty that he would just as soon have let it drop on to the red-hot coals.

'Where d'you want the party?' he asked.

Tinker turned from looking at a print by Schongauer. It had been left to Martin by a wealthy client and was the pride of his life. Near to it was a small watercolour by a local artist. He pointed to the print and picked up the watercolour.

'That's nice. How much is the watercolour?'

'Twenty-five pounds. Twenty-two fifty to you.'

Tinker said nothing. China leaned over the counter, the locks dangling on either side of his scrawny features giving him the look of a predatory weasel.

'Nobody been asking you about the job next door?'

Martin shook his head like a demented metronome. In fact the police had been round to ask if he had seen anything unusual, but he was too frightened to say so.

'You don't remember seeing me and Mac that night?'

Martin's head vibrated from side to side again. Tinker's fist levitated over the counter top. The fingers uncurled and the watercolour dropped from them, crushed to a tiny ball. Tinker put a twenty-pound note down and looked towards the Schongauer.

'Any chats to the police, and for that'—he nodded

towards the print—'I'm not going to pay.'

Martin felt the sweat drying cold on his neck. He put the note in the till, produced some polythene packets of white powder and pushed them across. His tongue rasped dry on his palate.

'On me,' he croaked.

Tinker palmed the packets with the dexterity of a Mississippi gambler and rewarded Martin with a friendly and reassuring smile. All trace of menace was gone, his handsome features radiated good fellowship. China leaned forward, grinning lewdly.

'Man, get that blonde nurse along. She's a turn!'

On the counter was a six-inch nail. Tinker was toying idly with it and threaded it beneath the middle finger of his right hand. As China spoke he made a fist and to Martin's fascinated horror the two ends of the nail bent up. He opened his hand and when the nail fell out it was almost a perfect U.

It did not take Martin long to organise a party. He had numerous contacts, and it boosted trade as everyone was charged. He had to make a special trip to London that week. Tinker's flat was a good place for a party as there were no nosy neighbours and the garage was closed at night.

Sandra Gotch arrived, to China's delight, and brought with her a friend from the nurses' home whose name was Lisa. She was a first-year nurse, with blue eyes and brown hair and the nervous air of a startled rabbit. When she saw Tinker rise up from the white leather sofa dressed in black leather trousers and a crimson shirt, she stared at him in awed fascination. He towered over her and smiled, showing gleaming white teeth, his whole being exuding a magnetic attraction.

Lisa felt her knees tremble.

'Could I sit down, please?'

Tinker took her hand and led her to the sofa. It was

so large she was almost lying down when she sat back on it. He sprawled beside her and handed her a glass of sparkling wine.

'Cocktail?'

She did not know what to say to this man who seemed like a being from another world.

'Er. . .thank you.'

He sprinkled some powder into her drink that made it fizz furiously. She drank it and opened her eyes wide.

'It's lovely! Makes your nose tickle.'

From the speakers came the dusky strains of '*Love Changes Everything*.' Tinker knew when to keep his Bach at home.

China applied himself to Sandra Gotch, who allowed herself to be monopolised while keeping a wary eye open for any good-looking newcomer. Dancing started at the end of the living-room. Tinker twirled the dimmer switch, put on synchronised lighting and reggae music with a pervasive beat that made the blue and green lights flash and Lisa dance in a way she had never dreamed. She pulsed her hips at Tinker. He grinned at her, picked her up in one hand and twirled her around like a circus act. She was wearing a blue skirt and jumper and her skirt fell back, revealing her white knickers.

The party applauded as Tinker twirled her faster and faster on his uplifted hand. Lisa shrieked with delight, high on the heroin, and when he lowered her to the floor and flipped off her pants with a practised motion of a big black hand she did a dance kick that landed her heel on his shoulder.

The party progressed.

More couples arrived, and Sandra Gotch espied a good-looking young man with a beard who took her fancy. China, however, was not to be put off. By this time he had inveigled Sandra on to his knee and had his hand well up her skirt. Over his shoulder she saw the young man watch their wrestling match with interest. He even went so far as to raise his eyebrows and smile at her.

That was enough for Sandra.

She was not inspired by the persistent approaches of China and was trying to think of a way of removing him when she saw a plastic packet on the table next to their glasses. Deftly she tilted the contents into his glass. When the effervescence had died down she picked it up and handed it to him.

'Have a drink, hero. It'll help you to keep your mind on your job.'

The bearded man caught her eye as she was doing this and gave her the thumbs-up sign. China, interpreting this as encouragement, swilled it down in one and returned to the attack. Already he had had a lot to drink, and Sandra hoped that the little extra she had slipped in would settle him so that she could pursue the intriguing man at the other side of the room. She was not prepared for what happened next.

China had a fit.

His face went blue, his mouth stretched into a sardonic rictus and he started to judder and then convulse. He foamed at the mouth, his head went back in spasm, his eyeballs bulged with the whites showing like a choking cod. Finally he fell on to the floor in a twitching heap.

Lisa ran across the room and the two nurses bent over China. Training took over with Sandra and she pulled his head back to allow him to breathe and maintain an airway. She looked up at Lisa.

'Ring 999 for an ambulance. Tell them it's an emergency.'

Tinker loomed over them. 'What cooks here?' he

wanted to know. He peered down at China, still blue and unconscious. 'That boy got too greedy on the coke. I seen that before.'

He bent down, picked up China without an effort and laid him on the sofa.

The ambulance men were knocking on the door within minutes. They put China on to a carrying chair and Sandra Gotch went with them.

'I'm a staff nurse at Manbury. I'll come with you.'

The two men exchanged glances as they loaded him aboard and they took off into the night with blue lights flashing and the gong rousing the town. Mark Slater was on Casualty duty that night. He too raised his eyebrows as they brought in China accompanied by Staff Nurse Gotch in a short dress and high-heeled sandals.

'What's the problem?' he asked.

She looked at him levelly.

'Cocaine overdose, probably. Self-administered.'

'You mean probably cocaine or probably self-administered?'

She went white.

'I mean, Dr Slater, that it's probably a cocaine overdose and that it was certainly self-administered.'

'You were there?'

He was busy inserting a Venflon needle to get a drip up.

'I can't see that that's any business of yours,' Sandra said coldly.

'It'll be plenty of yours if this guy drops off the hook! Now tell me what happened.'

'He was drinking and took a shot too many.'

Mark was looking in China's pupils. His breathing was getting slower. He seized a laryngoscope, inserted a tube into the trachea and connected it to the oxygen supply on the anaesthetic machine.

'Looks more like a massive heroin overdose to me,' he observed.

Sandra gasped. Maybe the white packet had been heroin. The thought had not occurred to her. If that was high-grade heroin then China was likely to die. Her mind flashed back to the scene and like a slow-motion picture she saw the good-looking boy watching her as she poured the powder into the fizzing drink. She even remembered his thumbs-up sign.

The thought struck her that he thought she was deliberately doing it, knowing what was in the packet. In that case, if China died she would be a murderer and the stranger would know.

'Oh, my God!' whispered Sandra, and slumped to the Casualty floor.

The following morning David was about to start a ward round, and as they were passing the intensive care unit Mark Slater stopped.

'Would you mind having a look at this patient while you're here? Came in last night with a massive heroin overdose. We filled him up with naloxone and had to put him on a respirator. He's alive, but he's in renal failure after his hypotension. Do you think we should dialyse him?'

He led the way into the unit. Staff Nurse Crisp handed him the notes and he looked down at China with a dawning sense of déjà vu. China looked terrible, and if it had not been for his dreadlocks David would not have recognised him from Sam Bennett's photographs. His dark skin was sallow, his cheeks sunken and his eyes unnaturally bright. He plucked constantly at the bedclothes, his nose ran copiously and he kept licking his lips, which were dry and cracked.

David scanned the notes, read the biochemistry results and then flicked to the front page to see the name. When he saw it his eyes widened. There it was in Staff Nurse Crisp's precise handwriting: Surname—St George, First name—China. David could not help himself. After Martin Webber's remark at the ball there had to be some sort of tie-up.

'Your name China?' he asked.

China nodded.

'Do you know anyone called Martin Webber?'

China looked desperately sideways as though wanting to escape. His voice came in a hoarse whisper.

'No. Never heard of him.'

'Was Mac, the Scotsman, a pal of yours?'

Another shake of the head, and a flash of spirit.

'What's this for? I don't have to put up with this. You're not a copper.'

David put the notes down and turned to Mark.

'On these figures I think you should dialyse him. Obvious renal failure, probably reversible.'

China's eyes followed David as he left the room. What he said brought a shocked reprimand from Staff Nurse Crisp.

'Shithead!'

To Staff Nurse Gotch, entering as David left, the word could not have sounded more beautiful. After her faint in Casualty she had recovered quickly, only to spend a sleepless night worrying about China and whether he would live. The bearded man had seen her put the heroin in China's drink, she was sure of that. If China died and the man told the police she was convinced she would be arraigned for murder.

When she nearly bumped into David the following morning at the entrance to the intensive care unit she was twittering with anxiety, and when she heard China shout 'Shithead!' she nearly wept with relief. She was at first appalled at his appearance, but that feeling was soon replaced by relief when she knew there would be no chance of her being on a murder charge. With the relief came a surge of adrenalin and, perversely, a determination, somehow, to get at Ginette. Sandra Gotch was not only jealous of Ginette's position as senior sister, she was also jealous of everything else about her.

Ginette, with her natural elegance and confident manner, was all that Sandra would have liked to have been, but knew she could never be. Where Ginette bred trust and admiration, Sandra roused natural antipathy; where Ginette sympathised, Sandra was full of reproof; when Ginette embraced a crying child it would stop, if Sandra did so it yelled all the louder. Whenever things went wrong for Sandra she would eventually lay the trail to Ginette's door.

Another time, if a ligature slipped, she would make doubly sure the fault would be traced back to Ginette. It was just a pity about the Scotsman and the way the post-mortem had come out.

David, on the other hand, was wondering about China. It seemed a remarkable coincidence that he should be on Sam's list and in with an overdose close to the time that the Scotsman had been admitted after robbing and murdering the chemist.

Had China been in on the robbery? Had he, in fact, killed the chemist?

He decided it was all very speculative and that it was not his job to run to the police every time he had an idea.

It could also lead to too many questions about Mac's death.

CHAPTER EIGHTEEN

AN INSISTENT tapping at the bedroom window awoke David earlier than usual. His eyes opened and his gaze flicked to the small side window overlooking the downs. It was uncurtained and inside the window was a ledge on which Laurel kept four porcelain figurines; characters from *The Wind in the Willows*.

Outside the window and striking furiously at it with his beak was a huge black crow, intent on getting at the tiny animals. David watched with interest until he feared the glass would shatter before the predatory beak. He sat up, the striking stopped and the bird, looming black at the window, stared at him with beady malevolence before flapping away. He followed its lazy flight to the nearby woods, looked at his watch and picked up the telephone.

Ginette's voice had the husk of sleep. He pictured her in bed, her copper hair spread over the pillow. In his mind's eye it made a beautiful and romantic picture.

'Did I wake you?' he asked.

'No,' she lied, smiling to herself with sleepy delight at his call. 'Where are you?'

'I'm at home.'

'What about. . .' She hesitated.

'She's in Henley Hospital. They kept her in for several nights for observation and to get over the shock of falling in the lake.'

'What happened?'

He told her briefly.

'David, are you sure James is all right? It must have been an awful feeling being dragged down!'

The concern in her voice was obvious, genuine and reached to his heart.

'He's fine physically, but he seemed more emotion-ally upset. Said he didn't like it there any more and wanted to come home. I only wish he could.'

'Why can't he?' Ginette's voice was hard.

'Laurel won't have it. No, that's wrong, she can't have it. The nursing side upset her so much she had a break-down, and she spent three months in a nursing home.'

There was a silence, and Ginette changed the subject.

'Are you still in bed?'

'Yes, are you?'

She nodded into the telephone. 'Yes.'

'I wish I was with you,' said David deeply.

'I wish you were with me too.'

'You'd be late on duty.'

'I can't think why,' smiled Ginette.

'Would you like me to tell you?'

She wriggled deliciously. 'Not now. When we're together.'

'What are you wearing under that uniform of yours today?' he wanted to know.

'Mr Compton!'

'Don't you Mr Compton me!'

Her voice was gentle and teasing.

'I think you'd better get up and have a cold bath, or you won't be fit on parade.'

David had a sudden thought.

'Would you like me to take you in?' he asked. 'I can drop you back tonight—save your petrol.'

'That would be fun, but you'll never make it.'

He looked at his watch. With a push he could just do it.

'Into uniform, Miss Irving, and I'll pick you up right away. 'Bye.'

He put the telephone down and leaped out of bed with all the excitement of a boy going to the circus for the first time. As he drove into the courtyard, past the lions on the gateposts, David saw Ginette standing on the steps of the Georgian building. She was wearing her sister's uniform and a cloak. With her white starched cap and her straight figure he thought she looked like a star on a film set.

He had barely stopped before she was in the car. He gunned the engine and they shot through the gateposts, leaving the lions keeping vigil through a cloud of dust.

Ginette put a hand on his knee.

'You're a mad, mad boy!' she laughed.

They skirted dangerously past a farm cart on the country road, their offside wheels thumping on the grass verge. She looked at the speedometer flickering at seventy-five.

'At this rate we'll have time to stop for breakfast!'

David grinned at her and shouted above the noise of the wind in the open car,

'If we stop at all it'll not be for eating!'

She drew her knees primly together and wrapped her cloak around them.

'Just get us there in one piece and no questions,' she begged. 'And you'd better drop me at the far end of the car park. There's no point in inviting too many knowing remarks.'

They slid quietly into the hospital car park and she got out before David went on to his reserved space. He looked at his watch.

'Ten minutes to eight. You're OK.'

'What about tonight?' Ginette asked.

'I'll ring you from Outpatients when I'm finished. I'll drop you back on my way home. Laurel will be back, so I'd better not be late.'

David had no operating list that day; just a morning

round, a lecture to the nurses and an outpatient session in the afternoon. He went to his office and dictated reports. When his secretary arrived at nine with his mail he skimmed through it and with a sigh slit open a familiar envelope. His secretary opened all his mail, except those she recognised as being confidential, and this one was easily recognised. It was marked 'Private' in black and it was from the bank.

'. . .pleased to confirm that as of this date your current account has been credited with the sum of thirty thousand pounds. This does not yet bring your borrowing within our agreed limit, and should the situation be anything other than temporary perhaps you would be kind enough to let me know.'

It was signed by the under-manager. David quirked an eyebrow at it. He usually dealt with the manager himself, but perhaps this meant that the heat was coming out of the situation. He knew where the money had come from. Sam was a man of his word, whatever his other failings.

He clasped his hands on the desk and looked out of the window. He had done his best for Mac at the operation, but despite the pathologist's report he knew that the cardiac failure was precipitated by blood loss following the failure of the 000 ligature. Accepting Sam's money did not make him an assassin, but it brought it uncomfortably close, and what if it came out? Nobody would believe the truth.

There was a knock on his office door and Mark Slater's chubby face appeared round it.

'Good morning, David. Am I interrupting?'

David waved a hand at him.

'No, Mark—come in. Problems?'

'For once, no. Just the opposite. That chap with the heroin overdose, you remember?'

David nodded. 'OK, I hope?'

'Fantastic. You were right about the dialysis. I did it yesterday and this morning he's as frisky as a ferret on fire. Insisted on going home and took his own discharge. Just thought you'd like to know.'

'Thanks, Mark. I'll see you on the ward at ten.'

As Mark closed the door David reached for the telephone and rang Sam. He had resisted the temptation to tell him about China thus far, but the bank letter stifled his good intent. An impersonal voice with the echo of the ether to it answered.

'This number is transferred to 0533–780001 at no further charge to you. Please wait until you hear the ringing tone.'

Surprised, he waited. After a pause came the burring ring and Sam's voice above a background rumble.

'Bennett.'

'Sam, this is David.'

'Good morning, David. What can I do for you?'

'I want to talk to you. I've had a letter from my bank.'

'Good news, I hope?'

'That's why I want to talk to you. And there's one other thing.'

'Carry on,' said Sam.

'We've had another admission from your rogues' gallery. Fellow named China St George.'

'The West Indian?'

'Correct, but he went out this morning. Took his own discharge.'

'That's a pity,' Sam said. 'You won't have time to pick up your bonus, but I'll see you're looked after for the information.'

'Thank you, but I don't want the bonus. I'm happy to give you information, but the bonus is a no deal. I've done nothing to earn it, and I wouldn't if I had the chance.'

There was a pause and David wondered if they had been cut off.

'Are you still there?' he asked.

'I'm here—sorry about that. Some sod was trying to cut me up on the roundabout,' Sam explained.

'You're in your car? I rang your home.'

'Automatic transfer, I'm on the M4.'

'I don't like talking on the telephone,' said David. 'Can't we meet?'

'Sure. I'll be with you in four minutes. Your office?'

'Yes. I'll wait here for you.'

As he put down the instrument David shook his head. Dealing with Sam was like using a rapier against a man with a claymore. It was just six minutes before there was a knock on his door and Sam barrelled in. His square figure was clad in a beautifully cut chalk-stripe suit that could only have come from Savile Row, his shirt lay perfectly against his short neck and his tie, with its Windsor knot, was impeccably tied. Nevertheless there showed through it all the rough, tough builder who had clawed his way to the top.

He sat down in front of David and pulled out a Burma cheroot.

'David, I don't give a bugger what you do with the money. I paid you as I said I would and that's the end of it.'

'But I haven't done anything to earn it,' protested David. 'If I had it would have been murder.'

'That's right,' admitted Sam cheerfully.

'You're asking me to murder three men, given the chance, at thirty thousand pounds a time?'

'No. I said that if they died I'd add a nought on to what I'd already given you. I didn't say anything about your murdering them.'

'It's the same thing,' said David reasonably.

'I don't agree. You think about it. You're interpreting it the wrong way. As I see it, you're lucky to be under the tree to catch the apple when it falls. Nobody asked you to shake the bough. If you do, that's your business.'

David began to see how Sam had made his millions.

'I'm going to return that thirty thousand,' he said firmly.

Sam shook his head.

'Impossible. I don't know anything about it. Didn't come from me—try tracing it back. There's no way you'll do it.'

David began to feel like a man in Cloud-cuckoo-land.

'What am I going to do about it?' he groaned.

Sam grinned at him.

'Lie back and enjoy the inevitable, as the lady said. By the way, how's your boy? I hear he had an accident.'

'He's OK, Sam. Who told you? Laurel?'

Sam nodded and got to his feet.

'Let's hope China trips and breaks his neck on his way home—that should go a long way to solving your problems. Goodbye, David.'

He was gone, and David felt as though he had been in a fight.

Sam sat in the back of his car as his chauffeur waited for a taxi in front to draw away. Had he known he would have looked at it more closely. It was taking China back to his digs in Marlborough. When it reached Kingsbury Hill, on the edge of the town, China leaned forward and told the driver to go straight to Tinker's flat. There was just a chance that the big black might be at home, as he worked shifts.

He was lucky. Tinker answered the door, holding a forty-kilo weight in one hand as if it were a Coca-Cola bottle. His face creased into a big smile, showing a set of perfect white teeth.

'China boy, good to see you! You're looking better than when you left here.'

China followed him into the living-room and wasted no time on preamble.

'We got lots of problems, man,' he said briefly.

'So what kind of problem?'

'They can reach us.'

Tinker's features were suddenly expressionless, his geniality gone.

'Who's they?' he demanded.

'A feller at the hospital—a surgeon. Guy called Compton who's one of the bosses.'

'What the hell are you talking about, China?'

Tinker looked impatiently at the nervous West Indian, his eyes following him shrewdly. He pulled a toke out of a box on the table and handed it over. China took it gratefully and lit it, dragging the smoke deep into his lungs. He offered it back to Tinker, who shook his head, but took a pinch of white powder from another compartment and sniffed it up.

'I'm working myself up today, crack only. Now tell me what's on?'

'This Compton's a smart guy,' China explained. 'He knows about me and Mac. Somebody's been telling him things. He's made a five out of two twos, and that's going to bring the pigs here if he gets on to them.'

Tinker's eyes narrowed. Absentmindedly he wound the heavy weight in circles in the air.

'Who would talk to him? That nurse you were grabbing at the party? She works at the hospital. Maybe she's been opening her gab to him. You sure about this, China?'

China nodded, his lean face tense and worried despite the effects of the toke.

'He's got me tied in with Mac, and that'll nail me for the job at the chemist's. Then they'll jump at me for that doll in the forest. After that they're into you.'

Tinker whirled the weight around in a great circle as he thought. The sweat began to shine on his brow. China sat on the white leather sofa and watched him. Tinker picked up another set of matching weights and swung them around in a series of complicated circles and arcs. He had a natural grace and handled the eighty-kilo weights as though they were flags. Finally he lowered them gently to the floor and picked up a towel to mop his face.

'This guy got a car?' he asked.

China shrugged. 'How should I know?'

'Find out.'

In the late afternoon David had just seen the last of his patients. There was a knock on his door and Donna came in. Her black hair was carefully arranged and the cleavage of her red blouse lower than ever. She had spent ten minutes in the ladies' room before coming downstairs to see David at Mr Shaw's request. Any break from the office routine was welcome, especially if it meant a few moments with David Compton. She felt herself going pink as he greeted her in his usual breezy manner.

'Hi, Donna. You look as if you're going out on a date. Got a new boyfriend?'

She produced a file and put it on the desk.

'No, Mr Compton. Mr Shaw asked me to bring you this, it's the approved list of new theatre equipment. He asked me to tell you that he'd like your expenses for the visit to Lyons if it's ready.'

David grinned. Shaw was holding out the olive branch. He had been preparing his expense account at home.

'Certainly, but it's in my car,' he told her. 'You wouldn't like to get it for me? A tan folder on the passenger seat; you can't miss it. The passenger door's not locked.'

Donna dimpled at him. She would have walked naked through the freezing Thames for David.

'Would you like it back here, or shall I take it straight to Mr Shaw?' she asked.

'You can take it straight to the boss. Thanks, Donna, you're a treasure.'

Donna left him with a brilliant smile and a dip of her cleavage. As she tapped her way across the car park she caught sight of Donald Shaw looking out of the window and gave him a bright little wave. She stopped beside David's Triumph and peered through the window. The tan folder was there on the passenger seat. When she gripped the door handle it would not shift and she thought David had locked it after all. She paused. It was a long walk back to his office, and she gave the handle a firmer tug.

The explosion created a fireball that illuminated Donald Shaw's office before the shock wave blew in his plate glass window and all the front windows of Manbury Hospital. He was lucky to escape being cut to pieces by the flying glass. When he picked himself off the floor and looked out on the scene there was no sign of Donna and very little remained of the car.

From the aerial of a nearby Ford flew a bright red flag.

It was Donna's blouse.

'Who on earth would want to kill you?'

Laurel sat in the high-backed chair in the living-room of Apple Tree Cottage, sipped a dry sherry and quizzed David, who was at the piano idly playing chords from *Clair de Lune*.

It was late, and the confusion of the last few hours was gone. The police had snapped rubber bands around their notebooks, the sanitation squad had cleared the car park, and nurses and cleaners had swept up the glass from the wards.

Donna's body had been taken to the mortuary.

After endless questioning David had been picked up by Laurel and they had just returned home. He shook his head as his hands wandered over the keys, seeking peace in the music. He found it difficult to concentrate. In his mind he kept seeing the bright smile and black hair of the attractive Donna whom he had sent to die on his behalf.

'Somebody with a grudge, I suppose. You can't heal everybody in this game. Sometimes you make mistakes without knowing it, and there are people who never forget or forgive.'

David thought of Sam, but dismissed it. Sam was in no danger from him—quite the reverse, in an odd sort of way. His sensitive fingers sought the melody of *'Pavane for a Dead Infanta'*. Ravel's haunting strain suited and soothed his mood.

'You think there may be someone who holds a grudge against you?' asked Laurel.

'Possible,' shrugged David. 'Some soul who reckons I did a poor job and ruined their life. Don't forget the old saw that bones are not full of good red marrow, but black ingratitude. Nobody comes to mind, but you never know.'

'What are you going to do about transport in the morning? It's your early list.'

'Perhaps you could run me in?'

Laurel swung a nylon-clad leg briskly up and down.

'I suppose so, but I can't do it every day. And you can't borrow the BMW, it's the firm's.'

'I hadn't considered it,' he assured her.

'I thought you might as I shan't be using it for a few days.'

David arched an eyebrow, saying nothing. This always nettled Laurel and put her on the defensive.

'I'm needed for a business conference,' she told him.

'Where's that?'

'Phoenix, Arizona. One of Sam's companies has a big development going there. He wants me to take notes and organise the entertaining.'

'I'm sure you'll do that all right. How long will you be away?'

'Only four days. We're using the Learjet.'

'Big time,' said David drily.

'That's why they pay me so much money—to be there.'

'It doesn't seem to do us much good.'

'I'm not going to argue with you about that again, David!' Laurel snapped.

'I'm glad. It stops us waking the neighbours.'

Laurel tossed down the remainder of her drink and went upstairs abruptly. As she fell asleep the delicate strains of '*Traumerei*' floated into the night air.

The next morning the tension in the hospital was obvious. David was conscious of extra attention in the covert glances and outright stares as he walked into the main hall and up the stairs to the theatre block. He was a marked man, and he could feel the question in everyone's mind. Would it happen again? And where? And how?

The police came back in force and spent endless time questioning him and others about who might want to kill him and who had been seen in the hospital grounds who might not be on the staff. They even quizzed him on the clubs he belonged to now and when he was at university in case there was a political connection or someone with a grievance.

They wanted the details of every operation he had done when the patient had not recovered. They appeared tireless, and no detail was too small for them to make a note of it. Everything went into their computer. David felt particularly uncomfortable as they asked him about operation failures and they noted that there had been a recent one on a Scotsman.

'Anything special about that one, sir?' The young constable's face had been blandly innocent.

'No, nothing. He had a poor chance from the start owing to blood loss.'

As he said it David had an uncomfortable sensation as he visualised the frayed ligature.

He was glad that they were not asking him details about his finances and for a look at his bank statement. They might have noted a proximity between Sam's thirty thousand and the death, or at least the computer might have done. Had it not been for that particular sword of Damocles over him he might have voiced his suspicions about China. As it was, the less the police knew the better as far as he was concerned.

The sight of Ginette raised his spirits remarkably. She was smart, as always, in the simple theatre uniform of green skirt and shirt and green turban. There was a gaggle of nurses in the recovery area, and he smiled briefly at them.

'Good morning, ladies. Are we on stage and ready for the first act?'

There were self-conscious giggles and the gaggle broke up. Ginette turned to him with a disapproving frown, although her tone of voice was sympathetic as she tried to let him know that the horrors of the day before had touched her too.

'Mr Compton, I don't think that's the proper way for a consultant to address the nursing staff. Your first case is in the anaesthetic room, and I think it's time you scrubbed.'

The morning list was interrupted twice when David

was called into Casualty for emergencies which had the Casualty Officer worried. The second time he had to wait for Staff Nurse Gotch. She tried to be pleasant.

'That was a near thing, Mr Compton,' she observed.

'Yes, Staff Nurse.'

'Lucky for the mechanic too. If he'd got there before Donna he would have died instead of her.'

David looked at her.

'What mechanic?' he demanded.

'The one who was coming to service your car.'

'How do you know anyone was coming to service my car?'

Sandra bit her lip and smelled danger.

'Somebody rang here for you. Said they had to take your car for servicing and asked where it was.'

'Who was that?'

She was getting hot and rubbed sweaty hands behind her back.

'I don't know—I didn't ask,' she said nervously.

'Why not?'

She got more flustered.

'I don't know. It isn't usual to get that sort of call, and we were busy.'

'I take it you told the police this?' said David.

'Yes.'

She had not, but she was not going to admit it to him, and when he left Sandra Gotch heaved a sigh of relief. It was beginning to dawn on her that she knew who owned the voice on the phone. But if Tinker or China were found out they would inevitably implicate her as their source of information about David's car. Furthermore, the less that was found out about her attendance at their parties the better.

When she had been telephoned about the car the man had introduced himself as from Greenwood's Garage. She had not thought of it as being unusual until after the bomb, and now it had come to her that the voice was familiar because it was China's. If the investigation got close it could implicate her as an accessary, although she had given the information in all innocence.

She remembered the bearded man looking at her as she poured the powder into China's drink. If there was an investigation and he was asked, he might have an unhappy recall of the incident.

During the lunch break David told Ginette,

'I do my own servicing. I hadn't arranged for a mechanic to call.'

Ginette's big eyes opened wider than usual.

'What do you think it was about?' she asked.

'I think whoever called Sandra Gotch wanted to know which was my car so that they could plant the bomb. And I think Sandra does know who it was. I think she's lying to cover it up.'

'Why should she do that?'

David pulled at his ear, a sure sign he was concentrating.

'Because it's somebody she knows and wants to protect, for whatever reason. However, she said she'd told the police when I asked her, so maybe I'm wrong.'

Ginette shook her head.

'It's pretty far-fetched. Car bombers aren't common company for nurses.'

'No, and innocent surgeons aren't usually their target. Belfast maybe, but not here in sleepy old Wiltshire.'

They finished the cold ham sandwiches from the canteen, and Ginette stood up.

'We'd better move, you've still got a cholecystectomy and a femoral graft to do.'

David turned to Mark Slater.

'Call Sister le Feuvre on Female Surgical and tell her

we'll be late doing the round, or she'll not be best pleased.'

Despite this precaution they were later than ever. Sister le Feuvre, dragon extraordinary, wasn't happy, and it was six-thirty before they finished and David went to his office. He had barely started dictating into the machine before the telephone rang.

'It's me.'

'Hello, me.'

Despite his fatigue he smiled. Ginette had a voice full of breathless anticipation.

'Have you got a new car?' she asked.

'No, why?'

'Then how are you getting home?'

He laughed.

'I just hadn't given it a thought. Taxi, I suppose, like you last night.' He brightened with a thought. 'Unless you'd like to give me a lift?'

'My God! You don't mind, do you? What would your wife think if you drove up with me? I'd need armour plate!'

'Not so. She's abroad.'

There was a silence, and in a different voice Ginette said, 'Where's she gone?'

'America—Phoenix, to be precise. Flew off this morning with her boss on some big property deal.'

'Oh.'

He heard her voice, heavy as lead shot with disappointment, and cursed himself. The day had been so busy, his mind so taken up with other things, he had not thought to take the opportunity to be with Ginette. He had considered discussing Sandra with the police, but on reflection had decided against it. You never knew where something, once started, was going to stop.

He clambered to make amends to Ginette.

'I thought we might have dinner tonight,' he told her.

'Are you sure you want to?'

From the voice he knew he had still some way to go.

'Of course I'm sure. How about the Highwayman near Cirencester? Nice big steak and a Gaelic coffee?'

Ginette had a healthy appetite and he knew these were two of her favourites. It was bribery, naked and unashamed.

'You go for a girl's weakest spots!' she laughed.

'Every time. If I can find them.'

'The car park in ten minutes?'

'Nine and a half.'

David put the telephone down and gabbled into the dictaphone, his tiredness gone. Ginette lost her brief pang of disappointment that he had not made more attempt to see her in Laurel's absence. The bomb incident had brought home to her how precious was their relationship. She did not want to waste a moment in foolish recriminations.

She made the car park in eight minutes exactly. David was only just able to fit into her Morris Minor. He sat in the passenger seat, his legs spiked up like a daddy-long-legs, and she laughed as she pulled at the starter.

'I don't think the designers had you in mind when they built this car!'

'I would have thought you would have gone for something rather more dashing.' He was unable to resist the little dig.

'I like to keep a low profile,' Ginette explained.

'Don't you think that's a form of snobbery?'

'No, I don't. Self-protection, if you like. I don't want the nurses to think I'm too toffee-nosed for them, and this way I don't attract men on the make.'

'You mean on the make for money?'

'Precisely.'

'Are you very wealthy, then?' asked David directly.

Ginette hesitated.

'Yes, as a matter of fact I am.'

He sat back in the car seat and said nothing after that.

The Morris hooted as they went round a bend and into the slope of Wootton Bassett. Ginette hooted again as they entered the drive to her flat and even the lions seemed to sit up straighter.

Ginette settled David on the big Knoll couch with its tasselled posts and put a large Scotch in his hand.

'There it is. Malt whisky, Bowmore, water and no ice.'

He raised an eyebrow at her. 'How did you know that?'

'Attention to detail, as you always say. It's a houseman's job to know his chief's likes and dislikes. So I asked Mark. Simple. Now stay there while I change.'

He sat and savoured the whisky. It was his favourite, smoky and with a hint of peat in it. He began to relax and looked around the room, some of the furniture familiar from his last visit. He stood and went to the mantelpiece to inspect the bronze dancer. He was so taken with it that he did not hear Ginette return until the music of 'La Traviata' swelled behind him.

She was standing by the sideboard, the hem of her green kaftan in her hand, and pirouetted towards him, her hair loose and swirling. She ended in his arms, her face looking up, her lips moist and parted. He held her close and whispered in her ear,

'What's this? Hardly the rig of the day for the Highwayman.'

'You've been hijacked, kidnapped, netted like a salmon. We're not going to the Highwayman. I'm giving you dinner here. Just us, with candles and romantic music and the servants' night off.'

He kissed her, holding her to him with unashamed hunger until she pushed him gently away.

'Steady! Come and help me do the dinner.'

Her kitchen was small and neat and equipped with all the most modern equipment. A blue Aga occupied the whole of one wall and the remainder were taken up with cabinets and gadgets. David leaned against the kitchen door, watching her work, enjoying the sight of her graceful, fluid movements under the kaftan.

Ginette felt his gaze on her and it gave her a warm sense of anticipation. She heard him take a step as she was bending over the refrigerator and her spine tingled, but he was only inspecting the herb rack.

She opened the door of a deep-freeze, extracted some chicken pieces and put them into a microwave to defrost. From a vegetable cupboard appeared onions, chicory, green and red peppers, celery and mushrooms. She produced a knife like a machete and an immense wooden block.

'You're the cutter—get busy on these. Onions in rings, across the chicory in one-inch bites, the peppers and mushrooms in slices.'

He used the machete on the onions with unconscious expertise, but spent so much time watching her that he narrowly missed chopping his finger. There was a sense of excitement in the narrow confines of the small room that they could both feel. Ginette's voice developed a high-toned breathlessness David recognised as a sign of mounting tension when they were in theatre. Why should it happen here in the kitchen of her own home?

That was when he nearly cut his finger, and when he exclaimed at the narrow squeak she turned, her reactions over-fast, and looked at him, her eyes wide and her pupils large.

'What was that?' she asked.

'Nothing. Just nearly ruined my career.'

Ginette returned to the deep-freeze and extracted a plastic bag of bilious green mixture. That followed the chicken into the microwave. She fried chopped garlic in a pan of butter, added the onions and then the peppers and mushrooms, with a generous sprinkling from several herb jars. The chicory she tossed in oil and put in the refrigerator. David cleaned the knife while she was adding the fried vegetables and wine to the chicken before returning it to the microwave. She kissed him lightly on the lips. He put his hands on her waist and tried to drag her to him, but she resisted.

'Now sit down and enjoy your drink while I do the fiddly bits.'

He watched her setting the table, carefully arranging porcelain plates, silver cutlery and delicate long-stemmed wine glasses. She lit two tall candles which reflected a flickering shine off the mahogany table and stood back to view it all. When she turned to him, smiling and happy, he wondered to himself what he had been given. She held out a hand.

'Give me your glass. I'll pour you a second drink and join you while the dinner's cooking.'

They sat, side by side on the sofa, holding hands like children. Rachmaninov's Second Piano Concerto entranced them both, sweeping them together in a thrilling crescendo. She looked sideways at his dark, clear-cut features, the eyes deep-set and closed now as he listened to the first movement. The strain of recent events and the crushing work load were etched in the lines on his face.

Ginette wondered what he was thinking now that she had told him about her wealth. Despite herself she felt an apprehensive twinge. She could not free herself from the memory of Simon Falconer. When the music finished she stood up.

'I'll bring it in and you can pour the wine.'

David went to the dining-table, picked the wine out of the ice-bucket, looked at the label and whistled—Chevalier-Montrachet 1971. The sort of wine he had only drunk on return visits to Magdalen for Gaudy dinners. Thoughtfully he poured it out.

Ginette came in with a French soup tureen, complete with lid and ladle. She put it on the table and ladled it out. It was green, almost matching her dress. David eyed it dubiously.

'What is it?'

'*Soupe de poisson*—fish soup. Try it.'

He did. It was a garlic-laden dream of the sea and rocks and faraway places. He raised his glass to her.

'Here's to the cook.'

'Here's to us.'

The wine smelled of oak and fruit, dry and full-bodied. He rolled it on his tongue.

'Do you always drink this?' he asked.

Ginette smiled at him over the candles.

'By the barrel. I buy it at the Co-op.'

'Seriously. This stuff is not a common item on supermarket shelves.' He was too intrigued to let it go.

'Present from Papa,' she explained. 'I've kept it for a special occasion.'

'And this is it? Do you think it warrants it?'

'Every bit.'

'Then good for Dad. He sounds a discerning man. What does he do?'

'He's a doctor, and a great wine buff.'

David laughed. 'I should have known!'

They finished the soup and Ginette served the chicken and the chicory salad. The salad was crisp and bitter and made the chicken taste as if it had come from a Creole kitchen in New Orleans. They both ate heartily and David, intrigued, asked,

'How did you learn to cook like Escoffier's aunt?'

'Papa. It's his hobby.'

'I think I'd like to meet your dad,' said David.

Ginette nodded approvingly.

'I think I'd like you to.'

'Not tonight, though.'

'I love him dearly, but tonight he'd be *de trop*.'

After dinner she made him coffee and they danced by candlelight, the flickering shadows moving seductively around them. When they stopped they were both breathless. As they stood together David could feel the heat of her breasts through her kaftan and his shirt. His hands on her back slid down to her buttocks. She was wearing nothing under the robe.

'David.' Her voice was low and husky. He could only just hear what she said. 'What are we going to do?'

Without replying he picked her up and took her across the room, kicking open the bedroom door.

CHAPTER NINETEEN

THE MOON was full, its silver beams through the big Georgian windows illuminating the fourposter bed which stood like a stage at the far end of the room. David laid Ginette gently down and sat on the edge of the bed. The moonlight gave her an entrancing, ethereal beauty. Saying nothing, she put out her hands, cupped his face and drew him down. This was their moment and they both knew it. This was the moment they would remember all their lives, their Rubicon. After this there would be no going back.

Ginette had a moment of panic as she remembered telling him she was wealthy. Had this spurred him on?

For his part, David looked at her and wondered. What, after all, did he know about her? Why was she wealthy? Had there been more to her past than she admitted? He put it away from him and reached for her silky neck, his fingers sliding around her in a grip that had barely the touch of a butterfly's wing. Delicately, his fingertips went behind her neck and he felt her arch at his touch.

Through the thin fabric of her kaftan he traced down the deep curve of her spine and whispered softly in her ear. Later they would argue as to what it was he said. It did not matter later, but at this moment it raised within Ginette a well of excitement the like of which she had never known and the remembrance of which would make her cheeks flame.

Her lips were moist and warm, his tongue urgent and invasive. From her throat came low moans of excitement. Under her kaftan he could feel her nipples, firm as fresh raspberries. He lifted the kaftan and, holding her breasts in his hands, moved his lips from one to the other. Her breasts were large and soft but firm, and he felt them quiver at his touch.

Finally he could bear it no longer, and drew off her kaftan. Her hands went to his shirt and quickly and deftly she undressed him. At the touch of their bodies they became man and woman possessed. Their legs entwined and their kisses and movements against each other became more and more urgent and frantic.

David felt her wetness on his thigh and bent his head on to her. His fingers parted her lips and when his tongue rasped gently over her she cried out in orgasm, gripping his head between her thighs in a convulsion of ecstasy.

When she lay still he thought the passion had died within her. He was wrong. She turned to him and whispered in his ear,

'My love, you drove me mad. Now I'm going to do the same to you. I want to drive you crazy.'

They drove each other crazy.

With strokes and insinuating fingers they explored. As the hours went by they pitched and tossed in peaks and troughs of delight, developing an exquisite intimacy new to them both. Words came and went; fierce, gentle, demanding, aggressive, loving, their tonality as varied as a Brahms symphony.

Twice they made love—first with a rearing, un-bridled demand that took them to a clawing, juddering climax. Later, after they had slept, it was slow and loving, with the gentle deliberation of a walk down a country lane. They fell asleep again, close, warm and entangled.

When David awoke, streaks of dawn had replaced the moonbeams. At first he could not think what was happening or where he was. Dream sequences of the

night mingled erotically with his awakening. Fiery
tingles sparkled between his thighs. He felt himself
erect, his tumescence growing with a warmth that
played over it like a lambent flame. When he opened
his eyes all he could see was Ginette's copper hair
spread over his belly.

He could not see what she was doing beneath the
copper curtain. He did not need to; he could feel every
lubricious sweep of her mouth upon his member and his
juices travelling like a floodtide through his loins. He
gripped the sheets, unable to stem the tide.

'Ginette. No!'

His plea went unheeded and David died the little
death. Ginette had returned the pleasure he had given
her the night before to the full. His return to life was
slow and luxurious. The pale streaks of dawn were
replaced by brilliant sunshine. Ginette had gone, and
through the door came the smell of grilled bacon. He
threw aside the sheets and strode through to the
bathroom. The shower needled on his skin and at the
finish he turned it to cold, gasping at the sudden
invigorating shock.

Ginette's razor was a flimsy affair in pink plastic, but
it sufficed. When he went into the kitchen she was
standing in front of the grill lifting rashers of bacon on
to a plate already covered with fried eggs, tomatoes and
mushrooms. She was wearing a green silk dressing-
gown, her hair tied back in a chignon. David lightly
walked across to her and kissed her neck.

She put the plate of breakfast on the table and turned
to face him, smiling gently.

'Come and have breakfast, David.'

He sat down as she poured hot coffee for them both.
Ferociously hungry, he demolished the breakfast and
followed it with toast and chunky marmalade. Ginette
had fresh orange juice and a plate of muesli. She

watched him eat with satisfaction and noted that the worry creases on his face were going. The tension was out of him and he looked relaxed.

'How are we for time?' he asked.

She looked at the delicate watch on her wrist. He had not seen her wear it before. It was a Rolex, and the face was ornamented with tiny diamonds.

'No rush. We did wake early, you may remember.'

He looked across the table at her, reached over and took her hand.

'I remember. I shall never forget.'

'That's what you say to all the girls. It's just the breakfast talking.'

'That's not the only talking there is to do,' said David seriously.

Ginette looked up at him quickly.

'Oh yes?'

'Oh yes. About us.'

'I don't see what there is to talk about. It's too tragically cut and dried. But I don't mind. I'd rather have you as things are than not at all.'

'I feel a cad,' he muttered. 'I'm letting you down.'

'You are a cad, but an adorable one, and I'm not about to do without you.'

She got up, kissing him lightly on the nose, and went from the kitchen to the bedroom to dress, careful not to brush the tears from her eyes in case he should see.

Her car refused to start. After several pulls at the starting knob Ginette gave it a rest, adjusted the choke and tried again. There was an immediate catch of the engine and it ticked over like a sewing machine. Ginette looked sideways at David, a smile lighting her eyes above the crests of her cheekbones.

'I told you—she's temperamental. Doesn't approve of early starts with male company.'

'Not like her mistress.'

'Not a bit!'

They laughed happily while the car trundled obed-iently past the sentinel lions and gathered speed down the road into Wootton Bassett. They turned into the car park of the hospital, and David was about to kiss her when she held him off.

'Careful, Mr Compton! Nobody will believe you're conducting a clinical examination in the car park.'

From the surgeons' room David telephoned a car hire firm in Swindon and arranged for them to deliver a car at lunchtime.

'Please make sure that your delivery man hands over the car to me personally,' he instructed.

'Don't worry, Mr Compton. Only you can sign the papers anyway.'

David did not want any repeat episodes. The car, when it arrived, was a red Volvo 740. He took the keys and looked at them.

'Are these the only ones you have?' he queried.

'No, sir. I have a spare set on me.'

'I'd like them, if you don't mind.'

As an added precaution he stuck a piece of Sellotape across the lower edge of each door. The hire car man went off with his mate, shaking his head at the vagaries of hospital doctors. At the end of the day David called Ginette.

'I need to pick up some things from the cottage,' he told her.

There was no need for them to discuss whether he was going to the flat that night. It was understood.

'Would you like me to drive you?' Ginette asked him.

'No. I'll take the hire car and you can go straight home in yours. It'll give you more time to pretty yourself up for me.'

'Chauvinistic pig! How do you know I want to?'

David smiled wickedly into the instrument.

'You told me so last night. You said. . .'

Ginette blushed at the other end of the line.

'That's quite enough, Mr Compton! I'll see you later.'

Uninhibited by anyone in the room, he whispered,

'I want to kiss you. . .'

There was a click as the line went dead. Sometimes, on the extension in the sister's office, it was possible to hear what was being said right across the room, and Ginette wasn't letting anyone in on what he was saying.

In the car park David inspected the doors of the Volvo carefully before inserting the key in the lock. They were undisturbed. He drove to Apple Tree Cottage with a pleasant sense of anticipation. It seemed an age since he had been there. Everything looked the same, and he noted that there were no broken windows.

As he opened the front door something felt unfamiliar, not quite right, and he could not think what it was. The front door opened freely. He closed it, looked around and knew what it was.

The door had opened too freely.

There were no papers to obstruct it as there usually were when he had been away. He looked down and saw them piled away from the door. His hair prickled at the back of his neck. Somebody must have been in the cottage since he and Laurel had left it. He stood still and looked for anything else out of place. Was there a booby trap? Another bomb? Would the telephone explode if he picked it up? Trip wires, perhaps, leading to a brown paper package big enough to blow the whole cottage to powder?

He put a tentative foot forward towards the drawing-room. There was no sound on the fitted carpet. The drawing-room door was ajar. He gave it a push, and when it came smashing back at him it was barely a surprise and he was ready for it.

He kicked at it with the sole of his foot, and it slammed into Tinker's stocking-clad head. The door split Tinker's eyebrow, and he staggered back towards the piano. David followed through the doorway and, seeing the big black man, was almost glad. At least it was not a bomb.

He kicked Tinker on the knee with the point of his shoe, and there was a grunt of pain as he went down on one knee. David followed this up with another kick at the stockinged face.

It was a mistake.

Tinker recovered quickly from the initial attack when he had been caught unawares and easily avoided David's second kick. He swayed sideways, gripped the ankle and twisted, using David's momentum against him. At the same time he rose to his feet and chopped viciously down with his right hand at David's lower ribs.

There was a double crack as two lower ribs fractured, and David felt as if a hand grenade had exploded inside him.

He picked up a chair and tried to swing it at the big black. It was a waste of time. Tinker was a master at this sort of fighting, and he grinned under the stocking. Despite David's size and fitness, this was going to be easy. The chair broke into pieces on Tinker's back as he turned, spun on the ball of one foot and loosed a high-flying kick that caught David at the base of his neck and dropped him to the floor like a felled ox.

Not for nothing had Tinker practised the art of *la savate*. He leaned over David, who was white and unconscious. Limping slightly, Tinker went to the kitchen, rummaged in some drawers and found a plastic bag. Back in the drawing-room he drew it carefully over David's head and stood up.

'David, are you there?'

There was a double hoot from a car outside. Tinker looked around quickly and went out through the back door. A racing cycle was propped against the wall. He jumped on it and cycled round to the front.

The Southeys' Sunbeam-Talbot was parked in the road. Tinker cycled round the back of it and was off. Molly Southey got out of the car and walked up the garden path. The front door was still open, and she went in.

'Anybody at home? Hello!' she called and went into the drawing-room.

'Oh, my God!' she exclaimed.

Quickly she ran to David and tore the plastic bag from his head. His lips were blue and his skin deathly white. Trying desperately to remember what she had heard about mouth-to-mouth resuscitation, Molly held his nose, put her mouth to his and blew into it with all the force she could muster.

She had no experience of emergencies and first aid, but she made up in desperate endeavour what she lacked in expertise. David was precious to her, although despite her provocative barking she had never actually taken a bite.

She could feel his chest moving as she blew into his mouth. His face was icy cold and she wondered if she was blowing into a corpse. Despite this she kept on until she was dizzy and her head began to spin.

She felt sick and had to give up. On all fours above him, she looked down at his face, just a few inches away. There was colour in his cheeks and she felt a draught on her face. David was breathing again. His eyelids fluttered. A wave of relief came over her and her tears dropped on to his forehead. Impulsively she put her cheek to his.

'Thank God! Oh, David, I thought you were dead!'

He moved slightly. Molly stood up and took a cushion from a chair to put under his head. The white telephone caught her eye and she dialled 999.

'Emergency. What service do you require?' The quiet, impersonal tones of the operator calmed her.

'Ambulance—ambulance at once, please. Right away.'

She gabbled the information to the operator and went back to David. He was still unconscious, but breathing steadily and looking better. The whiteness had gone, his hair curled damply on his forehead and there were deeply etched lines from nose to mouth, but he no longer had the pallor of death on him.

She took hold of his wrist and tried to find his pulse. When she finally got it, it thumped under her finger with a strong and regular beat. Far away she heard the ee-awing of the ambulance siren and fervently hoped they knew where to find the cottage. She did not need to worry. The siren grew louder and louder, died away, and then ambulance men were running up the garden path carrying a red box.

The leading man took in the situation at a glance, knelt beside David and opened the box.

'What was the trouble, madam?' he demanded.

'I don't know. I found him lying here with a plastic bag over his head. I tried to give him artificial respiration. He seemed so cold. . .'

The ambulance man had a mask over David's face by this time, adjusted a clip and turned a stopcock on top of an oxygen bottle. Pressurised oxygen flooded into David in rhythmic bursts and his cheeks turned rosy red. Within minutes Molly found herself following the ambulance over the downs to Manbury Hospital.

Mark Slater was on duty with Sandra Gotch. Both of them had a shock when they saw who it was on the stretcher. Sandra was the first to recover and, with the aid of a nurse, got David undressed so that Mark could examine him. David was semi-conscious, just able to speak and hear. He gripped Sandra's forearm and muttered,

'Ginette. Come here, Ginette. Aah. . .!' The pain from his ribs lanced through his chest and he stopped.

'Gently, Mr Compton. Try and relax.'

'I'm dying!'

Mark Slater smiled at Sandra. 'He's not too bad,' he told her.

He examined David carefully, his fingers gently pressing for other injuries, searching for internal bleeding. In the X-ray department he put the plates of David's chest on the viewing screen. The broken ribs were clearly visible beside the spine in the lower portion of the chest. Beside them was an area of white, and Mark tapped it thoughtfully.

'Look at that! Blood, almost certainly, and that. . .' his finger traced along a line up to the neck '. . .is air. He's got a haemo-pneumothorax. Needs aspirating and a drain with an underwater seal.'

They took David into a separate room kept for those too ill to be in the main ward. Mark gowned up and a nurse helped David to sit up in the bed. Mark tapped over his chest to determine the position of the blood, checked it against the X-ray plate and put local anaesthetic into the area. Then, with a large syringe carrying a wide bore needle, he slid it into David's chest. To his relief blood welled into the barrel of the syringe as he withdrew the plunger. He continued aspirating until no more came and then connected the needle to a plastic tube leading to an underwater seal so that air could not get back into the chest.

When they got David back on to the pillows and into a more comfortable position he looked white and exhausted. He smiled wanly at Mark Slater.

'Sorry to do this to you, Mark,' he said faintly. 'Not easy for you.'

'Don't worry—I'm glad you can talk. Now get a rest.' Mark turned to the nurse. 'Morphine sulphate, fifteen milligrams, please, Nurse.'

Against the rest of his pain David did not even feel the needle go in. He lifted an arm feebly on the counterpane.

'Tell. . .tell. . .' he muttered.

Mark looked at him enquiringly, his pink, chubby face still serious with concern.

'Laurel?'

David shook his head impatiently.

'No, Laurel's America. Ginette. Tell her.'

Mark thought for a moment before realisation dawned as to who Ginette was.

'Sister Irving?' he queried.

David nodded, too exhausted to reply. When Mark returned to Casualty he picked up the telephone in the office and spoke to the operator.

'Would you get me Sister Irving at home, please?'

Staff Nurse Gotch listened with interest.

'He's amazing, the boss. Comes in here half dead and all he can think of is to tell Sister Irving to cancel tomorrow's list!'

He shook his head, full of admiration. Sandra Gotch was less so. She turned to walk out of the room, her lips compressed.

'If you believe that you'll believe anything!' she muttered.

Ginette was beginning to wonder what had happened to David when the telephone rang in her flat.

'Sister Irving?'

She recognised the night operator's voice from the hospital.

'Yes, Walter. What is it?'

'Dr Slater for you. One moment.'

She felt a twinge of alarm. It was not usual for Mark Slater to ring her at home.

'Mr Compton asked me to ring you, Sister,' said Mark. 'He won't be doing the list tomorrow.'

'Why not? What's the matter?' Her voice was dry and squeaky with alarm.

'He's been damaged in a fight. He's in the ward now—haemo-pneumothorax with a drain, but he was lucky.'

'Lucky?'

'Yes. Somebody knocked him out and put a plastic bag over his head. He's lucky to be alive.'

Ginette felt herself go cold and faint. Mark's voice came anxiously over the wire.

'Are you there? Can you hear me?'

'Yes, I hear you. Goodbye.'

She got up, anger supplanting her previous anxiety, and went into the bedroom. Quickly she changed into a track-suit and trainers and ran outside. Her car started first go and shot through the gates like a formula one off the line at Le Mans.

As she drove to Manbury Hospital Ginette turned it over in her mind, and got nowhere until she remembered David's words about Sandra Gotch after the bomb. '. . .she's lying to cover it up.'

When she saw David she was shocked. He was lying propped up on pillows, his face grey and drawn. Plastic tubing led from his chest to a complicated apparatus containing water, stationed alongside the bed. As Ginette entered the room his eyes opened. He smiled at her and her heart twisted as he gave her a rueful, mocking smile with the uplift of his eyebrow she knew so well.

She was across the room in a moment, holding his

hand and bending to kiss him. Despite his condition his grip on her was firm. She laid her cheek against his and tried not to let the tears appear. Minutes went by, then she whispered to him,

'Tell me what happened.'

'I had a visitor—big, black and ferocious,' he told her. 'They say a good big 'un will always beat a good little 'un. I'm afraid it's true.'

She put her arms around him and kissed him again, as if to protect him from more damage.

'Good job you're not in uniform!' he grinned. 'Very improper for nurses to kiss the patients.'

'I don't give a damn,' she assured him.

'That's my girl!'

His eyelids drooped in a morphine haze, and Ginette felt a cold anger growing inside her against his attacker.

'David, have you any idea who it could be?' she asked.

'Nope.'

'You said you thought Sandra Gotch was lying about the mechanic who rang up for your car. That could be a lead.'

He nodded without saying anything, tired with the talk and the effect of the drug. Ginette sat with him for a while until he went to sleep and then tiptoed from the room. Molly Southey was sitting outside.

'How is he, Ginette?' she asked anxiously.

'He's going to be all right. Molly, tell me what happened.'

Molly did so, and Ginette's eyes went hard as the story came out.

'Could you recognise this man who cycled away?' she asked.

Molly shook her head.

'It was all too quick. He was big and black and he was wearing a cap with a long peak, that's all.' Molly nodded to David's room. 'Can I go in and see him?'

Ginette shook her head.

'I wouldn't if I were you, Molly—he's pretty whacked. But, Molly. . .' she paused, 'thank you for what you did. He's very precious to me.'

Molly smiled, drawing at her cigarette with an elegance only she could contrive.

'That goes for us both, my sweet. You're the lucky girl that's got him. Just don't tell Dick!'

Ginette squeezed her arm and went down the long corridor towards Accident and Emergency. When she arrived at the office and saw Sandra Gotch there the smile had gone from her face and she looked grim and determined. Sandra had her cloak on and was about to go off duty. She looked round in surprise when Ginette entered and closed the door behind her.

'Sister Irving?'

Sandra Gotch was not one to be put down easily, but she sensed trouble when she saw the expression on Ginette's face and saw her close the office door behind her.

'I want to hear what you know about the person who's trying to kill David Compton,' Ginette said coldly.

Sandra's eyes opened wide. This she had not suspected.

'Why should I know anything about that? Who told you?'

'David thinks you know who it was that telephoned about his car before it was blown up. Do you?'

'What if I do? He's not the one who's trying to kill David.'

That was a mistake, and as soon as she had said it Sandra bit her lip. Ginette leaned forward.

'So—you *do* know who it was who telephoned! That man was trying to find out which was David's car. You told him, and that was how they were able to put the bomb in it.'

'I didn't say I knew anything.' Sandra's tone was sullen and defensive.

'You know all right, and you're going to tell me who it was!' snapped Ginette.

'Why should I? It's nothing to do with you.'

'Oh yes, it is. And if you don't tell me I'm going to fix you so that you'll never nurse again!' Ginette's voice was iron-hard, her eyes narrow. She stood, hands on her hips, like an avenging fury. 'I'll bring up the frayed 000 catgut. I'll tell them about your drug sessions with that dirty little toad Martin Webber. I'll load them with so much information about you you'll never be able to clean it off your record!'

Sandra went white. She had never seen Ginette like this, and there was no mistaking her purpose. If she did not give Ginette a name it was more than likely that she would get it from some other source. She shrugged her shoulders under the cape.

'OK, if that's how you feel about it. There's no great secret. I think it was China St George.'

'Who is he, and where do I find him?'

'He lives in Marlborough—has a flat in Merlin Cottage on Kingsbury Hill. He works as a storeman for Andrew's the builders on the London Road. Does that satisfy you?'

'Perfectly, thank you.'

When Ginette left Sandra Gotch heaved a sigh of relief. She could have given Ginette Tinker's address, but she was so terrified of the big black she had not dared.

Ginette drove slowly along the road leading to Marlborough while she thought. She could not go to the police; they were far too probing and wide-ranging with their questions. They might ask her too many things, and she was worried about the sensitivity of Mac's death and the frayed catgut. There was no way she was going to risk having that little stone turned over.

No, the police were definitely out.

By the time she reached Ogbourne St Andrew she had made up her mind what she was going to do and put her foot down on the accelerator. If she could find who it was there was always the possibility of buying them off. Perhaps she could turn them into the poacher-turned-gamekeeper role and give them money only on condition that David remained safe? But why were they after him in the first place? Was there some secret he had kept from her?

She had a funny, instinctive feeling that Sam Bennett was involved with David in a way that she did not know. Despite her love for him it gave her an uneasy feeling. She liked everything above board.

She had no difficulty in finding Merlin Cottage. It was a small house with leaded windows and the name in faded script on a carved board tacked to the front door. There were two bells, one labelled St George. Ginette pressed it firmly and stepped inside.

She was in a narrow hall with a brick floor. In front of her was a passage to the back and a narrow staircase led steeply to the next floor. She had no difficulty in deciding where to go. Immediately on her right was a black-painted sign. The single word 'CHINA' occupied almost the whole of the face of the door.

She was reading it when the door opened and China himself appeared. He was having an unaccustomed night at home. Ginette caught the whiff of joss-sticks and marijuana and steeled herself to be nice. She smiled at him and said,

'Are you China St George?'

China was caught off guard. He was not used to

attractive women knocking at his door so late in the evening, and the grass he had smoked had dulled his normally keen perception, otherwise he would never have admitted his identity without further question.

'That's me. What can I do for you?'

He looked at her more closely in the shadow of the passage and decided that there was a good deal he could do for her given the opportunity. He stepped back and opened the door wide.

'Would you like to come in?'

'Thank you.'

With a feeling of approaching destiny Ginette took a step over the threshold. The room was low-ceilinged and small. There was a long sofa, two armchairs and an Oriental coffee-table in front of a television set. On the floor were a pair of brightly coloured flat-weave rugs; a voodoo mask and crossed spears graced one wall and on the mantelpiece sat a carved figure in black wood with big eyes and a huge grinning mouth. Next to it a slender vase held joss-sticks that emitted a thin trail of smoke from their grey tips.

Through a crack in the curtains Ginette could see the familiar white shape of the Morris parked outside. Somehow it reassured her.

China was wearing black trousers, and a red and black shirt open to the waist. He grinned at her, his prominent canine teeth showing white in the flickering light from a pair of candles on the sideboard.

'A nursing friend gave me your name,' Ginette told him. 'She said you might be able to help me.'

China knew a number of nurses and he looked over Ginette with a speculative leer.

'What sort of help do you want?' He gestured towards the sofa. 'Take a seat. Like a drink?'

Ginette nodded. She felt as though she needed something, and perhaps if he had one as well it would encourage him to talk.

'Whisky, if you have it.'

He produced it, neat and in a tumbler with a picture on it. She took a gulp and did not even notice the fiery liquid burn its way down. China watched her appraisingly, wondering what it was that brought this attractive woman knocking at his door so late in the evening. He viewed her shape under the track-suit and felt an urge stirring within him. This was pussy on a plate, and he was not one to miss out.

'You work around here?' he asked.

Ginette nodded. 'At the Manbury Accident Hospital.'

'So you're a nurse?'

'That's right.'

China ran his tongue round his thin lips. 'That's nice. I like nurses.'

That was true. China had known many nurses at Martin's parties. He had liked them all. He decided that he liked this one more than most and made the first move in a game which he had learned to play with the expertise of a chess-master.

'Toke?'

He leaned forward and casually picked one out of a wooden box on the coffee table. He put it between his lips, lit it and took a drag; then he passed it to Ginette. She had never smoked grass in her life, but under the pressure of the moment she took it from him, puffed at it tentatively and handed it back. She smiled at him, and he leaned towards her so that their shoulders touched.

'What can I do to help you?' he asked her.

'I want to find somebody.'

'You need the Salvation Army. Who is it you want to find, and why?'

Ginette had her story ready.

'One of my friends is pregnant. She wants a termination and can't afford it. I'm trying to find the father to persuade him to help.'

'And who is the father?'

'She doesn't know his proper name. She met him two or three times at parties and that was it. You know how it is.'

China grinned and nodded at her.

'Yeah, I know how it is. But how do we identify this boyfriend?'

'He's big, very big, and he's black. Wears a cap with a long peak—American style. Know anybody like that?'

China almost laughed. The thought of Tinker being pursued for a contribution to end a dubious paternity claim amused him. Especially when the pursuer was an attractive girl like Ginette. He decided he could afford to have a little fun without expense.

He nodded slowly and looked at her with real sincerity.

'You know, I think I know just the man you want. There can't be many with that description.'

Ginette felt herself trembling with excitement.

'What's his name?'

'What's your name?' he countered.

Taken aback, Ginette replied without thinking.

'Ginette—Ginette Irving.'

'Well, Ginette. What's the deal?'

'The deal? How do you mean?'

China spread his hands.

'Come on, Ginette. A deal is a trade. I give you something, you give me something. So far, there's no trade.'

Ginette began to feel breathless. They were getting to the crunch.

'What can I give you? I thought you might tell me, if you knew, for the girl's sake.'

She took another gulp at the whisky glass as he leaned closer and put his hand on her knee.

'You've got a lot to give. You're an attractive girl. I fancy you.'

There was a moment's hesitation; she looked down at the hand on her knee and then up at him. His black eyes were bright with excitement and anticipation.

'You mean if I go with you then you'll tell me his name?'

'That's what I mean.' He shrugged his shoulders. 'You get what you pay for these days. Nothing for nothing.'

'How do I know you'll tell me?'

'Good question. You don't. You'll just have to trust me.'

He thought for a moment.

'Tell you what—I'll write it on a piece of paper and put it on the mantelpiece. You can open it afterwards. How about that?'

It wasn't foolproof, but Ginette could see that it was the best offer she was going to get. The idea of going to bed with China iced her emotions, but the thought of David at risk from the shadowy black aggressor drove her on. She finished the whisky and stood up.

'Where's your pencil and paper, China? You can start writing.'

She let him lead her into the bedroom. It looked out on to a small and leafy garden, and for a moment she had an intense desire to escape through the french windows. China switched on a bedside light, illuminating a double bed with a flowered quilt. He undressed quickly, and Ginette looked with distaste at his skinny brown frame. He lay under the quilt and watched her with a greedy anticipation she could feel across the room. She sat beside him and felt his hands reach for her in a spidery exploration that made her clench her teeth. There was no kindness, tenderness or emotion in him, just a selfish intensity that left her icily alone and unmoved. She put her hand on his chest.

'Just a minute, China. The name before we start.'

He looked at her briefly, then rolled over to the side of the bed and scribbled on a pad. He folded the piece of paper and stood it on edge. Ginette leaned over and read the two words. As she did so a volcanic rage rose within her, erupting like a Vesuvian explosion.

'You little toad!'

She shook the paper at him. On it was written in spidery hand 'Mickey Mouse.' China was sitting up in bed, grinning at her.

'Take a little joke, kid.'

She swallowed, getting a grip on herself, and smiled at him. 'I like a joke, China, but a trade is a trade, as you said.' She slid her hand under the quilt, stroking under his thigh as he sat with his knees drawn up. 'You're not a welsher, are you, China?'

Her hand cupped his testicles, fondling them gently like billiard balls. The whisky and the toke had put her into a half world, but there was no dimming of her intent. For David's sake she was determined to find out who was behind the attack on his life. China faced her, a faraway look in his eyes.

'Some you win, some you lose. Today you lose, Ginette.'

'No, China, not today.'

With a convulsive grip she squeezed his testicles. She squeezed as hard as she was able with a hand made strong by thousands of hours of gripping surgical instruments.

He screamed like a woman in labour and rolled away from her, but she would not let go and rolled on to the bed with him.

He screamed again. Still she would not let go, and

heaved at him with savage jolts.

'What's his name, China?' she demanded.

'You bitch, let me go! Please let me *go*!'

His voice rose up the scale as she hefted her grip. She felt a sensation like tearing wet paper as his cords ripped and he screamed again.

'It's Tinker you want—Tinker.'

'Where is he?'

'In a flat over the warehouse by the river.'

He fainted, and Ginette left without a backward glance.

As she drove back she felt herself trembling, but her hands on the driving wheel were firm.

CHAPTER TWENTY

CHINA lay in agony the whole night. Despite smoking all the grass he could find the pain never stopped. It bored at him unceasingly and with a mounting pressure. Twice he was sick, and by morning, when he inspected himself in the bathroom, the whole of his genitalia was swollen to the size of a watermelon. His scrotum was tight, red and tense and he could find no position that was not acutely painful.

He considered going to the doctor, but realised that he would never be able to walk there and he had no telephone to ask for a visit. The following day dragged on, and by late afternoon he was ill and dehydrated with vomiting. It was all he could do to get to the door of the flat and shout upstairs to his neighbour.

There was no reply.

Eventually he lay in an armchair in the front room with a shoe in his hand and waited until he heard someone go by outside. Then he threw the shoe through the window. There was a muttered curse.

'Bloody idiots!'

The footsteps hurried on, leaving China cursing weakly at everyone and Ginette in particular. The second shoe through the window attracted the attention of an old lady pushing a shopping trolley, and when she heard his cry of 'Help!' she stopped and peered through the window.

All she could see was China sprawled in the chair, his fly open.

'Disgusting—what will people get up to next?' she snapped.

The old lady hastened away up the hill with her trolley, and China began to think he was going to die unnoticed. Each time there was a sound outside he shouted. After two hours, when he was reduced to a pleading wreck, a policeman stopped by the broken window. He saw China, who waved and croaked at him,

'Come and help me!'

The constable had to bend low and remove his helmet to get through the door. He viewed China's set-up and sniffed disparagingly.

'What's been happening to you?' he wanted to know.

'Please, Officer, get me a doctor. I'm dying!'

A closer look from the constable assured him that China was in a bad way. He took his UFH pocket phone from his tunic and spoke rapidly.

'Don't you worry, sir, the ambulance'll be here in a jiffy,' he assured him.

The journey to Manbury Hospital was a nightmare to China. Every jolt and sway of the ambulance brought him fresh torture. The Casualty Officer took one look and admitted him to the surgical ward, where Mark Slater was on duty. He whistled when he saw China and the extent of the problem. China was past caring what happened as long as he was relieved of the pain.

Mark spoke to the consultant on duty who was taking David's place.

'I'd be glad if you'd come in, sir. Chap here with what looks like a torsion of both testicles.'

Mr Brade was a tall, thin, grey-haired man with a manner as precise and spare as his figure. He had a piercing look and fixed Mark with his gaze after he had examined China.

'You're right, Slater. Better get on to theatre and tell them to set up for an orchidectomy as soon as they can.'

Fortunately Ginette was not on duty. When Mr Brade drew the scalpel down the side of the small watermelon that was China's scrotum he exposed the underlying testicle. Normally creamy and glistening like a wet billiard ball, it was dull and red and black in patches. He dissected it out with swift precision, cut and tied the artery and cord and dropped the whole mass into a stainless steel kidney bowl, instruments attached.

He held out a hand to the instrument nurse.

'Prosthesis, please.'

She handed him what looked like a white bantam's egg. He slid it into the sac and stitched round it.

'Very important, that, Slater. Fellows can put up with being castrated, but they jib like hell at an empty bag. Now let's see if he's going to lose the other one.'

The other side was much the same. The blood supply to the testicle had been cut off for so long the organ was too damaged to retain. With an icy indifference Mr Brade repeated the performance.

David heard about it from Mark, who visited him the following morning. He told him about it as a matter of clinical interest, but David was only half attentive until Mark mentioned that it was the same man who had been in with a heroin overdose. Immediately he was alert, his mind racing through a fog of analgesia.

This was one of the men on Sam's hit list. He seemed to be both very unlucky and to have a charmed life. Maybe Sam had someone else on his payroll more ready than he to assist China to shuffle off this mortal coil?

He looked at Mark quizzically. 'How is this chap?' he asked.

'OK. He's not very happy just now, but he's not in any danger.'

'How did he come by this? Bilateral torsion doesn't happen on its own.'

'Dunno. He was pretty clammy about it when he came in. Maybe one of his junkie pals paying off an old score. They can be a rough crowd.'

David tried to think through his drug-ridden state, but was so befuddled he gave it up. Ginette, he knew, was in theatre all day and would not be in to see him until that evening.

Sandra Gotch heard about China's admission when she came on duty at eight o'clock. During the lunch break she went up to the men's surgical ward. Mark was in the sister's office, writing case notes, and was alone. Since the time of their mutual problem they had maintained a reserved distance. Sandra did her best to be affable.

'I hear you've got China here, in a lot of trouble,' she began.

He looked up at her and nodded.

'Right. Somebody got to his wicked parts. Brade had to whip out both his testes last night.' There was a pause. 'He won't be any good to the girls again,' he added significantly.

Sandra ignored this and went into the ward.

China looked grey under his dark skin. His narrow face was thinner than ever. He turned his head on the pillow as Sandra came and stood by his bed. There was no smile on his face. His black eyes viewed her flatly, registering no emotion.

'How are you, China?' she asked.

He said nothing, and she began to feel uncomfortable. Finally he spoke.

'You know what happened?'

She shook her head.

'They've castrated me.'

Put in that raw fashion it brought it home to Sandra more than any clinical description. She put a hand on his arm.

'I'm sorry, China.'

It seemed inadequate, but she could think of nothing else. He gave her a sarcastic smile.

'I bet you are, but it's too late now.'

'What happened to you?' she queried.

'I was playing football with an elephant and he kicked me.'

'What?' she demanded.

'Mind your business. You can't help now.'

'If that's how you feel. . .'

She turned to go away and he called to her.

'No, stop. Maybe you can help.'

'What can I do?' asked Sandra.

'I'll tell you who did this. It was that redheaded bitch, Ginette.'

Sandra Gotch's eyes went wide.

'Sister Irving?'

'That's her. She screwed me to get Tinker's name. Left me to nearly bloody die, she did!'

Sandra remembered her conversation with Ginette and felt herself go cold. If China ever found out who had given his name to Ginette she trembled to think what he would do. China's scrawny fingers clutched at her apron.

'Find Tinker and tell him what's happened,' he said urgently. 'Get him to come and see me. He'll fix that bitch!'

Sandra shivered at the mention of Tinker. The big black frightened her in a way she could not define. The last thing she wanted was to be involved with him, however remotely.

'Where do I find him?' she asked.

'At his flat, of course. He's bound to be there tonight after work.'

Sandra left the ward, her mind going round in circles. She felt the situation was getting out of hand, the events coming faster, each one worse than the last, each one leading more directly to disaster. The thought of going to Tinker's flat on her own in the evening haunted her the whole day.

She was not overly fussy in her men, but Tinker she knew to be difficult to handle. He was like a big jungle cat, only more dangerous and less predictable. If she caught him on a high and alone it was quite possible she would not come back—at all. She had heard tales of Tinker from China when he had been drunk, and they were not pretty. She shuddered and decided she would go in uniform. No tinsel dresses tonight to tickle Tinker's fancy.

That evening, as Sandra drove out of the hospital grounds in her small Skoda, her pale face was set and anxious and her blonde hair was drawn tightly back in a chignon under her cap.

At the same time Ginette was sitting on David's bed, holding his hand. He was looking very different. The drain had been removed from his chest, his pinched cheeks had gone and his eyes were no longer sunk in their sockets.

Ginette was looking flushed and beautiful. After the previous evening she had gone back to her flat, taken off her track-suit and scrubbed herself all over in a hot bath full of perfumed suds. She felt soiled after China and was amazed at herself that she had been able to go through with it. Now she was going to bury the events at Merlin Cottage in a deep hole at the back of her mind, determined that they would not affect her relationship with the man she had found and loved to the exclusion of all else.

'Darling, I'm going to take you away to convalesce,' she told him.

He smiled at her and held out his arms, then winced as the pain from his ribs speared into him.

'You're a shameless hussy! Laurel will be back tomorrow.'

'You're not going back to her,' Ginette said quietly.

'Then she'll have me over a barrel in the courts. She'll cook my goose to a cinder!'

'That doesn't matter. It's your life I'm worried about.'

David sat up and grinned his crooked grin at her.

'Thanks very much, but I'm not exactly at death's door!'

'I don't mean that. I mean you're in danger. That's twice you've nearly been killed in the last week. The next time you may not be so lucky.'

'What do you know about it? You sound as if you know more than I do about what's going on.'

Ginette took both his hands in hers.

'Ralph says we can use his house in Jersey. It's a lovely place—I used to go there for holidays when I was a little girl. Please let's go!'

He smiled at her. 'I don't like the idea of running away.'

Ginette frowned impatiently.

'You're not running away. Don't forget the old adage about living to fight another day. And what's more, I've got some interesting news for you. I know who and where the man is who attacked you.'

David looked at her sharply in surprise.

'How did you find that out?' he demanded.

'Sandra. She has some dubious contacts.'

'I know that.'

'She told me his nickname and where he lives,' Ginette revealed.

David felt a sense of relief.

'In that case, all I've got to do is let Sam know and he'll do the rest.'

Ginette looked puzzled. 'Why Sam?' she queried.

With a start David realised he had made a slip. Ginette did not know about his deal with Sam, and she was unaware that Tinker was one of Susan's rapists.

'He's the sort of chap who'll sort things out,' he said, rather lamely.

He was right. Sam would sort out Tinker once he knew where to find him, and that would take the pressure off them.

'Give me the telephone and tell me who and where he is,' he ordered.

Ginette did both, and in minutes David was speaking to Sam.

'I can tell you where to find at least one of the gang right now,' he told him. 'The big black.'

He heard Sam's indrawn breath.

'You sure?'

David nodded.

'He's the guy who put me in here. Seems he thinks I know too much, but I don't know how. You get to him and my insurance company might take me on after all. What's more, the little West Indian's back in Manbury. He'll be safe in here for a bit.'

'Who's the black, and where is he?' demanded Sam.

David relayed Ginette's information, and as he did so Sam let out a laugh like the bark of a sea-lion.

'Feel safe, David. It won't be long before you can walk down the High Street in broad daylight. That ugly piece of work won't bother you again—ever!'

When Sandra Gotch tramped up the steps leading to Tinker's flat her heart was beating as loud as the sound of her footsteps on the wooden boards. She pressed the bell and stood back.

'Come in, Sandra baby. Just push the door—it's unlocked.'

Tinker's bass tones came booming out in front of her,

and she gasped with fright. There was a soft whirring sound from the door. When she looked more closely she saw that there was a grille by the bellpush. A microphone. Above her head a tiny camera pointed down. With an outward confidence she did not feel she pushed the door open and went inside.

Tinker was sitting at a computer console and beside it was a television screen showing the steps leading to the front door. He swung round to greet her, a big smile on his handsome Ashanti features. She saw that he had shaved his head completely and was wearing a long, multi-coloured robe with ebony beads. She had never seen him dressed like this, and as he came across the room towards her she stood in trembling fascination, like a bird before a snake.

'My new toy frighten you, baby? I like these electronic gimmicks. They come cheap now, and it's nice to know who's calling.'

With a sense of relief Sandra saw that he was acting normally. There was no sign of the brittle, drug-induced manner she recognised so well. She sat down on the edge of one of the white leather armchairs and Tinker stood before her, his big bare feet protruding under his robe. A large hand opened before her and she thought, inconsequently, how pale the palm looked.

'Drink or a snort?' he invited. 'Or would you like both?'

'No, thanks.'

She felt too nervous to accept anything. She could feel the vibrant aura from him, and when she looked up she could see from his face that he knew she was afraid and was enjoying it. He was playing with her, and yet he had said nothing out of place. He padded over to the hi-fi set and switched it on. Music came flooding into the room from the giant speakers—reggae music with a deep insistent beat. Wild music Sandra had heard here before at wilder parties. She cleared her throat, anxious to deliver her message and be away before Tinker set the scene more firmly.

'China asked me to come and see you,' she said. 'He's in hospital.'

'In hospital? What's going on? More trouble?' She could feel anger swelling already in the deep tones.

'I'm afraid so. He's had an operation and wants to see you.'

The big black looked puzzled.

'Operation? What sort of operation?'

Sandra told him, and as she did so Tinker's face looked grim and he nodded to himself. She made it brief, and when she had finished he held out a hand and lifted her to her feet out of the armchair. It was as if he had heard nothing of what she had said.

'Come and watch me work out,' he said. 'You never seen me work out.'

Sandra followed him into the gymnasium, too frightened to refuse. In any case, it was not an invitation, it was a command—a command delivered with the inherent authority of an Ashanti chief.

In the gymnasium Tinker stripped off his robe and stood on an exercise mat. He was wearing nothing but a tiny black G-string. At the edge of the mat were four massive Indian clubs. He took one in each hand and started to twirl them in a series of complicated manoeuvres that grew faster and faster until they were going too fast to follow. It was a masterly performance, and Sandra was fascinated.

His muscles, perfectly defined under the gleaming black skin, rippled, bunched and flexed as he went through the routine. He stopped and exchanged the clubs for weights. He held one out to her.

'Take it.'

She took it in both hands. It was so heavy she dropped it immediately. Tinker bent down and picked it up with one hand and went into a routine of raising, swinging, pushing and pulling that made her open her eyes in amazement. The sweat gleamed on him and ran in rivulets down his thighs. She was caught up in admiration of the animal intensity of him.

He was straining now for breath, his mouth open and his neck muscles corded. He went into the slow raise and lower with both arms outstretched, like a cruci-fixion, and Sandra felt herself straining with him. The strain was obvious and terrible, and she leaned forward, urging him on. At the very moment of maximum raise he caught her eye. Her open mouth and attitude had given her away. He gave her a triumphant grin, raised the weights high above his head, gave a suggestive double thrust forward of his pelvis and dropped them to the floor.

Sandra felt as though she had been caught in the nude.

Tinker grabbed a towel from a rail on the wall, wiped his face and walked into the shower. Over his shoulder he said to her,

'Tell China I'll see him tomorrow.'

The interview was over, and Sandra Gotch left feeling as if she had been taken against her will.

Which she had.

CHAPTER TWENTY-ONE

THE RUNWAY at Phoenix airport shimmered in the hundred-degree summer heat as the Learjet 55 teetered gently against the brakes, waiting for take-off clearance from the control tower. The pilot, comfortable in the air-conditioned cockpit, adjusted his headset and waited patiently.

'Golf-Alfa-Romeo-Alfa-Golf, you are clear for take-off on runway one-two.'

The throttle levers went forward, the thunder of the twin Garrett turbo-fan engines rose in concert, the graceful little aircraft hurtled down the runway and rose into the azure of the Arizona sky like a swallow from a cage. In the crystal atmosphere at forty-five thousand feet it arrowed north-east at five hundred miles an hour, its jet thunder heard only by solitary Indians of the desert. Sam Bennett sat in an armchair in the main cabin and looked at Laurel.

He realised that she was interested in him primarily for his money; meanness was not one of Sam's traits. In his turn he was only interested in Laurel as a bedmate. His rough, almost brutal approach to sex had aroused in her a sexual appetite that would have shocked her three months ago. This in turn had massaged his ego so satisfactorily he felt almost sorry for the many he knew who fancied her.

She had opened a bottle of champagne and was pouring it into two flutes. Elegant as ever, she was wearing a dress in barred red and black with high-heeled black leather shoes and stockings with tiny bows above the heels. She handed him a glass and sat down.

'Here's to you, Sam. You did it! Now for home and glory.'

He grinned back at her, his rugged face creased with pleasure, his gold tooth glinting in a shaft of sunlight.

'Not bad, Laurel. I reckon those greedy bastards in Scottsdale spent so much time looking at you they didn't have their mind on their job.'

It was close to the truth. In the quiet interiors of the banks of Scottsdale, where offices resembled drawing-rooms of luxury homes, there had been strenuous bargaining over the financing of a massive shopping development that was to net Sam's company a profit of over thirty million dollars.

Toughest and most difficult of the American nego-tiators had been the sixty-year-old president of Phoenix Commercial, Forrest M. Holbrook. Hard and inflex-ible, he looked as though he was going to block the deal. The night before the final day of negotiations he had held a party in the penthouse suite of the Phoenix Plaza.

He was a short, burly man with greying hair cut en brosse and a face that looked as though it had spent years in the great outdoors. He liked his whisky and was a widower. According to the gossip Laurel had heard in the ladies' powder-room he had more than an eye for the women.

Throughout several meetings Laurel had been con-scious that Forrest Holbrook had paid more attention to her than strict protocol demanded. Little things like including her in a conversation when it was not her place to speak, or finding her a drink and a sandwich when they stopped for a break. The party he gave at the Phoenix Plaza was lavish. Waiters circulated with trays of champagne. There was a buffet with caviar, black and glistening in ice-bedded silver bowls; lobsters from Maine, their great red claws still raised in anger;

Chincoteague oysters, pâté de foie gras Strasbourg, cold venison, wild turkey, tamale pie, stone crabs, clam chowder bubbling gently on a burner—the long table seemed to go out of sight.

Forrest Holbrook drank Southern Comfort, and a lot of it. He circulated among his guests, laughing and joking and having his glass filled regularly by a sharp-eyed waiter; but Laurel noticed that he kept returning to talk to her. Sam was busy lobbying and she hardly saw him. They both had separate suites in the same hotel and had arrived at the party at different times. Thus far they had been to bed together twice, just enough to whet his appetite. Laurel was playing her fish carefully.

'You're not thinking of going?'

She turned to face Forrest Holbrook. He was red in the face and sweating visibly. It was not a question, more of a command. As a matter of fact she had not been thinking of leaving. The atmosphere of wealth and sophistication appealed to her. This was what she craved and she saw too little of it. The women were dressed fashionably and superbly, their wrists and necks glittering with jewels that would have made Van Cleef and Arpels weep in their sleep. Their figures were the product of a dietary and fitness routine so rigid it would have made a Zen priest a casting candidate for Gargantua. Only their abrasive adenoidal twang got on her nerves.

To Laurel this was the high life. She smiled at Forrest and put a hand gently on his arm.

'Would you like me to stay?' she asked.

'Indeed I would, Laurel—the longer the better. I just have to run around here a shade more, say my piece to all the folks I've invited and then we can relax.'

Laurel wondered if he ever did relax. He was a hard-muscled bundle of dynamic energy if ever she had seen

one. She knew that his wife had died three years ago
and wondered if that was the reason he was so hard and
intransigent in business. Maybe he had channelled all
his energies into banking after her death. She began to
ponder.

'Hell and back, there's Samson of Standard Electri-
cal! Come and meet him. Valuable guy—a real dog for
a new bone.'

He took her off to meet a giant of a man with snow-
white hair and a nose like Cyrano de Bergerac. There
were others with him, and Forrest introduced her
without a moment's hesitation for a name. Despite his
small stature Laurel was impressed by the way his
personality dominated the group. He would listen, but
it was never long before he spoke, and when he did no
one else interrupted. He included her in the conversation, brought her to the forefront of every discussion
and generally made her feel important.

Some of the men she met, obviously admiring, tried
to get her to one side, but after a moment or two
Forrest would appear, put his arm through hers and
lead her off on the pretext of introducing her to
someone else. She found it flattering and exciting.

'Forrest, I think I'd better find Sam,' she told him.

'Sam? What d'ya want to find Sam for?' He looked
like a Staffordshire bull terrier bristling for a fight.

'I do work for him, you know.'

'Work for him? This is a social occasion. You're not
supposed to be working. What d'ya do for him,
anyway?'

'I'm his PA,' Laurel explained.

'What in the mother of hell's that?'

'Personal assistant—a sort of high-class dogsbody.
I'm just supposed to be around in case he needs
anything.'

Forrest looked at her, his jaw jutting out.

'Yeah, he's a smart one, that Sam. How'd'ya like to be my PA?'

'I couldn't do both jobs. And we're due to return home the day after tomorrow.'

'Well, let's say you're on secondment for the time being.'

Laurel laughed demurely.

'I'd have to ask the master!'

'Never mind him! I've decided it's part of the deal. He's not going to refuse that.'

'Very well, sir. Just until tomorrow, but in the morning, like Cinderella, I must return to my former post.'

'OK, Cinderella. Seeing as how we're driving such a tight bargain, what time's morning?'

She looked him straight in the eye. The wraps were off. There was no more time for fooling. From his expression and the look in his eye she could see this was a naked request. Not to be outdone, she looked quizzically at him.

'How about cockcrow?' she said.

The party did not go on late. The dedicated business community, like the film world, were too conscious that late nights do not make for sharp wits. At half past nine Sam came to Laurel and asked her if she wanted to go.

'Not yet, Sam,' she told him. 'Forrest has asked me to stay on and see his bronzes. Apparently he's got a great collection.'

He looked at her enquiringly.

'Make sure he doesn't get you dancing for him.'

'Don't worry. What time are we on parade in the morning?'

'Eight-thirty. It's going to be a rough old session if we're not going to go home fleeced. Goodnight.'

As he turned to go Laurel spoke.

'Sam—get an early night. Make sure you're on the ball tomorrow.'

Sam puzzled over her parting remark. It did not sound like Laurel. As he walked down the hotel corridor he shrugged his shoulders. Women!

By ten o'clock the last guest had gone. Forrest led Laurel out of the main room towards the bedroom suite.

'Would you like to have a look around?' he invited. 'This is quite an apartment.'

'I'd rather have a glass of champagne. I've spent so much time talking I'm as dry as a bone.'

'OK, Cinderella.'

The staff had gone and he went to a champagne cooler and poured her a glass.

'Thank you, Forrest. How about you?'

His glass was empty. Laurel picked it up, went to the bar, sloshed in a formidable quantity of Southern Comfort and filled it up with Perrier water.

'Cheers.' He raised his glass. 'Here's to the sexiest, slinkiest lady I've seen tonight.'

'Fie there, Mr Forrest, you do me too much honour!' She looked at him demurely. 'Now show me those wonderful bronzes I've heard so much about,' she smiled.

Bronzes were indeed Forrest Holbrook's passion. He had a world-renowned collection.

'Honey, the collection's at home. I've only got two here that travel around with me, just to keep me company.'

'I'd love to see them.'

'Sure thing. You know where they are?'

'Where are they?'

'Right through there in my little old bedroom. What d'ya think about that?'

He peered at her owlishly. The Southern Comfort

was beginning to get to him. Laurel raised her eyebrows.

'What am I meant to think about that?' she asked softly.

He shrugged.

'Dunno. Wouldn't like you to think I was playing the Pied Piper to get you between the sheets.'

'Forrest, I know you wouldn't stoop to anything like that. Would you?' She was teasing him deliberately. 'Can I have some more champagne?' she added.

Without waiting for him to reply she poured it out and then followed suit with more Southern Comfort for him. There was barely room for the Perrier water in the big tumbler. She raised her glass to him.

'Now, Prince Charming, take Cinderella to the ball. Or are you the Pied Piper?'

Laurel was getting used to opulence, but the sheer extravagance of the bedroom suite took her breath away. A vast double bed on a raised dais was surrounded at the head by silk swathes. A central glass chandelier sparkled above and on the walls silver candelabra were encompassed by oval mirrors. The furniture was Chinese Chippendale. The whole of one wall was taken up by a picture window that overlooked the city of Phoenix. It lay before them like a dense sprinkling of stars thrown haphazardly on to a black velvet cushion.

On a satinwood commode stood a pair of bronzes. One was of a satyr sitting beside a nymph. One hand of the satyr held a set of pipes and the other was around the nymph. The nymph was beset by shyness and the satyr was suffering from priapism. Forrest pointed at it with pride.

'By Riccio, one of the greatest,' he told her.

Laurel raised an eyebrow. 'I can see that!'

Forrest ignored that and pointed to the second

bronze. It showed a lion attacking a horse. The horse's skin was stretched into folds by the lion's teeth and claws. Its head was drawn back, the mouth was open and the eyes were bolting with terror. The effect was fierce, dramatic and, to Laurel, exciting. Forrest looked hard at her.

'What d'ya think of that, eh, Cinderella? Susini. I got a lot going for that guy. Reckon he knew what it was to be a lion.'

His hand was round her waist and she felt it slip down to her buttock. His big hand squeezed the cheek of her bottom tightly.

'I feel sorry for the horse. You can almost feel his pain.'

'That's the law of the jungle—the lion getting his share.'

His hand had slipped lower and she could feel his finger pushing the silk between her cheeks. She turned to face him and put her arms on his shoulders.

'You're like a lion, Forrest, but do you get your share?'

His tough brown features creased into a smile.

'I'd sure as hell like to get it now,' he told her.

'You've played the Pied Piper. See what it's like to play the lion.'

It was like being caught up in a whirlwind.

His hands went to her zip and her Bruce Oldfield dress fell to the floor in a heap around her ankles. The next moment Forrest had picked her up and carried her to the bed, his hands pulling at the straps of her slip. She put her hands to his neck and whispered in his ear,

'Steady there, Mr Lion! This filly isn't going to run away.'

She took off his jacket and tie, feeling the quivering energy within him despite the Southern Comfort. He

stood beside the bed, mute while she took off his shirt
and undid his belt. When she finally slipped off his
pants she gasped. He was built like a mountain gorilla
and his erection was gigantic. She took him in both her
hands and licked the great blue helmet, holding the
root of him tight in one hand, the other massaging him
gently. He gasped,

'For Christ's sake, Laurel!'

He stood, feet apart, rooted to the carpet as she
worked upon him. She could feel him approaching
orgasm and her tongue flicked faster. When she knew
he was not going to hang on any longer she stopped and
lay back. With a feverish haste he tore off her
underwear, throwing slip and knickers across the room
in his desperation. When he reared above her she took
him in her hands and moved him up and down against
her. He stood it for so long and then, with a growl, he
lunged into her.

She was so wet there was no stopping him. She felt
the great bulb of him filling her, pumping in and out
with the tireless rhythm of a nodding donkey. The
drink slowed the advent of his orgasm and he pursued it
with a relentless ferocity that had her breathless and
anguished. He came with a bellow that she thought
would put out the lights and collapsed beside her in a
mountainous heap of gasping exhaustion.

Laurel looked at her watch. It was midnight. At two
o'clock she woke him up, with the lights still on and a
glass of champagne in her hand. Forrest did not realise
he had been deliberately awoken. She had done it by
stroking the sensitive area behind the base of his
scrotum. He sat up and licked his lips, his mouth dry.
She passed him the glass of champagne.

'Try this and you'll feel better. How about a
sandwich?'

He drained the champagne and looked at her

appreciatively. She got out of bed, went into the next room and came back with a plate of pastrami sandwiches. They sat beside each other, under a sheet only, looking out over Phoenix and drinking champagne with the pastrami. Laurel kept his glass filled until the bottle was empty, then took his glass from him.

She brushed up the back of his neck with her hand and whispered into his ear,

'This time I'll be the lion!'

And she was. This time it took them longer, and Laurel marvelled at the way he performed after the alcohol he had drunk. They slept until six, when she woke him again.

'Time to move—I heard the cock crow,' she said. 'How about a shower?'

Forrest shook his head like a man who has been knocked down in a boxing bout.

'Sure thing, Laurel. You got real stamina, lady!'

He got out of bed and tottered to the bathroom. When she heard the shower running she followed him. His figure was visible through the frosted glass of the shower door. She opened it and went inside. The shower was roomy and as she stood beside him the jets needled refreshingly on her skin. He was covered in soap, and she stood close and sought his member through the suds and steam.

'Hell and back, Laurel! You never give up?'

'Do you sing in the shower, Forrest?' she asked.

'Never.'

'I'll make you.'

She did. It took time and a lot of hard work, but he sang—loud and long.

The meeting began on schedule. They trooped into the conference room at eight-thirty precisely. Laurel had just had time to get into her dress, return to her own room and prepare herself for the meeting. Sam, she noticed, was looking very sharp in a navy mohair suit and white shirt.

Forrest arrived looking an old, old man. Contrary to his usual fashion, he had little to say, and when the bargaining came Sam ran rings around him. Even Forrest's tan had turned to a murky grey. He did not even bother to read the agenda, and the meeting was concluded in half the time they had allowed.

When they had left the next morning Forrest had not appeared to see them off. Laurel still felt as though she had been in a four-day fight. Her whole body ached, her back hurt and underneath she was sore. That morning there had been an envelope in her room. The card inside read 'Who played and who paid the Piper? Forrest.'

Laurel smiled at Sam as they toasted each other in the Learjet. She knew and he knew, and she hoped it was going to prove worth it. They made two refuelling stops, and when they put down at Heathrow Laurel was grateful that she did not have to drive herself home. Sam dropped her at Apple Tree Cottage and carried her bag in for her. He stopped at the front door.

'Thanks, Laurel. That was a lot of business and a lot of fun. You can go back to being the dutiful wife.'

She watched the Bentley whirl off with a thoughtful expression. He was right, but little did he realise whose wife she intended to be.

The next day she went to visit David.

CHAPTER TWENTY–TWO

'RALPH? Yes, it's Ginette. We'd like to take you up on your offer of Argenteuil. Will that be all right?'

She held the instrument a foot away from her ear as Ralph foghorned his assent.

'Thank you, darling—you're a lovely cousin. 'Bye!'

Ginette smiled as she put the telephone down. Even Tinker would have a job finding them if she whisked David away to Jersey without telling anyone. She just had to stay out of trouble until they got away. David would be safe in the hospital, but she was not sure about her own safety at Netherby Place. The sooner they were gone the better.

Getting David out of the hospital was more difficult than she had imagined. He still had some fluid on his lung, and Mr Brade was adamant about keeping him in hospital until there was no chance of a relapse. Looking after a colleague always carried an extra responsibility, and he was not going to be swayed against his better judgement.

Mark Slater spread his hands at Ginette, who was cross at the delay.

'Sister, I'm sorry, but the chief says no and that's it,' he explained.

She looked at him.

'Dr Slater, you know what's going on behind this, don't you?'

Mark nodded.

'I've got an idea. He's in some sort of danger from a mob—God knows why.'

'I want you to make sure that there's nobody, but

nobody, allowed in here except the nursing staff,' Ginette told him earnestly. 'No visitors, no vicars, no librarians, no papermen. Just nobody who's not a nurse.'

Mark looked at her determined expression, the thrust of her chin and the glint in her green eyes, and pitied anybody who tried to creep past the net while she was there.

'I'll do my best,' he promised. 'What about Mrs Compton?'

He had not meant it as a barb, but it stuck in Ginette's flesh. Somehow, since David had been ill, her attitude had changed. Now she regarded him as hers. No longer was she the supplicant mistress. The thought of Laurel returning, with all matrimonial rights, hit her with a jolt. There was a cool hauteur about her as she looked at Mark Slater.

'Mrs Compton is in America, so the question won't arise.'

'Mrs Compton is right here. And it does arise.'

They were standing outside the door to David's room and Laurel had walked up behind them, picking up their last remarks. She was smartly dressed in a cream lightweight suit and a red pillbox hat. Her black hair was swept up and she carried a red leather bag.

'Good evening, Sister Irving. I'd like to see my husband—that is if you have no objection.'

'I'm sure he'll be glad to see you at last, Mrs Compton.'

Ginette could not resist that last little sting, as she walked away. The evening visitors were streaming into the main entrance of the hospital, crowding the main corridor, and she stood aside in an alcove to let them go by. She was standing not far from the entrance to the men's surgical ward and watched the motley groups.

She was still recovering from the surprise of seeing

Laurel and did not at first see the tall black figure in the crowd. When she did he was close, and she gazed, with a morbid fascination, at the handsome black Ashanti features and shaven head. As he went past he caught her staring at him and gave her a big, insolent smile and a suggestive wink. Instinctively she drew herself up and looked the other way.

David lay in bed looking out of the window of his fourth-floor room at the rooks nesting high in the nearby elms. From this level he had a direct view into their nests and enjoyed their raucous cawing and flapping. It took him out of the confines of his room. He moved cautiously and felt his side. It still hurt to move, but it was improving.

When Laurel came into the room, he was surprised. The events of the past few days had put her out of his mind. Time had been concertinaed. Having to cope with the pain of his smashed ribs, his mind had filed away the problem of the two women in his life. She bent over him and gave him a dutiful peck on the cheek.

'How are you, David? I hear you had a nasty dust-up with an intruder at the cottage?'

He smiled wryly at her. 'You could call it that.'

'Well, you seem to be healthy enough now. When are they going to let you out?' Sympathy had never been Laurel's long suit.

'Next week. Brade is being over-cautious because it's me,' he told her.

Laurel compressed her lips, a sure sign that she was coming out with something unpleasant. David waited patiently.

'This is not easy to come out with, but I think it must be obvious to us both that we're, to use a trite phrase, "all washed up". I don't think there's any point in us trying to disguise, or to continue, a dreary charade.'

She stopped and watched him to see what effect this had. David looked up at the ceiling. Problems like this he could do without just now. His first thought was for James.

'What about the boy?' he asked.

'To hell with the boy! First we have to sort out ourselves.' The exasperation in her voice made it shrill.

'It sounds as though there isn't much sorting out to do,' David observed. 'You appear to have it cut and dried.'

Laurel did have it cut and dried in her own mind. She was not going to divorce David until she had her relationship established with Sam. At the same time she wanted more leeway to make things smoother with Sam, and she was not going to be able to do that unless she was separated from David.

'We must agree on what we're going to do. The proper thing is for us to arrange a separation. You can move into a flat.'

'And run two households?'

'Certainly. And I shall require an allowance.'

'We might just as well get divorced as that,' said David reasonably.

'I don't agree.'

Laurel did not say why she did not agree, but she had thought it out carefully. She was well aware that David had been seeing Ginette. Molly Southey was not the most discreet lady when it came to human relationships.

'Laurel, you're just not in this world!' he sighed.

'Well, you are, David, and as long as you are you'll have to pay. I'm well aware that you're having an affair with that redheaded nurse, and I'm not about to stand for it! I'll leave you to think it over.'

David lay back on the pillows, too tired to argue it out and confront her with her affair with Sam. He closed his eyes and did his best not to think about the future. Laurel was barely out of the room when Ginette came through the door.

She had seen Laurel depart and could tell from her walk and expression that there had been trouble. David's pale features confirmed it. She took his hand and looked down at him softly.

'Now what's she been up to?' she asked quietly.

He told her, and as he did so he saw fire in her eyes. She took his dressing-gown out of the cupboard. It was a navy blue Jaeger with polka-dots, a present from Laurel in happier days.

'Put this on,' she ordered. 'I'm getting you up and doing. And I've got news for you.'

David shrugged into the garment she held out for him, turning as he did so and kissing her gently on the mouth. She clung to him briefly, then pushed him away.

'Not in front of the uniform, Mr Compton, please. Now, listen to me. Mr Brade says you won't be fit for a month, and I've fixed it with the administrators. You'll be on sick leave and I can accompany you.'

The tension in his face eased slightly as he replied,

'Quite the girl, eh? You don't waste much time! OK, I surrender. When and how do we go to this island paradise of yours?'

'As soon as you leave here. I thought we might drive and take the night ferry from Portsmouth.'

'What day of the week is it now?' he asked.

'Saturday.'

'Book us across a week on Sunday. I'd like to visit James. We can drive there in the morning, spend the day with him and still have time to get to Portsmouth to catch the ferry.' He looked at her, suddenly anxious. 'You don't mind, do you?'

Ginette sat on the bed beside him.

'My darling, of course I don't mind. I'm looking

forward to meeting him. Don't forget I love you, and that means anything to do with you.'

He picked up her hand and kissed it, unable for the moment to say anything. Ginette pulled a photograph from her uniform pocket and handed it to him.

'I thought you might like to see where you're headed. Ever been to Jersey?'

David shook his head.

'You'll like it. We used to go there for holidays as children. Ralph's side of the family have had that house for years.'

David studied the photograph. It showed a white-painted house with shuttered windows. It stood on a hillside and behind it was the arc of a wide bay. In the centre of the bay was a round tower, looking like a ruined fort. Ginette pointed her finger at the house.

'That's Argenteuil, and the little girl on the swing is me. Oh, David, you'll love it! You won't need to do anything—just sunbathe and swim and listen to the birds. And that awful Tinker won't have a chance of finding us there.'

She looked out of the window at the rooks, not wanting David to see the expression on her face. She did not want him asking more questions about her source of information. As it was, she knew that China was still in the main ward and uncomfortably close.

'Darling, if we go to Jersey and don't tell anyone this man can't possibly find you,' she urged.

David nodded.

'Let's hope not. He's not the sort of chap I want to see again, except on the other side of bars.'

Ginette looked at her watch.

'I must go—the list starts in half an hour.' At the door she turned and smiled at him.

'Don't talk to any strange women while I'm away! Love you.'

No strange women came to see him that day, but Sam Bennett did. He arrived that evening, sat in the only chair and started in without preamble.

'I gather Laurel's been to see you?'

'She has,' said David.

Sam debated whether to say anything to David about his relationship with Laurel and decided against it only because David looked so ill. David decided to shift the ground.

'Sam, I must tell you I'm fed up to the teeth with this business. I may have been in debt before, but since your troubles started mine have multiplied. It's one thing to be socked for unethical conduct, but now I'm in danger of being investigated for murder if the wrong story gets to the police about the Scotsman.'

'Money never came easy, David, and you're getting a lot of it,' Sam pointed out.

'It's time it stopped. Time you called it all off. The whole game's getting too messy—and look where it's landed me. You call off your contracts and get a message through to these men to lay off me. At present I've got the insurance rating of a tail gunner in the last war!'

'No chance.' Sam shook his head. 'You're in too far now, David. You might not like a Nantucket sleigh-ride, but you're on board and you're going to stay that way. Don't get out of line or you might go over the side.' He paused. 'When will you be fit to leave?'

'I'm out next week.'

'Convalescing? Or straight back to work?'

'Having a break in Jersey for a couple of weeks and then back,' said David.

Sam stood up and held out his hand.

'Cheers, David. Stay in touch while you're away – and have a restful time. I'll see you're not bothered by that black bastard again.'

Sam left the hospital to drive to a cocktail party at the Abelsons'. He spoke to Penelope and Daphne Webber, who were huddled together in doggy conversation.

'Sorry I'm late, Penelope,' he said. 'I've been seeing David Compton.'

Daphne let out a squeal of concern.

'Poor David! How is he?'

'Doing fine. As a matter of fact, he's coming out soon.'

Daphne shook her woolly curls.

'I'll dawn in on him with some of our honey.'

Daphne, among her other home industries, kept her own bees. Honey was her sovereign remedy for all ills. Sam shook his head at her.

'Wouldn't bother, Daphne. He'll be in Jersey for a convalescent holiday.'

'Jersey? Not staying at Ralph's, is he? Lucky old thing! I keep trying to persuade Martin to go there for a holiday, but he won't leave the shop.'

Ginette's car ran smoothly up the middle lane of the M4 at a steady sixty, heading for London. She was driving, pretty in a short white skirt and a blue full-sleeved blouse. It was nine o'clock on a Sunday morning and there was little traffic. The sun was bright and a haze over the fields presaged a hot day.

David sat back, enjoying the countryside. The green fields, dotted with copses and grazed by slow-moving ochre-dappled Herefords and black and white Friesians, were a relaxing delight after the confines of his hospital room. A big transport lorry overtook them in the fast lane, making the car rock with the wind-lash.

'Go on,' said David, 'give him a run. Show him the old lady's skirts!'

The speedometer needle remained unfalteringly at sixty.

'Certainly not!' retorted Ginette. 'This car doesn't indulge in such unmannerly antics!'

'Then I will.' David put a predatory hand on her knee.

The needle faltered to fifty and the Henley sign came up on their left. Behind them came the wail of a police siren and a blue and white car went past with lights flashing.

'Serve you right, Mr Compton—trying to procure an act of gross indecency on the Queen's highway! They have places for people like you.'

The siren wailed away into the distance as they took the Henley turn-off. David looked at her. Her cheeks were flushed, her eyes bright with concentration and her copper hair drawn back and secured with a ribbon. He thought he had never seen her look lovelier.

'Have I told you I love you?' he said.

'Never.'

It was true. Somehow he had taken it for granted that she knew. He had never actually said it.

'I'm telling you now,' he assured her.

Her colour went up a shade. 'I like that—it's nice. Say it again.'

'I love you.'

'Again.'

'I love you again, and again, and again.'

Ginette turned her head and looked fondly at him. Her thoughts were racing madly and she wondered how they would ever manage to drive the rest of the journey safely.

James was waiting in the hall at St Athelstan's when they arrived. Patently he was in a dither of excitement. His face fell when he saw Ginette.

'Where's Mummy?' he demanded.

David gave him a hug.

'Mummy's away on business. This is Ginette—she

helps me at the hospital. I thought you and I might show her the river. She's never been on the river before.'

James looked up at Ginette thoughtfully, then held out his hand politely.

'You're very pretty,' he said, 'nearly as pretty as my mummy.'

Ginette took his small hand in hers and shook it solemnly.

'Thank you, James, that was a very nice compliment. I hope you'll show me the river.'

The ice was broken.

They drove to Maidenhead, parked the car by the bridge and David led the way to Salter's boatyard. There they hired a cabin cruiser for the day. David had done this many times before and they knew him well.

'You don't mind having the *Florida Moon,* Mr Compton?'

The *Florida Moon* was something of an old scow, but David had taken her out before and knew most of her foibles.

'She's all we've got for today, I'm afraid.' The man in the faded white yachting cap and blue guernsey was apologetic.

'That's all right. She's full?'

'All you'll need for the day, sir.'

The *Florida Moon* had a cockpit at the stern and a long deck over the cabins. There was a wheel on the port side with a seat for the helmsman, a throttle lever, a gear lever for forward and aft and an ignition switch. A metal notice on the bulkhead announced that she was powered by twin Volvo Penta engines. That was the sum total of the controls.

David lifted James aboard, gave a hand to Ginette and settled into the seat. The boatman waited with the mooring lines until the engine rumbled and then flung them on board. A churning wake appeared at the stern and the *Florida Moon* nosed her way out into the main stream.

Across the water the patrons of an exclusive hotel sat at white tables under gaily coloured umbrellas on a lawn that swept down to the riverside, sipping their morning coffee and being entertained by the river traffic.

David turned the *Florida Moon* and went down river, under the arches of the bridge carrying the main London road. On either side were elegant houses, each with its little boathouse, landing platform and willow tree weeping into the water. The engines thumped steadily beneath their feet, the water gurgled alongside and the sun warmed their backs pleasantly.

David put James on to the driving seat and let him take the wheel.

'You're the captain now, my son. You have the controls.'

James's eyes sparkled and his cheeks flushed with excitement. He swung the wheel to and fro out of devilment and the *Florida Moon* lurched ominously. Ginette staggered, and David put a hand on her waist to steady her.

'Steady, Captain, this isn't a power boat race, you know!'

A large river boat loomed ahead, crammed with passengers. It seemed to take up the whole width of the river, and James looked nervously round at his father.

'What'll I do, Daddy?' he asked anxiously.

'Keep her over well towards the right-hand bank and give two blasts on your horn.' David pointed to a large chrome button on the bulkhead.

'What does that do?'

'It tells them you're keeping to starboard.'

James pushed his thumb doubtfully on the button and the *Florida Moon* let out a throaty croak. He repeated it, and as the river boat went by the passengers waved at them. James was thrilled. They rolled in the wash of the bigger vessel and he nearly fell off the seat. David steadied him, and the boy looked up at his father with a shining face.

'This is just wonderful, Daddy!'

'Keep her steady on course, Captain,' ordered David.

They passed a white-singleted sculler on a tiny matchstick of a craft, flitting across the river like a water-skater. Across the water a young man wrestled with a long pole at the end of a punt while his blonde girlfriend, lying on a bank of cushions, watched him with amusement. The young man got his pole stuck in the river bed, the punt drifted on and, in a desperate endeavour, he hung on to the pole too long. The splash was accompanied by a shout of alarm and girlish laughter.

David turned to Ginette in amusement.

'Never a dull moment on the river!'

He went down to inspect the main cabin and found a fishing rod lying on one of the forward bunks. It was complete with reel, line and hook, and he brought it on deck.

'How about this, James?' he smiled.

James turned in his seat and his eyes went wide.

'Ooh, lovely! Can we fish?'

'We can when we stop.'

They stopped at Monkey Island, a haven of tall trees shading a large lawn and an elegant hotel exuding an aura of quiet good manners and a feeling of yesteryear. They moored at the landing stage and trooped up the garden path to the hotel.

An attractive girl with cornflower blue eyes and

wearing a flowered print dress to match greeted them warmly. She had an upper-class accent that made Ginette whisper to David when she had departed for their drinks,

'Do they choose all their waitresses out of Debrett?'

He nodded. 'Looks like it.'

'Would you ask her for some bait, Daddy?'

Cornflower Eyes returned with two tall glasses of Pimms and a lemonade for James. David put on his most winning manner and asked her if she could supply them with some bait.

'With pleasure, sir. We have the best.'

She gave him a thoughtfully approving smile and returned with a Players cigarette tin.

'Your bait, sir. I hope you find them sufficiently fresh and wriggly.'

As she went away the print dress swung provocatively against the flowering oleanders. David took off the perforated tin lid and looked inside. In a bed of fresh sawdust was a moving heap of wriggling white maggots. James gasped excitedly.

'What are those?'

'Bait. Bring the rod and I'll show you.'

James was soon back, and David skewered two of the maggots on to a tiny hook.

'There you are. Now go and hang that in the water and wait and see.'

As James clumped off to the boat David raised his glass to Ginette.

'Cheers. Let's hope he catches something. That's good bait, they obviously know something about fishing here.'

'I'm sure they do,' replied Ginette keenly. 'It's not the only bait around here.'

David eyed her mischievously over his glass.

'Tut-tut, do I see a little green eye?' he laughed.

'I doubt it. You've been too busy peering into big blue ones.'

He laughed again and pulled her to her feet.

'Come on, let's go and keep an eye on James.'

James was sitting patiently on the bank, watching the red quill of his float on the water. As they approached it dipped uncertainly and he reeled it in with a squeak of excitement. Out of the water, dancing in the air like animated tinsel, came a small, silvery fish with a tiny head and rose-red markings. It flapped on the grass and James picked it up. It slipped away and he picked it up again.

'Look, Daddy!'

It was a shout of pure triumph. David patted him on the back and looked at the fish.

'Well done, Captain—you've caught a nice dace. Now try again.'

'Will you bait the hook for me?'

David handed over the cigarette tin.

'Not this time. Every good fisherman has to bait his own hook. You know how to do it now. It's all yours.'

James eyed the wriggling maggots dubiously.

'I don't think I like doing that,' he decided.

'That's the game, my son. The rough with the smooth. You can't spend all your time dragging them in.'

They walked back to the hotel, leaving James looking fixedly into the tin. When they looked back they were in time to see him plunge a determined hand in to extract a maggot. They both laughed at the little pantomime and returned, hand in hand, to finish their drinks. James caught no more fish, but it did not matter. One was enough to bring the elation that comes to the successful hunter. Tonight he would be the centre of attention in the school dormitory and the tiny dace would have grown to the size of a small carp.

When they had finished their Pimms David looked round for Cornflower Eyes in order to pay for the bait, but Ginette drew him away.

'Come on. Leave some money on the table—I'm sure she's used to it.'

Ginette could not keep the touch of sharpness out of her voice. She was not yet confident enough about David not to be jealous. They regained the boat, and James looked at them keenly.

'Are you in trouble, Daddy?'

There was anxiety in the young voice. Like most children, James was sensitive to any voice inflection. David put his arm round him.

'Don't worry, James. Trouble is only as big as you make it. We're not in trouble.'

'Good. I know you could fix any trouble.'

David smiled wryly to himself, started the engines and wished it were true.

They lunched at the Hind's Head at Bray off cold sea-trout and cucumber mousse. James did not fancy this and opted for sausage and chips followed by an immense, multi-coloured ice-cream called a Knickerbocker Glory. David looked at him across a mountain of white foam on top of the concoction.

'I hope you're not sea-sick, Captain?' he queried.

James waved a long spoon at him airily.

'I could eat another of these if you'd let me. Will you?'

'No,' said David firmly, 'not a chance. I don't want you sick on the way back.'

'I was sick the last time I came out, with Mummy,' said James.

'Oh, were you? I suppose you ate two of these then?'

'No, I didn't—I just felt queer. Matron got quite upset. She gave me some awful-tasting medicine and that made me sicker than ever. Then I was all right.'

Ginette darted a look at David, who raised his eyebrows back at her.

'Is Matron at the school now, James?' David asked. 'We missed her this morning.'

'Oh yes, Daddy. I forgot to tell you—she said she specially wanted to see you before you left.'

The journey back took the rest of the afternoon, with James alternately steering the *Florida Moon* and standing on deck pretending to be the captain of a pirate ship and ordering David to do unseamanly things to passing craft. When they had returned the boat and driven back to St Athelstan's he was clearly a very tired little boy.

Matron greeted them in the hall. She was obviously worried, and after they had seen James off she turned to David.

'I wonder if I may have a word in private with you, Mr Compton?' She looked apologetically at Ginette.

'Don't worry about me,' said Ginette, 'I'll go and look round your lovely garden.'

In the Matron's office that homely lady's Welsh accent was more pronounced than ever with embarrassment.

'Mr Compton, I don't know how to put this to you,' she began. 'I'm becoming concerned.'

'Concerned, Matron? What about?'

'About James. Please understand that I'm not making any accusations, only observations.'

David realised well that if anything was coming it was to be a full-blooded accusation. It was a preamble he had heard only too often.

'It's very difficult to say this,' Matron went on, 'but every time James goes out with his mother there's some difficulty.'

Wishing she would get to the point, David forced a smile at her and said,

'What sort of difficulty, Matron?' He tried to keep his voice patient and polite.

'There's been either an accident or he's been unaccountably unwell whenever his mother has visited him alone. I must tell you I'm beginning to wonder if it's non-accidental.'

Now she had said it the poor woman let out a breath of relief. David, not normally slow, found himself wondering if he had understood her properly. He put his hands behind his back, walked to the window and turned round, his face like frozen granite.

'What you're saying, Matron, is that my wife may be trying to harm my son.'

She bristled at his brutal directness and looked squarely at him.

'Yes, Mr Compton, that's just what I'm saying. Not in those words, but it amounts to the same thing.'

He looked out of the window, fighting for control. His mind went back to the conversation he had had with Laurel when she was in hospital. It was capable of interpretation in more than one way.

Had the pat James had felt on his back in fact been a push?

Laurel was not a brilliant swimmer, but getting stuck in the weeds had been a weak story. Had it been her excuse for not rescuing James?

Across the lawn Ginette was lifting her face to a rose, and the sight of her restored his sanity. He turned round and faced the anxious little Welshwoman.

'Thank you for telling me, Matron—it can't have been easy. Thank you very much.' He paused. 'I want you to keep a close eye on him at all times. I don't wish Mrs Compton to take him out without me, and if she insists would you please telephone me?'

He scribbled in a notebook, tore out the page and handed it to the Matron.

During the first part of the journey to Portsmouth David said nothing. He did not even notice when Ginette braked fiercely on the motorway to avoid being sideswiped by the swaying trailer of an overtaking truck.

She had sensed there was something wrong when he emerged, granite-faced, from St Athelstan's and led her to the car without a word. Wisely she had said nothing and had just driven with meticulous care. They were going through Petersfield when finally he spoke.

'What did you think of my son?' There was appeal as well as question in his voice.

'I think he's a delightful and gallant young man,' she told him.

She cast a sideways glance at him and saw his face relax. Suddenly she felt a fury rise within her against Laurel. She had no knowledge of the Matron's comment; it was only because of her attitude to the boy and what she had done to David as a result. She took a breath.

'David, would you let me look after him? I could do it. If Laurel doesn't want him he'd be so much better off with you and me. He could school at St Athelstan's, but come to us for holidays. He'd have a home again.'

David looked steadily out of the window and said nothing for so long that she looked across at him to see if there was something wrong. Eventually he turned to her, his emotions under control.

'That sounds suspiciously like a proposal of marriage, Sister Irving,' he observed.

Ginette smiled tremulously.

'If it suits you, it is.'

'Ah, but would I suit you?'

Her wide mouth curved generously as she replied,

'Like no other man I've ever known.'

David leaned over and kissed her on the neck and whispered in her ear,

'When will you marry me?'

'The day after you're free?'

'You're trying to shanghai me!'

'Yes,' she said happily.

They arrived in Portsmouth at dusk. The traffic down Commercial Road held them up, but they eventually bumped over the iron ramp down to the gaping doors of the roll-on roll-off ferry ten minutes before sailing time.

The car was parked behind a giant freezer transporter and in front of a red Ferrari Dino in the cavernous bowels of the ferry. There was an air of bustle, the rumble of engines and the clanging of steel reverberating throughout the great chamber. Ginette and David climbed the iron staircase leading up to the passenger deck and found their cabin. It was small, with bunks and a tiny ladder leading to the top one. A minuscule handbasin and a mirror completed the furnishings. David slung their grip on the lower bunk.

'Let's go on deck and see us pull away from the dock.'

They did, and leant over the guard rail as the ferryboat churned away from the quayside and headed for the Channel. The myriad lights of the town twinkled at them like a giant diamond bracelet flung into the night. Ginette squeezed his hand.

'Drake and Nelson and lord knows how many other sailors must have done just what we're doing,' she said dreamily. 'They might not have seen so many lights, that's the only difference. Don't you think that's exciting?'

'Not as exciting as us.'

'You're right,' she smiled.

'There's just one thing,' David began.

'What's that?' There was a sharp note of alarm in her voice.

'I've got to resolve this business before I marry you. I'm not having you a widow before your time. Drags down your market value, you know.' He said this with an attempt at lightheartedness.

'You're just finding excuses!' Ginette protested.

'No, darling.'

From the edge in his voice she knew he meant it. He tapped his fingers, his forehead creased.

'There's something else I must tell you,' he added.

'What else?' Alarm bells started to ring within her. She wondered what he was going to produce next.

'The Matron thinks Laurel may have been trying to harm James.'

As serious as this situation was, Ginette felt almost relieved. This she could cope with.

'Why should she do that?' she asked.

'Because she wants to marry Sam Bennett. And knowing Laurel, when she sets her mind to something then nothing, but nothing, will stand in her way.'

'That still doesn't explain why she wants James out of the way.'

'Sam doesn't like illness, or any form of weakness. According to Laurel, one of the intimate snippets she let out in one of our rows, Sam has an absolute horror about deformity. Hates the thought of it, and he certainly wouldn't marry Laurel with James in the offing.'

'That's dreadful—I can't believe it!' gasped Ginette.

'You may as well. Laurel has always regarded James as an encumbrance—that's why he's where he is. Now he's something worse than an encumbrance. She regards him as an obstacle to her making it with Sam.' David's voice had the bitterness of gall.

'What are you going to do about it?' she asked.

'I don't know. It's not anything I can prove. I can't get an injunction to stop her seeing him. The Matron is going to make sure that she doesn't take him out if she does turn up, but she's not likely to at the moment. It gives me some breathing space.'

'If we're going to have James she wouldn't have to worry about Sam,' Ginette pointed out.

'That's right. The sooner we let her know and get this mess sorted the better. There's another consideration,' David added. 'She's not likely to give me a divorce unless she knows she's going to get Sam. I'm her meal ticket, and a divorce would spoil it. And God help us if she finds out about your having money.'

Ginette flinched inwardly, but was careful not to show it. Again the spectre of her wealth.

'What will you do?' she asked him. 'You can't very well say to her "Stop trying to kill off our son – your problem is solved".'

'No, I'll say just that, but wrap it up. Then she'll be all sweetness and light.'

He put his arm round her waist. The sea breeze was becoming cool, and she moved instinctively closer to him.

'You're getting better,' she told him.

'That's right. Time to go below.'

She put her hand to his face and kissed him.

'Those bunks are awfully narrow. How about your ribs?'

'I'll worry about them. If they hurt I'll grit my teeth and you can shout for me.'

She did, but they were miles off the coast of Alderney and nobody heard.

CHAPTER TWENTY–THREE

THERE WAS a gentle chop on the sea. The breeze ruffled Ginette's copper hair and flicked frets of spray off the wave tops. They stood together on the boat deck, Ginette scanning the Jersey coast through binoculars as they approached the ice-cream cone of the Corbière lighthouse. She handed them to David and held his arm with excitement.

'Look—to the right of the green patch on the left of the lighthouse. You can see the house—white, with a blue roof and shutters.'

David did his best, but saw nothing but fields and gulls. He handed the glasses back to her.

'Here you are, Hawkeye. You'll have to be my guide.'

She kissed him quickly on the cheek.

'You're an ungrateful man, but I love you, and I'm going to show you all the places where I used to play when I was a little girl.'

'Spare me the dandelion days of your adolescence!'

He dodged the playful swipe, caught her in his arms and kissed her on the mouth. She relaxed against him and then pushed him away, blushing at a round of applause from a party of approving Americans.

'Well done, mister!'

'Can I have one too?'

David gave them a friendly wave, then pointed ahead.

'Looks as though we've arrived.'

They were rounding a rocky headland and before them was the town of St Helier nestling under the bulk of Fort Regent and spreading along the shoreline.

Ginette pointed to an island in the centre of the bay, with a long breakwater and an ancient and impressive fortress.

'Elizabeth Castle, home of Jersey's first governor, the great Sir Walter Raleigh.'

'Looks good,' he commented. 'Who uses it now?'

'Fishermen and tourists. The new order.'

The ferry swept around Elizabeth Castle and made a majestic entrance into a harbour filled with a collection of boats ranging from cargo vessels, sailing boats, and cabin cruisers to the States tug, resplendent with the arms of the Duchy of Normandy. A hydrofoil came up behind them at high speed and settled into the water off its stilts as it slowed down.

Above them towered the granite walls of Fort Regent and, across the harbour, quayside cranes rattled loudly as they lifted cars and crates into the hold of a derrick-bedecked cargo boat. Ginette and David went below and got into their car. The loading door was raised and they moved up the ramp towards Customs. A perfunctory wave and a smile let them through without stopping and they were along the dual carriageway out of the town within minutes of entering the harbour.

David took in the leafy scenery of St Peter's valley. The road was narrow and in places the trees on either side turned it into a tunnel. Geese and mallards decorated a water-meadow, plonking their webbed feet happily among wild irises and bulrushes. As they passed a lake there was a disturbance in the trees and David raised his finger.

'My God, look at that!' he exclaimed.

'That' was the great grey shape of a heron, flapping his wings lazily as he sailed low over the waters of the lake to seek a less disturbed vantage point. With his outstretched wings, dangling spindly legs and long pointed beak he reminded David of Concorde coming in to land.

The car climbed its way up a steep hill flanked by tall beeches that turned the bright sunshine of the morning into speckled shade. A scampering shape ahead of them crossed the narrow road in three waving bounds, its long furry tail a graceful announcement of its identity. He turned to Ginette.

'Am I seeing things, or was that a red squirrel?'

'That's why I brought you here,' she smiled. 'I've called this road Squirrel Lane ever since I was four.'

At the top of the hill was a granite farmhouse, redolent of manure. The smell wafted into the car as they drove by. A telltale trail of mud-encrusted hoofmarks led from the crew yard across the road to a pasture field. There were six cows in it, each tethered to a stake in the ground by a long rope that gave it a grazing circle of some thirty feet. Each cow wore a light green canvas coat.

David stared at them in amazement.

'I know what Alice in Wonderland felt like. Now I've seen it all—cows with coats on!'

Ginette smiled, happy to enjoy his surprise.

'What else are you going to hit me with?' he asked.

She changed into top gear and took them past the airport, along the Avenue de la Reine Elizabeth II, at a brisk forty miles an hour.

'Lots. Minna for one. She and Sancho are Ralph's housekeepers. They live at Argenteuil and they'll look after us. Minna's a real character—old-fashioned Portuguese, and a wonderful cook. Her fighting weight is about two hundred and twenty pounds, and Sancho manages eight stone wet through.'

'They sound too good to be true!' grinned David.

'They are. Wait till you've had one of Minna's cheese omelettes and tried her *bacalao al pil-pil*.'

'What's that?' he queried.

'Dried salt cod. They sell it in the fish market and it looks revolting—like great boards of old firewood.'

'I can't wait!'

'Don't worry. What Minna does with it in the dark recesses of the kitchen I tremble to think, but it comes out a dream,' Ginette assured him.

She coasted down the hill at La Pulente and stopped on the turn halfway down. David gasped at the breathtaking view. A giant bay swept before them, disappearing towards a craggy headland in the far distance. A round tower on a granite plinth in the centre of the bay looked like a chess piece placed there by a giant artist to balance the picture.

White-topped surf, powered by the hidden forces of the Atlantic, thundered down on to sand that shone like a strip of white porcelain before sandhills dressed in spiky marram grass. Huge rollers boomed into rocky islets in front of them, sending up vertical towers of spray.

On the horizon loomed the grey hump of the island of Guernsey. It was a picture drawn on a giant canvas, and David had not seen its like before. Ginette sat and watched him, enjoying the expression on his face.

A bird of prey hovered above them, its splayed tail holding it static in the wind, its head bent as it scanned the ground. It was a kestrel. The next second it dropped, but rose again almost immediately. Silhouetted against the blue sky, a mouse dangled pathetically in its talons as it flew away to feed its young.

David shook his head in wonderment.

'What a scene! I can't believe it.' He turned and caressed her hair. 'What more spells have you in store for me?'

'That's all for now. Can't have it all at once. Now we'll find Argenteuil.'

They drove down the Five-Mile Road that ran along the shore and turned off on to the Chemin de L'Ouzière towards Mont Matthieu. The road wound past a German bunker that was still clearly labelled 'GESTEINSBOHR-KOMP.77' in concrete letters over the gun port.

Their engine noise disturbed a flock of lapwing feeding in the cow pasture and they flew off, their wings semaphoring black and white with each protesting flap. Argenteuil was a two-storeyed house built in the old colonial style. It was white, with black slatted shutters flanking the windows and a roof of shiny blue Belgian pantiles.

They drove into a spacious courtyard covered with pink granite chippings. Roses, pink, red and yellow, draped the front of the house. On the left ran a granite outhouse blazing with the vermilion blooms of a trumpet tree. The front doors opened and through the pillared portico came an immense lady looking like a pale version of a black mammy from the Southern states. She wore a green turban and a flowered pinafore over a black dress. Her sleeves were rolled up, revealing the forearms of a heavyweight boxer. Her face was round and beaming and she held out both hands to welcome Ginette.

'*Ai meu Deus*, is my little Gin' again!'

She wrapped Ginette in a voluminous embrace that would have made a polar bear flinch. Behind her, smiling and nodding with equal delight, was a slim, handsome man with delicate features. Sancho.

Ginette introduced David, who felt the survey of black button eyes from the big round face. Mentally he decided that if he ever had a row with Ginette he would want Minna to be a long way away.

'Ver' good. Your bags you leave to Sanch'. Sanch' carry them bags to der big room.'

Sancho did not look strong enough to lift a pixie's purse, but appearances were deceiving and he had the car unloaded before they were inside. The hall was large and furnished with antique chests and Persian rugs. Minna led them up to their room. It was tall and airy and had a balcony overlooking St Ouen's bay which had so caught David's imagination when they rounded La Pulente. French windows led on to the balcony and net curtains waved gently in the sea breeze.

Beneath them was a lawn with a curved swimming pool, the surface of the water twinkling in the sunlight. A swing hammock stood beside the pool and at the end of the lawn a tiered Italian fountain spurted water high into the air. The noise reached them through the french windows and within it was the faint tinkling of a bell.

David cocked his ear. 'Do you hear that?'

Ginette nodded. 'Do you know what it is?' He shook his head, and she took him to the balcony and pointed to the cascading fountain. 'Look at the top of the spray.'

Dancing on the column of water was a ball the size of a large grapefruit.

'That's it,' she said.

He watched and listened intently. There was no doubt that the tinkling was related to the movement of the ball.

'Tell me,' he invited.

'It's a fountain bell, made of metal, and inside the ball is a bell on gimbals. Ralph found the drawings in an old book and had it made years ago. I love it. Minna keeps it on all the time when I'm here. It helps me to sleep at night.'

'Doesn't it ever fall off?' asked David.

'Not as long as the fountain keeps going. If you remembered your physics you'd know why.'

'Thanks—I'd rather just listen to the music.'

Ginette led David downstairs and would not let him unpack.

'Don't worry about that,' she told him. 'Sancho will do it. He's meticulous—better than a lady's maid any day. I want to show you round.'

By the time they had done the grand tour David was beginning to feel the strain. He went pale, and Ginette hustled him to the swing hammock.

'I'm a selfish woman—so busy with wanting to show you everything I forgot you were only just ambulant.'

David lay back on the cushions, swinging gently, and blew her a kiss. Their idyll was interrupted by the ponderous footsteps of Minna, who appeared with a huge silver tray bearing a tall coffee-pot and a silver bowl full of chocolate finger biscuits.

Ginette pulled the teak table closer to the swing and Minna set the tray down.

'Thank you, Minna,' she smiled. 'I could just use a cup of coffee.'

'There's none coffee, Gin'. There's chocolate 'm better for yore poorly man. 'm coffee too jazzy.'

Minna's ideas on what was good for patients were firm and fixed, like her menus. Ginette poured liquid chocolate into two enormous breakfast cups. David eyed his speculatively.

'Am I meant to jump in or drink out of it?' he queried.

Ginette laughed. 'Just don't strain yourself lifting it. This is Minna all through. She paints life with a broad brush.'

They spent the day sunbathing by the pool. It grew hot, and David dived into the water to cool off. The exercise stretched his muscles and felt good after his long period of inactivity. As he lay on the swing seat, looking at the white, shuttered façade of Argenteuil, he pondered on the background necessary to maintain this luxurious house and the Porsche he had seen in the garage, on a tax haven island just as a summer residence.

It spoke of quiet family money and lots of it. He wondered how much of it had rubbed off on to Ginette. He thought uneasily of how she was going to react when he told her of his financial problems. Worse still, what would she say about his arrangement with Sam?

If he was her idol now she was soon going to discover what feet of clay meant.

He was determined to pay Sam back, but how? Should he wait until he had done so before telling Ginette about it? That could take a long time.

If he married her without telling her and without paying it back would she ever believe that he had not married her for her money? Did she really have a lot of money?

He felt confused, frustrated and guilty, and dived back into the pool and swam furiously up and down until he was exhausted.

In the evening Sancho brought them frosted mint juleps as they sat on the terrace listening to Mozart on the stereo. David sat back in a big basketweave chair and looked out over the bay.

A flight of mallards wheeled in the sky and planed down to settle for the night. In the trees on the hillside an owl hooted and from the end of the lawn came the fairy-tale tintinnabulation of the fountain bell. At eight o'clock Minna announced that dinner was ready. As they sat down David looked at Ginette across the table.

'What did you order for dinner?' he asked.

'I didn't. I left it to Minna.'

He raised an eyebrow. 'Do you always do that?'

'Always. Minna's the greatest cook on earth. She can produce any dish you care to name, but choice isn't one of them.'

Minna appeared with a tureen and ladled out a plate of pale yellow soup garnished with lemon and mint and thickened with egg.

'*Canja*,' she announced, and then, seeing David's lack of comprehension, 'chicken soup,' she added.

It was the finest chicken soup he had ever tasted, the lemon and mint stimulating his palate and appetite. Minna's ideas on invalid food might have been rooted in Zion. This was followed by a long dish containing tender pieces of kid in gravy. It had been roasted with sweet peppers and served surrounded by a ring of sautéed mashed potatoes. The meat was soft, succulent and rich and enhanced by the peppers. Alongside it Minna produced creamed chard studded with wedges of fried bread. The slight bitterness of the chard offset the sweetness of the peppers.

For dessert Minna placed before them dishes of small yellow egg cakes smothered in an amber syrup. They tasted brown and deep and the smothering syrup lifted their depth. David pointed to them enquiringly and appreciatively, and Minna's face was a picture of happiness.

'*Papos de anjo*,' she told him.

He looked at Ginette.

'She says they're Angel's Breasts,' she explained.

David nodded. 'She could be right.'

After dinner they curled up on the sofa and listened to more music. Ginette poured David a cognac and as he swilled the brown liquid round the glass bowl he looked at her.

'Would you like to have children?' he asked suddenly.

'I already have. . .'

She put her hand to her mouth. All along she had been frightened to tell him about Peter and her affair with Simon. At first she had not done so because it was so painful a subject that she did not want to bring it back to life by talking about it. Later, as their relationship developed, it was because she feared that David would not understand, and that it would break their precious new understanding. She could not have continued it if his reaction had been anything other than sympathetic. He darted a look at her, sensing that there was something to come.

He did not have long to wait.

'I had a son, David. He was so beautiful, but he died three years ago when he was two.'

Slowly and hesitatingly Ginette told him about Simon and what had happened to Peter. When she had finished she held her breath, trying not to let the tears come, willing herself to be in control.

When she looked at him her heart went cold. Where she had expected tenderness and compassion she saw only a hardening of his mouth and a flaring of the aquiline nose. A vertical furrow etched his forehead deeply and confirmed her worst fears.

He was jealous and getting angry.

She could not believe it. It had happened years ago, and yet he didn't like it. What sort of a man could react like this because of an old affair years before he even knew her?

David could not help himself. He knew it was illogical, he knew he was being inconsiderate, cruel even, but there was no stopping his emotion. The best he could do was to hold his tongue and not utter those biting phrases that, once loosed, could never be recalled. He stood up, with a face like black marble.

'You seem to make a habit of consoling aspiring surgeons!'

He walked away, his hands clenched in his pockets, and Ginette shook her head in bewildered misery, the tears blurring her vision as she watched him turn the corner of the house. Moments later she heard the engine of the Porsche revving and the screech of tyres as he took the sharp bend on the hill too fast.

They spent the night in wretched and unspeaking isolation. Ginette was hurt and David was tormented by emotions he could not control. They awoke early, each of them wrapped within a confining blanket of suppressed anger. Finally David made an attempt.

'Would you like to go for a swim in the sea?' he asked stiffly.

It was the first move, and it had cost him a lot to make it. Ginette restrained an impulse to tell him to go and jump in it and nodded instead. She gathered towels and they changed into costumes and parked the red Porsche on the cobbled slipway in the centre of the bay.

The tide was well out and they had to walk a long way over the sands before they reached the water's edge. The early morning sun turned Corbière light-house into a stick of sea-foam candy set upon a granite plinth and made La Rocco Tower look like a castle from the *Morte d'Arthur.*

They had the great beach to themselves. As they walked they started well apart, but gradually, without realising it, they came closer together. The sun and the sea breeze helped to wash away the dusty cloud of their discontent, and by the time they were at the edge of the tide they were holding hands.

Suddenly David pulled Ginette after him as he ran into the waves. The water felt cold and she shivered and tried to stop, but his grip was too firm and she had no alternative but to run with him. Soon they were up to their waists and together they dived into the on-coming surf. It was cold, but refreshing, and they frolicked and tumbled in the Atlantic rollers until they were tired.

Ginette saw David's head emerge from the wave alongside her and put both hands on it and pushed him under. Then she ran from the surf, her copper hair wet and tangled, her legs flailing desperately from David's vengeance for the ducking he had received. Not yet fully recovered, he weakened as they ran into soft sand and stopped, his fists raised.

'You can run, but I'll get you. You'll never get away!'

She turned, laughing, and went on her knees, her hands outstretched, supplicating.

'Please, sir, I'll be good—I swear I will. I'll never do it again.'

He stood above her and looked down. Her breast was heaving, her mouth smiling, her eyes wide and shining. He went on his knees, his arms around her. Her skin was cold, but warmed to his touch, and when his mouth covered hers and he felt the heat of her tongue, there came a surge into his loins. He tore at her costume, baring her body to the waist.

His hands cupped her breasts and he felt the rising hardness of her nipples. She moaned deep in her throat as she felt his hardness against her belly. He slid his hands behind her back and pushed her costume over the curve of her buttocks.

'No, David, not here.'

'Mmmm!'

He was kissing her neck, knowing its effect, and his hands dragged her costume to her thighs. She felt a heat flaring beneath her and no longer cared. As aroused as he, she tore at his costume and they coupled on the soft white sand, oblivious to the oncoming tide. It was fierce and fast; each greedy for the other in a surge of desire that swept over them with scalding intensity. The cold ripple of the tide, questing forward in the sand, did nothing to stay their climax; but when they were done, and a wave splashed over them,

Ginette sat up and looked around.

'Oh, my God, look there!'

Approaching, with pedantic stride, was an elderly gentleman carrying a walking stick. They picked up their costumes and ran, laughing, into the sea. As he passed them, porpoising in the waves, the man doffed his cap courteously.

Ginette, struggling back into her costume, looked at David.

'Do you think he saw us?' she asked.

'Not if he was carrying a white stick.'

She thought for a second, then there was a heaving splash as David got another ducking.

The walk back up the beach was as lighthearted as the walk out had been dreary. David looked at Ginette walking before him, saw the spring in her step, the tautness of her figure, the brightness of her smile as she looked back at him and realised that he still had his own son and that she did not.

He ran after her and took her hand.

'Ginette. . .' It was not easy for him, but he tried.

'Yes?'

'Ginette, I'm sorry.'

Misunderstanding, she looked at him with a puzzled crease in her forehead.

'David, I'm not a young girl. You don't have to apologise for making love to me.'

'No—I'm sorry about Peter. I just wanted you to know that I'm not the uncaring bastard I must seem. It's just that you're so important to me and I get carried away. I'm just selfish about you, I'm afraid, but I do care. . .And when you're ready to tell me, I should like to know more about your son.'

She put a finger to his lips, fearful that he should spoil it by saying more.

'Dearest David!'

They rescued towelling robes from the seat of the car and drove back to Argenteuil, fresh-faced and re-freshed. The Porsche backfired and crackled as David put his bare foot down on the accelerator, but then took off with a satisfying thrust in the back.

He turned his head to look at her and grinned as the sandhills flicked by on either side.

'You'd be pushed to make the Morris fly like this,' he remarked.

Ginette pursed her lips at him.

'I should hope so! The Morris is a lady. This thing is a scarlet woman—far too fast.'

He blew the horn loudly as they snaked round the hairpin bend before 'GESTEINSBOHR-KOMP.77' and into the drive of Argenteuil.

'Ting-a-ling!' he shouted, finding himself suddenly free of all care.

Minna had breakfast ready on the terrace. When they had showered and dressed she brought in a monster silver coffee-pot and a glass jug of fresh orange juice, the sides dew-frosted in the warm air. Sancho followed, pushing a heated trolley. Minna gave Ginette a maternal pat on the shoulder, a big smile, and they departed without a word.

David, with an appetite sharpened by his early morn-ing swim, inspected the contents of the trolley by lifting the lids off a row of containers. Bacon, eggs, sausages, mushrooms and grilled kidneys lay before him.

'Good old Minna! She doesn't stint, does she?'

Ginette laughed.

'You won't believe it if I tell you she was going to produce Arbroath smokies to start with! I told her you had to be careful about your diet.'

He shook his head as he attacked his breakfast.

'I just don't believe all this!' He waved an empty fork at the fountain with its bell tinkling eternally on top of the column of water. 'You'll tell me next you can make the bell play "God Save the Queen".'

'Not quite. Now what would you like to do today?'

'Nothing. Just lie by the pool and look at you.'

'Anything you say.'

And that was what they did, but not for long. David was too restless and active to stay still. He rolled off the sun bed and ran a finger down Ginette's spine as she lay basking in the warm sun.

'Let's do something,' he said suddenly.

Ginette looked at her watch. It was nearly eleven o'clock.

'We'll go and look at the port,' she decided.

David nodded.

'I like ports—they give me the feel of travel and going somewhere. But not another of Minna's meals just yet, please!'

'Don't worry, she never produces two main meals. Dinner will take all her time, so you're safe until eight o'clock.'

Twenty minutes later they were driving past the harbour at Gorey, crammed with small boats and nestling under the shadow of the mediaeval castle on Mont Orgueil. They sat on the harbour wall, warmed by the morning sun. At least, Ginette thought, here was somewhere where they were safe. She found his fingers and laced them lightly with her own. David felt tired, but relaxed.

'How do you feel?' she asked him.

'I feel I love you more every minute.'

'Do you think James would like it here?'

'He'd love it. It's just made for him.'

'Then why don't we bring him over for a holiday?' she suggested.

He sat up, his face alight and alive.

'Wonderful!'

'In the meantime I'm going to fix us a fishing trip,' Ginette told him. 'Something you'll like.'

He watched her swinging walk as she went towards the car and admired her straight back. She walked gracefully with a hint of self-conscious elegance. His eyes were not the only appreciative ones to follow her progress.

The tide was high and threw towers of spray across the road, spattering the windscreen, as they headed along the coast road leading to La Rocque. David looked at the sea washing up the slipway, threatening to engulf the main road.

'Pretty high tide tonight. Does this happen often?'

Ginette nodded, her copper hair glinting in the evening sun, her eyes shining.

'One of the biggest tides in the world, nearly forty feet. You'll get a better idea tomorrow.'

'What do we do tomorrow?' he asked.

'We're going for a picnic on the Ecrehous.'

'What's that? Sounds like a giant sea-creature.'

'Nearly right,' Ginette said. 'It's a rocky reef a few miles off the coast towards France.'

'Anybody live there?'

'Only in summer. There are some holiday homes on one of the islands. Otherwise it's just the birds and the fish and the odd lobster lurking in a rock hole.'

At La Rocque, on the east of the island, was a tiny harbour encased by rocks on one side and the protecting arm of a curved jetty on the other. Several boats bobbed at anchor, and David viewed them with interest as Ginette parked the car by the slipway.

'What now?' he wanted to know.

'I'm going to fix our transport.'

Sitting on the wall, mending a fishing net with a ball of twine and a wooden bobbin, was a grizzled old sea-dog wearing a blue peaked cap and a navy blue jersey. He had a creased, weatherbeaten face and bright blue

eyes that twinkled as he eased himself off the wall, put
his pipe in his pocket and raised his cap to Ginette.

'It's been a long time, Ginette,' he beamed.

She shook hands with him and introduced David.

'This is Richard Valpy, the finest fisherman on the
island. He's been taking me out since I was three.'

The fisherman grinned and nodded.

'That's right, Ginette. Caught your first bass when
you was four, you did—right off Seymour Tower
there.' He waved in the direction of a Martello tower
rising from the sea about a mile away.

'Richard, can I beg a favour?' she asked him.

'Whatever you like, Ginette.'

'May I have the *Osprey* tomorrow? I want to take
David to the Ecrehous.'

The old sea-dog looked at her fondly and nodded.

'As long as you can remember your marks and you're
careful going up the channel.'

Ginette threw her arms around his neck and kissed
him.

'Richard, you're a dear! Of course I can remember
the marks—you've shown me often enough.'

The coast was full of rocks and reefs, and the marks
were navigation points to safe channels. They were
usually prominent rocks, a church steeple or a stripe
painted for the purpose on to a wall. Lining up marks
was essential for a safe passage. David raised an
eyebrow.

'Which is the *Osprey*?' he asked.

Ginette took his arm and pointed to an open boat
moored near the harbour entrance.

'There she is.'

David looked dubious.

'Not very big, is she?'

The fisherman put his pipe in his mouth and puffed
reflectively.

'She's eighteen feet of North Atlantic fishing boat—safer than the *Queen Mary*. Pal of mine escaped during the occupation in a boat half that size.'

David hastened to mollify the old fisherman.

'I'm sorry, I didn't mean to belittle your boat. It's just that. . .'

Ginette smiled at him fondly.

'We know—you're just chicken! Don't worry, the *Osprey* really would take us across the Atlantic.'

Richard Valpy blew a cloud of malodorous smoke out to sea.

'She'll be ready for the morning tide, Ginette. You want to fish?'

'Yes. We'll have a go for a while.'

'The lines and bait will be in the rear locker,' he told her.

'Richard, you are good! What can I do to thank you?'

'Maybe a nice bass for my supper when you're back on the evening tide?'

Ginette laughed.

'If we get it you shall have it.'

They stopped for a sandwich at the Seymour Inn and played a round of golf on the nine-hole course in St Ouen's Bay before returning to Argenteuil. Minna's dinner proved to be up to her customary standard, and after it David was tired and they went to bed early.

That night they needed no rocking. Ginette put her head on the fresh linen-covered pillow and was asleep at once. She would have slept until morning if something had not woken her. She sat up in the dark, wondering what it was. Eventually the silence told her.

It was the fountain bell.

The tinkling had stopped.

CHAPTER TWENTY–FOUR

GINETTE felt her flesh, her skin, her inner self go cold. Part of her love affair with Argenteuil had been the fountain bell, which never stopped. That it had done so now set every fibre of her nervous system on the alert. It was an unconscious alarm. It was not the noise that had alerted her, but the lack of it.

It was pitch black in the bedroom. There was no moon, no wind, no sound. She sat up and listened, holding her breath so that it would not mask the slightest noise. She heard nothing, but she could feel an atmosphere, a presence. She reached for the bedside lamp and clicked the switch.

Nothing happened.

The feeling within her grew more intense and she wanted to pull the covers over her head. Instead she got out of bed, felt for her negligee on the chair and put it on. David's steady breathing told her that he was still asleep.

The soft carpet under her feet made no noise as she moved carefully to the bedroom door and opened it. On the landing above the marble staircase was a light switch. She felt for it and flicked it down.

No response.

She felt the coldness of the marble under her feet as she glided down the staircase. Twice she stopped and listened. Not a sound. Once she opened her mouth to call for David, but stopped. With each step down she grew more frightened, the feeling within her more terrifying. Her nightdress was lawn and her negligee filmy. She felt as protected as a naked slave before a knight in armour.

The impulse to turn and flee back to bed and wake David grew almost irresistible. Instead she went forward to the door of the drawing-room, her inner alarm now bleeping like a Geiger counter.

She passed the bank of switches operating the hall lights. The clicks as she threw them over sounded like rifle fire, but the response was nil. Never had she been so conscious of the black blindness of the night. It covered her in a blanket of unreasoning fear.

The doorknob turned in her hand and she opened the drawing-room door slowly, hearing the delicate scrape of the carpet fibres as the wooden edge brushed across them. The smell of furniture polish came pungently to her nostrils with the enhanced perception of her senses. Normally she never noticed it.

She froze.

Somebody was in the room.

She knew it with utter certainty. Perhaps it was a temperature change so slight as to be imperceptible to the conscious mind, perhaps the pressure wave of an exhaled breath, perhaps some molecules of male pheromones sensed only by the female subconscious. Whatever it was, she knew that a man was in the room as surely as if he had been standing there on fire.

She was ice. Immobile.

She hoped, like a frightened hare, to be camouflaged by immobility. She was wrong. A voice came out of the darkness, muffled but clearly audible.

'I see you.'

The next moment a cold pencil of dazzling white light speared across the room into her face. Ginette raised her hand protectively. Beyond the beam of light she could see nothing.

'Don't move and don't scream, or you're dead.'

The voice was soft, but a hard authority in it told her that if she did scream she would be dead. The voice whispered on. It taunted her, told her in intimate detail what would happen to her if she did not do exactly as she was told. It went on and on, and she did not realise what was happening. She was being hypnotised.

It stopped her realising that the pencil was moving closer. The voice was so compelling that she did not notice its insidious approach.

'Bastardo!'

The shout came from behind and the room lit up. Illuminated before her was a giant black figure with the head of an ape. For a brief moment Ginette thought it was an ape, but it was not.

It was Tinker with a rubber gorilla mask over his head.

The torch beam shone upon him as he stood in the middle of the room, an ape-headed figure with a gleaming black torso clad only in black tights, a pencil torch in one hand, the other hand stretched forward to ward off the light which illuminated his pink palm.

Ginette looked round.

Behind her stood Minna, a huge torch in her left hand. In her right hand was a knife the size of a machete. She advanced upon Tinker, the blade raised and gleaming in the light. With her green turban and a white wrapover she looked like an avenging angel.

'Sai daqui antes que te mate!'

Tinker did not understand Portuguese, but he got the message.

In a fight Minna would not have stood a chance, but she had caught him wrong-footed and her blazing anger showed that she was past reason. With two giant strides he was through the french window and gone.

Ginette turned to Minna and burst into tears. The motherly Portuguese put her arms around her.

'OK, my little Gin'. He gone.'

'Minna dear, it's just as well. I think you really would have killed him if he hadn't!'

Minna nodded.

'I tell him that. That why he go.'

Her confidence in her powers of persuasion was total. They went to the granite outbuilding and Minna looked at the fuse boxes. They were switch-type and all the relays were down. For Tinker it had been child's play.

Minna made a pot of tea and they sat in the kitchen together, drinking out of mugs.

'You call police?' Minna asked.

Ginette shook her head.

'No, Minna, I don't think so. Not now, anyway.'

Minna raised her eyes and shrugged her shoulders, but nodded agreement. Ginette stood up and kissed her.

'Thank you, Minna—for everything,' she said, and went back to bed. She could not sleep and lay in the dark, her mind jumbling over what to do about this latest problem. She knew that it was a waste of time trying to obtain police protection. The local honorary police were not into that sort of thing on the island, and to invoke them would involve more extensive questions which she did not want. The problem went round and round in her head and she could not sleep. David awoke eventually and eyed her across the pillows.

'What's got into you this morning?' he asked sleepily. 'Suffering from insomnia?'

Ginette tried not to say anything, but could not. The fright she had received and the lack of sleep had worn through her self-control. She moved over on to his side of the bed and put her arms round him.

'Ginette, darling! What is it?'

He was worried, he had never seen her like this. Her good intentions about keeping him in the dark deserted her.

'David, he was here,' she said urgently. 'Last night, in the drawing-room.'

'Who? What are you talking about?'

'Tinker. I thought there was something wrong downstairs, and he was there with a gorilla mask. Oh, David, I was so frightened!'

He held her tightly, gentling her fears away as she told him what had happened. At first he was angry with her for not waking him and with himself for sleeping through it all. She was too upset for him to show it and his anger passed, replaced by the cold awareness that they were both in danger. Tinker, having found their hideaway, would be sure to act quickly against them. He was not a man to be ignored.

'What shall we do, David?' Ginette asked.

'I think we should have a talk with Sam Bennett,' he told her.

'What can he do?'

David knew that Sam would produce something in the way of protection for them, if only because the best form of protection is attack, and he was sure that Sam's contract men would arrive very quickly. They would almost certainly be more efficient at providing protection than they had been in hunting out the gang.

'Wait and see.'

He picked up the telephone and dialled Sam's number. He was not there and the maid was unable to give him a contact number. When he told her, Ginette felt an icy apprehension. Every moment they would be waiting for something to happen—an explosion, a shot, an accident in the car. She knew, with utter certainty, that there would be something.

What could they do?

She remembered then their projected trip to the Ecrehous.

'Don't forget we're going to the Ecrehous today—that's one place Tinker won't find us. We'll be safe there for the day, and when we get back we can have another go at contacting Sam. The safest place for us is away from the island where he can't get at us.'

They packed their bathing clothes and Minna put up a picnic for them. David walked around the grounds of Argenteuil, carrying an ash walking stick, until Ginette had everything organised for their fishing trip. Any moment he half expected the giant black to appear out of the bushes. After the events of the previous night and his earlier encounter with the man he was keen to avoid another confrontation.

After an age of preparation, and a journey across the island when he was looking at every crossroad for a car to block their path, they reached La Rocque. The *Osprey* was riding at anchor in the harbour, and they paddled out to her in a rubber dinghy.

Only when they were aboard and had the Mercedes diesel engine steadily beating under their feet and could see the harbour mouth behind them did they relax.

The *Osprey* rode the waves smoothly, the sun glittered off the water and to port reared, with monstrous pride, the mediaeval castle on Mont Orgueil.

David sat in the prow, his arms spread along the gunwale, and looked at Ginette. As she stood against the tiller, her hair streaming in the breeze and her eyes scanning the water, she looked like a latter-day Valkyrie.

They drew away from Jersey and eventually it lay as a shadow on the horizon. Ahead of them was a low line of reefs. When they approached she pointed to a rock looking like a great nose.

'See that rock? It's the Bigorne. We get that between the white one—the Sablonière—and the one that looks like a Roman galley—the Grand Galère.'

David looked anxiously around. They were surrounded by a maze of rocks. At this distance from Jersey it seemed ludicrously dangerous. Ginette appeared quite unconcerned. They swung to port on their mark and coasted up a stretch of water leading to an island bearing a cluster of huts.

'There's La Marmotière, the only one with houses on it. Now we'll line up the flagstaff with that black stripe somebody has so obligingly painted and we'll be into the lagoon. It dries out at low tide and we can go ashore for our picnic.'

The *Osprey* creamed along the rock-ridden waterway with David silently praying as the reefs surrounded them. Ginette tapped his arm and pointed to a high reef on their starboard bow.

'See that? It's called the Prières des Femmes. An immigrant ship was wrecked there. The men swam over to La Marmotière to get help and a storm blew up overnight. When they returned in the morning to fetch the women and children the rock was bare.'

'What a terrible tale!'

'Valpy says you can still hear the wails of the women when there's a storm. That's how it got its name.'

They swung to port and entered a calm stretch of water—the lagoon. David heaved the anchor overboard and a lady crab scuttled away sideways over the sandy bed, her claws raised protestingly in the clear water. David pointed down.

'See that?'

'That's nothing,' smiled Ginette. 'Wait till you tread on a turbot! They bask in the shallows, and a big one feels like an earthquake.'

The water was not deep and receding fast. They

waited, warmed by the mounting sun, then splashed ashore, Ginette leading the way.

'This is Maître Ile. It's a bird sanctuary now, but there was a priory here years ago. The monks lived here to tend a lighthouse.'

It was another world. They climbed over the rocky edge of Maître Ile on to the flattened top. Thousands of gulls rose screaming into the air at their approach, and the noise was deafening. They had to shout to hear each other. Ginette cupped her hands to her mouth.

'Don't tread on the chicks!' she warned.

In the low green shrub covering the ground were seagull chicks by the hundred, fluffy little brown and white bundles, spotted like leopards. They were everywhere. David bent down, picked up a pair and held them on the palm of his hand while Ginette took a picture with her camera. To get away from the noise they left the gull area and explored the rocky peak of the island. Ginette pointed down a shallow crevasse. Two small beaks pointed up at them, cheeping stridently.

'Baby cormorant. Now look here.'

David viewed several small towers, about three feet high, made of straw and seaweed and about eighteen inches across.

'The greater blackbacked—king of the gulls. It's a good job the young are gone, the parents can be ferocious.'

They tramped around and found a quieter spot where they could sunbathe. Ginette opened the picnic bag.

'Minna's idea of a snack,' she laughed. 'I had to trim the menu, otherwise we'd have needed a wheelbarrow!'

She produced a bottle of wine and a piece of string. David took it from her.

'I'll deal with that,' he told her. He knotted the string expertly round the neck of the bottle so that it would not slip and lowered it into a rock pool. 'Nice to have a built-in cooler around us.'

He looked at the label. 'Clos de la Mare—Jersey.' Ginette produced a whole cold chicken, hardboiled eggs, smoked salmon sandwiches and fresh tomatoes. At the bottom of the bag was a tablecloth, paper serviettes and two glasses. They sat cross-legged, facing each other, and David carved the chicken with a clasp-knife. He hauled up the wine and they toasted Minna. Then they ate the chicken with their fingers and toasted Ralph for letting them have Argenteuil.

They threw the chicken bones down into the sea where they were pounced upon by wheeling gulls. They plummeted to the water and the bone would disappear down a big yellow beak with a toss of the head. When they had finished they went back to the *Osprey*, now lying on her side on the sandy bed of the lagoon.

'Let's explore and go for a swim,' David suggested.

Ginette spread her hands.

'No costume, no towel.'

'Do we need them?' he grinned.

They crossed over the lagoon, on to La Marmotière. A white strip of shingle stretched before them like a racetrack alongside a strip of water separating them from the Prières des Femmes. David stripped off his clothes and ran naked to the water's edge.

'Last one in's a cissy!' he said, and plunged in. Ginette looked around cautiously, took off her clothes and followed David into the sea, leaving them in a pile on top of the white shingle. The water was cold and they could feel the rip of the tide. He caught her round the waist so that she was sitting on his lap in the water. She could feel the warmth of his belly against her buttocks and his hands slid up to her breasts, buoyant in the sea water. His mouth nuzzled her ear and she felt the warmth of his tongue within it.

Despite the cold of the sea she was excited at the closeness of him, and more so as she felt the hardness of his erection between her thighs. He swivelled her round easily in the water and she floated before him, her legs around his waist. She felt his hardness pushing against her and shook her head at him.

'You can't, it's too cold, and I'm sure there'll be somebody in the huts.' The holiday huts on La Marmotière looked down on them.

'Nonsense!'

He pulled her to him with an urgency she could not resist and the next moment they were locked, and coupled with a fresh urgency undeterred by the cold sea.

It was fierce and brief, and as they floated apart he said to her,

'Come on, Ginette. We don't want to be candidates for the Prières des Femmes!'

They emerged from the water and clambered to the top of the white shingle ridge. Of their clothes there was no sign. Bewildered, David trudged up and down looking for them. Fortunately the sun was warm, but there was a cooling breeze over the ridge. Ginette ran down the shingle towards the shelter of the lagoon, brushing water off her with her hands. David followed, still looking around for their clothes.

'What's going on?' he demanded. 'Is this place haunted?'

Ginette shook her head.

'I know who it is. Let's get to the *Osprey* and we can dry off in the sun.'

They reached the *Osprey* and Ginette looked inside and laughed.

'I knew it! The old devil!'

David leaned over her and there, on the duckboards in a neat pile, were their clothes. Beside them, as if on guard, was an enormous lobster waving a long pair of querulous antennae. David scrambled into his trousers with a sense of relief.

'Now tell me what's been going on. I could see us making a stark naked return into La Rocque.'

'I bet it's Alphonse,' laughed Ginette. 'It would be just his way of telling us who's boss around here.'

'Alphonse?' he queried.

'Alphonse le Gastelois. They call him the Hermit of the Ecrehous. He came here years ago because he was being hassled by the police. They thought he was a rapist and he wasn't. Anyway, he's lived here ever since—lord only knows how.'

'He put the lobster here?'

'Of course. He finds them in the rocks. He's telling us to be more careful; in a nice way.' Ginette took in a breath of fresh air and looked about. 'It's so free here, so undisturbed. It has a wonderful sort of peace.'

David cupped his ear to the noise of the gulls wheeling and shrieking over Maître Ile.

'Very. They make so much noise you can't hear to speak under them.'

'Philistine! The gull noise is a sort of peace. Let's go and explore Maître Ile before we go. There are some remains of the old priory there still.'

'How about the tide? It's coming in now.'

'Time enough,' Ginette assured him.

They splashed through the shallows of the lagoon on to Maître Ile and tramped through the low under-growth. Seagull chicks scurried before them in panic in all directions. They found the remains of the old priory, now the site of an archaeological dig, but deserted today. David was fascinated and prowled around until Ginette became bored.

'Would you like to take some gull's eggs back?' she asked him.

David looked up and nodded.

'Good idea. I've never tried a gull's egg.'

'I'll find us some while you're pottering round here.'

She walked to the other side of the small island and scrambled down some rocks on to a jutting promontory. She knew this was a place favoured by the gulls for nesting. Sure enough, there were several nests, each of them little more than a scraping on the rock and each containing three or four olive eggs with diffuse chocolate markings that camouflaged them against the fearsome greater blackbacked gull. Ginette took one from each of four nests and was carefully finding a toehold up the rock face when there was a sound above her.

'David,' she called, 'I've got four eggs for us.'

'That's just great!'

She looked up in alarm at the unaccustomed voice, to see above her a dripping black frame, a shaven skull and a grinning wide mouth.

Tinker.

There was a heart-stopping moment when neither of them moved. It seemed to last for ever until Ginette turned from him and scrambled wildly down towards the sea.

At first she clung instinctively to the clutch of eggs, but when she lost her footing she dropped them all. They made a yellow, smeary mess on the surface of a flat rock. Tinker bounded down after her. She was six feet from the waterline and preparing to dive into the sea when there was a shout behind her that made her look round. It was not a threatening shout or a shout of warning. It was not really a shout at all. It was a scream of agony.

Tinker had stepped on the flat rock, one of the few, and slipped on the eggy mess. He was lying in one of the many small crevices that made up the rocky promontory. Ginette paused at the water's edge, ready to dive in, and looked back.

Tinker looked like a great black bird struggling to get off the ground. Most of him was hidden within the crevice, but his head and shoulders projected above it. His face was contorted in an agonised rictus. His arms were outstretched. He was trying to push himself out of the crevice, but it was clear that every time he moved it caused the most intense pain.

Again and again, like a flapping bird, he tried to extricate himself. Ginette stood watching, in awful fascination. He was barely five feet from her. The water lapped at her ankles. Sweat streamed down his face and finally he stopped struggling and stared at her.

'You've got to help me!' he shouted.

Ginette stood and did nothing. It was as though she was paralysed, robbed of all power. She could not even speak. Tinker put his hands out and tried again to lift himself up, but it was no good.

He was trapped.

'It's my leg—I've broken my fucking leg! Get me out!'

She stared at him and moved at last, the water swirling round her knees as she did so. Despite the summer, it was cold. She sloshed her way up the rocks and he bellowed at her with the fury of unbelief. She was walking away from him.

'Look at the bloody tide! It's coming in like crazy. You leave me and I'm going to drown!'

She stopped, turned, and looked at the massive muscles on his arms, the great black hands gripping the rocks, and shuddered. He was only a few feet away and she had to get even closer if she was going to get past him.

She looked down at the tide level. With the forty-

foot swing it rose here, as in all the islands, with
terrifying speed. Ginette stepped slowly and carefully
on to another rock that took her closer still. She could
see beads of sweat on Tinker's forehead and every pore
of his skin. She was trembling, and as she took the last
step that would bring her closest to him, he gripped the
rocks in one last titanic heave to get free.

She bent down and held on to the tip of a granite
peak, desperate in case she came within the grasp of
those huge hands. His effort brought only a further
scream of pain. Despite her fear and the danger, she
could not leave him to drown; all her nature and
training forbade it. She looked at him again, briefly,
and the next moment she was away and scrabbling up
the promontory, shouting,

'David, David, David!'

She found him, on hands and knees, scratching the
earth from a date stone with great excitement. He
barely looked up as she approached.

'Darling, look here! I think it says 1257.'

She could have wept. Here he was, playing at being
an archaeologist while she had been nearly murdered
by Tinker! When he saw her face he leapt to his feet
and put his arms around her.

'My darling, what is it?' he demanded. 'What's
happened to you?'

She could say nothing and buried her face against his
chest, holding him tight.

'Come on, Princess. What's been going on?'

Ginette took a breath and gained control of herself.

'David, it's Tinker. He's on the rocks over there.
He's followed us somehow. He came at me and I know
he was going to kill me!'

He held her tight, smoothing her hair and cradling
her in his arms, trying to calm her near-hysteria.

'Where is he now? How did you get away?'

'He fell, David. He's stuck in a crevice with a broken leg, thank God.'

'Is he alone?'

'I suppose so. I didn't see anyone else.'

David thought quickly. Should they go and rescue Tinker? If they did, would he not attack them again?

Not if he had a broken leg. He would need their help to get him away. With the tide rising as fast as it was he would need them badly. On the other hand, it was a God-given opportunity to see the last of him without actually doing anything. Not a sin of commission, and who would know that it had been a sin of omission?

Only themselves.

Two people too many.

'Where is he?' he asked briefly.

Ginette pointed to the promontory a short distance away.

'Over the brow there.'

He looked at her for a long moment and put her aside. With slow and indecisive strides he walked towards the promontory and looked down to where Tinker lay. By now the water had reached his chest. He looked up at David when he heard the step on the rocks and the two men stared at each other.

There was no fear in Tinker's face, only the implacable stare of a bird of prey caught in a trap. David looked thoughtful. It was Tinker who broke the silence.

'What you going to do, smart boy? Sit and watch the dog show?'

He coughed and winced as a wave heaved over him and moved his body against the side of the crevice. Automatically he tried again to push himself free with his hands and failed. David moved a step closer, his better nature overriding the cold logic of the situation. Tinker grinned up at him scornfully.

'What's it, whitey? Never seen a nigger die? Not got the balls to walk away?'

There was no fear in him. He was a trapped feral animal. David tightened his lips.

'Give me your hand.'

He stepped into the water and waded towards the big man. Within seconds he was chest-deep. He held out his hands to Tinker, who grasped them, and as David groped with his feet for a firm foothold he felt the grip on his hands tighten like a steel vice. The swell of the water nearly lifted him off his feet and he pulled with all the strength of his twelve-stone frame.

Nothing happened.

Tinker must have weighed in at eighteen stone, and he was not to be moved. The shift of the wave and David's pull only served to twist the broken leg within the grip of the granite stones and despite himself he threw back his head and shouted with the pain.

'Aaiiwah!'

David got behind him and put his arms round the great chest, lifting his legs in the water and getting a purchase on rocks at waist level in order to lever Tinker upwards. It was like trying to grapple with a hippopotamus. A wave broke over the pair of them and David inhaled a mouthful of water that made him cough and gasp for breath. He lost his footing and the next moment was treading water, having lost his grip on Tinker.

He heard Ginette's voice from above.

'David, get out! For God's sake!'

In front of him the face of Tinker appeared, a scornful sneer on his handsome Ashanti features. The water was lapping his neck and the immense black rounds of his shoulders. David was kicking away when a hand gripped his wrist and he winced as the bone-crushing grip of Tinker's fingers tightened on him. The thick lips pursed and shot out a spout of sea-water.

'If I'm going, whitey, it's going to be in company. Stay for the ride, boy.'

'David!'

Desperately he tried to wrench his wrist out of the grip that was paralysing his arm. He was several inches shorter than Tinker and although the man's head was just above the water David's feet could not touch ground. Tinker was determined that he should die with him. He wrestled with his free hand to undo the implacable grip, but Tinker merely brought his other hand across and he was then gripped by both wrists. Tinker twisted his wrists down and he went under, seeing green walls laced with a million white bubbles. There was a commotion in the water as the wave receded, and when David surfaced he saw Ginette standing over Tinker.

'Let him go!' she shouted.

It was like reasoning with a ravening lion. Tinker spat at her and threw his head back to avoid being washed over. She saw another wave approaching up the channel, higher than the last. Impulsively she picked up a rock at her feet and threw it at Tinker. By a lucky chance it hit his shoulder, and David heard the crack of splintering bone before the grip on his wrist relaxed. He kicked with both feet in a convulsive effort and spun away from Tinker as the giant wave came up the channel, taking him with it and throwing him over the rocks like a bundle of rags.

He was grazed and bruised, his knees and elbows slamming viciously on the barnacled rocks. He stayed briefly on all fours, trying to get his breath, and then Ginette helped him to his feet. He stood groggily and looked around. The water was washing around his ankles and at first he could see no sign of Tinker, but then the tide receded and he saw him.

He was straining with one hand against the rocks in a final endeavour to free himself. Only his neck and head were visible as the water went down, and David saw the cords of his neck standing out with the strain. His lips were drawn back and his eyes bulged with what was his last possible attempt, because another wave was surging up the channel. The whites of his eyes grew huge, the pain of it was written savagely over his face, and as he strove with the fierce intensity of a trapped animal he looked at David.

His mouth opened to say something when the swell of the wave washed over him in an all-encompassing wall of green that shut him off in mid-shout

'Whitey bast. . .'

Ginette held David's hand and they stood together in horror, because when the wave receded Tinker did not reappear. In the depths of the clear cold water they could see the gleam of his black shaven head. Bubbles spiralled around it, but whether they were from the wave or from Tinker David was not sure.

On the other side of the approach to Maître Ile China was waiting apprehensively in a dory fitted with an outboard motor. They had hired it from a weekend fisherman at La Rocque when they had seen the couple preparing to go to sea in the *Osprey*. In the little area of La Rocque, where nothing is secret, they had been told that Ginette and David were intending to go to the Ecrehous, and Tinker had decided to follow and await his opportunity in the remote and rocky wilderness.

The couple returned to the *Osprey* in silence. David was disturbed and his wrist ached abominably where Tinker's grip had nearly taken him to the grave.

Was it murder?

Tinker's fall had been due to an act of his own volition. Ginette had only been protecting him by throwing the rock. It was a form of self-defence, and although it might have injured Tinker, it had not been the cause of his death. Ginette was still shaking. As they had stood together, looking at Tinker's shaven head under the water, she had clung to David in horror. They had retreated before the tide and had to climb up the rocks to the top of Maître Ile before they could make their way across to the lagoon where the boat lay in the lee of La Marmotière.

'What are we going to do, David?' Ginette whispered. 'We killed him.'

'He drowned. You only stopped him killing me— there's a world of difference.'

'What are we going to tell the police when we get back?'

'Nothing. There's nobody here to see us and it would only invite a load of trouble.'

Ginette thought of the lobster and remembered Alphonse.

'What about Alphonse?' she asked.

David turned to face the way they had come. They were nearly at the boat. From where they were it was impossible to see over the edge of the steep decline to the place where Tinker had died. On the beach of La Marmotière, on the other side of the lagoon, a bearded figure was sitting on the white shingle. Alphonse.

They waved and a hand was raised slowly in response.

'There's no way he could have seen us,' David assured her.

The tide was coming in fast and they sat in the boat and waited for it to lift off. David put the lobster in the rear locker, its huge pincers a menace to his bare feet. When the *Osprey* gave a lurch and started to swing on her anchor rope Ginette started the engine and they cruised slowly out of the lagoon into the channel between the reefs.

The tide was higher than when they had arrived, but the reefs still towered above them as they sailed down the channel. David watched Ginette concentrating on her marks and said nothing until they were into open sea.

'This is like walking down a street full of broken glass with bare feet,' she told him.

'Are we going straight back?' he asked.

Neither of them wanted to do anything other than return home.

'Are you sure we're not going to say anything about Tinker?'

That was Ginette's question. David thought carefully.

'If we do there's bound to be the most tremendous investigation and public hullabaloo.'

'And questions about why he should attack us.'

'Which leads us back to more investigation about the Scotsman and China.'

'Did you see anybody else on the island?' asked Ginette.

'Not a soul.'

'Then the whole thing is untraceable. When he's found the cause of death must be drowning, and he could have got all sorts of damage by then from the rocks.'

They looked at each other and nodded in accord. Ginette, with a natural practicality, turned the boat towards the Conchière.

'We'd better do some fishing,' she decided. 'It'll look strange if we get back too early.'

She slowed the engine, they got the fishing lines out and slung them over the side with lead weights, hooks and spinners. Slowly they trolled for half an hour and caught six mackerel, the bright blue and silver fish with their forked tails looking like tiny sharks on the floor of the boat.

Ginette gave the tiller to David, showed him the course to follow and pushed up the revs until they were slapping over the wave tops. As they neared La Rocque she took over again and guided the *Osprey* through the rocks into the harbour.

'We'll give the bass a miss today, it's getting late. Richard can have the lobster as a thank-you.'

China saw them depart from the Ecrehous and was puzzled. Something was wrong—he could feel it. He climbed out of the dory into the shallows. It did not take him long to look round Maître Ile and find no sign of Tinker. He looked everywhere and shouted loud in all directions, but his voice was drowned by the noise of the ever-screaming gulls.

Finally he went back to the boat and motored round to La Marmotière in case Tinker had gone over there. By the time he had finished and found no sign the tide was high and it was getting late. He was no boating man, and the thought of a voyage back to Jersey in the dark made him sweat with fright.

When Ginette and David came ashore Richard Valpy was standing by the sea wall, puffing his pipe and watching their return. Ginette fished into her duffel bag and handed over the big crustacean.

'A present from the Ecrehous, Richard,' she smiled.

The bright blue eyes glittered. It was a considerable prize.

'I always said you were a good fisherwoman, Ginette.'

Behind his back David raised an eyebrow at Ginette, who had the grace to blush. They drove back to Argenteuil, tired, sunburned and windblown, their legs aching from hours on the moving deck of the *Osprey*. After his efforts to help Tinker and his fight against the oncoming tide on the Ecrehous David was tired out.

Added to which his legs had been grazed on the rocks.

Minna scooped up the fresh mackerel with cries of delight, and when they were bathed and changed she served them grilled from a barbecue on the terrace amidst clouds of herbal smoke. David had never tasted fish quite so delicious, and said so. Minna beamed with pleasure.

'This how we cook them in Estoril, like sardines, fresh from the sea, on the carbon. You make good fishing today, yes?'

David looked up and saw Ginette shaking her head slowly, tears in her eyes.

'Yes, Minna, I think the fishing was good today.'

CHAPTER TWENTY–FIVE

GINETTE had nightmares long after Tinker's death. The first was when she woke up that night with a start from a dream that was a phantasmagoria of ape-headed men drowning in heaving seas, flying machetes and voices in the dark, accusing her of murder. It was bizarre, but the feeling of stark reality made it terrifying.

'David!' she cried.

He awoke at once, saw her sitting up in bed, terrified, and moved to comfort her. With his arm around her shoulders he could feel her shaking. Gently he stroked her hair and calmed her down.

'You don't think he's outside, do you?' she whispered.

'Who?'

'China. He might be trying to get us now that Tinker's dead.'

'Nonsense, darling. China's no Tinker. Don't worry.'

'Hold me tight, David,' she begged. 'I didn't kill him, did I?'

'No, darling. And he was trying to kill me. If it hadn't been for you I'd be out there.'

'David, don't say it!'

He moved closer, holding her tight. Her trembling stopped and she relaxed against him. His hand cupped her breast and he whispered in her ear.

'Listen!'

A delicate fairy-like tinkling reached them from the garden. It was the fountain bell. Ginette smiled to herself in the dark and went back to sleep.

The day after the trip to the Ecrehous David telephoned Sam, and found him at Offa's Hall.

'I have some news for you, Sam. Nothing I can tell you over the phone, but it's something you'll welcome.'

'Sounds good, David.'

'We're still worried about safety from the last man on your list,' David added.

'The last? Do you mean that. . .?'

'I do.'

There was a silence as Sam digested this piece of information.

'I'll fix a trip on my boat the *Peregrine*. You'll be safe on her at sea. I'll invite the Abelsons, the Southeys, and maybe Laurel could bring young James. I've not got anything special on at the moment and was planning to take the boat out. We'll sail from Southampton tomorrow—pick you up at St Helier tomorrow night. How about it?'

David thought quickly. He did not want to join the party, but he was not going to let James go without him and it would keep them out of the way of China, who might well be plotting something. While not as dangerous as Tinker, China was still to be feared.

'Thanks, Sam—very kind. OK if I bring my nurse along?'

'Bring the whole of the nurses' home if you feel bad, David. I hope you're getting better?'

'Fine, thanks.'

'Tomorrow afternoon at the harbour,' said Sam. 'We should be in about four.'

With the telephone in his hand David thought to ring Mark Slater.

'Everything OK, Mark?' he asked.

'Of course, David. How are you?'

'Fine. Just thought I'd keep in touch. If you need me my number is. . .' David paused and read out the number on the instrument, 'but we shall be off for a few days on the *Peregrine*, Sam Bennett's boat.'

'Sounds like the life!' said Mark. 'Forget about Manbury, David. Just get yourself better.'

David rang off. Despite the fact that he was on sick leave the habit of a lifetime was hard to break. He had to keep in touch. They spent the day walking to get David's strength back. Ginette took him to the north coast where cliffs rose a sheer two hundred feet from the sea. A long path, cut by prison labour, snaked along the top, wound through bracken, traversed valleys and cut through shrubland. From here they looked down on oystercatchers sunning themselves on the rocks far below.

As they walked along, their feet treading on the soft loam, two ravens flew majestically by, their shaggy-tipped wings ruffling in the thermals. They contrasted with the whiteness of the gannets, plummeting like Stukas deep into the ocean. Bobbing on the surface in groups of two or three were dark birds with orange parrot-like bills—puffins.

Ginette caught David's arm and pointed.

'Look!'

Flying low over the waves came a pair of cormorants, their wingtips almost touching the water as they skimmed over the waves, their necks outstretched. They swooped to a rocky islet and perched on it, their wings outstretched like umbrellas drying in the sun.

The path led them through a wood bright with bluebells and refreshed by a stream that turned into a waterfall, misting the air. Ginette led the way and as he watched her cross the stepping stones, David thanked his gods for bringing him together with such a beautiful woman.

Ginette turned, sensing his thoughts, and called out,

'Come on, slowcoach! You're carrying this invalid thing too far. That game's over now.'

He sprang after her, realising that it was indeed

nearly over. He was better, and he could feel that it would soon be time to get back to work. The path brought them out at Grève de Lecq, a tiny bay encircled by high ground. Brightly coloured floats bobbed on the sea outside the harbour wall, marking the position of lobster boxes. Ginette pointed them out.

'See that dark thing just under the water?'

David put the glasses on it and saw a wooden box about ten feet by four, floating under the surface.

'I've got it.'

'That's where they keep the lobsters. The fishermen catch them in pots and what they can't sell they put in these *nourrices*. They tie their claws so they can't attack each other, and when the catch is poor they can still keep up a supply to the hotels.'

'What happens if one gets his claws undone?' he asked.

'Slaughter. The others haven't a chance.'

They plodded down to the beach, found an old granite pub with a giant water-wheel still operating and sat in the sun, slaking their thirst with cold lager. Ginette hoisted her skirt slightly and held out a leg. It was a golden brown. She looked at him saucily.

'How about that?' she queried.

'Not bad for a coppernob. You don't burn?'

She shook her head.

'I'm lucky. Most girls with my colouring stay white and red and get sore.'

'I suppose you're dying to show off your nice deep tan when you get back to Manbury,' said David.

'Not at all. I'll just be glad not to have to wear stockings.'

'You lie.'

'Yes.'

They both laughed together. David held her by

the shoulders, suddenly serious.

'Will you come and live with me when we get back?' he asked urgently.

'Do you think that would be very proper?'

'No, but I'm not concerned with propriety. I'm concerned with you.'

Ginette smiled her assent and he kissed her briefly.

'You've just got yourself a flatmate.'

They sat in silence, watching the water-wheel circling, creaking and dripping. Finally David said,

'Sam said he was going to ask Laurel to come on his boat and bring James. Do you mind?'

'Of course not.'

She did not like it one bit, but was not going to say so. At the same time, the turn of their conversation revived her concern about how much David wanted her for herself. Did her money play a part in his rapidly developing scheme? She looked at his strong profile and her fears dissolved. David squeezed her hand.

'We'll have to watch her carefully and keep a close eye on young James.'

'She'll be too busy working on Sam to worry about us, and she wouldn't dare to do anything to James with us all there,' she assured him.

'Do you know what I'd like to do as soon as we're married?' David asked.

'What?'

'I'd like us to buy a house. Then we could get James back, have a nanny to keep an eye on him and start a new life.'

'Sounds marvellous,' Ginette smiled. 'Where shall we live?'

'I don't know, but there are lots of lovely places in Wiltshire. I'd like one of those thatched cottages with patterns on the thatch and a cock pheasant on the gable.'

'And a barn with great knotted cross-beams.'

'A lawn and a stream with ducks galore.'

'How about a swing and a walnut tree? All gardens should have a swing and a walnut tree.'

They stood up together, smiling with the conjured excitement, and David took her arm.

'Come on, let's start now.'

They walked back to Argenteuil and found Minna in a state of agitation, her ample features creased with worry.

'Mister Dr Compton—lady telephon' you, very worry. You ring her quick, this number.'

She held out a piece of paper with a pencilled number. When he saw the prefix David went cold. 0491 was the code for Henley-on-Thames. He was at the instrument and dialling almost before Minna had finished speaking.

'Hello, Matron. This is David Compton.'

'Thank goodness, Mr Compton!' said Matron in relief. 'It's about James.'

'What's the matter with him?'

'Nothing as far as I know. At least, I hope there isn't. It's just that Mrs Compton wants to take him away for a holiday.'

'When?'

'Tomorrow. She says she's coming to see you. After what you said I thought I'd better speak to you before he went off with her.'

'Quite right, Matron,' said David. 'She's bringing him to meet me on our friend's yacht. It's all right.'

He put the instrument down with a shake of his head. Ginette looked at him quizzically.

'What was all that about?' she wanted to know.

'The Matron was worried about letting James out with Laurel alone. I told her it was OK as she was bringing him to meet me.'

'At least we'll be safe for a bit, and maybe Sam can get his men to find China while we're at sea,' said Ginette.

'That makes this our last night here. Better not waste any time.'

He reached for her on the wide couch as Ginette cried weakly,

'Not in front of the serv. . .'

Her protest ended as his lips closed over hers, and across the hall Minna was kind enough to close the kitchen door with a resounding click.

Susan Bennett sat on the broad stool of her dressing-table and looked at herself in the mirror. Her blonde hair was growing back. There was now about an inch of stubble and it would not be long before her hairdresser could make something of it, although it would not be to Sam's taste. He had met her with long hair and he liked her to keep it that way.

She ran her hands through it anxiously and concentrated on her face. Mercifully the burns had not scarred, but there was still a dull flush on her skin that was not easy to disguise. It was fading, but it was going to take weeks yet, and in the meantime she laboured under the feeling of being handicapped. Sam had given her presents and fussed about her, but she sensed that it was a show and not from the heart. He had not yet made love to her, and she needed him so desperately, to show her that she was still attractive to him and that he still loved her.

She shook her head at herself in the mirror. He had made a wonderful recovery from his injuries and was again full of bounce and aggressive energy. Why wasn't he his usual demanding self as far as she was concerned? Where else was he satisfying his greedy sexual appetite?

Susan's eyes narrowed as she thought of Laurel. She was not a jealous person, but Laurel was attractive and she could see from the way he acted that Sam fancied her. In addition, her injuries made her feel at a disadvantage. She tried to be rational. After all, Laurel was Sam's personal assistant and it was natural that they should spend a lot of time together. David Compton was an attractive man. Why should his wife want to stray with her boss? Was this just a sexual fling on Laurel's part, or was there something more to it?

She thought of Laurel's wardrobe and the few pieces of jewellery she had seen her wearing. They were all expensive. Susan buffed her nails and looked at the engagement ring on her left hand. It was a square-cut, flawless emerald, worth a fortune. Sam had bought it in Burma during their heady courtship days. She held it up, admired it and thought again of Laurel. Despite her attraction there was a tightness about her mouth, a hardness about the eyes and a precision about her movements that suggested that her actions were calculated and motivated. Motivated by what? Not by emotion—Susan had yet to see Laurel make a spontaneous gesture of any kind. Perhaps it was power? As Sam's personal assistant she would be sure to wield power, being close to the throne.

Involuntarily Susan shook her head. It did not feel right. What was there that Sam could give her that she did not have already? Her mind strayed back to David and she had a vision of him driving out of the hospital courtyard in an old Triumph car the day she had been discharged. Unusual sort of car for a consultant surgeon. It could almost be called an old banger.

Susan sat up abruptly and snapped her fingers. That was it! Why should he drive an old banger unless he was short of money? Laurel needed money—that was obvious from her clothes and jewellery. Even as she thought it, Susan felt her stomach sink.

If Laurel was motivated by money in going for Sam it meant that this was no lighthearted fling. She meant business. She would be trying to get Sam for herself.

For ever.

Susan was holding a long, pearl-handled nail file in her right hand, and with a savage motion she stabbed it through the expensive fabric of her seat into the padding beneath. Her wide mouth hardened into a firm line and she leaned forward at the mirror and lightly touched her flushed cheeks. This was jungle law. When you were down a predator was upon you before you could get to your feet. In her case the predator had arrived in the unlikely guise of her own surgeon's wife.

A movement in the grounds below caught her eye. The Mulsanne was coasting slowly along the drive from the main gate. She stood up and went to the window. The chauffeur was driving.

Susan picked up a pair of binoculars from the windowsill and focused them on the interior of the Bentley. As the car drew into the courtyard she got a good view of Laurel in the back. The chauffeur opened the door and she caught sight of a hand on Laurel's knee. It was removed even as she looked.

The hand was Sam's.

Laurel got out and stood momentarily, a picture of elegance in a tailored navy suit, and a star brooch on her lapel glinting in the sun. Her dark hair was drawn back tightly, finishing in a smooth chignon on the back of her head. Although the style was severe it was immaculately done and the effect extremely smart. As usual her make-up was perfect, and Susan clenched her fists, hating every inch of her.

Swiftly she reached for her foundation cream and began to apply the special make-up she was using to cover her marks. As she did so her mind was travelling along her wardrobe, deciding what to wear. She decided to fight fire with fire and chose one of the outfits she knew Sam liked her to wear, which was far removed from the studied elegance of Laurel Compton. She worked quickly, and ten minutes later was walking out of her bedroom in a Technicolor outfit that suited her flamboyant looks and her mood.

Sam had gone into his study and Laurel was sitting by the marble table going through the contents of a slim crocodile briefcase. Susan walked over and greeted her with a smile.

'Laurel, I wonder if I could have a word with you?'

Laurel looked up and raised pencilled eyebrows.

'Of course, Susan. What can I do for you?' She made it sound as if she was conferring a favour, and Susan forced herself to be pleasant.

'Shall we go into the conservatory?'

She did not want Sam intruding on what she had to say, and the conservatory was well away from the study. It also tended to get very hot and Susan was used to the heat, but with a bit of luck Laurel's pan make-up would run and in that suit she would find it more than uncomfortable.

'Please sit down, Laurel.'

She indicated a wicker chair well in the sun and Laurel took it. Susan sat on the edge of the table and looked down at her.

'I'm going to be brief, Laurel, and if you repeat what I have to say I shall deny it. Nor am I going to indulge in argument. This is a plain statement of fact.'

Laurel looked at her coolly.

'Go ahead,' she invited.

'Don't think you're going to take Sam off me. He's too sharp not to see you coming at him.'

Laurel took in a drag from a cigarette and blew it out slowly.

'That's straight,' she observed calmly.

'I'm an Aussie,' said Susan. 'We are straight.'

'Then I'll be straight with you. I don't give a monkey's whether he's too sharp or not. If I want him I'll take him. And if he sees me coming it'll be only because he's kept his eyes open, bless him.'

Susan felt her anger blaze up like an incandescent blast furnace.

'You'll leave him to me, Laurel. Because if you don't you won't live to enjoy him!'

'Just what am I to infer from that crude little comment?' drawled Laurel.

'You'll infer nothing. You'll know that I'm prepared to do anything to stop you wrecking my marriage. I'll lie, maim, cheat, grovel—anything to make sure of him. You just know that.'

'Sounded to me as if you were willing to do more than that,' Laurel shrugged.

'You're damn right I am. There's nothing, absolutely nothing, I won't do. So watch it. Just watch your step.'

'The only step I'm likely to watch after this is yours.'

Laurel stood up, turned her back on Susan, and walked out of the conservatory. Susan looked after her, her face hard with hate, her hands gripping the edge of the table. After a moment she took hold of herself and walked slowly through the hall towards Sam's study.

She knocked on the door—it was something he had always insisted on for his study—and when she entered he was talking on the telephone. He waved her into a large leather armchair and turned to her when he had finished his conversation.

'Hi, gorgeous, you're looking good. How do you feel?'

He got up and bent over her to kiss her cheek. Susan put her lips up to him and received her first proper kiss since their last disastrous effort at lovemaking. They had said little to each other about that particular frustrating evening or about the night of the disaster, and those were some of the reasons they had not been close. The rape still sat darkly between them like Goya's brooding giant. Susan smiled a wide smile and forced her eyes to crinkle to make it look good.

CHAPTER TWENTY–SIX

THE *Peregrine* sat sturdily at her berth in Southampton docks. Her name, in bold gold lettering, decorated her stern. She was big and beamy, sported a short red funnel and she was all white. Not graceful, her short prow and rounded stern took her out of the front line of the chorus, but she was all comfort and could go anywhere in the world.

Captain McKeen kept her in a state of almost instant readiness. Her tanks were always fully fuelled and the twin V12 turbo-injected Detroit diesels would take her across the Atlantic at a steady fifteen knots in any weather. Her Vosper stabilisers ensured that the vagaries of the weather were not transmitted to the passengers. She carried a swimming-pool at the stern, and steel motorised covers would slide across it in heavy weather and do double duty as a helipad.

Sam liked to be mobile and he liked to be in touch. The VHF radio, with a single sideband set alongside it, saw to that. Also on the bridge was Decca satellite navigation that could pinpoint their position worldwide within seconds.

Susan and Sam stepped out of the Bentley and walked up the short gangway, to be greeted by the Captain, immaculate in white uniform with blue and gold epaulettes.

'Welcome aboard, sir.'

Captain McKeen was ex-RN, had captained a minesweeper during the Gulf war and sported a beard that made him look like the man on the Players cigarette packet. Susan watched his face carefully as he shook hands with her, wondering if he would see any change in her appearance. The Captain looked straight at her and his eyes did not flicker. She felt a wave of relief and gave him a big smile, although her face felt as though it was cracking.

They went to the master cabin, furnished in polished mahogany with a huge double bed and a Fragonard above it of a shepherdess listening coyly to a boy playing a flute. The bathroom was en-suite and contained a shower and a jacuzzi. The portholes were large and curtained with a Colefax and Fowler fabric that matched the bedspread. The carpet was a pale pink and the only touch of male interference was an eagle Kazak rug before the dressing mirror. Sam's choice.

Ash, the cabin steward, brought their luggage aboard, deposited it in the cabin and retired discreetly. Susan knew that if she did not unpack he would do so, and very expertly; he had not worked for twenty years with Cunard for nothing. She turned to find Sam looking at her appreciatively. She was wearing a flowered dress in glazed cotton that she knew he liked. It showed off her superb figure to its best advantage and the swirling skirt enhanced one of her best features, her shapely legs. They at least had not been damaged in the accident, she thought grimly to herself.

'You're looking good, girl,' beamed Sam. 'How do you feel?'

'Fine, darling. Just great!'

He came towards her and put his arm around her in an all too rare gesture of affection. She leaned against him and he did not move away, but neither did he make any further move towards her. She sensed he was at a crossroads. She would have to be careful and not frighten him away, but the feeling for her was there within him. She knew it. Once again she felt herself seethe against Laurel. If that bitch thought she was going to romp in and carry him off when the going was tough between them she was going to get a shock! This was one nut she was going to crack her pearly teeth on.

Susan held his hand for a moment and gave it a squeeze in a way they used when there was a special message they wished to convey. He came back with the same response, and some of the harsh bitterness within her began to leach away. All was not lost.

'Shall we go on deck?' she suggested. 'I like to watch from there when we leave.'

He looked faintly disappointed, and she was glad. It would not have taken much for him to be lured into bed, Sam was not one to take note of time or place when he wanted to make love, but she was not going to rush her fences.

Sam followed her on to the upper deck and stood beside her against the rail, watching the quay for the arrival of their guests. He felt a warmth towards her, engendered by her increasing wellbeing and the resumption of her looks, but also a guilt at the way he had estranged himself from her at a time when she needed him most. It was time he made amends, and he had invited James not entirely from altruistic reasons. He realised that Laurel was going to be a danger to him and with typical practicality he had decided she was not worth it.

Bedworthy she was, but he realised she would not be satisfied with the occasional expensive present, and that sort of nuisance he was not prepared to face just now. James would defuse the situation, and David's presence would help. He could see his old Susan returning every day and he was not planning to swap her for Laurel.

They stood on the upper deck, outside the bridge, and looked around the dock. A cruise liner was moored further along the quay and across the other side of the dock were two immense supertankers, their giant bulk making the *Peregrine* seem like a toy craft. There was a good deal of fuss and motor traffic on the quayside as the liner was due to sail on the same tide.

A band of Marines, resplendent in their white helmets and blue uniforms, were assembling by the Customs hall. Baggage trolleys scuttered to and fro among a throng of passengers and friends who had come to wave farewell.

The Abelsons arrived in their Volvo estate, driven by Thomson and carrying a mountain of heavily labelled baggage that looked as though it had been several times around the world, which it had. While Thomson was dealing with the baggage Sir Ralph stood on the quay and studied the *Peregrine* with his hand shading his eyes. He caught sight of Susan and Sam standing with Captain McKeen and waved. His foghorn bellow reached them as clearly as if he was standing beside them.

'Stand by for a boarding party!'

Penelope Abelson came up the gangway in an outfit that was a miasma of flowing silk and georgette and made her look like a long-haired Saluki. They were followed by the Southeys, who appeared out of the back seats of the Volvo, Molly Southey in a blue and white suit that looked decidedly naval and Colonel Southey in a blazer and regimental tie, the sun glittering off his polished black toecaps. Molly greeted them and looked enquiringly round.

'No David, no Laurel?'

Susan patted her arm.

'Don't worry, Molly—he'll be around. We're picking him up in Jersey—he's convalescing there. Laurel will be here soon.'

'Not with him, eh? Do I smell a rat?' asked Molly archly.

Susan looked at her pointedly and pursed her lips.

'Perhaps something. You'll see.'

Captain McKeen came to them. 'Your guests will be delayed, then, sir?' he queried.

It was as close to a complaint as the Captain was likely to come to. Laurel was late.

Trust the bitch, thought Susan, just to make an entrance, that's all it is.

She saw James first. It was his unusual gait that caught her eye among the crowd on the quay. He was trying to run, but with his calipers it was difficult and ended in a sort of ungainly shuffle. Several yards behind him walked Laurel, elegant as ever in a scarlet suit and black toque hat and accompanied by a sweating porter overloaded with luggage.

'You'd think she was coming to a Paris collection instead of a boat! Those high heels will wreck the deck!'

Susan could not resist getting in a dig about the shoes. Laurel's heels would pit the deck noticeably and Sam would be furious. Despite that she saw him follow Laurel's progress carefully until she arrived at the bottom of the gangway. James was there first, and his relief when he came up it made Sam grin.

'Thank goodness! I thought you'd sail without us 'cos we were late. Hello, Mr Bennett. Thank you for having me along.'

Sam was taken aback by this. He did not know what he had expected, but it had not been this fresh-faced young boy who spoke like an angel and was so unselfconscious of his disability. He shook the prof-fered hand and gave James a welcoming smile.

'Nice to have you aboard, young man. I hope you're going to enjoy the trip.'

'I'm sure I will. I've never been on a boat like this before. All the chaps at school are crazy with envy!'

'Then we'll try and give you something to talk about when you get back.'

Laurel patted him on the shoulder.

'Come along, James. We'd better get out of the way so the Captain can cast off before we miss the tide.'

Captain McKeen, standing just behind Sam, took in the situation quickly.

'How would you like to help me take her out?' he asked James.

The boy's eyes shone with excitement.

'Is that allowed?'

'Certainly is. I could do with another hand on the bridge.'

The Captain climbed the few steps to the bridge and James followed, nimble as a squirrel despite his calipers. The gangway was already up and the shore hands were unleashing the mooring ropes from the iron bollards. They all crowded on to the bridge for the departure. The marine band was playing 'Hello, Dolly' for the cruise ship and streamers were being flung. The *Peregrine* got away first, and as they crossed the dock a signal came from the liner. The mate handed a slip of paper to the Captain.

'Signal from the *Prinz Eugen,* sir.'

Captain McKeen glanced at it and handed it to Sam, who read it with a smile. 'A SMART BIRD IN THE SUMMER SUN.'

'It's nice to be noticed,' he grinned.

Captain McKeen thought briefly.

'Make a reply, Mr Struthers. 'I FEAR THE PRINCE'S FLATTERY. STEER CLEAR OF MY STERN.'

A blast on the ship's siren accompanied this little sally and the *Peregrine* sailed out on to Southampton Water like a goose before a swan, with the mate at the helm being assisted by an excited James. No ship ever had a prouder pilot.

They sailed down the Solent and into the Channel, on course for Jersey. A south-westerly breeze brought a slight chop to the water, but the *Peregrine* rode it without demur. They passed the Cherbourg peninsula and by teatime they were rounding Noirmont Point at the north-west corner of Jersey.

There was no berth available big enough for the *Peregrine*, and Captain McKeen decided to moor in St Helier Bay. They carried a Dell Quay dory as a tender with two seventy-five-horsepower Mercury outboard motors as well as a twelve-foot clinker-built dinghy for funning. It would be no trouble to go ashore in the dory and would save fiddly manoeuvring within the harbour and perhaps some paint. It would also save them from the prying eyes of visitors who gathered alongside to gawp whenever the *Peregrine* docked.

As they were approaching Elizabeth Castle they were all collected in the main living area. Sam looked at Laurel.

'Better give David a call and let him know we're here,' he told her.

Laurel nodded and picked up the telephone. One minute later David was on the line, and she handed the instrument to Sam.

'David. We've just passed your front window. You coming aboard?'

'Sure. We'll be at the Albert Quay in fifteen minutes. Where are you?'

'Moored in the bay. I'll send the tender for you. Did you say we? You got somebody with you?'

'My nurse. I mentioned her, you remember,' said David.

'Yes, of course. See you soon.'

David turned to Ginette.

'Better get our skates on, the *Peregrine*'s in the bay.'

Ginette had some brief qualms now that they were due aboard. She did not enjoy the prospect of Laurel being there in the motley party Sam had engineered. There was also the underlying anxiety about James. She would have to be doubly vigilant on this score.

The Dell Quay dory was creaming its way towards the *Peregrine* only twenty minutes later. James was standing on the foredeck, keeping watch for his father, and waved excitedly as soon as the dory appeared around the bulk of Elizabeth Castle.

David was nearly bowled over by his son in his enthusiastic welcome, and when Sam recognised Ginette out of uniform she got an equally warm one from him. Ralph, too, appeared happy to see her. Susan fussed over her and was glad to put a little extra into it for Laurel's benefit. Ginette quickly sized up the situation between Susan, Sam and Laurel, recognising in Susan an ally and a warm-hearted girl with whom she could communicate.

Susan was surprised, nevertheless, when Ginette sought her out and asked her if they could have a private chat. She took her into their cabin and Ginette looked at her very straight.

'Susan, I won't insult you by mincing words. You don't like Laurel much, do you?'

Susan laughed harshly.

'Right there, Ginette. I hate the bloody woman's guts!'

'So do I. Susan—David and I are worried about Laurel and James.'

'Why should you worry about the two of them?' asked Susan. 'Hell, she's his mother, isn't she? Or is she?'

'Yes, she is, but she's not a bit motherly to him. In fact, we're not sure that he's entirely safe with her.'

'You're not telling me. . .?'

Ginette nodded.

'Yes, I am. We haven't any definite proof, but James has had some funny accidents, and always when Laurel has been around. It may be coincidence, we don't know, but it's very worrying.'

'Too right, but what can I do about the little squeaker?' Susan asked her.

'Well, I thought it was likely that you'd be keeping a close eye on the lady and that it might help to increase the safety factor if you knew about it. That way there would be more scrutiny and he'll be safer. I can't say it to everybody, for obvious reasons, but I thought that you, with your special relationship. . .'

'Right, girl, I'll keep a smart eye on the pair of them,' Susan promised. 'What's more, I'll tell the crew to watch the boy. Just as a matter of routine.'

Ginette pressed her hand. She liked the big Australian girl and she felt sorry for the way she was being treated. With her on their side she knew that James would be watched like a hawk, and when she told David he agreed. It would make things easier for her to marry David if Laurel ousted Susan, but Ginette did not want to think about it too much.

David spoke to Sam and told him about Tinker. He made it brief and omitted details, but he was shocked when Sam said,

'I reckon that rates the same as an operation. Well done, David!'

'You don't understand, Sam. I didn't kill him. He slipped and drowned because he couldn't get out of the rock crevice. I tried to save him.'

'Don't be modest, David. You're just trying to talk yourself out of thirty thousand. Your conscience is too tender! Tell you what—I'd have given a hundred for a ringside seat on that.'

'You're trying to make me into your bloody hit man!' complained David.

'Nothing of the sort,' Sam assured him. 'You don't need any help from me. You're doing fine on your own. Two up and one to go.'

'For God's sake, Sam!' David protested. But he saw it was no use arguing with him. 'What about China?' he asked. 'He's still dangerous.'

'I should have thought he ought to be the one to do the worrying.'

'Can't you get anyone to find him?'

'And then what, David? Don't tell me you're after his blood as well?'

Sam's smile was grim, and David gave up. He walked away in disgust and was almost out of earshot when Sam called to him.

'David!'

He turned. Sam was raising his glass to him, an enigmatic smile on his face.

'Cheer up. I've given him a week. Wait and see.'

Ash had set up the rear deck for pre-dinner drinks and served them chilled Veuve Clicquot with the quiet discretion born of years of ocean practice. Sam held up his glass as he looked at his wrist-watch.

'Ladies and gentlemen, the sun is soon to go below the yard-arm. May I toast the one among us to whom many of us owe a great deal? To David.'

They all raised their glasses, and David sat there feeling foolish and uncomfortable. They had hardly sat down when Ash appeared with a telephone.

'Call for you, Mr Compton.'

David took it, and recognised at once the heavily accented tones of Professor Langevin.

'Is that you, David? I have been telephoning everywhere for you. It is Anne-Marie—she is ill, David. She is asking for you.' In his excitement the

Professor's English had deteriorated.

'What's the problem?' asked David. 'Has the graft gone sour?'

'*Oui*, and she is not good. Toxic.'

'Do you want me to come and see her?'

'We would be very grateful,' the Professor told him. 'I know it is difficult to get away, but for you to come soon would be good for her.'

'Give me your number,' said David. He made a note of it on the damask cloth of the drinks table, and Ash winced. 'I'll get back to you, Professor.'

As he put the telephone down David was in a cleft stick. His natural duty took him to Lyons to help Anne-Marie. At the same time, he was concerned at leaving James on the *Peregrine*. He looked at Ginette and with the communication that existed between them she divined that there was something bothering him. She stood close to him and whispered,

'What is it?'

'Anne-Marie. We'll have to go, but I'm worried about leaving James.'

'Don't be. Susan will keep an eye on him. He couldn't be safer with a pair of Rottweilers.'

'Should we take him with us?' he asked worriedly.

'That wouldn't be easy,' Ginette pointed out.

'Then I'm going to have a word with Laurel.'

Ginette firmed her lips and shrugged her shoulders. David sought out Laurel.

'Laurel, I'd like to talk to you,' he said quietly.

Laurel was with Dick Southey and raised her eyebrow at David's brusque interruption.

'Carry on,' she invited.

'On deck—it's private. Sorry, Dick.'

Dick Southey gave him an understanding nod and excused himself. Over the stern rail David told Laurel he was going to Lyons.

'What's so special about that?'

'I just want to tell you that if anything happens to
James while I'm away I shall hold you responsible. Do
you understand what I mean?'

'No, David, quite frankly I don't,' said Laurel coldly.

'Then I'll tell you more clearly.' He gripped both her
wrists with an intensity that made her wince. 'If that
boy comes to any harm I'll kill you. Do you understand
now? I've had my suspicions about your actions for
some time and any move against the boy now will
confirm them.'

She looked at him, her eyes wide with pain and
fright. This was a David she had never seen. She tried
to pull away, but his grip on her wrists was implacable.

'You must be drunk!' she gasped.

'Drunk or sober, and I'm not drunk, you'd better
believe it.'

He let her go and went back into the main cabin,
surprised at his own intensity.

Sam was looking for him. He had overheard David's
conversation with the Professor and put two and two
together.

'You want to be there tonight, David?' he asked.

David shrugged. 'Nice, but impossible, I should
think.'

'Not so. Pass me the telephone.'

There was a quiet in the party at this sudden
interruption, the holiday spirit evaporating before the
spectre of surgical drama, however far removed. They
had all heard the story of the Lyons trip. Sam dialled,
spoke swiftly for a few moments and turned to David.

'The Lear will be ready for take-off at Jersey Airport
in an hour,' he told him.

David put down his champagne.

'That's wonderful! In that case we'd better be off.'
He looked across at Sam. 'Thanks, Sam. I'll ring you

from Lyons when I know what's up.' He pointed to the number on the damask that had so distressed the meticulous Ash. 'Will you tell the Professor we're on our way. I expect he'll meet us at the airport.'

'Don't worry, David. There's plenty to occupy us round here for a few days. You'll just miss out on a few good meals and the sunshine.'

Ginette looked up at David enquiringly and he nodded at her. She got up and smiled all round.

'Goodbye, everybody. Sorry it was so short and sweet.' She turned to James, who was looking disconsolate. 'Don't worry, James, I'll bring your daddy back in a day or two safe and sound.'

David gently tousled his son's hair.

'In the meantime, young man, I expect you to keep the *Peregrine* well stocked with fish. I'm told there's a great line in bream round here. That'll keep you busy.'

He was still unhappy about leaving James, but with Anne-Marie's hand at stake there was no choice. In any case, he would only be gone for forty-eight hours.

They were away in the Dell Quay dory in minutes, leaving a foaming wake behind them as the high-speed propellers of the twin Mercury outboards bit into the water. David held Ginette round the waist to steady her as they crossed the wake of hydrofoil Condor 1 entering the harbour. She leaned against him, her copper hair blowing in the wind, and smiled to herself. She had watched Laurel in the short time they had been on board the *Peregrine* and it had been obvious that she was entirely absorbed in Sam.

As the *Peregrine* receded she wondered how the situation would develop between Susan and Sam and Laurel. What changes might there be when they got back? They stepped ashore at the Albert Quay and walked quickly to her car. At Argenteuil they packed with Minna's help and were ready on the tarmac at the

airport before eight o'clock and in time to see the
elegant Learjet, with its twin rear engines and upturned
wingtips, land on the main runway and taxi towards
them.

When they took off Ginette looked at the chrono-
meter on the cabin bulkhead. It read 20.05 hrs. She
looked out of the window as they took off over St
Ouen's Bay and saw the long line of white breakers and
was just able to make out the roof and swimming pool
of Argenteuil before they were arrowing through the
misty cumulus clouds and levelling off at forty thousand
feet, heading for Lyons at five hundred miles an hour.

Ginette had never flown in an aircraft of this kind,
and she revelled in it. The seats were covered in soft
white leather. They reclined and swivelled in every
direction. She got up, prowled around the cabin and
found a refreshment cabinet. In it were an assortment
of drinks and individual tins of foie gras Strasbourg and
Iranian caviar. She found a tray, and within minutes
they were spooning out the caviar and drinking cold
Perrier.

She looked at David. He seemed better for his rest,
but there were still lines around his eyes that had not
been there before. She hoped the trip was not going to
demand too much from him. He was not yet up to an
eight-hour session in the operating theatre.

Beneath them the patterned quilt that was France
slipped by swiftly, and the first intimation she had of
their arrival was the sensation in her ears as they started
their descent. The countryside became starkly visible
instead of a tapestry of pastel greens and browns, and
then there was a blur of passing buildings as they
landed. She saw a large sign which read 'AEROPORT
LYON–SATELAS' as they taxied to a halt.

The pilot came back to see them. They had barely
had time to introduce themselves at Jersey Airport, and

Ginette thought he looked more like a sixth-form schoolboy. His name was Barry Rawlins and he had blond hair and a fair moustache and the look of an expectant spaniel.

'Thank you, Captain Rawlins. That was like being on a magic carpet!'

'My pleasure, Miss. . .er. . .Irving.'

He blushed, having nearly forgotten her name, and she gave him a reassuring smile in return. Professor Langevin appeared round the wingtip and his anxiety was apparent.

'Almost you are here quicker than I! It is twenty-seven kilometres, and the traffic—*morbleu!*' He mopped his forehead with a handkerchief and looked at the aircraft. 'You do not mess about, David. To arrive so quick, in the company of such a beautiful woman—that is "*le style*", as we would say.'

Ginette considered this. It was true. David did have style. She watched him walk across the tarmac to the arrival buildings, talking earnestly to the Professor, and she felt proud of him. They drove in the Professor's old Citroën. Ginette, in the back, almost died of fright several times as they wove their way into Lyons, the Professor illustrating his conversation with gestures that left little opportunity for him to grasp the driving wheel. When Soeur Camille greeted them on the ward she whispered to her,

'Ginette, what is the matter? You look like a ghost!'

'You're right, Camille. I nearly became one—several times! As a Professor he's great, but as a taxi-driver he'd kill the city, given time.'

Camille gave her a leathery smile of sympathy.

'*Eh bien*, shall we go to see Anne-Marie? She is not very good.'

They all nodded and went with her down the corridor. She opened the door to Anne-Marie's room quietly and slowly. David stepped inside and looked at the tiny form propped on the pillows. His first emotion was one of fury that they had arrived too late.

On her face was the whiteness of death. Ginette too was upset by what she saw, not only because she was concerned for Anne-Marie, but because the colour of her face reminded her strongly of the last time she had seen her son Peter.

CHAPTER TWENTY–SEVEN

DAVID took a step towards the bed, and as he did so there was the slightest flutter of Anne-Marie's eyelids. Gently he stroked the skin of her right arm and she opened her eyes. They were large and brown, accentuated by her wasted face, but if anything she looked more ethereally beautiful than ever. She smiled faintly at him as his eyes flicked to her left hand. It looked pink and healthy, and he nodded towards it, relief spreading over him like a warm tide.

'How does it feel?' he asked gently.

By way of answer she moved the tips of her middle and index fingers, then she said,

'Thank you for coming. I knew you would.'

Soeur Camille handed him the thick folder which comprised her clinical notes. He read the last few pages carefully, his eyes scanning the pages fast. When he came to the pathology findings and the blood biochemistry his eyebrow went up. Anne-Marie watched him anxiously, noting his every expression. Finally he handed them back to Soeur Camille, and Anne-Marie spoke in a soft voice.

'What's happening to me, David? I'm not going to die, am I? I mustn't—there's so much I have got to do.'

'You're going to be fine, Anne-Marie. We'll just have to pull a few stops out. Let's just have a little look at you.'

Gently and swiftly his hands went over her. He noted the texture, temperature and colour of her skin, her respirations, the look and feel of her abdomen. He examined her throat and chest and noted the dark brown fur on her tongue. He turned to Soeur Camille.

'Can we get some urgent pathology done? Like now?'

She turned up the fob watch attached to the bib of her uniform. It was ten-thirty in the evening local time.

'*Oui*. Dr Duval will come out any time you ask him if there is a good reason.'

'I can't think of a better one.' He smiled at Anne-Marie. 'I'll be back!'

In Soeur Camille's office they gathered together while waiting for Philippe Duval. David thumbed thoughtfully through the case sheets, then looked up as Dr Duval came into the room. They shook hands and David apologised for dragging him out so late. The good-looking young Frenchman smiled.

'If you can fly from Jersey I can certainly come in from Venissieux!' he said.

'Can you do some bio-chemistry right now?' David asked.

'*Certainement.*'

'I'd like the blood urea, electrolytes, and creatinine, together with full haematology and a blood culture.'

'At once. Apart from the culture you shall have it all within the half hour.'

Ginette watched David. He was detached, occupied entirely with the urgent and desperate problem. She could tell from the way the Professor looked and the chat she had had with Soeur Camille that they were all worried. This was an operation in another sense—an operation where drugs and intellectual expertise took the place of instruments and surgical incisions.

Michel Drouin appeared, and David asked him about Anne-Marie's post-operative course after they had left. It was now six weeks since the operation. Michel Drouin stroked his protuberant chin thoughtfully.

'For the first month, everything went well. Then we

got infection—bad. Septicaemia. We gave gentamycin and she got better quick. Then trouble—no urine passed, and then too much.'

David nodded, as if he had expected it. Ginette wondered what was going on in his mind, but was careful not to interrupt. When Philippe Duval returned and handed David a sheaf of forms he ran his finger quickly down the list, nodding as he did so.

'Look here. Her blood urea is thirty-five, potassium six and creatinine fifteen hundred. Haemoglobin nine.'

Ginette could not restrain herself and blurted out,

'What does it all add up to?'

'Renal failure. She's got acute tubular necrosis of the kidney, vasomotor nephropathy, they call it now. Her kidneys are just not working and her electrolytes are up the creek. This will give her cardiac problems and a gastro-intestinal haemorrhage soon, if not already.'

'What can you do?' she queried.

'Correct the electrolyte state through a drip and use peritoneal dialysis. Her peritoneum will act as a dialysing membrane. If we can reverse this quickly she should be fine.'

'Chances?' Ginette asked.

'At her age, about fifty per cent. Is that what you'd advise, Professor?'

Professor Langevin nodded.

'We had trouble like this when I was in Chicago,' David said. 'Septicaemia treated with a nephrotoxic drug that hits a kidney compromised by the operation because of the globs of myoglobin sticking in the filter mechanism.'

Ginette looked at him.

'Where does the myoglobin come from?'

'Muscle breakdown from the grafted limb. That gives the kidney a bad time, and the halothane anaesthetic doesn't help. Along comes the septicaemia and makes it worse. After that the gentamycin kills the infection, but puts the *coup de grâce* on the kidney. Then it's downhill all the way. Finally there's a haemorrhage in the gut from the potassium rise which also sends the heart into fibrillation and arrest.'

David looked at Michel Drouin.

'You all right for Travenol dialysis fluid?' Drouin nodded. David turned to Soeur Camille.

'Can we set up for peritoneal dialysis, intravenous fluids and rectal cation exchange?'

'*Tout de suite*, Monsieur Compton.'

She was gone, and Ginette knew that everything would be ready within minutes. David stood up to go to Anne-Marie and turned to Ginette.

'Would you care to give me a hand? I think Soeur Camille will be running around in other directions.'

They went back into Anne-Marie's room. David took her hand and spoke gently and softly to her. Ginette recognised the same softness in his voice that was there when they made love.

'You're going to be fine soon, Anne-Marie, but there's one unpleasant bit to come. I'm going to pop a needle into your stomach and put you on a drip, and Soeur Camille is going to give you an enema.'

'The pricks I don't mind, but the enema I can do without,' said Anne-Marie nervously.

'It's not that sort of enema. It's just a way of getting some special stuff into you that will help your blood and your electrolytes.'

'Anything you say, David,' she sighed.

Souer Camille had the intravenous giving set ready and David slid the Venflon needle into a vein in Anne-Marie's arm, waited until the blood appeared in the container and connected the giving set.

'Fifty per cent glucose solution, please, Sister. Soluble insulin, one unit to four grams of glucose and then a large syringe and an ampoule of ten per cent calcium gluconate. Michel, would you tie her on to the ECG monitor?'

The insulin-glucose solution would reduce the dangerously high potassium level, as would the calcium gluconate he was going to inject via the drip line. This had to be done slowly and carefully under ECG control in case there was an undue effect on the heart muscle. causing a rhythm abnormality. David would see this on the monitor and stop the injection immediately if it happened.

'I'll need some eight point four per cent bicarbonate solution after this, Sister,' he told her.

Ginette watched him inject into the plastic drip line very slowly, his eyes never off the green oscilloscope screen. When the bicarbonate solution was in he turned to her.

'Now we'll do the peritoneal dialysis.'

They both scrubbed and she took the sheet off the sterile trolley for him. On it was a kidney bowl with two large needles, four inches long, and plastic tubing. Swabs and gallipots of cleaning fluid and cotton wool completed the collection. Ginette unpeeled a syringe from its paper case and David took it without touching the exterior. She snapped an ampoule of one per cent xylocaine and turned the open neck towards him. He drew it up into the syringe, picked up a spirit swab and approached Anne-Marie.

She smiled at him, wanly but bravely. Soeur Camille had her prepared, and he swabbed the brown skin of her belly and slid in the needle just to the right of her naval, raising a bleb as the local anaesthetic went in. He drove the needle down into the deeper layers of muscle, injecting as he went, until he was satisfied that he had a cylinder of anaesthetised tissue reaching down to the abdominal cavity.

He turned and picked up one of the peritoneal needles and pressed on her skin with the middle fingers of his left hand. The needle he held in his right hand like a knight with a lance.

'You're not going to stick that nasty thing in me?' she asked in alarm.

'Don't worry, you won't feel it,' he assured her.

'I bet that's what you tell all the girls!'

He smiled at her courage and pushed the needle firmly into her abdomen until he was sure that it was through the peritoneum, the filmy lining of the abdomen. He connected the plastic tube and that again to a litre bottle of dialysing fluid. The fluid in the abdomen would attract metabolites out of the blood by osmosis and the fluid would then be removed from the abdomen, full of the waste products that the kidney would normally filter out. This would be repeated many times until the kidney itself took over. The needle would stay in the abdomen until the process was finished so that Anne-Marie would be spared multiple punctures.

David peeled off his gloves and threw them on the trolley.

'Thank you, Soeur Camille. Perhaps you'd administer the enema now? Over to you, Michel. I think it would be as well to give her some frusemide and dopamine. That should improve her renal circulation and her output.'

Anne-Marie looked at him, and Ginette noticed the tears in her eyes.

'You really know how to treat a girl, don't you?' she said faintly.

David smiled at her reassuringly.

'Wait until you see how you feel tomorrow before you complain!'

They went out and met the Professor in the corridor.

'What do you think, David?' The face behind the glasses suddenly looked very old.

'She has a good chance,' David told him. 'Better because she's young. The mortality rate is seventy per cent if you're over forty.'

Ginette noticed that he was looking tired. She looked at her watch. It was midnight, eleven o'clock in Jersey. It had been a demanding time and he was not yet fully recovered.

'Is there somewhere we can stay here, Professor?' she asked.

'Ah, I am so sorry! It is arranged. Soeur Camille says she will be privileged to have you, and there is a room in the hospital for you, David.'

They exchanged glances, but there was nothing they could do about it and it was late. Soeur Camille appeared.

'I have a flat across the road. It is only two minutes to walk.'

There was a mischievous twinkle in the kindly leathery face. Ginette gave David's hand a squeeze.

'See you in the morning!' she whispered.

He went off with the Professor, looking aggrieved, while Camille patted her on the arm.

'Do not worry. He is not likely to come to any mischief with the Professor.'

Ginette nodded resignedly, and they were walking up the corridor in the opposite direction when a voice behind them halted their footsteps.

'Are you going away without saying goodbye?'

It was Philippe Duval. The attractive doctor smiled and spread his hands in a Gallic gesture of remonstrance. Ginette hoped David was out of sight round the bend in the corridor.

'Of course not, Philippe. We shan't be going until we know that Anne-Marie is on the way to recovery.'

'Then you may be here for a little time. I have something that might amuse you,' he added.

'What's that?'

'The intent to take you two ladies for a tiny nightcap in the café on the corner. I am sure you could do with it after your journey.'

Camille nodded.

'*Bon—merci. C'est très gentil,* Philippe.'

Ginette was just about to try and avoid it, but realised that she could hardly do so when Camille had just accepted and she was staying the night in her flat. Philippe took them to a bistro in the Boulevard Pinel and they drank coffee and *marc de champagne* brought by an elderly waiter wearing a striped apron and old-fashioned armlets on his shirtsleeves. There was a smell of Gauloises and a copper samovar steamed gently on a corner of the bar. The tables were partly hidden by a mahogany partition surmounted by a double brass rail and an array of *faïencerie* containing fern and aspidistra. In the corner table four old men were playing dominoes and a young man sat on a bentwood chair by the entrance playing *La Mer* on an old accordion.

To Ginette, the *marc* tasted like firewater, but Camille and Philippe pronounced it excellent. They persuaded her to have a second, and when she had finished it her head felt more than swimmy. She realised that the only thing she had eaten since a frugal lunch was a pot of Iranian caviar on the Learjet.

'I think it's time I went to bed,' she decided.

Philippe walked with them to Camille's flat. As Camille was waiting for the lift in the dark hall Ginette felt herself caught by the waist, and the next moment the amorous Frenchman was kissing her. Too tired to resist, Ginette briefly kissed him back, but when he began to pull at her skirt from behind and she felt his hand on her bare thigh she pulled away.

'No, Philippe. Thank you for taking us out, but that's enough.'

'You are a woman too attractive to leave, Ginette.'

His voice was hoarse. Ginette looked across the hall. To her surprise and dismay she saw Camille going up in the lift. As she disappeared she saw her give a wave and a smile. Camille thought she was being discreet. Ginette found Philippe an attractive man, the *marc de champagne* had blurred her judgement and he was a persistent Frenchman. He kissed her neck, something that always aroused her sexually. He whispered in her ear and she felt the tingle of his tongue exploring it. His hands stroked her back and her buttocks, and she felt his arousal through her dress as he pressed against her. Something in her hesitation told him that she was not entirely resistant, and he kissed her on the lips again. This time his mouth was open and his tongue slid over hers. She could feel the heat of his erection through his trousers and her dress, and when his hand went to his zip she knew what he was going to do.

'No, Philippe, absolutely not!'

Guilty at allowing him to kiss her in the first place, she tried to push him away. He was strong and held her close to him, his hands on her back had a strength she would not have suspected. He tried to kiss her again, but she turned her head away.

'Stop it, Philippe!' she said crossly. 'Don't be a fool!'

His voice whispered hoarsely in her ear, but she could not catch what he said. With all her strength she tried to get away, and there was a silent, panting struggle in the darkness of the stairwell. Just as she was about to shout for Camille Philippe let out a cry of pain and let her go.

'*Merde!*'

He was hopping about on one leg, his hands clasping his foot. Despite their struggle Ginette was alarmed for him.

'Philippe, what is it?' she asked anxiously.

'My foot. My damned foot!'

He sat on the floor, slipped off the shoe he was wearing and stripped off his sock.

'What's happened to it?' She knelt anxiously beside him, her anger dissipated.

'What are those shoes you are wearing?' he demanded angrily. 'They've just broken my metatarsal!'

Only then did Ginette realise what had happened. She had changed at the hospital into semi-stiletto heels, and in the struggle she had stepped on his foot with one of them. Stiletto heel injuries were well recognised in casualty departments. Exerting a pressure of around fifteen hundred pounds per square inch, they could be formidable.

'Philippe, I am sorry,' she apologised. 'I didn't mean to. Let me help you.'

He put his arm on her shoulder and got gingerly to his feet.

'You're a bad boy, Philippe, taking advantage of a poor young nurse!' Ginette scolded.

He smiled at her ruefully.

'Let us go and see Camille for a minute or two.'

Ginette shook her head. She was not going to be caught twice.

'Not tonight, my friend. Now it's *au revoir*.' She stepped to the lift and pressed the call button. 'Goodnight, Philippe.'

When she knocked at the door of the flat she knew there was something wrong when she saw Camille's face.

'What's the matter, Camille?' she asked urgently.

'It is David Compton. He rang for you. When I told him you had gone out for a moment he was not very happy.' The French nurse's agitation had rendered her accent more pronounced.

'What did he say?'

'Just what he's going to say now. Where the hell have you been?'

David's voice behind her made her spin round. Ginette had not heard the whirr of the lift and the two women were still talking in the doorway of Camille's flat. David stood there like an avenging angel, with an expression on his face that made Ginette quail.

Before he spoke again she wondered if he had seen Philippe Duval walking up the street, and prayed that he had not. If the two men got to rowing there was no knowing what would happen, or what Philippe would let out.

'We've been to a café. Have you any objection?' Attack, she felt, was the best defence.

'When you go off getting yourself half drunk with some damned French doctor, yes, I have!'

He was beside himself with rage and jealousy. He didn't normally behave like this, and the fact that he had done so made Ginette both cross and frightened. Her anger overcame her fear and she challenged him.

'And I too object when you let your schoolboy immaturity turn you into a rude and jealous boor. You insult our hosts! Goodnight.'

She stepped quickly backwards into the flat and closed the door straight in his face. There was a scraping noise for a moment and she thought briefly that he was going to try and kick the door down. Then there was a silence, and she heard his footsteps cross the corridor and the whirr of the lift and sighed with relief.

Camille raised her eyebrows and pursed her lips at her in a low whistle.

'That was a close thing! If he had caught you with Philippe I think you would have been hurt—both of you.'

CHAPTER TWENTY–EIGHT

WHEN Ginette and Camille arrived at the hospital the next morning they went to Camille's office to get the night report.

It was good. Anne-Marie had received repeated exchanges of the dialysis fluid and the night staff reported that her general condition had improved remarkably. Ginette listened hard as the night nurse spoke rapidly to Camille, but she was able to understand only part of what was said. She watched Camille's face intently as she was receiving the information, and her expression told it all. The auguries were favourable.

Ginette's jealousy of Anne-Marie had long departed and she was as anxious as anyone that the lovely young medical student should make a good recovery. Apart from her professional concern, Ginette knew how much David's reputation was involved and how it would be enhanced if Anne-Marie came out of this not only alive, but with a functioning hand.

Thinking of David brought her thoughts back to the previous night, and her heart sank as she wondered what she was going to say to him when they met. How could she explain her absence from the flat? If he had the slightest idea of what Philippe Duval had been doing with her he would go berserk.

Would it end their relationship?

She firmed her lips and looked out of the window as she debated within herself. God, what a piece of stupidity! Getting half drunk and running into a trap that a student nurse could have avoided. It had seemed trivial at the time. The trouble was that David would not see it that way.

She wondered if Philippe was coming in that morning, and devoutly hoped that he was not. The less the two of them met the better. They brindled at each other like stiff-legged dogs, and after last night it would be just her luck that something would come out. The difficulty was that she and Philippe were going to be working in close proximity as long as Anne-Marie was dangerously ill and he would take every advantage of it. She knew instinctively that, with his perseverance in the pursuit of women, he would not give up because she asked him to do so.

As if on cue a voice behind her said,

'*Bonjour,* Ginette. You look beautiful today.'

Philippe was standing in the office doorway, a devilish smile on his handsome face. He looked smart in his starched white coat, with the collar rakishly turned up, a tray of bottles and syringes in his hands. He looked towards Camille.

'And you too, of course, Soeur Camille,' he added.

Ginette did her best to look stern, but did not succeed. Soeur Camille was better at it, and she was on her home ground.

'Doctor Duval, if you spent less time with nurses you would have more time for your patients,' she told him severely.

'Soeur Camille, I am here to see Mademoiselle Langevin. That is if you have a member of your staff to accompany me.'

Soeur Camille revolved in her chair and fixed him with a steely look and a hint of malice in her voice.

'*Certainement,* Docteur. I am sure Soeur Irving will be pleased to accompany you. My nurses are all busy at the moment.'

Ginette glared at Camille but she had turned back to

her desk. Philippe walked beside her down the corridor to Anne-Marie's room. Before they entered, Philippe laid his hand on her arm.

'Ginette, I have thought about you all night—you are such an exciting woman. Tonight I will take you to dinner, yes?'

'No,' she said firmly.

'Tomorrow?'

'Not tomorrow.'

'You will meet me after dinner? For a *petit café-cognac*?'

'Not even for a *café,* and certainly not for a *cognac*,' Ginette assured him.

'Ginette, I will not leave you alone. You excite me, I excite you. I know that, I felt it.'

She felt herself going hot and shrewdly suspected he was playing with her deliberately for kicks.

'Look, Philippe,' she said firmly, 'what happened last night was a mistake, when I'd had too much to drink. It will never happen again. Not ever.'

He stepped closer to her and she could sense the warmth of his breath. She thought he was going to kiss her and put her hands up defensively to stop him. As she did so she saw, over his shoulder, a movement down the corridor.

It was David and the Professor.

'You do not mean that, Ginette.'

He gripped her elbows and she hissed at him,

'The Professor's coming!'

He released her immediately and opened the door to Anne-Marie's room as if nothing had happened. Ginette preceded him, and was amazed to see Anne-Marie sitting up in bed looking quite different. Despite the lines of plastic trailing in and out of her and the draped cardiac monitor leads, it was clear that she was a different girl from the one they had left the previous day.

A plastic bag containing a unit of blood hung slackly from the drip stand. The transfusion had brought colour to her cheeks which no longer bore the dark whiteness of Lazarus. Her face was less pinched and there was a new life in her eyes. Her hair was not now straggled on the pillow; it had been combed and lay sleekly around her face. Ginette could not suppress a gasp of delight.

'Anne-Marie, you're looking marvellous!'

'Hello, Ginette, good to see you. I hardly knew what was happening yesterday, so may I thank you for coming?'

Ginette shook her head in amazement. The transformation in speech and attitude was so marked. Philippe Duval stood by the edge of the bed and regarded her professionally.

'Dracula is here again, I'm afraid,' he smiled at her.

Anne-Marie held out her good arm.

'Treat it carefully, Philippe. I'm a little short on arms at the moment!'

He looked at her closely for a minute and then nodded, slipping a tourniquet over her wrist. He swabbed an area over the back of her hand and within seconds had withdrawn a syringeful of blood and transferred the contents to three different bottles. He inverted them gently and wrote on them.

'This will tell us if you are good, or if you are bluffing,' he explained.

'I'm good—I'm very good. You should try me some time.'

She was openly flirting with the doctor, and Ginette had to admire the courage of the girl who only twelve hours before had been so desperately ill.

While Philippe was trying to find a reply, uncharacteristically short for words, the door opened and Professor Langevin came in with David, followed by

Soeur Camille and Michel Drouin. There were nods of acknowledgement all round, and David stood beside Anne-Marie.

'You're better today?' he asked.

She smiled. *'Magnifique!'*

'Sleep well?'

'Better than a condemned man.'

'Mind if I take a little look at you?'

'Of course. You can look at the lot, there's not a lot to see.' She was right, her previously elfin form had wasted to a pathetic scrawn.

'There soon will be,' David promised. 'More fluids and you'll pump up like a balloon.'

'So then I'll be too fat.'

'No satisfying some ladies!'

He leaned over her and Ginette looked at the back of his head with a drop in her heart. He had not looked at her. He was totally professional. When he was like this he was a man far removed from the one she loved. The little creases around his mouth told her that he was strung up tighter than a violin string. She hoped it was because of the responsibility of Anne-Marie and nothing more, but something inside her told her that was not so.

She raised her eyes to the ceiling as she caught Camille's eye. It was going to be a difficult day.

After the examination the surgical team departed for discussion in the office. To her relief Philippe went to get the tests under way as soon as they left Anne-Marie. The Professor was ecstatic. Clearly his emotional involvement had clouded his clinical judgement, but now he was a man walking with the gods.

'You have worked a miracle upon her, David! It is the *don de Dieu* you have.'

'It's not all over yet, Professor, but she's a lot better,' David agreed.

'She is going to live—that is enough.'

David nodded.

'She'll do that. Another forty-eight hours should see her well out of the crisis.'

His speech was tight and clipped, his voice had an edge that Ginette had rarely heard. Still he had not looked at her or made a gesture towards her. It was not like him. By now they would have made eye contact frequently. She remembered David's flaring jealousy when she had said that Philippe had invited her to look around the laboratory. He had become a savage stranger, a man she did not know, a man she could not control. If that had happened because of a light remark the last time, what now?

The Professor pulled a gold watch out of his waistcoat pocket and flicked open the case.

'*Tiens,* I shall be late for the ward round if I do not go at once. Perhaps you would care to accompany me? Between us we may be able to teach these students of mine something they will remember for more than five minutes!'

It was a courteous accolade to a visiting surgeon, and Ginette could see that David was aware of it. Perhaps that mellowed his mood, because before they departed he glanced towards her with a raise of his left eyebrow and nodded briefly.

'I'll see you for lunch in the main hall. Midday.'

It was like a teacher speaking to a naughty schoolgirl and made Ginette clench her fists. Nevertheless she acquiesced with a look, and they were gone like a gaggle of stately geese.

She spent a miserable morning, and not even Camille's pragmatic approach could cheer her up. Ginette had confided to her what had happened, and her confidence had been met with a disdainful shrug.

'So you are upset with yourself because you have

kissed the handsome Philippe? Next you will tell me
you cry when you buy a chicken because it has been
killed for you!'

Ginette knew she meant well, but it did not seem to
help. Sex for Camille was obviously something she
enjoyed like a good dinner. She was not a romantic.

When the cathedral bell tolled noon Ginette was
walking across the large entrance hall of the hospital.
She saw David admiring a large flower arrangement on
a round table in the middle of the hall. He was wearing
his cashmere jacket, a cream shirt, knitted tie and fawn
trousers. As she approached him she thought how
impossibly attractive he was and her heart reached out
towards him. He was looking in the opposite direction,
and when he turned at her step she saw that he still had
the tight mouth and the hard eyes that marred his looks
and made him appear stern.

'Where would you like to eat?'

No greeting, no 'I love you, Ginette', no silly
sympathy. Just the straightforward question.

She stiffened in response.

'I don't know. I'm not very hungry.'

'We'll go for a walk in the garden, then.'

He strode out of the hall without waiting further and
she had difficulty in keeping up with him. Only when
they had crossed the lawn and were walking among the
oleanders did he slow down. Ginette could contain
herself no longer.

'David, why are you being like this?' she demanded.
'What's got into you?'

He turned his head sharply and stared at her, his eyes
flinty and pained.

'You should know. You're the one who's provoked
it.'

She felt sick. She did know. She only hoped he did
not.

'What were you doing at Camille's?' David demanded.

'Nothing. I just slept there.'

'You took a helluva time getting there! I rang and
there was no reply for ages after you left.'

'We went for a drink in the bistro,' Ginette explained
again. 'Philippe invited us and Camille said yes. What
would you expect me to do when I'm staying with her?'

'I don't expect you to scoot off like an alleycat as
soon as we say goodnight!'

Ginette felt herself getting cross.

'I am not an alleycat, and I will not be called one!'
she snapped.

'Then don't try and deserve it!'

Hot and impulsive as she was, this was too much for
Ginette. She turned abruptly and left him, the hot tears
welling into her eyes against her will. She did not want
David to see her like this, and she ran down the gravel
path towards the main road. She did not know where
she was going.

David made no attempt to follow her, and having
crossed the main road she just walked on and on. The
tears in her eyes almost blinded her, and twice she was
hooted at as she crossed a road without looking for the
traffic.

It was warm, and despite the cool cotton dress she
was wearing she became hot. A café-bar, its frontage
bedecked with chairs and tables, swam in front of her
tear-filled vision and she sat down in a wicker chair
beneath a canvas awning.

'*Madame?*'

The waitress before her had the patient concern of
the very young, and it showed in the tone of her voice
as she stood and looked curiously at the attractive
woman in the expensive dress with the tear-stained face
and far-away look.

'Un chocolat, s'il vous plaît.'

Ginette dabbed her eyes with her handkerchief and looked around. The café faced on to a square lined with plane trees and within their circle was a fountain and a tiny market with stalls selling vegetables. A white van with the side down carried a variety of pigs' heads and trotters decorated with frilly paper, while sausages of every size, colour and thickness dangled within its interior.

Most of the stalls were covered over because it was the lunch hour, their owners crowded into the café. Ginette had taken the last available table. It was a typical lunchtime scene in any French town. There was background chatter, and the smell of food, wine and cigarettes combined to give the impossible to describe but easy to recognise atmosphere of a French bistro.

Ginette began to relax and picked up the menu out of idle curiosity. Despite her normally healthy appetite she was not hungry. She was too upset, so she sat back to try to absorb and enjoy the atmosphere, the sights and sounds that belong only to a French provincial square. She was trying to decide what kind of trees they were that provided such welcome shade to the market stalls in the centre of the sqaure when she saw David.

He was walking disconsolately, hands in pockets, in front of the white van with the pigs' heads. She was about to wave and call to him, but then stopped. Let him stew for a while and get over his anger.

To her right a French family were enjoying a celebration lunch, and Ginette had watched them as they assembled. There was an elderly couple who were always greeted first, and she noted that they received three kisses, one on each cheek and one again on the first cheek. Younger couples received a peck on each cheek and some only one. Clearly a highly defined pecking order. There were about twenty of them, and

Ginette decided it was the old couple's golden wedding party. There was even a baby in a high chair enjoying titbits from anyone near who felt like feeding it.

She was horrified to see one young girl lean across and give the baby a piece of snail, but her fears were obviously groundless, because the baby chewed away at it happily.

As she was watching a toddler slipped down from its chair and on to the pavement. In the general hubbub of the lunch nobody noticed, and when the toddler strayed away from the table Ginette became worried.

She was rising from her seat when the little girl caught sight of the white van with its display of meats and sausages and, evidently attracted by the bright colours and shapes, decided to investigate. The van was on the far side of the wide, cobbled street. David saw the toddler look round uncertainly when she had crossed the street and burst into tears. Having watched her cross the road with some concern, he picked her up and carried her back to her family. Only when he was under the awning of the café did he see Ginette sitting there.

'There you are!' he exclaimed. 'I've been looking for you.' He sat opposite her at the table. 'What made you rush off like that?'

His reaction to her was frustrating. One minute savage as a mad dog and the next coming after her full of injured innocence!

'You were so damned rude, that's why!' she retorted.

'What do you expect when you start flirting with somebody? You don't expect me to sit meekly by and look the other way?'

'I was not flirting, and I don't expect you to get angry over nothing. How can we have a stable relationship if your anger gets triggered so easily? You must be reasonable!'

'I am reasonable. I'm also in love with you, and if you expect me to. . .' The pulse was beating in his left temple and his hand made a fist on the table top.

'I expect you to behave like a rational man,' said Ginette coldly.

'I am rational most of the time. But where my emotions are concerned you send me out of control!'

His voice was raised, and some of the café patrons began to glance in their direction.

'You're acting like a boy!' Ginette told him angrily.

'I'm not acting, I'm reacting; and in a way that any normal male would react when provoked.'

She looked around and tried to calm the volatile situation. 'Please stop shouting, you're creating a scene.'

'I'll create a scene all right!'

He stood up abruptly, jostled the table, and her cup smashed on the stone flags. She watched his tall figure march down the street, glanced in embarrassment at the French family group and put a note on to the saucer that held her ticket.

She was back at the hospital before she realised she had not waited for her change.

CHAPTER TWENTY–NINE

As the Dell Quay dory raced across the waters of St Helier Bay Ginette sat and watched the *Peregrine* glow in the rays of the afternoon sun. She saw a small figure in the prow waving excitedly at them: James.

The sea air blew her hair back from her face and she felt tiny droplets of spray salty on her lips. A row of faces appeared on the rail. All the party were gathered to greet them like long-lost travellers. She smiled to herself. She certainly felt like one.

David's hand felt for hers and she returned his gentle squeeze. As they came up the companionway it was James who pushed his way to the front to greet them first, his eager little face beaming with delight and excitement.

'Hello, Daddy, did you make that lady better? You've been gone a long while.'

To Ginette it felt as though they had been gone half a lifetime, and after her experience outside the café only a few hours ago she still felt bruised.

David had been waiting for her in front of the hospital entrance and had grabbed her by the arm and into the semi-privacy of an alleyway.

'Ginette, this is no good. I'm sorry if I upset you. You know I love you. It's just that a devil gets into me when I think of anyone with you.'

It was not the apology she wanted, but it was the best she was going to get and she realised it. She put her head on his chest, and when he lifted her chin up to kiss her the anger melted and it was all good again.

The Lear had brought them back so fast that with the

time change they arrived in Jersey almost at the same time as they left Lyons. When they walked into Argenteuil from the airport Minna had seen her fatigue in her face.

'My God, Miss Gin! What bin going on with you? You look like you bin chased by n'elephant!'

Ginette gave her a hug.

'I'm all right, Minna. Just tired. It got a bit rough in places.'

'Rough? Looks like it was a storm you was in!'

Minna clucked and shook her head, convinced that there had been goings-on of which she would not approve.

Once on the boat, the party were clustered round David, wanting to hear of their trip, and Ginette was left with Susan, who looked at her closely.

'You had a good time of it, Ginette?' she asked.

'Not exactly, it was pretty busy overall.'

'Looks like it was. The man seems to thrive on it, though.'

She was right. David looked a picture of health now and was talking animatedly with Molly and Dick, with James hanging on to his hand. He seemed to thrive on action. His dark hair hung forward on his forehead and he was gesticulating towards the town.

'It's just as well he does, with what he's had to put up with,' Ginette replied without thinking. Normally she did not refer to Laurel either directly or indirectly in her conversation, but the recent activities had dropped her guard.

'He doesn't look the sort of guy who's found life too troublesome,' said Susan. 'I suppose you mean that wife of his?' Ginette nodded.

'She's a tough cookie and no mistake. Now she thinks she's found better fish to fry. She's going to have to be more than lucky.'

'That's not what's got him down, Susan,' Ginette told her. 'They haven't been much good to each other for some years. It's the boy he's had to worry about.'

'Well, that's a pity about the little squeaker, but it's not the end of the world.'

'It's the finances that have crippled David, and she doesn't help with her fancy wardrobe,' Ginette explained.

'I tell you straight, Ginette. That sheila might look smart now, but when I'm finished with her she won't be good for dingo bait! Sam's a fool over women, but he's my fool and it's going to stay that way.'

Ginette looked at the beautiful Australian girl, saw the expression on her face and did not doubt it. Molly Southey came up to them, glamorous in a white sailor suit.

'We're going to have a look around St Helier—David says there are some terrific buys in the leather shops. Coming?'

Ginette looked across at David and decided to go with him. Susan shook her head.

'Crowds aren't my scene. I'll stay here and let Sam feel guilty and bring me something nice.'

Molly turned to Laurel, who was sunning herself on a long chair.

'Coming with us, Laurel?'

James answered for her.

'You're not going to leave me as well, Mummy, are you?'

Laurel flicked a look across at Sam and David.

'No, darling, I'm not going to leave you on your own.'

Bitch, though Ginette, never fails to score. The tide was high and where Captain McKeen had anchored the *Peregrine,* there was a chop on the water and the beginnings of a sea running. A strong current from

Noirmont Point had swung her so that she was head-on into the current, and the tide made a swirl around the anchor chain, which dipped into the sea at an angle. From the forestay, at the halfway mark, was a black sphere indicating that the *Peregrine* was at anchor. James put his rod together, baited the hook with a worm from a tin with holes in the lid, reeled out the line and waited patiently.

'Hey-up!'

Suddenly he had got a bite. Susan saw the rod bend and James started to reel in the line as fast as he could.

'Gently, James, you don't want to lose him,' she warned.

His face was bright with excitement. There was a ripple, then a flap on the surface of the water as the fish was pulled in. He swung back the rod and the fish, flapping on the line, landed on the deck with a thud.

It was a grey, ugly fish; flat with a big head and mouth, and a mark on the body like a thumb-print. As it thumped on the duckboards of the dinghy James looked at it uncertainly.

'He looks pretty vicious—what is he?'

Susan leaned forward and took the fish behind the head with one hand and the hook out of its mouth with the other.

'It's a John Dory. You're lucky, he's good eating. See that big mouth of his? He gets lots of other fish with that. And the mark on him is the thumbprint of St Peter. Here you are.'

She handed the hook and line back to him and he baited it with another worm. As he cast the line out a second time he looked at Laurel triumphantly.

'That's a good start, Mummy. Now I'll catch one for you.'

He cast out from the foredeck again, but this time his hook snagged on the black ball on the forestay. Laurel,

dressed in a flowered wrap, was sitting reading under
an awning. Susan was lying sunbathing in a new red
swimming costume that showed off her superb figure.
Neither of them saw James climb on to the ship's rail
and reach up to the forestay to try and free his line. He
reached too far, missed the line, lost his balance on the
rail and fell overboard with a cry of fright.

Susan, half asleep when it happened, was slow off the
mark. Not so Laurel, who went after James immediately. Already the pull of the tide had swept him
alongside the ship. He was splashing ineffectually with
his arms and coughing when his caliper caught on a
chain hanging underwater from the accommodation
ladder at the side of the ship.

The *Peregrine* was rolling in the sea and James was
lifted in and out of the water with each roll. This was
one occasion where her Vosper stabilisers did not help.
The lift was over six feet and James was being dunked
in a frightening fashion.

When she heard the twin splashes, in quick succession, Susan turned and saw what had happened. She
saw Laurel splash towards James and when she reached
him there was a commotion. It was impossible for
Susan to see precisely what was happening, but it was
obvious that James was in trouble. He seemed to be
disappearing under the water for moments and then
reappearing.

She heard him cry, 'Mummy! Help!'

Laurel was there almost beside him, and a thought
struck Susan as she remembered Ginette's comments.
Could she be watching a mother drown her own son?
What was going on down there?

She stepped on to the ship's rail and dived into the
water. The only crew on the *Peregrine* at the time were
Ash, who was resting in his cabin, and the mate, who
was on the bridge. Ash saw Susan step on to the rail

and execute a perfect dive into the water, assumed she was doing it for fun and took no action. When James fell over and Laurel went after him the mate had been checking the Decca navigator and had seen nothing.

David Compton saw it all.

He was standing on the breakwater over the Albert Quay and looking at the *Peregrine* through a pair of high-powered binoculars while Ginette was busy in one of the shops on the Esplanade. He saw the boy topple in, followed by his mother. He saw them drift down the side of the ship and Susan dive in after them.

In impotent horror he saw James being ducked in and out of the water, hanging from the platform of the accommodation ladder. Finally, after one deep swing, James did not reappear.

David's anxiety increased.

He saw a splashing on the surface of the sea that was moving along the side of the *Peregrine*. Occasionally there was a brief glimpse of Susan's red costume, but he could discern nothing more.

He put the glasses down and started to run. A short distance away was the Harbour Office—he had noticed the sign as they came ashore. The duty officer, to his eternal credit, lost no time in picking up the thread of David's story. He reached for the telephone that called out the Zodiac rescue craft. Four minutes later the Zodiac was entering the water and the forty-horsepower Mariner outboard burst into peak revs at the first touch. The increasing sea made it difficult for the rescue craft. Clouds of spray showered on the two men in their orange jackets crouched low on the duckboards as they bounced over the white horses.

They circled the *Peregrine* and finally located Susan, who was holding up James with one hand and waving with the other. Of Laurel there was no sign.

The boy was pulled aboard first. He was unconscious and blue around the lips. One of the rescue crew pulled out a Brook airway, slipped it into his mouth and started to inflate his lungs. Susan came aboard, and immediately the craft was sweeping round and heading back for the shore. At the same time a crewman radioed for another craft to go out and continue the search for Laurel.

They came up the slipway at Bel Royal and out of the back of the Range Rover extracted a Minuteman oxygen apparatus. James's colour improved dramatically as the pressurised oxygen intermittently flooded his lungs. Susan was wrapped in a foil blanket and they were into Accident and Emergency at the General Hospital five minutes later. She was in good shape, but down the side of her face was an ugly scratch from temple to jaw.

The following day Susan and James were little the worse for their experience. James was subdued after the fright he had received, and when he was discharged from hospital after twenty-four hours and taken on board the *Peregrine* he was promptly tucked up in his bunk.

It was obvious that he did not yet appreciate that his mother was missing. Ginette applied fresh antiseptic to Susan's deep scratch in the privacy of the cabin.

'That's nasty, Susan,' she said. 'How did you get that one?'

Susan looked her straight in the eye.

'How the hell do you think I got it? Young James was thrashing round with his calipers, that's how.'

Ginette looked at it carefully. In her days in Accident and Emergency she had seen many such injuries. Most of them had been on men, and all of them had been caused by women's nails.

* * *

Laurel's body was found two days later, battered almost beyond recognition by the savage rocks in the local waters.

Not long after Susan and James were back on board a launch arrived with the States of Jersey police and a balding man in a sports coat. He announced himself as Centenier Ecobichon of the honorary police of St Helier and appeared to be in charge of the investigation.

Susan was questioned about the events and told them how she had gone into the water as Laurel was in difficulties with James. She told them that James was frightened and thrashing about in the water and she had taken him from Laurel as she was the stronger swimmer. She had been so intent on getting James to the *Zodiac* that she had not paid attention to Laurel, assuming that she would be able to fend for herself.

She demonstrated how difficult it had been by pointing to the scratch on her face which had come from one of his calipers. David was able to confirm most of what she said because he had watched it all, although he had not been able to identify the persons at that distance. Nobody thought to ask him if there had been any period when he was not viewing them, as when he ran to the Harbour Office.

The uniformed constable took notes, and the Centenier nodded sympathetically at Susan's story.

'I don't think we need to bother you any further, Mrs Bennett. You've had a trying time. We'll need you at the inquest, of course.'

Susan nodded her assent, and Sam put his arm protectively round her.

'Thank you, Centenier. We'll be there, of course. When is that likely to be?'

'Just a few days, sir.'

The police departed and there was a general relaxation. Ginette looked at David, who looked as though he was in a dream.

'Right,' said Sam, 'I think we all need a drink after that. Where's Ash?'

Ash appeared like a genie out of a bottle and after giving their orders they gathered in the lounge. There was an uncomfortable silence. Nobody seemed to know what to say. Laurel's absence gaped at them like a hole in the ground. Even after Ash produced a second round of drinks it was only Molly who had anything to say, and that was to enquire what they were going to do next. They looked at Sam.

'I think we go home,' he decided. 'I'm sure nobody feels like carrying on after this.'

They all nodded.

That night David moved into the double cabin with James. He had been occupying a single and James had been in a double with Laurel. He looked at the boy, who was sleeping peacefully, and wondered what he was going to say to him in the morning. Despite their differences Laurel's death had come as a shock, and he felt emotionally drained. Ginette realised that when he forgot to say goodnight to her.

David was saved the difficulty of what to say to his son by James himself the following morning. David awoke to see his son looking sadly at him from the other bed. There were tears in his eyes and he could see that the boy had been crying.

'Daddy, do you know where Mummy is?'

'Yes, James, I do.'

'She's not coming back, is she?'

'No, my boy, she's not,' said David gently.

'She drowned, didn't she?' asked James in a small voice.

David swallowed.

'That's right, James—she did, I'm afraid. How did

you know?'

'I was awake early. I heard two of the crew talking on deck.' James struggled across to David's bed and snuggled up to him. 'You mustn't be too upset, Daddy. You've still got me.'

David was glad there was nobody else there just then, because he was unable to speak.

After breakfast there was a message from police headquarters that the inquest was to be the following day.

They all attended.

The coroner was called the Viscount and he had an inquisitorial expression on his face. Susan was commended by the Viscount in the highest terms. In delivering his summing up the man leaned back in his ornate leather chair, and with an air of firm benevolence said,

'There is no doubt that Mrs Bennett showed commendable courage in going to the rescue of the boy and Mrs Compton, and had it not been for her prompt action there would undoubtedly have been a greater tragedy.'

Sam, sitting next to Susan, gripped her hand and looked like the winner of a championship prize at a dog show. From the way he looked at her Ginette could see that he was proud of her. He had every right to be. She was wearing her cover make-up, and had chosen an attractive, sleek blonde wig. Her navy suit was piped with white and she wore a wide-brimmed hat with a trailing navy ribbon. She was every bit his beauty queen.

A verdict of accidental death was recorded.

They lunched on board the *Peregrine* and afterwards Sam took David aside.

'No problem about the West Indian. I just had a message from those idle buggers I pay a fortune to that he's been seen in England, so you needn't worry about staying in Jersey.'

The *Peregrine* sailed that afternoon, leaving Ginette, David and James in Jersey. They had decided to have a few days more with James before taking him back to St Athelstan's. Minna had taken him under her wing, and James slipped into her care as if it was the most natural thing in the world, despite the fact that he had the greatest difficulty in understanding anything she said.

That night was the first time that David and Ginette had been together since they had last left Argenteuil. They were like two magnets, straining to be together, but held apart by invisible forces. With unspoken accord they had climbed into bed and lay there in the dark, listening to the fountain bell. Neither of them spoke. The shadow of Laurel lay between them like an invisible spectre.

Ginette waited, but David said nothing. This was a ghost that needed exorcising or it would destroy them both. She put her head on his chest. The moonlight dappled them and he kissed her lightly on the top of her head. She put her arms around his neck and moved sinuously against him. Her breasts touched his and she gently moved to and fro so that he would feel their softness.

Their mouths opened and their tongues flickered round each other. She felt his hands encase her buttocks and she pushed her pelvis against him with a seductive circular movement. Her knee went between his and she began to rock gently with him. She felt herself hot and moist and her desire for him flared. Her hand went to his pyjama cord, and with a swift movement she undid it and felt between his legs for the erection she knew he must have.

There was nothing.

His organ was soft and flaccid, limp as a rag. Ginette took hold of it and began to massage him with her moistened hand. He held her tight and she heard his teeth grit as he put his head to her shoulder. She tried harder, but he was so soft and small she had difficulty in keeping hold of him.

He grunted with exasperation, and she whispered in his ear,

'Don't worry, darling—don't try. Just lie back and let it happen.'

He gripped her even tighter.

'Ginette darling, I'm sorry. It's not that I don't love you. I don't know what it is.'

'You've had too much, dearest. Lie back and let me love you.'

He lay on his back, and she slid down the bed and took him in her mouth and sucked him gently. Her hand massaged him and she felt him twitch involuntarily. She heard him moan with impotent rage and stopped her lovemaking. As she lay beside him and felt his body, rigid as a board, she tried to make him relax.

'Don't worry, darling. Tomorrow's another day. You'll be fine, wait and see.'

She went to sleep and dreamed that Laurel was standing at the end of the bed, laughing and pointing at them. In the morning, when she awoke, David was gone. Ginette got out of bed and went to the balcony overlooking St Ouen's Bay. The sun was brilliant and the surf was a white ribbon across the blue of the sea. Above it rose a fine blanket of sea-spray.

David was standing beside the pool with James. They were examining a surfboard, and James's treble voice reached her clearly.

'Why can't I surf, Daddy?'

She watched David's expression and her heart went out to him. A nerve in his temple twitched and his jaw set firm.

'There's no reason why not, my son. I'll take you out and show you right now.'

James's face lit up and he clapped his hands.

'Wonderful! Do you mean it?'

'Of course I mean it. I mean it so much you'll plead to come out!'

Ginette watched the pair of them go indoors to look for the other surfboard, then David and James were fitting them on to a roof-rack on the estate car kept for general running around. She put on a swimming costume and ran downstairs.

'Hey, you're not going to leave me behind?' she called.

David smiled at her, only a hint at the embarrassment of the night before in his eyes.

'Do you surf?' he asked her.

'Like a seal!'

James jumped up and down excitedly, and Ginette wondered how David was going to manage it. She need not have worried. On the beach James took off his calipers and David carried him to the tide, where he lay floating in the water while David fetched the surfboard. When the water was deep enough he sat the boy in front of him on the surfboard and they paddled out through the breakers together.

Ginette had some anxious moments as she watched the surf break over their heads, but they always emerged the right way up. She paddled out after them on the second board until they were in the calm water beyond the surf line. James waved to her and shouted,

'Look at me, Ginette! I'm surfing!'

His confidence, with David behind him, was complete, although they were in deep water. Ginette was anxious because she knew that the big surf could well throw them off, and what then? David paddled the board towards the shore until they were riding high up and down on the swell and the breakers were beginning to form behind them.

'When I start to paddle fast you hold tight on to the edges of the board and lie as flat as you can,' he instructed.

James nodded, and the next moment they were sliding down a wall of water and his father was paddling hard. James gripped the sides of the board and saw the foam of the wave around them as they hurtled towards the shore. He felt frightened, but exhilarated. It felt as though he was on top of a giant express train. He felt his father's arms around him as the board tilted, but it righted just as he thought he was going to come off into the boiling surf. They hurtled on, and then the ride slowed and they were in the shallows and Ginette was beside them, relieved to see James safe and apparently not frightened by the sea which had recently almost claimed his young life.

He shouted with delight, and his father picked him up and carried him back into the sea.

They did it again and again. Each time it was different, and once they came off. For James it was terrifying. The board swivelled, rose in the air on the crest of the breaker and they went down under a wall of green water. James felt the board go from under him, and panicked. He swallowed water, felt his father's arms gripping him firmly about the waist as the pair of them were tumbled and somersaulted in the surf, and then he was on the surface with his father beside him. He managed a smile to show he had not been frightened and was relieved when they reached the shallows.

David grinned at him.

'That was a bit scary, wasn't it, James?'

'Not really. I quite enjoyed it.'

'Then we'll do it again.'

They did it again, but this time it was good and they did not fall off. When he came ashore, with James riding high on his shoulders, David felt a satisfaction he had not known for years. There had been a significance in the surfing with his son that had left its mark on them both. Father and son had become closer together in sharing an experience that had the spice of danger in it.

Ginette had been out of the foaming sea for some time watching the two people she loved most risk their lives in the water, and her anger had been building steadily. James was dressing himself in the car when she turned on David.

'Of all the silly, irresponsible capers, that takes the cake! You should have more sense! After you took that big tumble in the sea you should have both come out! What on earth made you do. . .'

She stopped suddenly. It was not that he had done anything, it was the expression on his face. Hard, set and angry, it frightened her. His jaw jutted and his eyes pierced at her from under his dark eyebrows. When he spoke his voice was harsh and commanding.

'When I want you to tell me what to do with my son I'll ask you! It's time you learned to hold your tongue and not sound off with the first little thought that comes into your head.'

'I only felt. . .' she began.

'I don't care what you felt, or thought, or wanted. There are times when you should hold your tongue, and this is one of them. That "irresponsible caper" was a special moment between a father and his son, and I won't have you spoiling that for us. Don't ever take that tone with me again!'

Ginette retorted furiously, '"Take that tone"? Who do you think I am? Some sort of bloody whore-cum-housekeeper, to be told what to do and when to do it?'

David looked at her with the steel in his eyes that she had come to know and fear.

'Where my son is concerned what I say goes. You have no part in him. There've been too many petticoats around him as it is.'

'So you put me alongside Laurel, then?'

His eyes dilated and she saw his nostrils widen as he sensed danger. Danger to both of them. Danger to their newly found relationship.

One wrong word now and they would be finished.

The tears welled into her eyes and he drew back from the brink as they walked along the sand.

'No, of course I don't. You must know that.' He waved his hands in a gesture of hopelessness. 'Ginette—this is getting out of hand. Our emotions are high after all we've been through recently. Let's just leave it for the moment.'

When they got back to Argenteuil Minna produced breakfast by the swimming pool. They ate bacon and eggs and sausages, and James attacked the honey and toast like a starving lion.

'This is marvellous!' he grinned. 'I wish we could stay here for ever.'

David and Ginette looked at each other, once more in accord. David took a breath and dived in.

'I think something like that could be arranged—not all the time, but during some of the school holidays. Would you like that?'

'I would too. Does that mean I wouldn't have to stay at St Athelstan's all the time? Could I come away for school holidays like the others?'

David nodded.

'If you want to, but not here all the time. We'd have somewhere in England as well.'

'That would be terrific!'

James shook his head as if he could not believe the change in his world. He was missing his mother, but adapting to it with the curious facility that children have for dealing with things that hit them hard. He had had a lot of practice in his few years.

Later in the day they took him to the nine-hole golf course in the bay and David gave him his first golf lesson. It was not easy as he tended to lose his balance at the end of the swing, but he soon got the hang of it. It was hard work, especially after the surfing, but at the end of the round he did not want to give up and insisted on going on to the driving range to see if he could hit the ball further than Ginette.

They stayed several days at Argenteuil, with father and son growing ever closer to each other. Ginette was careful not to crowd David, and she held her tongue. In any case, they were so exhausted each night by the swimming, the golf and walks along the cliffs bird-watching that when they tumbled into bed they were asleep at once.

When they did leave they flew to Southampton, and took James back to St Athelstan's before returning to Ginette's flat in her car. As they passed between the two lions flanking the courtyard entrance David saw a pale blue Lagonda parked by the entrance.

'Looks as though you have wealthy neighbours,' he remarked.

The sleek low shape of the Lagonda looked just what it was, powerful and expensive. David viewed it with envy and Ginette eyed it with consternation. She had seen it outside Ralph's home when Dirk den Pol had been visiting.

As they stopped, the door of the Lagonda swung open and Dirk emerged.

CHAPTER THIRTY

DIRK came towards them over the courtyard, a smile on his broad, handsome face, immaculate in his grey suit and light tie. He gave Ginette the customary continental greeting of a kiss on each cheek.

'I am so glad to have caught you, Ginette.' He turned and shook hands with David as Ginette introduced them. 'Ralph told me you were getting back now, and as I am returning to Holland I thought it would be nice to call in and say goodbye.'

'That's lovely of you, Dirk,' smiled Ginette. 'I'm so glad we didn't miss you.'

Privately she wondered what she had done to deserve this. She could feel David tensing beside her. Dirk obligingly told her.

'After our enjoyable time at the Ritz I could not just fade away. I hope you will come to Amsterdam one day. It would be a pleasure to show you my city.'

'Thank you, Dirk—I would like that.' She inclined her head towards the front door. 'Come in for a drink before you go.'

He shook his head and looked at his watch.

'Very kind, but I must be off. Already I have waited half an hour and I must not miss my connections.' He held out his hand to David. 'Goodbye. Ginette has spoken of you. You are indeed a lucky man.'

David shook hands with him, watching speculatively as Dirk then took Ginette by the shoulders and gazed closely into her eyes. Having received the sign he seemed to be looking for, he kissed her gently and said,

'Do not forget what I say, Ginette. Amsterdam is

very beautiful, and I would be happy to entertain both of you there.'

The Lagonda purred between the lions and there was a heavy-throated roar as Dirk accelerated down the road. David turned on Ginette and his look was both suspicious and accusing.

'What was that little scene all about?' he demanded.

She eyed him coolly, but her heart was beating fast.

'He's a friend who came to say goodbye. Didn't you hear?'

'I heard all right—but I hope I didn't hear correctly. What was so enjoyable at the Ritz that he wants to draw you over to Amsterdam?'

Ginette turned away and walked up the steps to the front door.

'Would you bring the bags in?' she asked frostily.

He was after her in a bound.

'The bags can wait! I want this business sorted out before anything else.'

She opened the door with her key.

'Then I suggest we do it in private. I have no wish to entertain the neighbours.'

They went up to the flat, and when the door closed behind them David stood in front of her by the fireplace.

'It seems to me you've been playing two ends against the middle—and I thought you were someone I could trust!'

There was a wealth of bitterness in his words that brought from her an automatic response.

'That's not fair!' she protested. 'If ever you could trust anyone in your life it would be me. And what about you? Don't tell me there haven't been times when you've wanted to or have made love with Laurel!'

It was that last barbed remark that brought David to earth and stemmed his jealous rage, because it was true.

'Just who is that Dutchman, then?' he asked more reasonably. 'And what were you doing with him at the Ritz?'

'For your information, he invited me to the Toulouse-Lautrec exhibition—he's an art dealer—and then took me to lunch.'

She did not think it wise to mention the proposition that Dirk had put to her after the meal, but it did increase her indignation with David. He turned away from her and looked out of the window, not really seeing the movement of the trees, so caught up as he was with his inner turmoil.

'Ginette, there's no way we can go on like this,' he finally said.

'Well, what is it? Can you tell me what's really bothering you?'

He hesitated. This was the right time, if any time could be right, to tell her about his arrangement with Sam.

He regarded the Islamic pattern on the rug for a moment before looking up at her. Ginette was disturbed by his expression. She had seldom known him anything but confident. This was the face of a man in a dilemma.

David began, 'I must tell you about Sam.'

'Go on. I've been waiting for you to tell me more about your involvement with him.'

Slowly, but with increasing firmness, he told her of the financial arrangement with Sam and the problems he had had with the bank before it. When he had finished he looked at her with a sadness born of remorse.

'So there you are. I was a fool to do it, but then the road to hell is paved with good intentions, and mine were of the best because it was for James.'

At first Ginette did not know what to say or feel. She

had always looked on David as a knight in shining armour. Now he was showing her, telling her, just how tarnished the armour was. Disappointment, indignation, rage capered one after the other within her mind.

How could she now believe that he was not after her for her wealth? Already he was doing worse things than deceive her for money. Adding her to the list was a feather on lead-weighted scales.

'David, this frightens me. How can I be sure that you're not after me for my money after all? You've certainly got reasons enough,' she pointed out.

'Maybe for the same reasons that I can't be sure about you and the Dutchman. You can't. And there's Philippe as well, for that matter.'

It was that last barb that stung her. She thought they had buried that particular bone, and the grain of truth that there was in it made it sting the more.

'What is it that makes you react like this about other men?' she asked him.

She had shifted her attack. Something in her told her his insensate jealousy stemmed from Laurel and her ice-cold attitude, and she was sure she was right. Perhaps now he had found something so precious after so long in an emotional desert the thought of it being imperilled, however slightly, brought out the jealous insecurity in him.

This came to her in a wave of comprehension. This man was no Simon—she knew it with a certainty bred from their emotional exchanges. Simon would never have confessed to her in the way that David had. He would never have put himself in her power as David had done.

While he was looking at her, trying to collect his thoughts over her last piercing question, she took his hands in hers.

'David, money shouldn't come between us. What

you're involved in with Sam *is* morally wrong, but I can fully understand your dilemma. You didn't want the money for yourself, only for James's happiness. Ginette squeezed David's hand as she went on, 'I agree, you must find a way to get the money back to Sam, although he needs it as little as we need the plague.'

'Do you realise what it means?' he demanded.

Ginette raised her eyebrows. 'I don't follow you.'

'There's no way we can marry when I have a financial incubus like that,' David told her. 'Even if I build up a large private practice it's going to take me years to pay it off, and even then I shall have to live like a hermit.'

Ginette looked at him closely. This was her moment of truth. Was she sure enough of him to give him access to her money? Would he want her if she had nothing? It did not take her long to decide. She was as sure of him as she could be of anyone. Was he not even now walking away from her to save her from a decade of semi-poverty?

'Darling, if this is all the problem, then we have no problem. With my inheritance that's nothing. Godfather William can come to the rescue.'

'I can't let you do that!' he declared.

'Why not? When we're married we share. I'm not one for having my own and sharing yours. I know it's difficult to receive and easy to give away, but if we're going to be happy we'll have to come to some agreement on this.'

David hesitated, and she held her breath. If he was going to be intransigent about it they might well be lost to each other. He looked at her and for a moment she thought he was going to refuse. Suddenly he nodded.

'I know you're right. We've a lot of adjustments to make, and my standing on pride and being difficult won't help.'

'We must also overcome your tendency to become jealous about any man who gets within six feet of me!'

This was cards on the table time and Ginette had to say it. She knew now that he was no Simon, but if they were to make a success of their relationship they had to be honest and open with each other. His anger over James she understood. That she could deal with, but his unreasoning jealousy was something else.

David's eyes narrowed as unreasonable anger once again overcame him.

'I am not having you pursued by every man in sight and playing up to it!'

The ghost of Philippe's kiss appeared again.

'You're being impossible, and I resent what you're implying!' Her emotion rose with the tone of her voice.

'I'm not implying anything—I'm saying it. You play up to other men's flirtations.'

'You're so bloody jealous you're a cripple—an emotional cripple! You don't know the meaning of the word trust. I can have nothing to do with someone who treats me like a possession. If you stay like that you can go to hell!'

She glared at him, roused to a fury as much by the mixture of her own emotions as by his attitude.

The stared at each other, and she felt herself going over the edge at the way he was destroying what they had by his obstinate stupidity in the face of her own understanding.

Without thinking she raised her hand and hit him across the face.

David looked at her with a stare that cooled her almost as quickly as she had erupted.

'I'll do better than that. I'll get out, even if it is to hell!'

He turned swiftly on his heel and was across the

room and through the front door of the flat almost before Ginette realised what he had said.

She opened her mouth.

'David. . .'

The bang of the door cut off what she was going to say, and she looked up at the picture of the shepherdess over the fireplace in an agony of uncertainty. The Georgian windows of her drawing-room overlooked the courtyard, and she ran to one of them to try and lift it up and call to David when he emerged.

She was struggling with the heavy frame, almost weeping with frustration as it would not move, when she heard a footstep behind her. She whirled in surprise.

It was David.

'Forgive me,' he said humbly. 'We'll work it out.' Then he took her in his arms and kissed her; softly at first and then with a mounting passion. Silently he picked her up and carried her into the bedroom. Their hands moved over each other and they began to tear their clothes away in a frenzy of sexual desire that made them oblivious to all else. Ginette felt her dress rip as he sought her breasts and did not care.

She put her fingers on the belt of his trousers and soon they were standing naked before each other; she with her eyes brilliant, and he more than ready to pleasure her.

This time there was no play, and no gentleness, only a fierce mating to ease the want within them both. It was almost a fight, with no quarter given. Ginette shouted as he drove into her and when he drew back she saw the long shaft of him, corded and glistening. She gripped him and saw him shiver before plunging back into her with a long, penetrating slide she thought would go on for ever.

Her legs wound around him and she clenched his

buttocks with her fingers as she felt her orgasm mounting. Each thrilling stroke brought an exquisite pleasure that was almost a pain.

Sweat made them slippery and they were gasping with the effort. Ginette bit into his neck and felt herself coming with the warmth of his ejaculation, and her cry of pleasured torment brought a juddering response before he collapsed beside her.

Twice during the night he woke her, and each time it was different. The ghost of Laurel had been truly exorcised. As the sky paled with the dawn Ginette opened her eyes to see him sleeping deeply. Gently, with a feather-light touch, she slid her hand down the muscles of his belly to his groin and took him gently in her palm.

He slept still and she massaged him, feeling his response with her fingers. Suddenly he was awake. He turned to her and she kissed him, feeling his erection rise yet again against her forearm. He felt for her, his fingers searching, gently but firmly, in a way that made her breathless with anticipation.

When he found her the thrill of his finger on her sent Ginette into an abandoned frenzy. Her pleas for mercy in his ear were muted by his lips and when it came her orgasm was savage in its intensity. David let her lie and then turned to her, holding her with strength made gentle by loving. She closed her eyes as she opened to him and felt him within her. She went with him as he took her faster and faster up a staircase of ecstasy and delight that had her crying to the morning sun.

That same sun, through the slatted blinds, made a zebra pattern upon them as they slept. The pattern moved across their bare skin and they did not stir until the chime of the carriage clock on her dressing-table struck ten.

Ginette extricated herself, leaving David still half

asleep. She slipped on a wrap and went to make some tea. She felt tender and bruised. Her muscles ached in places she had never known, but they gave her a sense of deep content. All was well between them, and she had reached a peak of unbelievable sexual delight.

Things looked good.

David picked up the telephone and dialled Sam, who was busy and would not talk. Instead he invited them both to dinner at Offa's Hall the next day.

When he greeted them into his home Sam was a different person. There was less aggression about him. He was calmer and had lost the abrasiveness that made people wary of him. When they met Susan they realised why. She, too, had changed. No longer was she withdrawn, as she had become after her operation. She glowed, and her expression made one unaware of her scars, which were fading fast. Sam put his arm around her.

'Isn't she looking good? She should be, after what that Viscount said about her. She deserved a medal for what she did. Jumping into the sea when you're far out is no joke. I wouldn't be surprised if she doesn't get a life-saving medal for what she did.'

Sam's attitude to her had undergone a change since the cruise. Now he regarded her as a heroine for her sea rescue, and that transcended his attitude to her injuries. Sam was nothing if not pragmatic. He saw things in black and white. His values in life were balanced the one against the other, and in this case the scales had come down in a way that was a favour to them both. Particularly as there was now no Laurel to run interference on him.

After dinner Sam and David left the ladies and went into the study. David looked Sam in the eye.

'Tell me, Sam, why was it forty thousand pounds?'

Sam grinned and slapped him on the back.

'I reckon the way he went it was worth extra. You should worry!'

'I do worry, Sam,' David said seriously. 'I must tell you, I'm going to return the money. I've decided I can't keep it.'

'What are you talking about? David, to me the money is peanuts. To you it's important. Never turn down a good offer.'

'I have to, Sam. I feel compromised, and I couldn't live with myself if I kept it.'

Sam shrugged his massive shoulders.

'That's your decision, David.'

'I'll have it to you in a few days,' David promised.

'OK, but where are you going to get it from?'

'I've found a fairy godmother.'

'I hope she's good-looking!' grinned Sam. 'Money and looks don't usually go hand in hand.'

'They do with this one, and I'm going to marry her.'

'You dark horse. What do you think Ginette will say?'

'She's already said it,' said David. 'She's the fairy godmother.'

Obviously Sam didn't know Ralph Abelson's cousin was a woman of considerable independent means.

Sam's mouth opened, and for once he said nothing.

CHAPTER THIRTY–ONE

THE DAY after dining with Sam, David and Ginette went to Apple Tree Cottage. They arrived early in the afternoon and spent painful hours sorting out Laurel's things. Finally they sat in the drawing-room and debated what to do for supper. There was nothing in the cottage to eat, and David was about to suggest they went into Marlborough when Ginette held up her hand. He stopped in mid-sentence and they both cocked an ear.

Silence.

Ginette shook her head.

'I could have sworn I heard something. Must be imagining things. Now what are we going to do? How about an omelette at my place? We've both had enough.'

David shrugged his shoulders and held out his hands, nodding his head.

'You're always right,' he told her.

Ginette got up and went out of the room. Seconds later there was a crash as the front window imploded, showering him with broken glass. A dark object thumped on to the carpet, and David stared at it in horror. From its end a priming handle stuck out like a lollipop stick. The oval shape and the casing, like squared chocolate, told him what it was.

A Mills bomb.

There elapsed a brief moment when he stared at it like a rabbit before a snake, but then he acted fast. His arm shot out, grabbed the bomb and lobbed it back through the broken window immediately.

Almost at once came the thunder of an explosion. His eardrums crackled painfully, and a shock wave blew in the remaining windows, sending shards of glass flying across the room like silver darts. The mirror over the fireplace cracked and the porcelain figurines on the window shelf fell to the floor.

The night air blew in coolly through the empty windows, and when David opened his eyes he shouted,

'Ginette!'

He got to his feet and dusted himself down. There came a moaning from outside. David went to the window and looked out. By the light of the moon he saw a figure lying on the front lawn. It moved and moaned again. He smiled grimly and called to the kitchen,

'Looks like the biter bit! Let's go and see.'

He flicked on the outside lights and at once recognised the figure of China lying on the front lawn. What he did not see until he stepped out of the front door was the body of Ginette lying in the flower-bed.

Instead of going into the cloakroom for her coat she had taken a look outside the front door to see what had caused the noise she was sure she had heard. That was the moment when David had lobbed back the Mills bomb.

It had exploded in mid-air in front of China.

Ginette was shaded from the blast by the angle of the porch, but had been caught by a piece of metal. It had hit her in the temple and she had collapsed without a sound.

David knelt by her like a man in a bad dream. She was white and cold with instant shock. He picked her up and carried her into the drawing-room and put her on to the sofa. He was no longer a surgeon, but a man reacting as any man would who has had the woman he loves apparently killed before him.

Ginette was alive, but she looked as though she was

going to die, and he had seen many people die. He could see the entry wound and he knew what must be going on. Rupture of the fine arteries, bleeding within the brain tissue causing pressure within the skull which allowed for no expansion. Pressure on the basic centres controlling respiration and heart rate, leading to rapid death.

He made her comfortable on the couch and reached for the telephone to put out an emergency call for an ambulance. Only when that was done did he think to look at China and went outside, his medical training overcoming his basic instincts.

China was a pitiable sight. Part of his scalp had been ripped away by the force of the blast and the dreadlocks from the ripped portion hung on his shoulder like a torn wig. The white and red of the exposed skull gleamed nakedly in the light. He was wearing a red shirt, black trousers and a white pullover. The pullover was covered in a multitude of red spots that looked as though he had been sprayed by a water pistol filled with red ink. More spots appeared on his sweater as David looked at him. The red ink was blood spraying from a tiny artery.

David knelt by him. China was lying on his left side, and as he gently turned him on to his back there came a splurge of blood over the white sweater from his left arm, which had been compressed beneath him. The left arm was almost completely severed above the elbow and the movement had released it from the pressure of his body, causing torrential bleeding. The hand and elbow dangled from a piece of skin and muscle, turning like the handset of a telephone on a twisted cord. David took the stump of the arm in a grip of steel and the haemorrhage stopped. He took off his tie and twisted it into a rope. Swiftly he slipped it under the arm and round the stump, then tied it tight. Slowly he released his grip and watched the mangled end anxiously. There was no more bleeding.

He took the hand and forearm, severed the string of skin and muscle, took it into the kitchen, wrapped it in a teacloth and put it in the refrigerator.

Then he picked up the telephone and dialled Manbury Hospital. Mark Slater was on duty, and David breathed a sigh of relief. This was no time to argue with a brash young houseman who still had the examiners' voices ringing in his ears.

'Mark, get theatre set up as soon as you can. I'm bringing in Sister Irving with a serious head injury and a chap with a severed left upper arm. We have the limb and it should be suitable for grafting. He's lost a lot of blood, so have some O-negative ready, and get the duty lab technician out.'

'Yes, sir. How long will you be?'

'Half an hour, maybe. No longer.'

When he returned to Ginette her condition was unchanged. He bandaged China's stump with a torn piece of sheet and wrapped him in a rug. When the ambulance arrived they made the journey to Manbury faster than David had ever done.

At Manbury Hospital a small army of staff were waiting at the Accident and Emergency entrance despite the late hour. David spotted Mark in his white coat and went over to him while Sandra Gotch supervised Ginette and China's removal from the car by the porters.

Mark greeted him with concern.

'Not the best way for you to return to work,' he said.

David nodded and immediately asked, 'Everything set up?'

'Very nearly. Should be ready to go by the time you're scrubbed.'

'Splendid! Now get some blood into him quick and I'll see you in theatre.'

There was nothing David could do at this stage, and he left Mark Slater to get on with transfusing China. The last thing any houseman wanted was his boss breathing down his neck.

He went to see Ginette. She was still unconscious, her face white, her eyes closed and her breathing shallow and swift. The Casualty Officer was peering into her eyes with an ophthalmoscope. He straightened up as David entered the examination-room.

'I've called out the duty radiographer, sir. I think we shall need stereo views here. A bomb, was it?'

'Right.' David was terse with anxiety.

'She's going down fast. There's an ongoing intracranial bleed here—needs the neuro-surgeons in quick.'

'Get them—now!'

David's voice was like a whiplash, and the Casualty Officer looked as though he had been hit. This was not the tone of an emergency department. The greater the emergency the softer the request. He picked up the telephone. There was no neuro-surgeon at Manbury, the amount of neuro-surgery did not warrant it, and he had to be brought in from Oxford, or the patient transferred there if their condition allowed. Ginette's condition clearly did not allow. She was now deeply unconscious.

'Get Dr Sandifer,' ordered David.

Dr Sandifer was a neurologist, not a surgeon, but his opinion would be invaluable to decide what was going on and how much cerebral damage Ginette had suffered. He lived only half a mile away and was there within ten minutes. His examination was brief and his opinion similar.

'Get in quick, or don't bother,' he said briskly.

A white-uniformed theatre orderly appeared and approached David. 'Excuse me, sir. I've been asked to tell you that theatre's ready for the grafting. They're waiting, and Dr Coppard would be grateful if you could get along soon.'

After delivering this fearsome message the quaking orderly disappeared before David could reply. The Casualty Officer put the telephone down with a curse.

'Bloody hell! They can't get anyone here for at least six hours—there's been a major motorway incident and all theatres are at full stretch.'

Dr Sandifer snorted, 'You might as well not bother. By then she won't be worth rescuing.'

'Like hell!' David's face was white. He turned to the Casualty Officer. 'Tell theatre to set up for a craniotomy. Put back the graft until Mr Brade can get in to do it.'

'I wasn't aware that Mr Brade did whole limb grafts, sir.'

It was not a statement, but a question. Was David going to let the limb go in order to operate on Ginette? Mr Brade certainly did not do limb grafts, and even if he did the extra delay would jeopardise its success.

David did not hesitate.

'Just do as I say!'

He left the room and was in the theatre block within five minutes. On the way up he stopped in the theatre sister's office. Only a junior nurse was there.

'Where's the duty sister?' David demanded.

'She's not here yet, sir. She lives outside Ramsbury and it takes her time to get in if her car won't start.'

The telephone rang and the nervous young girl picked it up. She listened for a few moments, said 'yes' and 'all right', and put it down.

'That was Sister,' she said. 'She can't get her car started, I'm afraid, Mr Compton.'

David clenched his hands in his trouser pockets and said in a quiet voice,

'Who's second on call?'

'Sister Gotch. She was promoted during your absence and she covers nights for theatre as second on call.'

'What about her post if she's in theatre?'

'They've got an extra staff nurse and she takes over.'

David lifted his eyes up and vowed to visit Mr Shaw in the morning and discuss the financial priorities of Manbury Hospital in depth and preferably at the point of a knife. If he was going to operate on Ginette and do a craniotomy it would require top staff. There was no way he was going to start with theatre staff like the little girl in front of him.

Whatever else there was about Sandra Gotch, she was good. He only hoped her professionalism would overcome her ambition. Operating on Ginette was bad enough, but to have Sandra Gotch as his theatre sister was something he could have done without.

'Ask her if she'd be kind enough to take over here, and at once,' he said.

To do her justice, Sandra Gotch had the theatre ready faster than he had thought possible. David studied the stereo X-rays on the viewing screen. In the left temporal region was a metal fragment about the size of a wren's egg.

The theatre block was like Trafalgar Square on New Year's night. Somehow word had spread that there was to be a major brain operation and rumours were varied about the accident, but everyone knew that it had involved David Compton. Staff who were not strictly required on duty at this time of night suddenly found their presence indispensable.

Mark joined David in the scrub-room, selected a brush from the vertical rack, and trod on the rubber bulb of the liquid soap dispenser.

'He's looking better now,' he said. 'I got two units

into him fast and he's on his third now. How did it happen?'

David told him, and Mark's eyes went wide.

'You know who it is, don't you?' he guessed.

'I've got an idea,' David admitted.

'China St George. He's the guy who came in with a heroin OD and was hardly out before he was back in with a traumatic torsion of the testes. Bilateral orchidectomy.'

David was not surprised. Only one person remained who would take an action like throwing a Mills bomb into his house. It served to remind him that China was on Sam's list. If he died, David wondered if he would find another credit of thirty thousand pounds in his current account. It did not help his peace of mind that he had delayed operating on China in favour of Ginette; it also occurred to him that if Ginette died he was going to need it.

Mark Slater looked anxiously at his chief as they changed in the surgeons' dressing-room. David's expression was taut, his features compressed, the lines from his nose to his mouth deep. There was nothing of the casual attitude he so often assumed on operating days. As he fiddled with the elastic of his disposable face mask the tie broke.

'Damn!' He threw it into the bin and picked another out of the box. Mark drew a deep breath.

'Are you all right, David? Don't you think you should leave it until the neuro boys can do it?'

David looked up at him abruptly, his grey eyes bright and deep within their sockets.

'She won't last. And if she did she'd be a vegetable. Don't worry, Mark, I'm fine.'

He was not fine and he knew it. He was as tight as an overstrung fiddle string. Even a short time away from major surgery took off the fine edge, and he could feel it. He shrugged his way into the sterile operating gown and a nurse tied his strings. As they walked into the theatre, hands held out before them like supplicant priests, David was conscious of an atmosphere.

He pictured, in his mind, the complicated arterial supply to the brain. The circle of Willis, running like a radial motorway beneath the brain. The enveloping membranes of the brain—the pia, the arachnoid and the dura mater, the functions of the cortex of the brain on which the fragment of the bomb lay.

He hoped fervently that it had not penetrated into the substance of Ginette's brain. That would bring in a host of horrific possibilities—personality change, paralysis, sensory disturbance.

He stopped thinking about them.

Wordlessly he strode to the head of the table where Ginette lay, her shaven head gleaming like a white billiard ball, a black tube projecting from her nose and leading to the anaesthetic trolley. Here gleamed a cornucopia of dials, glass flowmeters with dancing bobbles, tubes and valves and a stainless steel drum that wheezed gently up and down—the artificial respirator.

Sandra passed him a series of green towels and he draped them around Ginette's head, leaving bare a circular white dome. David flicked an enquiring glance at the anaesthetist and got a nod in return. He picked up the scalpel and drew a semi-circular incision in the side of the exposed skull. They picked up the bleeding points, and David turned to Sandra.

'De Soutter, please, Sister.'

She handed him the heavy drill, driven by compressed air. There was a high whine and a sprinkling of bloody sawdust appeared in the wound. The drill was so designed that it would go through the bony cranium, but would not damage the delicate membrane covering the brain underneath.

David made a semi-circle of holes in the skull.

'Stryker saw.'

The narrow oscillating blade of the specially designed saw joined the burr holes. He had now cut through the skull in an arc like the periphery of a scallop shell. Under the edges of the burr holes he inserted flat stainless steel levers—osteotomes. One osteotome in alternate holes.

Mark took two and David two, and together they pressed firmly down. Slowly the scalloped edge of the skull began to rise. There was a cracking sound as the base of the scallop snapped across. The blood-rich covering was unharmed and the blood supply to the flap maintained.

Beneath the flap was a dark clot lying like a piece of liver on top of the dura mater, the thick membrane covering the brain. Gently David scooped it away with his fingers and a swab.

'Ready with the sucker.'

He knew that when the whole of the clot was away there could be increased bleeding from a ruptured artery. The pressure from the clot had slowed it down, but when that came off it could restart like a gushing oil well. The last of the clot slithered away from the creamy dura, and the serpentine folds of the brain showed through. He peered into the cavity, eyes narrowed, searching for the metal fragment which he had to find.

There was nothing. The whole area was white, gleaming, bloodless.

David began to feel alone. Gently he moved the brain aside in a different direction, and suddenly there it was—a black, irregular foreign body, a dark stranger in a white world of moist and gleaming serpiginous folds. He took a pair of toothed forceps and picked it up. It came away easily and David was relieved to see that it lay on the surface of the dura mater—little likelihood of any cerebral damage. He looked for a bleeding vessel. The bleeding had to come from somewhere; that size of clot did not just ooze its way there. There was no sign of one, and he gently used his gloved finger to move the lobe of the brain to and fro to show up the bleeding point.

Nothing.

'Bring her blood pressure up,' he instructed. 'I can't define the bleeding point.'

'OK, blood pressure rising.'

They stood there, doing nothing, for several minutes. Sandra cleared the area of unrequired instruments. David kept peering into the cavity, which remained obstinately clear and bloodless. The anaesthetist's voice, muffled behind his mask, came through.

'Hundred over seventy. She's coming up.'

Suddenly it was there—a scarlet thread of silk that fountained and flowered on to the surface of the dura with deadly elegance. David smiled under his mask and brought down the steel nose of fine Spencer-Wells that cut off the fountain with the first click of the ratchet.

'Got him!'

There was a wealth of satisfaction in those two words, and the atmosphere in the theatre relaxed noticeably. The fine catgut ligature went on with care and as he pulled the knot tight, pressing down firmly with his left forefinger, David nodded at Mark Slater. 'Off, very slow.'

He completed the knot, swabbed and watched the area carefully. There was no leak.

'Let's get out.'

The skull flap was re-positioned and pushed into place. The covering membrane, the galea, now had to be stitched to hold the bony flap in place. Sandra selected long-handled needle-holders, took a cutting needle, threaded catgut through the eye, clipped the needle-holders near to the eye and slapped them firmly into his outstretched hand. He had not had to wait, his hand had been held out for barely a fraction of a second.

She watched him stitch, lifting the edge of the galea with forceps and with a quick rotation of his wrist, push the needle through it, unlatch the needle-holders, grip the nose of the needle and pull it through, then take the end of the catgut with his left hand, his right in the air grasping the needle-holder. The fingers of his left hand then went through a rapid series of manoeuvres, like a violinist playing an arpeggio, as he tied a one-handed knot.

This was repeated many times until he was satisfied that the incision of the galea was secure.

Sandra handed him a sterile cotton swab and he dabbed lightly to make sure there was no bleeding. After that there was the skin incision to close and she had a finer needle ready for him, threaded with blue monofilament nylon. She noted how precisely he brought the skin edges together and then put in a back stitch so that the under edges of the skin were opposed and would heal swiftly. Inverted skin edges, with the outside area of the skin opposed, did not heal properly.

His stitches were small and frequent. Not for him the practice of large and distant sutures leaving an ugly scar, even if it was to be hidden by hair.

It had been long, and demanding, and for a man who was barely recovered from serious injury it had been a marathon; a marathon run under the scorching heat of an emotion held in check by the rigid discipline of his training years.

When they were finished the morning sun was blazing through the big theatre windows, but there were dark shadows beneath David's eyes.

Mark Slater looked anxiously at him.

'David, do you feel all right?' he queried.

He ran his hand through his dark hair and grinned wanly.

'Frankly, no, but I'll survive.'

'I'll get some sandwiches sent up with the coffee.'

David turned to Sandra and looked her straight in the eye.

'Thank you, Sister, that was good—very good. I'm obliged.'

It sounded stilted, old-fashioned almost, but he could not think of any other way to put it in his tense state. He saw, by the flush on her face, that she was pleased and that his message had got through.

Mr Brade arrived and operated on China. He did his best and there was an adequate co-aptation that would give China a chance of keeping his arm, but it was not the same as David's work and everybody knew it.

China was taken to the intensive care unit to be looked after by Staff Nurses Crisp and Best.

'Ever get the feeling that you're getting to know a feller?'

Staff Nurse Best looked over the unconscious form of China at her colleague on the intensive care unit, Staff Nurse Crisp. They were standing on either side of China, adjusting the padding on his pressure points, checking the flow rate on the drip line, watching the circulation in his fingers, and entering on a chart his temperature, pulse and respiration rate every ten minutes.

Best's chubby, attractive features were puckered into a questioning gaze at her friend. Crisp replied with a cool smile on her slim, cat face,

'I don't know. I've never known a feller.'

Best ignored the gentle dart.

'You're going to know this one well enough. This is

his third trip in no time. Once is more than enough for most people.'

Crisp arched a pencilled eyebrow.

'How did he get like this?'

'Blown up. And there's something funny about it too. Mr Compton came in with him in the ambulance— that's too much of a coincidence for me. You don't drive around finding bomb victims littering the country-side. It's fishy.'

'Mr Brade did a good job on him, considering it's not his field,' said Crisp.

China's eyelids flickered and stopped the conver-sation as the women turned their attention to him. The swing doors to the unit opened and Sister Gotch walked in. Starched and immaculate in her dark blue uniform and with an air of ruthless efficiency, she stood at the end of the bed and watched the two staff nurses.

They were the best on the surgical ward. She knew it and they knew it, but she was going to check them, if only to demonstrate her authority.

Sandra Gotch had just been promoted to one of the senior and most sought-after posts in the hospital— Sister of the male surgical ward, which carried with it responsibility for the intensive care unit. She was too old a campaigner not to start in a way that left anybody in doubt as to who was the boss.

'Treatment card, please, Staff Nurse.'

Silently Crisp handed over the card showing all the drugs ordered for China. Sister Gotch scanned it rapidly.

'He's not written up for diamorphine?'

'No, Sister.'

'This patient is a heroin addict. The first time he came in here was for a diamorphine overdose. Is Mr Brade aware of this?'

Staff Nurse Best firmed her lips.

'I don't know, Sister, but I assume he can read. It's in his folder.'

Gotch glared at Staff Nurse Best.

'On this unit you should assume nothing, Nurse. We don't want him suffering from heroin withdrawal in the post-operative period. Leave it to me—I'll remind Mr Brade.'

She swept out, leaving the two staff nurses fuming.

'That cow! She'd give God advice on running Heaven!'

Staff Nurse Best was not one to mince words. Crisp smiled at her.

'She's not likely to get the chance. She'll end up as handmaiden to Mephistopheles!'

In the other bay of the intensive care unit lay Ginette, unconsious and breathing slowly. David entered the unit and looked enquiringly at Staff Nurse Best. Wordlessly she handed the charts to him. Automatically he looked at the drip stand, noting the flow rate. The chart showed a slow pulse rate and low blood pressure.

He moved to Ginette's side, gently lifted her eyelid and flashed his torch on to her pupil.

'How do you rate her, Staff Nurse?'

'Stable. That's the best I could give her, Mr Compton.'

Staff Nurse Best was known for speaking her mind. At least, David thought, he wasn't going to get any wrapped-up news from her.

'Let me know at once if there's any change in her condition. Up or down. And I mean at once.'

He left, and the two nurses looked at each other significantly. David was acting out of character and they both knew why. Staff Nurse Best shrugged her shoulders.

'Can't blame him getting sharp, under the circumstances.'

The telephone rang as he went into the surgeons' room. Wearily he picked it up, praying that there would be no more demands on him that night.

'Mr Compton.'

'Call for you, Mr Compton. I'll connect you.'

'David?' He recognised Anne-Marie's voice.

'Yes.'

'David, it is Anne-Marie. I just wanted to tell you how well I am and to say thank you once more. And I must tell you I am going to be married.'

'Glad to hear it. Anybody I know?'

'It is Philippe Duval. He has asked me for a long time and I kept saying no, but now I have said yes.'

'I'm delighted. Congratulations.'

'You will tell Ginette? And give her my love.'

'Thanks, Anne-Marie. I'm sure she'll be overjoyed to hear.' He could not bring himself to tell her what had happened.

'*Au revoir,* David. You will come to see me again?'

'Of course. Invite us to the wedding.'

'*Certainement.* Goodbye, David.'

As he put down the telephone David bit his lip and thought what a fool he had been to fly off the handle about Philippe when all the time he had been pursuing Anne-Marie. Ginette's desperate state had sharpened and defined his values and attitude, made him acutely aware of how much she meant to him and how foolish he had been to put it at risk with his mindless jealousy.

He put the telephone down and looked out of the window on to the Wiltshire downs to ease his thoughts. When Mark Slater returned he found his chief sitting reading the paper. David raised an anxious eyebrow at him.

'Everything OK, Mark?'

'Fine, David. She's doing fine.'

Despite his general condition China made good progress. The graft looked like being successful. The tips of his fingers stayed pink and the long suture line across the top of his shaven head, where his scalp had been stitched back, showed every sign of healing well. Drip lines trailed into his upper chest.

Sister Gotch had been right about the diamorphine. Within twenty-four hours China had begun to show withdrawal signs. He became agitated and sweaty and complained of pains everywhere. His nose ran copiously and he was so restless in the bed that the nurses were concerned about his drip line.

Mark Slater wrote him up for diamorphine, ten milligrams eight-hourly, and his condition changed at once. He became rational and relaxed. His ashen, sweaty face disappeared and he no longer rolled to and fro. He even managed to tap Staff Nurse Best on the bottom with his good hand as she adjusted the drip line. She smiled at him.

'You're getting better, my lad! Time we got you into the ward. No more of this two-to-one nursing—you can join the mob.'

'Come on, Besty! I'm one of your star turns. If this arm stays on you'll all be famous. See the headlines: Surgical team tours country doing spare-part surgery. I'll be your agent.'

He was chattering away, high on the heroin. Best smoothed the sheets over him gently. She felt sorry for him, especially after the police had been in and questioned him. There was still a uniformed constable on guard in the corridor outside the door of the unit.

'Just you settle and get better first,' she told him.

'I'd get you lots of work. After all, I'd be a good advert—I've had enough done,' China added bitterly 'to satisfy a flagellant saint.'

Best, who knew of his castration operation, compressed her lips in sympathy.

'Take it easy, China,' she advised. 'At least you're alive.'

He darted a look up at her, his black eyes bright with hate. 'Who'd want to be, with what I've got left? My screwing days are done.'

His voice was bitter with hate and she could see that he was working himself into a fury. She asked,

'Would you like me to get you anything?'

'Yes. I want to talk to Sister Gotch.'

'What do you want to see her for?'

'I just want to. For Christ's sake, do I have to give you a reason to take a pee?'

He turned his head away, and she patted his hand gently.

'Don't worry, I'll ask her to come and see you.'

When Sister Gotch arrived beside his bed, a parade-ground version of a compassionless Florence Nightingale, China did not beat about the bush.

'I'm going to get back at that bitch Ginette—and you're going to help me,' he declared.

Sandra raised an interested eyebrow. China had no idea that Ginette had been injured by his bomb, or that she now lay in the next bay in the unit. She still wanted Ginette's job as theatre sister, but was no longer disposed to go to the same lengths to get it, especially after China's attack on Ginette and her operation.

'How am I supposed to do that?' she asked.

'Come closer and I'll tell you. I don't want to bellow it to the bloody world.'

She stepped closer and bent her head down. His hoarse voice whispered urgently at her, and what he said made her blood run cold. Sandra was no mealy-mouth, she was tough and hard and amoral, but what China whispered to her was so grisly her whole senses revolted. Furthermore, it would involve her in deliberate action that stood a chance of being detected. She shook her head.

'No, China, I'm not being party to that game. You want your own back on Sister Irving, you do it your own way and you do it yourself!'

He looked at her, his eyes bright and cold under the turbanned bandage.

'Tinker's dead,' he told her. 'You know that?'

She felt a lurching shock of surprise. Tinker had awed and frightened her, but she had been fascinated by his dynamism. It seemed impossible that a man with such ferocious energy could be demolished.

'No. What happened?'

China told her about their trip to the Ecrehous and Tinker's disappearance.

As he did so Sandra experienced the chill sensation of an animal drawn implacably into a net from which there was no escape. She felt a coldness down her back and looked down at China, who was trying to drag her into the net.

'It's no good, China. That won't make any difference. I'm still not going to do what you want.'

'Yes, you will.' He gave her an unpleasant smile.

'What's going to make me?'

'I am. I'm going to ask for a chat with the Matron when she next comes round. What I'm going to tell her about this ward sister, and her goings-on outside the hospital will make her think hard about your proper fitness for your post, Sister. Especially when I make a few extra complaints about what you've done to me in here.'

China's face left Sandra in no doubt about the sort of things he would say to the Matron about her. Her eyes narrowed and she looked down at him, her mind running like a mouse in a maze.

'I'll think about it,' she said.

'Not for long. I'm in a hurry, and I shan't be here for ever with the same chance I've got now.'

Sandra turned and left the unit, her starched uniform rustling as she went through the swing doors. The policeman sitting there gave her a smile.

'How's he doing, Sister?'

'As well as can be expected after all he's been through.'

Her reply was automatic. The presence of the police worried her. She went to her office and sat at her desk, tapping a pencil on the polished top and letting the shaft slide through her fingers as she did so.

China represented a serious problem. Obviously he was obsessed with his revenge on Ginette. Equally obvious was his high profile, and even more so was her chance of being found out if she went along with his plan. If she did not go along with him he was capable of trying to do it all himself, and that, she was sure, would end in disaster. During the interrogation he would receive she would be dragged in, and with one thing leading to another China would not hesitate to play up her part in giving Tinker information that had led to Donna's death. She could even end up on a murder charge as an accessory before the fact, and years in jail.

The tap and slide of the pencil grew slower and more deliberate as Sandra looked out of the window at the cerulean sky, her thoughts hardening into a less attractive hue. She took out a thick folder from the notes trolley. Along the edge, under a clear plastic cover, was labelled 'ST GEORGE, CHINA'. She opened it and thoughtfully flipped over the pages.

One of the pages was devoted entirely to reports from the pathological laboratory which were stuck on to the sheet. They were numerous, and as she flipped down them her attention was caught by the asterisks

which was the computer's way of bringing abnormal
results to the doctor's notice.

There were many asterisks alongside his electrolyte
levels. The potassium figures were particularly vari-
able. China's electrolyte replacement had to be carefully controlled and closely monitored. He was still on a
dextrose-saline drip which gave him the necessary
sodium and chloride he needed, and the potassium was
made up by potassium chloride solution put into the
drip through the injection port. How much potassium
he was given depended upon the results from the
laboratory and had to be minutely calculated because
potassium was dangerous in excess. Too little potassium and the patient suffered weakness and a fall in
blood pressure, too much and his muscles became
hyper-irritable, especially the heart muscle.

The effect of other drugs could be multiplied many
times in the presence of excess potassium.

Sandra Gotch's fingers slid slower and slower down
the shaft of the pencil as she considered the problem. It
was the thought of fat Staff Nurse Best that gave her
the answer. She needed less salt in her diet to help her
with her problem. She should use that salt substitute—
you couldn't tell the difference.

Her fingers gripped the pencil suddenly. What was
salt substitute but potassium chloride? A common,
everyday substance. Not on the drug list, not account-
able, and an abnormal potassium level in the body at
post-mortem a not unusual finding even if it was
measured.

Sandra put the pencil carefully away, stood up and
looked at her watch. Coffee break. She went back into
the unit. Staff Nurse Best was there alone with China.
Sandra handed her a treatment card.

'Would you go to pharmacy with this, please, Staff
Nurse? The ward staff are all occupied at the moment

and we need it at once. I'll stay here until you get back.'

Best shrugged and took the treatment card. It was unusual, but she was glad for an opportunity to have a break. As soon as she was out of the door Sandra turned to the trolley and removed a large green vial labelled KCl-Potassium Chloride. Swiftly she peeled open the wrapper of a plastic syringe and drew up the potassium solution.

'What's that I'm having now, eh?' China wanted to know.

'Just some more of your heroin mixture.' She knew he would welcome that.

'They don't usually give me as much as that.'

She smiled at him.

'You objecting, China? Not like you. This is more dilute than before. We're starting to reduce your dose slowly, so you're really getting less.'

With a firm thrust on the plunger she squirted it all into the injection port of the dextrose-saline bottle, then put the guard back on the needle, swept up the paper cover and put it into her apron pocket together with the empty glass ampoule. They would all go into the contaminated sharps container and vanish, impossible to trace.

Staff Nurse Best appeared and handed over the box from the pharmacy.

'Thank you, Staff Nurse. I'm going for my coffee break now.'

As Sandra passed the policeman on duty she smiled at him. 'Pretty boring for you, this duty,' she remarked.

'That's right, Sister. Nothing ever happens. As a guard dog I'm wasted.'

'I hope you are, Constable.'

Best caught a blip on the oscilloscope, the exaggerated wave form of an ectopic beat. It was not repeated, and she glanced at China, who was lying with his eyes closed. She checked the charts and as she noted the fluid balance her eye caught another blip on the screen followed in quick succession by two more.

She stood up and went over to him, watching his respiration rate. It had increased by four respirations per minute. She felt his pulse. The rate had quickened to a hundred per minute and she could feel the now regular ectopic beats coinciding with the exaggerated blips on the screen.

Best was an experienced nurse. With Sister at coffee she was not going to wait for her return before taking a decision, and she picked up the telephone and dialled 0.

'Exchange.'

'Dr Slater to intensive care—immediately, please.'

In front of her China was becoming restless, he was sweating and she could see his breathing becoming laboured. The blips on the screen were now in a ratio of one in ten.

Mark Slater arrived through the swing doors in a rush.

'What is it, Staff Nurse?'

She pointed to the screen and his eyes opened wide. The rate was up to a hundred and twenty, with the ectopic wave forms making the screen look like a child's scribbling pad.

'Lignocaine, Staff—quick!'

China's heart muscle was showing the signs of irritability. The lignocaine would reduce it. Swiftly Mark injected it into the drip tube. It was important to get it in as fast as possible to forestall a rising heart rate that would end in cardiac arrest.

'Increase the flow rate, Staff. Let's get this stuff through fast.'

Best opened the drip tap and the dextrose-saline with its deadly dose of potassium flowed faster into China's veins. They watched the screen anxiously. The peaks became faster and smaller. Two hundred, two-fifty, uncountable, and then the green waves became a straight line. The high-pitched pipping, sounding like a demented piccolo player, went suddenly silent.

Mark grabbed the paddles of the defibrillator and placed them on China's chest, looked at Staff Nurse Best and nodded. She pressed the button and China heaved convulsively on the bed.

They looked at the screen. The straight line continued.

Twice more they tried with the same result, and Mark shook his head.

China was dead.

Staff Nurse Crisp arrived back and was shocked to hear what had happened.

'Where's Sister Gotch?' she asked.

Best raised her eyebrows.

'Coffee.'

'She's never going to believe this!'

CHAPTER THIRTY–TWO

DAVID spent the night in the hospital, and at seven o'clock was up and dressed and walking along the corridor towards the intensive care unit when he saw Mark Slater coming towards him. For a moment he felt a surge of apprehension. Mark was not usually up at this hour unless there was trouble. David raised an eyebrow at him.

'What's happening? Problems in the unit?'

'You could say that. China St George is dead.'

David's immediate reaction was one of alarm. China's death might invite an inquest and further police interest if there had been anything unusual.

'What happened?' He tried to sound casual.

'Went into ventricular fibrillation and cardiac failure. Hardly surprising in view of everything.'

David could not help a sense of relief. Even if the police did have second thoughts about further investigation and wanted to question China there was no way they could do it now. Furthermore, it took away the unpleasant possibility of Sam wreaking his own revenge and the can of worms that might open up.

'What about Ginette?'

As he said it, he felt the butterflies of fear within him.

'Come and see for yourself.'

David pushed past him abruptly and went through the swing doors, unable to interpret Mark's meaning. He could hardly take in the scene in front of him. If he had not been aware that patients recover quickly after brain surgery he would not have believed what he saw before him.

Ginette was lying propped up against a mountain of pillows. Her head was bound about with crêpe bandage and her face was pale, but she was conscious and alert—he could see that from the brightness in her emerald eyes. She smiled at him and made a little gesture with her fingers on the coverlet.

The only piece of equipment around her was a central venous pressure line leading from a drip stand to a spot just above her collarbone, where it disappeared into the skin. He walked towards her, and those few feet were the longest walk he ever made.

Was she recovered, or was she going to be a brain-damaged dummy? He took her hand and she gripped it firmly.

'How do I look?' she asked faintly.

'Like a beautiful princess.'

'Still peopling your dreams, I see,' Ginette smiled.

'Certainly. And you feature in every one.' He bent and kissed her gently on the tip of her nose. 'I'll be back.'

He was back. Frequently, but briefly so that she was not tired. She recovered rapidly and soon was fit for discharge. During her time in the hospital they had little opportunity to talk together and David was, in any case, anxious that nothing should disturb her emotionally. He played it flat deliberately, and she began to wonder what was wrong.

Finally the time came for her discharge. There had been no argument as to where she was going. There was only one place to go.

Argenteuil.

Minna would look after her and David could fly out from Southampton on a Friday evening to be with her every weekend.

When she left Manbury it was a Saturday morning,

and there was a crowd at the entrance to see her off. She saw Staff Nurse Best and Staff Nurse Crisp next to Donald Shaw—amazing turn-out for him—and Pat Coppard gave her a thumbs up sign while digging Mark Slater in the ribs.

Their story had flared round the hospital and caught everybody's imagination. Their relationship was no secret, and the fact that David had performed an emergency operation on the woman he loved had added to his charisma. Ginette had insisted that they went in the Morris, and as she stood by the door, about to get in, a figure detached itself from the group at the entrance. Sandra Gotch. She held out her hands to Ginette, who wondered at the gaunt lines that showed in her face.

'Goodbye, Ginette. Come back soon.'

Ginette took her hands and nodded, overcome by the unexpected sentiment. She and Sandra Gotch would always be poles apart, but here was a different woman, and she wondered what had brought it about.

At Eastleigh airport David ushered her carefully through reception into a private room and left her while he organised their bags. When he returned it was with an attractive young man, and she was shaking hands with him before she remembered who he was. Barry Rawlins—the pilot.

Sensing a plot, she looked quickly out of the window to the tarmac. Behind the hangar, just visible, was the sleek Learjet.

'Mr Bennett asked me to wish you "bon voyage", and would you let him know when you want to return.'

She turned to David excitedly.

'Darling, isn't this all too much?'

He took her arm as they walked to the aircraft.

'Certainly not! It's just the start.'

Argenteuil was the same as they drove through the

gates in the taxi. The late summer sun shone on the shutters and Minna and Sancho were there to greet them. They could even hear the delicate tintinnabulation of the fountain bell from the other side of the house when they got out of the car.

That evening, replete after Minna's cooking, they sat hand in hand on the swing seat. They had spent the evening talking, like a couple thirsting for drink after a desert crossing. David squeezed Ginette's hand gently.

'Well, when is it going to be?' he asked.

'When's what going to be?'

'Our marriage,' he said simply. 'Philippe wants to know. I promised him he could come.'

Over the bay came the haunting cry of the lapwing, 'pee-wit, pee-wit, pee-wit!'

She looked at him with tender love. Her doubts had finally vanished. The ghost of Simon had gone.

'How about October the seventeenth?' she asked.

'Sure, but what's special about that?'

'Peter's birthday—a precious day to me, and together we can make it even more of a special occasion.'

EPILOGUE

SAM BENNETT is alive and well and living at Offa's Hall. He accepted a peerage from the government after the completion of a major development in Docklands.

Susan's beauty is undiminished and she and Sam are rarely seen apart. She has become closely involved with a local convent which has benefited from her generous donations.

Sandra Gotch died in 1991. She took up parachuting and one Sunday morning, over Watchfield, her 'chute failed to open. An investigation showed that her D-ring had not been operated. The inquest returned a verdict of death by misadventure.

Mark Slater obtained his FRCS, emigrated to Australia and now lives and works as a surgeon in a small town in New South Wales.

Anne-Marie and Philippe were married in Notre Dame de Fourvière with David and Ginette their very special guests.

David and Ginette were married in Glastonbury at the church where Peter was buried. Sam and Susan did not attend the wedding, they were in Atlanta, but they did send a wedding present—Barry Rawlins and the Learjet for a fortnight.

Minna and Sancho still look after Argenteuil. The only time they argue is over the children when they come for a holiday. James is tall now and the little girl, Susannah, is seven. She has a retroussé nose and bright auburn hair, just like her mother.